A Bold Encounter

His fair hair was tied behind with a wide satin bow, and he had deep brown eyes. The dramatic burgundy coat and green breeches offered a counterpoint to the pure whiteness of Lavinia's gown.

"I never expected to see so glorious a sight in this damp, gray city," he told her, coming closer. "You belong in sunny Italy, *bella signorina*."

His bold appraisal was unnerving and flattering at the same time. Ignorance of town manners put her at a disadvantage, but she knew better than to encourage a man who flirted with her in the street, however handsome he might be.

Beaming down at her from an immense height, he said, "I well know how people of your country greet one another." He captured her chin in his long fingers, and kissed each of her cheeks. Then, very lightly, he brushed his lips against her mouth.

Who was this madman?

Other **AVON ROMANCES**

MARGARET EVANS PORTER

KISSING A STRANGER

AVON BOOKS ◆ NEW YORK

AVON BOOKS, INC.
1350 Avenue of the Americas
New York, New York 10019

Copyright © 1998 by Margaret Evans Porter
Inside cover author photo by Pierre F. Durand/Chameleon
Published by arrangement with the author
Visit our website at http://www.AvonBooks.com
Library of Congress Catalog Card Number: 98-93177
ISBN: 0-380-79559-0

First Avon Books Printing: December 1998

AVON TRADEMARK REG. U.S. PAT. OFF. AND IN OTHER COUNTRIES, MARCA REGISTRADA, HECHO EN U.S.A.

Printed in the U.S.A.

WCD   10 9 8 7 6 5 4 3 2 1

Acknowledgments

I'm grateful to many people in different places for a variety of reasons.

In England: Margot and Robert Pierson, for years of treasured friendship and Xanthe the cat; Diana Scarisbrick, author and jewelry historian, for research advice; Frances Coakley of Surrey University, for so generously sharing Manx history and lore; The National Horseracing Museum, Newmarket, Suffolk; The Estate Office, Mapledurham House, Oxfordshire; The Victoria and Albert Museum, and the Wallace Collection, London; *and Chris.*

On the Isle of Man: Lisa and Dave and Mike Nixon, for warm hospitality and a horse called Fling; Colin Brown and the Manx Experience; personnel at the Manx Museum, the Reference Library, and Manx National Trust; *and Chris.*

Elsewhere: Emma, who listens; the Avon Ladies, those cyber-comrades; Robin Rue and Ann McKay Thoroman, my professional support; *and Chris.*

Prologue

Isle of Man, September 1793

Time to go home, thought Lavinia Cashin. Gray clouds curtained Mount Snaefell's distant peak. And if she didn't hurry, she'd get a soaking. Before climbing back onto her pony, she tucked a flowery sprig of mountain heather and a young ivy tendril into a buttonhole.

A purple, bell-shaped blossom dropped off, and she brushed it from her mud-brown skirt, woven from the fleeces of native Loghtan sheep. Originally the garment had belonged to her sister, and the fabric was thin in places, carefully patched and mended. Although the side seams had been taken in and the sleeves shortened, the faded crimson riding coat was rather large in the shoulders, for it had first been her brother's.

The old leather sidesaddle, another family relic, creaked when she mounted. "Walk on, Fannag." Then, knowing that in the future she'd rarely have a chance to speak the language he understood the best, she added, *"Immee er dty hoshaight."*

1

The animal picked his way carefully down the steep mountainside path, past the crumbling remains of a *tholtan*, an abandoned Manx farmhouse. In fields bound by ragged stone walls, reapers were at work scything ripened oats and barley—it was *Mean Fouyir*, the middle of harvest, a busy time on the island.

A strong breeze whipped Fannag's mane and Lavinia's dusky curls—impossible to say which was more unruly or more tangled. This homeward journey over the hills and through the glens was the last time she would be so cavalier about her appearance.

Her spirits sank lower when she came to the rocky headland crowned by the seaside castle her ancestors had acquired centuries ago. Seated on the front steps were her parents and brother, comfortably informal. Her sister perched before them on a camp stool, sketchpad open and pencil sweeping across the page.

A talented, dedicated watercolorist, Kitty was working on Lavinia's going-away present. "Did you ride to Snaefell?" she asked.

"To the summit of North Barrule but no farther, for there's a storm coming. Haven't you finished yet?"

"Impossible, without you. This is a family portrait; we all must be in it."

Dismounting, Lavinia led her pony across the ragged lawn to join the threesome posing on the steps. Her father perused his *Manx Mercury*, the weekly newspaper that circulated in the island, occasionally stroking the head of the tailless cat stretched out beside him. Her mother sorted the contents of the garden basket, separating and binding together the spent flower heads of mugwort and feverfew, costmary and wormword.

Kerron lounged on the bottom step. Glancing up from his open book, he told Lavinia, "We feared the *mooinjer veggey* had caught you up there in the hills."

"I keep away from the little men in green," she answered, matching her brother's playful tone. "Whenever I see their red caps, I run away quick as I can."

"Lhondhoo," Kitty called, "don't let Fannag's head droop. And try not to look so gloomy."

"I can't help it. By this time tomorrow, Father and I will be on our way to England. *Dys Sostyn*," she repeated softly to herself in Manx Gaelic.

With a strangled choke, Kitty laid down her drawing pencil. She reached for her handkerchief and coughed into it. Her parents exchanged worried glances.

"Worse today," said Lord Ballacraine.

"I gathered yarrow," said his wife. "It's as beneficial to a weak chest as any of the doctor's potions, and it costs us nothing."

"We'll soon have money enough to make her well," he replied. "And send Kerr off to his university. The woollen mill is productive; my cargo of woollen cloth ought to fetch a high price in Liverpool. And before year's end, our Lhondhoo will have her pick of the most eligible gentlemen in London."

Lavinia was doubtful about his last prediction. Their journey to England was an expensive gambit; its desired outcome was her marriage to a wealthy gentleman. But she worried that her family's great faith in her attractions was misplaced. In the years since her release from the schoolroom, she'd roamed the countryside like the vagabond she resembled rather than the nobleman's daughter she truly was. Worse, she had no dowry. That her face could compensate for these troubling defects, as her siblings frequently asserted, seemed unlikely. In future she would be judged by London standards, not Manx ones.

Her father, of Celtic heritage, might be described as one of the island's dark people; her fair-skinned mother's pedigree could be traced back to the Norse occupation. From the former she had thick black hair, tumbling down her back in windblown curls, and from the latter a light complexion and pale gray eyes. This combination of traits, the twins agreed, was arresting and unique. Lavinia remained unconvinced.

"If no man will wed me, what's to become of us?" she wondered aloud. "We won't be able to keep the castle."

Her father's smile was confident, full of pride. "You've never lacked for partners at the assemblies in Ramsey and Douglas and Castletown," he reminded her. "The London ones will be no different. You'll have a multitude of admirers."

She hoped so, for her family's sake. They depended upon her.

Her mother reached into the basket and held up one of her cuttings. "Sleep with this under your pillow tonight, and your future husband will appear in your dreams."

Lavinia accepted the yarrow stalk and added it to the heather and ivy already adorning her jacket.

Could she find contentment and lasting love in a marriage of convenience? It seemed too much to hope for. A bridegroom who was truly fond of his bride, she reasoned, would probably be gentle and kind on the wedding night. But if a couple were barely acquainted, and if their motives for marrying had nothing to do with affection. . . .

She abandoned this depressing speculation to study the ragged coastline, the boundary of her small world for almost nineteen years. A strong blast of damp air chilled her to the core, another sign of the approaching tempest. Fannag's ears twitched, and he swished his tail apprehensively. Lavinia patted his neck to soothe him, desperate for comfort herself.

Hers was a close-knit family, bound together by their adversity and their poverty. Her parents were devoted to each other. The twins, far from identical in both looks and temperament, were her best and dearest and truest friends. She knew that Kerr, with his well-trained mind and dark good looks, envied her more than a little; he waited impatiently for his turn to make the journey she would shortly embark upon. Kitty, domestically inclined and plagued by ill health, pitied her and tried not to show how much.

Lavinia understood that her destiny lay else-where—she'd been told so all her life. Yet never had she imagined the heart-wrenching regret of these last days at Castle Cashin.

A blackbird soared across the clouded sky.

"Oh, look—listen!" she cried. "It's *lhondhoo*, come to say *slane lhiat*."

For to her sensitive ears, the bird's plaintive call sounded exactly like a Manx farewell, and the finality of it made her even sadder.

Part I

In kissing, do you render or receive?

William Shakespeare
Troilus and Cressida, act IV, scene 5

Chapter 1

London, October 1793

A stream of pedestrians crossing Bond Street brought Lavinia's coach to a standstill. Watching them pass by, she marveled anew at the prosperity and assurance of London's residents. People of all classes were well dressed and adequately shod. On her small and impoverished island, only the richest could afford fine fabrics. Everyone else wore plain and serviceable woollens and primitive shoes, and were often unruly from strong drink.

English horses bore no resemblance to the stunted, rough-coated working animals kept by Manx crofters. They were uniformly large and perfectly groomed, whether pulling a gentleman's carriage, a brewer's cart, or a hired vehicle like the one returning her to her father's rented townhouse in Cork Street.

And the buildings! In fashionable Mayfair, dwellings of honeyed stone and warm brick lined the streets, testimony to the wealth of their occupants

9

and the talents of English architects. Each time Lavinia passed a towering classical edifice supported by columns, she recalled the engravings in her brother Kerron's Greek and Roman texts. Pointed church steeples were visible in all directions.

Her gaze shifted from the busy street scene to the oblong box balanced on her maidservant's lap. It held a garment of surpassing elegance, worthy of a princess—if not a queen—and would join a growing collection of gossamer gowns, plumy hats, smart jackets, and heeled shoes. Today she'd been measured for a proper riding habit. A necessary expense, her father declared, for she couldn't hack about Hyde Park wearing her siblings' castoffs.

The carriage's progress along Cork Street was slow, and a sedan chair speeded past it to appropriate a highly desirable space at the curb. Shouting curses at the pair of liveried chairmen, the jarvey accused them of piracy. Ignoring the lively exchange of insults and threats, Lavinia climbed carefully down from the coach, hampered by tight sleeves, confining stays, and layer upon layer of muslin.

The chair's passenger exited his conveyance at the same moment. Facing her, he cried, *"O, mio Dio!"* His fair hair was tied behind with a wide satin bow, and he had deep brown eyes. The dramatic burgundy coat and green breeches offered a counterpoint to the pure whiteness of Lavinia's gown.

"Never did I expect to see so glorious a sight in this damp, gray city," he told her, coming even closer. "You belong in sunny Italy, *bella signorina.*"

His bold appraisal was unnerving and flattering at the same time. Ignorance of town manners put her at a disadvantage, but she knew better than to encourage a man who flirted with her in the street, however handsome he might be.

Beaming down at her from an immense height, he said, "I well know how people of your country greet one another." He captured her chin in his long, strong fingers and poked his head under her hat brim to kiss each of her cheeks. Then, very lightly, he brushed his lips against her mouth.

Who *was* this madman?

Possibly sensing her desire to bolt, he captured her forearms with strong hands. Lavinia, now thoroughly alarmed and incapable of speech, stared helplessly up at him. His grin was so infectious that for a moment she had a mad desire to smile back at him. Then her senses returned, and she shook him off. When he stepped toward her again she glared fiercely and edged away.

His chairmen snickered. Her surly hackney driver let out a braying laugh and called, "Catch her and buss her again, guv'nor!"

Before the stranger could repeat his assault, Lavinia raced for the front door. As impudent as he was handsome, she fumed, face flaming after her very public mortification. He'd been making sport of her. A man so exquisitely and richly dressed— and so amazingly good-looking—couldn't possibly be sincere in his admiration. At first glance he'd realized she was a provincial, despite her modish finery, and therefore had mocked her most cruelly. Not all Englishmen, it seemed, were coldly reserved and stiffly correct in their behavior.

"He's a devil, that one," Polly grumbled, struggling with the cumbersome box.

A most dashing devil, thought Lavinia.

As they entered the narrow brick dwelling, the servant warned, "He's up to no good, m'lady. Prob'ly he's payin' back Widow Bruce for playin' him false." With a derisive sniff, she added, "This mornin' I saw her other lover creepin' up to her door again. In broad daylight!"

Lavinia had also witnessed the comings and goings of her neighbor's most regular caller—older, shorter, and fatter than the fair-haired libertine. Taking her box from Polly, she carried it into the parlor, eager to show off her latest and most splendid acquisition. To her surprise, her father was not alone.

"Here's my daughter now," he told the visitor, which indicated that she had been the topic of discussion. "Lavinia, this is Attorney Webb."

A swarthy man wearing a black suit and a wig stood up in polite acknowledgment. Keen, dark eyes assessed her face and form. Whether he admired them as much as the man who had accosted her in the street was impossible to tell.

"Honored to meet you." Mr. Webb frowned when she placed her burden on the sofa, saying reproachfully, "Lord Ballacraine, you had better curtail your daughter's shopping expeditions."

"I've resolved to limit my own purchases," the earl replied. "But I cannot be parsimonious where Lavinia is concerned. That would be false economy."

The attorney looked skeptical. "In that case, you should accept a loan from our mutual acquaintance Mr. Solomon."

The earl shook his head so violently that his

queue whipped back and forth. "He charges too much interest." When Lavinia's tortoiseshell cat leaped onto his lap, he permitted her to stay there. "I've been waiting for my Liverpool bankers to forward additional monies, but there has been a delay. I own a woollen mill, you see, and my inaugural shipment of cloth was refused by Customs officials and therefore cannot be sold. A dispute has arisen about the legality of importing Manx goods in a raw state, and I don't know when the issue will be resolved. I am thus entirely dependent upon my daughter for financial relief."

"I don't understand."

"Marriage settlements," Lord Ballacraine replied succinctly.

"She's engaged?"

"Not yet. But I'm confident that she'll quickly find a husband, and a rich one."

His frankness brought a hot flush of shame to Lavinia's face. Bad enough knowing she was a fortune hunter, without hearing the embarassing truth spoken aloud.

"My estate is large by the standards of our island," her father continued. "A succession of bad harvests has beggared my tenants; their rents come in at irregular intervals. My late father left me no capital to speak of. My son, Lord Garvain, will inherit still less. Our ancestral home is in a ruinous state."

That stark assessment was all too accurate. While the two men continued their discourse in low, grave tones, Lavinia recalled the discomforts and inconveniences of Castle Cashin. For the greater part of the year, it was so cold and drafty that her family habitually wore their heaviest garments indoors as well as out. The only marginally cozy chamber was their *thie mooar*, where a turf fire burned perpetually. Like the humble crofters, the noble Cashins ate their meals in the kitchen and spent most evenings gathered around the *chiollagh*, the open hearth of the great stone fireplace.

Her parent stroked the somnolent cat, slowly passing his hand from her round head to the tailless rump. "The merchant Onslow extended credit to me without question. But when I chanced to mention that I reside in the Isle of Man, notorious as a refuge for debtors, he demanded instant payment. And he was most insulting when I tried to explain why the money was not immediately forthcoming."

"Many tradesmen," Webb interjected, "have suffered from the tricks of unscrupulous imposters."

"Can he make trouble?"

"I shall endeavor to find out, my lord."

The attorney took his leave, assuring Lord Ballacraine that he would return for further consultation when his schedule permitted.

After the visitor was gone, Lavinia addressed her father. "I didn't realize our situation was serious enough to require legal assistance."

"That meddling moneylender, Solomon, sent Webb to counsel me." With forced cheer, he added, "Fret not, Lhondhoo. All will be well."

The pet name bestowed in her childhood took her back to a distant time when bills and bank accounts had been adult problems, discussed behind closed doors.

"Let's have a look at your new gown." He persisted in using the bright, false voice that told her he was very worried indeed.

She lifted the rustling mass of ivory silk and lacy gauze from the nest of tissue and held it up for inspection. "I've never seen anything so pretty as these lace butterflies—just look, they're sewn all round the overskirt."

"You'll be very grand. Especially if you also wear the Ballacraine rubies."

Together they fingered the materials and admired the workmanship, agreeing that such an exquisite creation could not fail to attract the rich and generous man who could rescue the Cashins from impending financial disaster.

The footman who received Lord Garrick Armitage grinned slyly, saying, "The mistress is laying down."

"Is she at home to visitors?"

"Gentleman visitors," the youth answered impertinently. "She's in her bedroom; you might as well go up."

Jenny Bruce, clad in a semitransparent chemise, generously granted Garrick a tantalizing glimpse of pink flesh before coyly covering herself with the sheet. Her disheveled golden tresses and wildly disordered bedclothes surprised him. He supposed she must be an active, restless sleeper, although the trait was more common to men.

"Why, Garry," she purred, "what a surprise to see you again, and so early in the day."

"It's two hours past noon, Jenny."

"Really?"

He refrained from pointing out that a clock occupied a prominent place on the bureau across from her bed. "I came to deliver this."

"Oh," she gasped when he presented the miniature leather box. "For me?"

His smile was calculated to charm. "You demanded a token of my esteem. I hope this will suffice."

When she opened his offering, she gave a rapturous sigh. "They're magnificent!" Letting the sheet fall from her scantily covered bosom, she inserted the earrings into her lobes. "Hand me the mirror; I want to see them!"

He watched her admire herself in the glass, tipping her head from side to side and making the large, pear-shaped pendants dance. Quality diamonds, perfectly faceted and extremely valuable. "Are you pleased?" he asked, never doubting it.

"How could I not be!" Her blue eyes darted from her reflection back to Garrick. "But I hope you won't insist that I—that we—" She shook her golden head. "Not now. For I'm—I'm feeling most unwell."

"Then we must wait till you're better," he answered, accepting her postponement of the inevitable. "I trust your recovery will be complete by the time I return from Newmarket. I leave tomorrow, to watch one of my racehorses run for a cup." He seated himself on the bed and claimed her hand. "There's a different sort of favor I need from you, Jenny."

"Anything," she promised, fluttering her lashes.

"I mean to celebrate my return from Italy with a card party. Would you be willing to arrange it for me and serve as my hostess?"

"There's nothing I'd like better," she said eagerly. "Who should I invite?"

"All our mutual friends. The Anspachs. Albinia Buckinghamshire. Prawn Parfitt—he's as fond of cards and pretty ladies as I am."

Flushing, Jenny said, "I wish you wouldn't use that silly name. It makes him sound like an *entrée* at a banquet."

"And the guest list must also include Lord Everdon. I've long aspired to meet him."

"Not many people feel that way. His reputation is so foul. He used to be quite the rake, you know; he seduced blushing virgins and bored noblewomen from one end of the Continent to the other. So they say."

Garrick was well aware of Everdon's history of debauchery. The woman he'd loved best and most selflessly had been one of the baron's victims.

Jenny went on, "He left Paris after King Louis was executed and we began warring with France. He hasn't received a very warm welcome in London."

"An experienced gamester, Everdon. I admit, I should like to test his skill at cards. What's his game, or does he prefer dicing?"

"How should I know?"

In a casual tone that belied his great interest, he said, "I thought he was your son's guardian."

"Yes. But I don't want him here," she stated flatly. "He's quite the most disagreeable person I know, the plague of my life, and is always poking his horrid long nose into my affairs. I'm a careless parent, he says, because I once took Bobby with me when I visited Brighton in the company of my—of a gentleman I know. My late husband always boasted that his cousin Everdon was one of Marie Antoinette's lovers, but I'll never believe it. Those cruel, dark eyes!" She shuddered.

"Nearly every foreign nobleman who visited the French court was identified as the queen's *galante*," Garrick informed her.

"Well, I can't imagine anyone fancying Everdon."

"Do you know his wife?"

"Susanne? She's a Frenchwoman and her father was a banker. The baron married her for her fortune after he spent most of his own." Jenny fingered one of the earrings. "If you insist, I shall ask them. To please you."

Garrick decided to push his luck still further. "Perhaps you should send a card to that new neighbor of yours. I met her just now, out in the street— black hair, white skin, rather shy. Who is she?"

"The daughter of a foreign nobleman," Jenny reported absently, entranced by her reflection.

Convent-bred, Garrick surmised, which would account for her horrified reaction to his kisses. He regretted committing himself to a more expedient liaison with Jenny, for he would have liked to introduce that beautiful young *contessa* to the pleasures of the flesh.

"They came here from some island," she added.

"Sicily?"

Jenny shook her head. "I don't think that was it. For the past fortnight silk merchants and milliners and tailors have waited upon her. Whoever he is, her father must be extremely rich."

"Then we defnitely want them to appear at our little assembly. A pair of titled, fashionable Continentals would lend a certain *cachet*, don't you agree?"

"Oh, yes." Swayed by his shamelessly self-serving observation, she said, "I shall call on them tomorrow."

By the time Garrick climbed into his sedan chair, he was beaming his satisfaction. The bearers hoisted their poles, grunting with the effort. It wasn't Jenny Bruce's house that he stared at so intently as he was carried away, but the identical one beside it.

The forceful knock at the front door made Lavinia jump. Hot tea washed over the edge of her cup, staining her white gown.

"Open up!" a gruff, masculine voice demanded.

"In the name of the law!" cried another.

She blotted her skirt with her napkin, then looked up at her father. His wild eyes and fearful expression alarmed her far more than that insistent thumping.

Rising to her feet, she said, "I'll tell Polly to send them away."

But it was too late for that. Heavy footsteps were coming down the passage.

"Here's his lordship," the housemaid said in her quavering treble.

"What a simpleton you are, girl," said the first intruder. He held a parchment decorated with a red wax seal and a dangling ribbon.

The other man, holding a stout cudgel, lingered at the door. "You've been taken in by a most cunning swindler."

Polly, mouth gaping, hurried out of the parlor.

Referring to his document, the first man asked, "Would you be John Cashin, who calls himself the Earl of Ballacraine?"

"I am."

"We are placing you under arrest for an unsecured debt to one Frederick Onslow, silk merchant of the city of Westminster. Will you come peaceably?"

"My father has broken no law," Lavinia declared.

"Is that so? Well, he's about to be charged with insolvency in Court of King's Bench."

"Keep quiet, lovey," said the man with the stick. "We're bailiffs, we are, and have to carry out our duty."

"You mustn't address her ladyship in that fashion," the earl protested.

"She's got no more title than Ned or me," the other bailiff retorted. "I dunno know 'bout where you come from, but here in London we don't stand for folk passing themselves off as nobs when they ain't. Come along now."

"Father, you needn't go with them," Lavinia said urgently. "Mr. Onslow is merely trying to frighten you into paying him."

The officer called Ned snorted derisively. "If he's taken matters this far, he means to have his money—or his revenge. You'll be held to bail, Cashin, and if you don't pay, you'll be imprisoned and brought to trial."

"Send for that attorney," she pleaded. "He left his card." She snatched it up from the table where Mr. Webb had placed it.

Said the earl, "You must go yourself and explain what's happened. An astute fellow—I daresay he'll settle this business so swiftly that I won't even miss my dinner."

"I say, Cashin, you're a cool one," Ned commented. "Been through this before, have you?"

Lavinia's father failed to dignify the question with a response. Calmly he handed the cat over to her and accompanied the officers out of the room. She followed them down the corridor to the front door and watched forlornly as he was bundled into a hackney coach and driven away.

He'll be back soon, she reassured herself. And she'd make certain a good meal was ready and waiting for him.

She was halfway down the service stairs when she heard Polly whine, "I ne'er *really* b'lieved he was an earl, not me. I've heard as how aristocratic gents is always after their maids, and he never paid me no mind 'cept to say, 'G'day, Polly' or 'You may take away the bottle now.' As for the daughter—"

"Hush," hissed the cook. "She's comin'."

Lavinia squared her shoulders and stepped into the kitchen, bravely meeting her servants' curious stares. "I must leave the house for a little while, and I'm not certain exactly when I or my father will be back. We shall dine later than usual tonight."

"Yes, my *lady*," the cook replied with sarcastic emphasis. "But we been thinkin', Polly an' me, that we ort to give our notice. Things bein' so uncertain 'cause of them bailiffs comin' round."

"They came in error," Lavinia insisted, concealing her apprehension.

Pausing on the stair, she consulted the attorney's card and read the inscription. His first name was Daniel, and he kept chambers in Stanhope Street.

Brisk and businesslike, just the man her father needed to champion his cause.

On her way to the door, she peered into the parlor and cast a remorseful glance at the cloud of creamy lace and silk billowing from the dress box— all the costly materials had been purchased at Mr. Onslow's warehouse. The splendid ballgown no longer figured in her dreams of glory; it stirred her resentment and her shame. If not for her extravagance, she wouldn't be so alone and unprotected in this vast and dangerous city.

Chapter 2

The mournful toll of a bell and her companion's restless prowling distracted Lavinia. Looking up from her book, she caught the particolored Manx cat batting a gold-fringed drapery tassel with her paw.

She rushed to the window and gathered the culprit into her arms. "*Cha nhegin dhyt,*" she scolded. "You mustn't. If Mrs. Bruce turns us out, we've nowhere else to go."

Lacking the funds to pay bail, her father had been taken from the court at Westminster Hall to the King's Bench Prison in Southwark. There he would remain until his case was tried, or until he found a way to satisfy his vengeful creditor. Fortunately for Lavinia, their neighbor was not as harsh and unfeeling as the bailiffs and court officials. She'd gratefully accepted Mrs. Bruce's offer to serve as a temporary chaperone.

Daniel Webb had also been very kind to her, delivering her father's long letters filled with instructions. She must never, both men stated emphatically, visit the prison. She couldn't tell anyone about the earl's imprisonment. If pressed, she should say that urgent business had required him to leave town—which was perfectly accurate. In short, she was to behave as though nothing unusual had occurred.

A sedan chair halted in front of the door, and a lean, long-limbed figure emerged. Lavinia drew a sharp breath, wincing as the boned bodice pinched her waist. The gentleman who had kissed her.

Memories of his taunts, physical and verbal, remained painfully clear. Just as troubling, she'd failed to banish the amorous, well-dressed stranger and his wicked smiles from her mind. Today his attire was no less exquisite than when she'd met him. A white cravat, intricately tied, swathed his neck, and he wore a mulberry-colored coat over buff knee breeches and a striped waistcoat. His bright gold buttons and the buckles on his shoes gleamed in the sunshine.

His self-assured march to the door made her aware of her own dismal lack of consequence—and her inexperience with men of this type.

Recent events had instilled a heightened awareness of impending trouble. Should she stand her ground or flee? With no time left to make her escape, she tucked the book under the chair cushion and patted her curls into order.

"Lord Garrick Armitage," the footman barked.

The unwelcome visitor regarded Lavinia with the same fascinated curiosity her cat had displayed when toying with the drapery tassel. "We meet again, *bella signorina*."

She'd not forgotten the teasing quality of that low

drawl, or the velvety brown eyes, or the predatory smile. His elongated nose made him look very lordly indeed. He had high, prominent cheekbones and a deeply cleft chin. Blond hair, unpowdered and unbound, grazed his broad shoulders.

"Never fear," he said, "I shan't greet you in the Italian manner. Unless," he added devilishly, "you prefer it. I've spent the past three years in your country."

Hastening to correct his false impression, Lavinia said, "I'm not from Italy. Or England, either. I live—lived—on the Isle of Man."

"How very unexpected." He removed his round-brimmed hat and tossed it onto the chair where she'd hidden her book "What are you doing in Jenny's house?"

"My father had to leave town," she explained, hoping he would be satisfied. "I'm staying with Mrs. Bruce until he returns."

The faintly satiric curve of Lord Garrick's lips became even more pronounced. "Incredible," he murmured, "that she extended hospitality to a lady so young—and lovely."

Lavinia lowered her eyelashes, flustered by his implied compliment.

"Is the benevolent Jenny receiving today?"

"She went to the milliner to collect a new bonnet."

"I forgot to send a message from Newmarket." He shrugged. "*Pazienza, niente da fare.* It can't be helped." He sat down on the sofa. When the cat sauntered past, whiskered nose high in the air, he asked, "Does this sadly disfigured feline know about my transgression of last week?"

Disregarding the reference to their previous encounter, Lavinia replied, "She was born without a tail. The Manx breed descends from the cats who survived the great flood in the Bible. They were the last two beasts to board the ark, and Noah was so impatient that he slammed the door quickly, cutting off their tails. I never quite believed in the fable, but during our crossing Xanthe proved to be such an excellent sailor that I think it might be true."

Lord Garrick inspected the cat, posing prettily on the hearth rug as she licked a paw. "Poor little Xanthe, you must take a lot of teasing from all the long-tailed London moggies." To Lavinia he said, "I sailed from Naples on a ship flying the Manx flag."

"The *Caesar*?"

"How did you know?"

She smiled. "Captain Stowell is famous on the island. He trades our salted herring for foreign silks and wines."

"As we've already got two acquaintances in common, Jenny and the captain, I trust it isn't overly presumptious of me to ask your name."

"Lavinia Cashin."

"Jenny said your father has a title."

"Earl of Ballacraine." On the island, where nearly everyone was related, her family's nobility had very little significance, and she was amazed by how much it mattered here in London.

"Pardon my ignorance, but I know only that the Isle of Man lies somewhere in the Irish Sea, and her people have a preference for odd-looking cats. Tell me more," he invited.

After a faltering start, Lavinia described the wild splendor of the mountains and how they'd been purple with blooming heather the last time she'd seen them. She spoke of the narrow glens, with rivers emptying into the sea. "I live near Maughold Head," she added, "in a castle by the cliffs."

"And do mermaids really dwell in the surrounding waters, as Captain Stowell claimed?"

"So our sailors report." Not wanting to seem too fanciful, she added, "I've never seen a *ben-varrey*, a woman of the sea. But my grandfather used to boast of an encounter with the witches of Kirk Maughold—very beautiful and terribly wicked and fond of dancing."

"Is there much social activity? Have you any assemblies as we do here?"

"Oh, yes, at Douglas and Castletown and Ramsey. But my dancing partners were nearly always hard-drinking military men who stumbled and stepped on my toes."

Lord Garrick threw back his bright head and let out a merry and infectious laugh. "So you came to London seeking more congenial company." Leaning forward, he asked, "Do you know you have silvery eyes?"

Confused by his *non sequitur*, she shielded them with her lashes. "They're gray," she corrected.

"I must warn you, Lady Lavinia, Jenny has an unfortunate habit of tumbling into trouble. Usually involving a gentleman. Or even two," he added direly. He bounded up from the settee. "I'm not waiting. I think it would be better to—leave a message for her."

"I'm not sure where she keeps her pens and paper," she told him apologetically.

"No matter. I'll find what I want in her bed-room."

Eager to complete the business that had brought him, Garrick marched up the stairs and into Jenny's cluttered sanctuary. Stepping over the lacy night-shift lying on the floor, he went to the madly dis-ordered dressing table. A dusting of face powder flecked the rosewood surface. Crystal perfume bot-tles were arranged haphazardly, and a rainbow of silk ribbons cascaded from a half-open drawer. Tucked into the shield-shaped frame of the mirror were several letters. Garrick inspected them, his mouth pinching into a disapproving grimace. Jenny shouldn't leave her intimate correspondence lying about—fodder for blackmail by a servant. He re-claimed a highly incriminating composition of his own.

With a furtive glance over his shoulder, he opened an ebony casket and sifted through the tangle of chains, bracelets, and rings. Taking the diamond-studded earrings, he slipped them into the pocket slit of his striped waistcoat.

He'd bestowed them upon an unworthy recipi-ent. In Newmarket, he'd learned exactly why Jenny had looked so tousled and tumbled last week. He wasn't hurt by her deception, but it annoyed him. However, he still meant to take advantage of her useful connection to Lord Everdon.

Alas, the scintillating Italian *contessa* who might have consoled him existed only in his fevered imag-ination. His black-haired charmer was merely a homesick provincial, so beautiful and naive that she'd surely come to grief with the giddy and im-moral Jenny Bruce for a chaperone.

* * *

Lord Garrick Armitage must be quite wealthy, thought Lavinia, to wear such elegant and expensive clothes, and he was an aristocrat. But despite these attributes, she must not view him as a prospective husband. He knew the way to Mrs. Bruce's bedchamber—evidence of a liaison. Did he also know that his mistress had another lover? Oh, but London was wondrous full of intrigue!

"There, that's done." Lord Garrick entered the parlor, looking quite cheerful. "I'm off. But I'll be back again—to see how you're getting on and to hear more tales about that island of yours."

His warm regard made her feel as restless and apprehensive as Xanthe during a thunderstorm. Would he kiss her again? A strange and terrible hope filled her, crowding in upon her heart and altering its normal rhythm.

He reached for her hand. When his lips grazed her fingers, she realized an unforseen danger of living in the widow's house: the likelihood that she would meet this handsome rogue on a regular basis.

Lifting his fair head, he murmured inscrutably, "What cursed bad luck that I found you in this house, *dolcezza*." Gently prodding the cat with the toe of his gold-buckled shoe, he added, "*Addio*, little Xanthe."

As soon as he left her, Lavinia perched on the brocade chair to ponder the significance of his cryptic comment and parting gesture. The bulging cushion was a reminder that she needed to put the book safely away before Mrs. Bruce returned from the shop.

She carried Xanthe upstairs to her bedchamber

and deposited her on the hearth rug. Going to her trunk, she knelt down and opened it. Pinned to the curved lid was her sister's watercolor, eliciting bittersweet memories. There was Kitty on her camp stool with the sketchbook, Kerr and their parents seated on the castle steps. Lavinia, in her makeshift riding costume, stood beside her sturdy Manx pony.

She reached for a tiny linen sachet and held it up to inhale the lingering scent of the heather she'd picked on the mountain that day. Then she seized her Manx Bible and searched for the ivy leaves and yarrow sprig pressed between its pages. Then, delving deeper, she pried up the trunk's false bottom to reveal a secret compartment holding her small hoard of coins and her father's heirloom rubies.

"Here you are!" chimed a triumphant voice.

Hastily Lavinia dropped *The Debtor and Creditor's Assistant* into the hiding place and closed the trunk.

"Goodness, but your cheeks are pink," Jenny Bruce observed. "You've been sitting too long by the fire, like that daft cat of yours." She untied the broad ribbons of a hat lavishly adorned with lace and nodding plumes. "I ordered James to bring tea and biscuits. Come along to my room," she invited, patting her puffed and powdered hair, "for I've walked my feet off this afternoon and must have a lie-down."

The diminutive widow favored towering coiffures and high-heeled shoes. Her skirts were fuller than fashion dictated, to set off the dainty figure she achieved through corseting.

In the presence of such highly cultivated femininity, Lavinia felt drab and colorless. If only her hair were fair rather than black, and she had a complexion like pink roses instead of chalk. Lord Garrick had generously described her eyes as silver, but plainly he preferred limpid blue ones.

Mrs. Bruce excused the untidiness of her bedchamber, saying airily, "My maid is a lazy slut." She unbuttoned her tight-fitting caraco. "Such a trying afternoon I've had," she declared, collapsing on the rumpled bed. "I couldn't find a single vacant sedan chair to carry me back from Piccadilly, can you believe it? All London had to be rushing about today, and everyone I met was bemoaning the dreadful news."

"What news?" asked Lavinia.

"Marie Antoinette was executed a few days ago, at Paris. Madame Anatole told me about it. Poor woman, she was in such despair that I don't suppose I'll get my new bonnet for ages. A great tragedy."

Assuming that she referred to the French queen's execution, Lavinia said, "So that's why the bells are tolling."

Jenny nodded. "There's a Catholic chapel near Golden Square, popular with the *emigrés*. It was just the same last winter, after King Louis went to the guillotine—clang, clang, clang, all day long. How did you amuse yourself while I was out?"

"With my reading. A little while ago a gentleman came to see you—Lord Garrick Armitage."

"Garry's back from the races? I suppose he missed me too much to stay longer at Newmarket. Ever since he returned from Italy, he's been courting me."

Recollecting his lordship's blatant interest in herself, Lavinia maintained a neutral expression while listening to Mrs. Bruce boast about her conquest.

"He's a shocking creature, very wild. For a time he was engaged to the Halsey heiress and had the audacity to jilt her. What an uproar there was! She'd no choice but to marry the very next gentleman who asked, when everyone knew her heart and her pride were hopelessly shattered. 'Twas the biggest scandal of that season. That's why his family forced him to go abroad."

Lavinia couldn't imagine anyone forcing the cavalier lord to do anything.

Jenny went on, "His brother, the Duke of Halford, owns Langtree, a grand estate in Oxfordshire. They both partnered me at the Reading assemblies, before I married Colonel Bruce."

"You must miss your husband," Lavinia commented.

"I suppose I do," Jenny answered vaguely. "But he was old and extremely bad-tempered. He caught a malarial fever fighting in the Colonies during the American War, and it wrecked his health. He was fonder of our son Bobby than of me. Even when he was alive, I had to rely on other gentlemen to take me to the play and to dance with me."

"Didn't that make the colonel jealous?"

"Oh, he didn't much care what I did. Or with whom."

Lavinia eyed her unconventional chaperone with awed fascination. Mrs. Bruce had evidently cuckolded her husband. Now she had two lovers dancing attendance, the dashing lord and the plump, pink-cheeked man who paid infrequent but furtive visits.

"I'll have to practice being discreet, now I'm your

duenna.'' Fingering the fall of lace over her full bosom, Jenny declared, "You've arrived in London at the worst season for husband hunting, but I don't doubt many men will vie to win your favor. I'm planning a little card party, at Garry's urging, and I think I'll send the very first invitation to Mr. Oliver Parfitt. You're going to like him; he's so very rich." She giggled softly, then exclaimed, "Matchmaking is really quite amusing!"

The footman arrived with a tea tray of inlaid wood, placing it on the table nearest Lavinia. She poured out two cups of the steaming brew while Jenny rattled off the many virtues of her friend Mr. Parfitt. The ongoing dirge for the departed queen of France was an ominous accompaniment to her lighthearted chatter.

"I do wish those bells would stop ringing!" she cried in annoyance. "That dismal sound makes me feel quite low." Her blue eyes settled on her cluttered dressing table. "Fetch that ebony case, my dear, and I'll show you the diamond earrings Garry gave me."

Remembering the kisses she'd had from him, and the compliments, Lavinia felt a wounding—if illogical—sense of betrayal. He had a roving eye, she cautioned herself. His ruptured engagement pointed to an unsteady character. He was a libertine.

"Quite the most expensive gift I've ever received from an admirer," Jenny declared as Lavinia delivered the requested box. "I vow, you've never seen such magnificent stones in your life!"

Chapter 3

The fashionable occupants of a second-tier box at the Theatre Royal, Covent Garden, greeted Garrick's entrance with murmurs of recognition. Attention wandered from the sufferings of the *Ward of the Castle* even after he and his cousin took their places.

For the remainder of the first act, he was the target of disapproving glares from two elderly dames seated nearby. They raised fans to mute their whispered discourse, and the tall plumes atop their turbans waved madly. He overheard that timeworn phrase, "jilted her and then ran off."

His companion gave him a sympathetic glance. He grinned back, unmoved by his notoriety.

His senior by nearly a decade, Frances Radstock was wed to a devoted, albeit regularly absent diplomat and was respected by her entire acquaintance. A paragon among females—and determined to repair his shattered reputation. She did him credit tonight in a gown of apricot satin embellished with pleated ruffles of canary silk. He'd purchased the materials in Venice, knowing how admirably they would flatter her coloring, but he regretted that her rich auburn mane was dusted with white.

Garrick assiduously avoided the powdering closet, and tonight was no exception. He wore a favorite black velvet coat and pearl satin knee breeches, the understated background for a silk waistcoat with intricate gold-thread embroidery.

During the interval between acts, Frances counted the various notable personages in the audience. Indicating the crimson-draped box reserved for King George and Queen Charlotte, she observed, "Their Majesties have stayed away out of respect for the poor queen of France."

Garrick, surveying the crowd, spied a lady he'd encountered during *Carnevale*. In Venice, she'd flirted with him in a gondola. Here she refused to acknowledge him—additional proof that he was *persona non grata* when in London.

He murmured, "You'll have to give me up as your pet charity, Francesca."

"Never."

"I've not been forgiven for my many sins, and probably never will be." He didn't mind, although at times he wondered why he'd bothered to return. England's war with France had placed him in no great danger, nor had it restricted his travels. He'd been born in Cherbourg, after all, and his passport gave Venice as his place of residence.

How he missed his beloved city's cooling breezes and the comforting sound of the Canale Grande waters lapping at the front steps of his *palazzo*. He yearned to hear the familiar church bells ringing in succession throughout the day—San Samuele, San

Vidal, San Stefano, San Maurio—an unvarying pattern he'd known since his boyhood.

Abruptly Frances stopped fanning herself. "Well, what could be more perverse! There sits Lord Everdon."

Everdon. Garrick's fit of nostalgia subsided the instant she mentioned his enemy. And he remembered what had drawn him back to London.

"He's making a liar of me, for when you asked about him I told you he rarely appears in public."

"Where is he?" Garrick peered through his quizzing glass.

"In the box across the way. A gloomy-faced gentleman, next to a lady in gray satin—his wife. The Comte de Calment is bending down to speak to them. Oh, they're leaving," she said in disappointment. "Well, now you've had a look at him. You can't be sure you ever will again."

A plan quickly took shape in Garrick's active mind. "Would you like a glass of champagne?"

"Why, yes, thank you, that would be delightful."

He stepped past the two elderly females, who averted their faces as if fearful of contamination, and exited through the rear door of the box. A winding stair took him down to the carriage entrance.

As he'd expected, the Everdons stood in the vestibule, waiting for their coach. The baroness dropped her fan when she saw him. He sauntered forward to pick it up, presenting it with his smartest bow.

"*Merci, monsieur.*" Her shy smile forced him to like her, despite her hated name. She was significantly younger than her glowering husband.

The baron's age was difficult to judge. Years of dissipation showed in the deep lines about his eyes and mouth, and in the sallowness of the skin stretched so tautly over the high cheekbones. His chin was narrow and deeply cleft.

"Lord Everdon?" Garrick permitted himself a triumphant smile. "I can't imagine that I need to introduce myself."

In a gravelly voice, the older man replied, "You are the late Duke of Halford's wastrel younger son, whose acquaintance I have no interest in pursuing." Yet his piercing stare was anything but ambivalent.

When he turned away, his wife murmured, *"Mais non, monseigneur, ce n'est pas convenable."*

"I don't care. Come, Susanne, here is our carriage."

With an apologetic glance at Garrick, she said in her thickly accented English, "We do not stay after hearing of the death—*hélas*, the *murder* of her sainted Majesty, the queen of France."

"Do not waste your breath with explanations," Everdon growled. "And if this young man should be unwise enough to come to our house, he's not to be permitted inside. *Comprends-tu?*" He laid a proprietary hand upon her arm and guided her to the door.

Fuming, Garrick ran through his repertoire of Italian curses, adding some choice French ones for good measure. The venomous baron had no secrets from his lady wife; her nervousness proved she was aware of his identity.

Garrick returned to the box-holders' lobby and swiftly gulped two glasses of champagne. They failed to douse the flame of his wrath.

Later, while they drove back to the Radstock house in St. James's Square, Garrick asked Frances if he might keep her carriage.

"Where can you be going so late?" she wondered. "Or am I better off not knowing?"

"I'm in the mood to quarrel with someone," he told her frankly. "Rather than impose my foul temper on you, Francesca *mia*, I'll seek out someone more deserving."

Reaching Cork Street a short time later, he saw that Jenny Bruce's parlor curtains were drawn. No ethereal, white-garbed creature stood at the window, breathtakingly lovely—but so dauntingly youthful.

The footman reported that Mrs. Bruce was feeling out of sorts. "Pitched her shoe at me, she did," he grumbled, rubbing a fresh scratch on his cheek.

Jenny lounged on the settee in her parlor, stocking feet supported by a low stool. Making no effort to rise, she extended a fluttering hand and wailed, "Garry, I'm so relieved you're here. Never have I felt more wretched." She pressed a lacy handkerchief to her temple. "Were you at the play tonight? I wish you'd taken me with you. I'm so dull sitting here all alone."

"Where's your guest?"

"I neither know nor care. When I was out shopping today, she stole my new diamond eardrops— the ones you gave me. Heaven only knows what else the thieving slut has taken!"

"Lavinia Cashin didn't steal the earrings. I did."

"You?" Jenny placed a hand over her rounded bosom and stared up at him with wide eyes. "But why?"

Annoyed by her melodramatic pose, he said harshly, "I learned why your bed was so mussed on the afternoon I left for Newmarket. And why you didn't invite me to join you in it."

"I felt unwell," she said, her swiftness a contradiction in itself.

"So you said at the time. I even believed you— until my illuminating conversation with Prawn Parfitt. He'd had a great deal too much to drink, otherwise he probably wouldn't have confided the details of a liaison you forgot—or neglected—to clarify. I may not be the most honorable of men by the usual standards, but I do live by a code of sorts. It prohibits poaching another man's mistress."

"And to get your revenge, you stole my diamonds?"

"Well, if you'd been home this afternoon, I would've politely requested their return. In your absence, I acted impulsively—and unwisely, I admit. I never dreamed you'd blame the Cashin girl. Send for her, and we can both apologize."

"I can't. She and that dratted cat of hers have gone."

"Surely you know where."

"To perdition, I hope," Jenny answered pettishly, tossing her golden curls. "This is all your fault. You wanted her to come to our card party, otherwise I would not have called on her or invited her to stay here. There was something odd about her—she claimed to be *Lady* Lavinia, but I daresay her father is no more the Earl of Ballacraine than you are. To think that I almost let her have Oliver Parfitt! For I meant to break with him, truly I did." Her wide blue eyes pleaded with him to believe her.

"What do you mean, let her have Prawn?"

"As a husband. She wants to marry someone rich; that's why she left her dreary little island."

"But Prawn doesn't want a wife. Surely you know that."

"Well, I couldn't tell the girl he'd much rather be her protector, now, could I?"

He stared at her. "Ah, I begin to understand. While he was seducing your companion, I was supposed to replace him in your bed. How cozy for us all."

Her color high, Jenny begged, "Let's not talk about Oliver. He's tiresome, and so tightfisted. All that money, and he never buys jewels for me."

"Neither did I," Garrick admitted. "I won those earrings from a female gamester. You're quite mistaken if you assume that I can afford to shower you with trinkets."

"Don't be absurd. You're an Armitage of Langtree."

"The duke cut me out of his will. What's more, he expressly forbade Edward to give me money or property. While on his deathbed, he drew up a document and made my brother sign it."

Jenny sat straighter in her chair. "I never heard of anything so monstrous! And yet you wear fine clothes and have a stable full of racehorses. And you own a grand house in Venice."

"I inherited the *palazzo* from my mother. I manage to support myself on my winnings at the card table. My clothes were fashioned in Italy, where materials and tailors are less costly than here. Edward is my silent partner in the stud; that's a joint venture." Garrick grinned. "He swore an oath he wouldn't help me, but he sees that my thorough-breds are fed and shod and trained."

She stared at him in astonishment. "You can jest about it?"

"I can jest about anything. I'm sorry if the disclosure of my desperate circumstances has robbed me of your heart, *cara*."

"It wasn't my *heart* you've been after, and we both know it."

Fair enough, he acknowledged. But she didn't guess that her easy access to Lord Everdon had attracted him even more than that ripe and rounded body of hers.

"So now you're giving me up," she continued, "without once taking me to bed. I vow, I've never met a more aggravating man! When Oliver Parfitt comes to me, I shall throw my arms 'round his neck and pledge my undying devotion!"

Poor Prawn. Garrick's pity for his crony mingled with his distate for the lady whose favors he'd rejected before winning them. But uppermost in his mind was the troubling question of Lady Lavinia Cashin's whereabouts. As a direct result of his unthinking action, she'd been tossed out into the street. Young, ignorant, unprotected—the various fates she might suffer made his blood run cold. Whatever dire fate befell her, he would be responsible. *Che disgrazia!*

His concern for the missing girl's welfare overshadowed his anger at the duplicitous Jenny and his hatred of the infamous Lord Everdon.

Lavinia pulled her Manx shawl over her head as the rain poured down upon her and the other pedestrians. The comforting aroma of damp Loghtan wool made her think of the sheep byre at home. Even more necessary than keeping the rain off her gown, the plain brown garment shielded her face from anyone who might be pursuing her.

At any moment, a constable could seize her and place her under arrest for stealing Mrs. Bruce's earrings. She'd learned that the justice meted out by English courts wasn't determined by facts or truth—if she were convicted, her fate would be far worse than her father's. Death was the customary sentence for theft of property, athough a comely female defended by a smooth-tongued barrister might be transported to some distant colonial outpost. During the past week, she'd suffered recurrent nightmares featuring leg irons, convict ships, and Botany Bay.

Halfway across Westminster Bridge, she stopped and stared down at the dark and unfriendly waters of the Thames. How many unfortunates, she wondered bleakly, had pitched themselves over the rail in desperation? In this great city, there must be numberless cases of heartbreak, pregnancy, disease, poverty.

She was beset by troubles. But at least her heart was whole and her maidenhead intact—and she possessed ten golden guineas. She held her head up and walked on.

On the other side of the broad river lay the unfamiliar borough of Southwark. She soon entered a ramshackle neighborhood, its streets lined with dilapidated houses and shabby shopfronts. From a dedicated study of the volume she gripped in her freezing hand, she knew the most privileged debtors lived here, within the Rules of the King's Bench.

Her breath emerged in a gasp of dismay when she saw the cruel spikes that topped the prison's brick wall. Reluctant to venture through the arched gateway alone, she took shelter beneath it and waited for Mr. Webb. He could afford carriage-hire, yet he was late. She'd traveled across London on foot, through a steady downpour, and had arrived on time.

A turnkey emerged from his office, a foaming mug of ale in his red fist. "And who might you be visitin' this evenin'?"

"John Cashin." As far as the court and prison officials were concerned, her father was a commoner until proved otherwise.

The man grinned. "That Manxman who boasts he's an earl? Belongs in Bedlam, that one—madder'n a March hare."

"He's not!" Her angry outburst was cut off by the party of Cockneys who shoved rudely past her, demanding attention. A loud discussion ensued, and coins changed hands.

Lavinia was bitterly conscious of the fact that in this place where people were confined for their inability to pay debts, the expense of living was inordinately high. Fees were imposed for entry and exit, food, drink, improved accommodations, the hire of bedding—even for a space to put the bed. When her father had been remanded by the court, he'd paid out over six pounds. Each prison official had taken his share—marshal, turnkey, gatekeeper, and guards. According to her guide book, the limited resources of a debtor would be further depleted during internment by every visit to the coffeehouse, the prison bakery, or the market stalls.

A hackney rolled up the carriageway, splashing mud and water. Mr. Webb stepped out, white neckbands and black coattails flapping in the breeze. The gray powder frosting his dark hair contrasted with the thick, inky brows that gave him such a resolute aspect.

"Forgive my tardiness, Lady Lavinia," he begged, his voice low and sonorous. He never failed to use her rightful title. "I was unavoidably detained."

After exchanging a few words with the keeper, he escorted Lavinia out of the lobby and through an enclosure surrounded by offices.

Another gate opened onto the prison yard. The market sheds that Lavinia had read about were deserted. A pair of men and a single woman huddled forlornly at the taproom window, gazing at the revellers within. The female's face was smeared with rouge; her gown revealed bare bosom and shoulders. Lavinia had been in London long enough to recognize a prostitute when she saw one.

Mr. Webb guided her around the many puddles in their path. The looming brick *façade* of the principal building was not unattractive, despite a coating of soot. Once inside, Lavinia recoiled at the apalling stench. Glancing up at her escort's stony countenance, she supposed he must be inured to it.

Without quite meeting her eyes, he said, "The earl's quarters are on the common side, and up two floors."

People filled the passages, standing, sitting, leaning against the wall, lying upon pallets. Their faces and arms and legs were pocked by fleabites. A young boy tempted a large rat with a morsel of cheese, making it stand and beg.

Her book described the King's Bench as the most comfortable of London's debtors' prisons. To her, it seemed a hell on earth—overcrowded, filthy, infested with vermin. A place where diseases flourished.

So did vice, she discovered when they reached the landing. A couple huddled in the corner had hastily rearranged their clothes, signalling the conclusion of their furtive sexual congress. The man's garments might have been modish once, but now they were shabby and soiled.

"Don't you tell my woman," he muttered to his blowsy partner, whose saucy grin exposed a mouthful of rotting teeth. "Hullo, Webb," he greeted the attorney. "Did I send for you? Damn me if I haven't drunk so much I forgot why."

"I'm here to confer with one of my other clients, Mr. Bowes."

The man's red-rimmed eyes fell upon Lavinia. "A prime wench," he commented, stroking his sharply aquiline nose. "Leave her with me, there's a good fellow."

Said the attorney repressively, "We must not tarry." He took Lavinia's elbow and propelled her up the stairs.

"Ho there, Master Barrister," called out an elderly man seated on the topmost step, "take on my case, do! I'm an honest fellow; 'twas my cheating partner who ran our business into debt. Kind lady, won't you spare a penny for a hungry man?"

"Thirsty is what you are," Daniel Webb shot back, showing no sympathy for the supplicant.

He took Lavinia to a tiny room with barely enough space for a narrow bed and a single chair. Tears filled her eyes when she saw her father, and she couldn't repress a great sob as his arms closed around her. She couldn't tell whether he was giving comfort or seeking it.

As he released her, he said, "I shouldn't ask you to come here, but I was desperate to see you. What's this?" he wondered when she handed him her book.

"*The Debtor's and Creditor's Assistant.* In it, you'll find much useful information about prison life."

Smiling, he patted her cheek. "After another week here, I'll be qualified to write such a treatise myself. Well, Mr. Webb, will you make my appeal to the court?"

"My lord, after careful consideration of the facts, I find sufficient cause to pursue your claim of injustice. Even now my clerk is drawing up a brief, which I shall deliver to a barrister on whose expertise I often rely. A tough little terrier, Shaw, successful in cases civil and criminal. Our first and most pressing task will be proving your identity. Can anyone presently living in London confirm that you are the Earl of Ballacraine?"

"No one, I regret to say."

"Lady Lavinia tells me you're acquainted with the Duke of Atholl, governor general of your island. I've already paid a visit to his house in Grosvenor Place, but the porter informed me that His Grace is at Blair Castle."

"Atholl never fails to attend the annual county meeting in Perthshire. He is a good deal less devoted to the interests of his Manx tenants. Damned Scotsman."

"Father," Lavinia interjected, "you could write to the duke and request a loan." Her suggestion was received with so fierce a look that she quailed.

"I'll not send a begging letter to a man I despise!" the earl thundered. "The Murrays were never friends to the Cashins. Besides, Atholl is a chatterer. We can't have any gossip." Frowning, he asked the attorney, "Will you be able to keep my arrest out of the newspapers?"

Webb considered this. "For the time being, perhaps. But editors sensationalize any case of dubious identity, so publicity will be inevitable when you stand trial."

"He won't be tried," said Lavinia. "Father, can't Mother or Kerron send the money to pay that merchant?"

He shook his head. "Neither has my power of attorney, so not a single sheep or cow can be sold. I doubt they've got enough cash on hand to pay off even one of the tradesmen."

Said Webb, "In addition to that fifty guineas owed to Onslow, there's an outstanding bill for half that much from seamstresses who made your ladyship's gowns. By the end of the quarter, lesser sums must be paid to a milliner, a staymaker, and his lordship's tailor. A rent of forty-five pounds on the Cork Street house falls due at Lady Day. By my reckoning, at this date, the total is in the region of two hundred pounds."

"So much," Lavinia sighed.

"That doesn't include legal fees," he added, "or

the monies your father will have to pay the prison officials on being released."

"If only my cargo in Liverpool could be auctioned," the earl said morosely.

While he and his attorney discussed the troublesome fate of the woollen cloth, Lavinia fluffed the flattened pillow on the bed and wiped soot from the windowpanes. There was no view, she noted sadly; the prison wall was too high.

Consulting his timepiece, Daniel Webb told Lavinia it was almost time to leave.

"I'm staying to cook Father's dinner."

"You'd better go with him, Lhondhoo, else you'll be locked in here for the night."

"I wouldn't mind," she told him staunchly.

"But I would. I'll not have you tainted by this place."

She persisted, "If you moved into the Rules, I could come and live with you."

"First, I'd need to buy my way in, and once there, that ten guineas wouldn't last very long."

"We could get money by selling your rubies," she reminded him.

The attorney, overhearing this exchange, told them, "If there are gems to be disposed of, I'll gladly assist you."

"The Ballacraine rubies have been in the Cashin family as long as the title," the earl declared. "They must never be sold."

"They might be pawned," Webb countered.

"Too risky." The earl turned to Lavinia. "I count on you to guard them well, Lhondhoo."

"Isn't there anything else I can do?" she asked.

"I'm in no great discomfort." Smiling, he added,

"I've spent all my life at Castle Cashin, so I'm hardly accustomed to luxurious living. And I needn't keep up appearances in a place where nobody believes I'm a lord."

"I can bring you some candles," she offered. "I lodge above a chandler's shop now, and—" Too late she realized her slip.

"Aren't you living with that woman, Mrs. Whatsit?"

He had worries enough, thought Lavinia; she couldn't tell him about her humiliating departure from Cork Street. "Mrs. Bruce didn't treat me kindly," she improvised, "so I've taken a room—a cheap one—near Charing Cross. I'll only be there till I can find a position as lady's companion."

"I won't allow it, unless you can assure me that your employer is a respectable female," he said emphatically.

"An aristocratic female," she embellished, giving him her most hopeful smile. "With an abundance of wealth and an ample supply of unmarried sons."

An alarm clanged harshly, prompting Mr. Webb to say, "The visitors' bell. Time to depart, my lady."

"*Jean siyr*, Lhondhoo." Her father pressed a farewell kiss upon her forehead. When she didn't move away, he repeated, "Make haste."

Obediently, she followed the attorney.

The old man on the stair was hunched over in a doze, his grizzled head lolling to one side. The warning bell had dispersed the crowds in the lower passages, and the smell of cooking food wafted from the inmates' rooms.

Mr. Webb offered to hail a hackney for Lavinia, and he insisted on paying the fare himself. The Borough Road coach stand was deserted; inclement weather supplied the jarveys with more customers than they could satisfy. Weary and heartsick, Lavinia tried to keep up her end of the conversation while she and Mr. Webb waited for the next available vehicle.

Breaking an awkward silence, he said, "My lady, you have all my sympathy in this trying time."

"Father suffers more than I, sir."

"I greatly admire your ladyship's courage in the face of adversity. Seeing your beloved parent in so wretched a domicile must pain you."

She scarcely heard him, her mind was so busy. The Ballacraine rubies weren't hers to sell or pawn, but she did possess several trinkets of her own: a pair of gold earrings and a triple-strand pearl bracelet she'd inherited from her grandmother.

"I was reluctant to say so in front of his lordship," Mr. Webb continued, "but I cannot approve of this plan to hire yourself out as a companion. You'd be treated almost as a servant and would receive a very low wage—or none at all. The only persons willing to pay generously for feminine companionship are men. And you, a virtuous lady of noble lineage, could never consider selling yourself."

"That's precisely why I came to London," she stated calmly. "But no man shall have me unless he first gives me a marriage ring and promises to support my family."

"A high price indeed," he said in a dry voice. "Prohibitive, some might say."

Would Lord Garrick Armitage think so? He was the only wealthy gentleman Lavinia had met. By now he must be aware of the theft that had occurred in Mrs. Bruce's house—and probably he believed, like his mistress, that she'd taken the diamonds.

The handsome lord who had paid such generous compliments would have nothing to do with her now, that was certain. But somewhere in that fog-shrouded city on the other side of the Thames was the person who could help her. All she had to do was find him—and soon.

Chapter 4

Garrick, perusing the many volumes in a walnut bookcase, failed to notice his cousin until she asked, "What are *you* doing in Radstock's library?"

"Hunting for a *Peerage*."

"Look on the third shelf down," she said helpfully.

His hand closed on a broad spine. Frantically thumbing the pages, he muttered, "Ballacraine, Ballacraine. *Ecco*—here he is!"

The directory confirmed the existence of a living earl by that name. The third Cashin to hold the title, he'd wed Laura Quayle, by whom he had issue. The names and ages of their children were not given.

"Interesting," he commented. "Also convenient."

During his continental wanderings, he'd encountered more than one *chevalier d'industrie*—swindler, to use the English term—and knew that anyone could impersonate an obscure aristocrat. This Manx earldom was ideal, for it was unaccompanied by a hereditary seat in the House of Lords and its possessor lived on a remote island.

The few facts he gleaned from Mr. Radstock's *Peerage* neither proved nor disproved that Lavinia Cashin was what she purported to be. He could only rely on her statements and his direct observations. Her recognition of Captain Stowell's ship the *Caesar* and knowledge of his trading practices proved she was a Manxwoman. She was well-spoken and mannerly. Her modish and expensive gowns indicated a monied background. Whether her father held a title and owned a castle was impossible to say.

The only way to solve the mystery was to locate her.

"You'll wear a rut in my carpet if you don't stop pacing," his cousin complained. "Is something the matter?"

"I'm in the devil of a scrape."

"What now?"

After he imparted the essentials of the tale, he subsided into thoughtful silence again and resumed his energetic march back and forth over the colorful Axminster.

"Will you *never* learn to govern your impulsiveness? Invariably it leads you—and others—into disaster."

"I'm going to find the girl, but I just don't know how or where to begin. Jenny was no help at all." When no easy solution presented itself, he flung himself into the nearest chair. "Suppose you were cast out into the street, Francesca. What would you do—where would you go?"

"I'd seek the comfort and protection of my relatives, or friends."

"If she had any, her father would've placed her

in their care before he left London." Inspiration flashed. "The newspapers. I'll place a notice in *The Morning Post* and *The Times*, requesting that Lady Lavinia Cashin contact me. She might already have placed an advertisement herself," he mused, "seeking employment as a governess or companion. Isn't that what young women commonly do in these situations?" He bounded to his feet.

"Before you dash off to rescue your damsel in distress, we must discuss Halford's invitation to keep Christmas at Langtree. I've no reason to remain here, for Radstock will still be in Naples. And I assume you don't care to offend the head of the family by refusing."

"I'll go," Garrick answered unenthusiastically. "God knows I won't get another invitation."

Before leaving on his errand, Garrick went upstairs to select a coat more appropriate to his excursion into the city.

"*Scusi*, milord, but you cannot go out without your cane or sword," his Italian valet remonstrated.

"They'll be no use where I'm going," he replied, shoving his round, tall-crowned hat onto his head. "*Pazienza*, Carlo, you shall dress me in the highest style for dinner."

He spent a frustrating and unproductive hour in the Strand, badgering clerks and printers' devils. None had noticed a young lady matching his verbal sketch. He asked to see the most recent solicitations for employment, but all were composed by females "of mature years" who had "long experience in the duties of a gentlewoman companion."

Needing a physical outlet for his desperate frustration, Garrick decided he would walk back to St.

James's Square rather than hailing a chair. As he passed beneath Temple Bar, he peered through the gates of the Middle Temple. The quadrangle was busy with gowned barristers, fluttering like rooks in a freshly mown field. Many were younger sons of the nobility, like himself.

He didn't bemoan his lot, although he sometimes tried to imagine the sort of life he might be leading if he'd studied for the bar. He could've gone into the church, like his paternal uncle, who had ministered to Langtree village, or purchased an officer's commission in the army or navy.

The duke, a most disinterested parent, had packed him off to Eton at the earliest possible age. Oh, the uttery misery of those years—when survival had depended on his ability to bully and brawl. He'd borne it until he turned twelve, and then he had run away from school. Miraculously, he'd not been sent back in disgrace; his mother had taken him with her on an extended foreign tour.

He'd passed his adolescence in countries more fascinating than dreary old England, receiving a comprehensive education in human nature at the gaming houses and assembly rooms of the various watering places the duchess had visited. Also in expensive brothels and lavish private boudoirs, he reflected shamelessly. Rather than preparing for a profession, he'd played cards and attended race meetings and danced at masquerade balls, all the while plotting the seduction of similarly frivolous females.

As he continued his walk along the wide and crowded thoroughfare, he spied the sign of three golden balls that denoted a pawnbroker's establishment. The jumble of goods in the bow-fronted window reminded him of items he'd surrendered in the dark days after freeing himself from his engagement. Watches and fobs, jewelled rings and stickpins, enamelled buttons—all had been lost, along with his reputation.

Did Lavinia Cashin own any valuables worth pawning?

Abruptly taking his search in a fresh, more promising direction, he entered the shop.

"I'm searching for a young lady who might have stopped here—yesterday or today," he announced. "Quite beautiful—dark hair, pale skin."

"Black gown, brown shawl," said the proprietor with a nod. "She's come and gone this past quarter hour. Her pearls were fine ones, but I didn't offer as much as she wanted for 'em. Told her to try Willis of Charing Cross."

Garrick left the shop, hot on her scent now. This hunt was more exciting than any he'd known with the Langtree hounds. In the Charing Cross district, he found another set of golden balls, and over the door a placard bearing the shop owner's name printed in black letters.

Through sun-dappled glass, he dimly saw a female inside, waiting for assistance. When he entered, she turned her head in his direction, and he gazed upon a face twice seen and never forgotten.

Her fingers closed protectively around an object she held. Prying them apart, Garrick stared down at a bracelet formed by three rows of gleaming pearls.

"Mine," she said, gray eyes flashing. "Left to me

by my grandmother, so you needn't cry for a constable."

"I won't," he assured her.

"I didn't steal those earrings, Lord Garrick. I swear it!"

"Yes, I know that. So does Jenny Bruce." Aware of curious stares from the pawnbroker and his customers, he said, "I'll explain everything, but not here."

Pressing his physical advantage, he steered her out of the shop and into a nearby coffeehouse. A cursory inspection of the patrons assured Garrick that all were strangers, but prudently he chose a table in the dimmest corner.

"What would you like?" he asked, placing his hat on an empty chair.

"Nothing," she answered feebly, with no trace of the vehemence she'd displayed in the pawnshop.

"The lady will have a pot of tea and a rack of toast," he informed the aproned waiter. "Coffee for me." When the man ambled off, he said, "I'll wager you've not eaten today. You're sadly shaky."

She withdrew her trembling hands from the tabletop and hid them in her lap.

"I arrived at Jenny's house after your departure and confessed to her that I took the diamonds."

"You?" She lifted her delicate, arching brows. "But why?"

Thinking how well they would become her, he said brazenly, "Perhaps I wanted to give them to another lady."

"But Mrs. Bruce is your—your—" Flaming color replaced her pallor.

"If Jenny implied she was my mistress, she did so prematurely."

She lowered her head in obvious embarassment. Hers were the longest, blackest eyelashes Garrick had ever seen, and he had time to admire them while the waiter laid out the food and drink. He couldn't quite believe he was actually sitting across from the object of his frantic search. Her brown and black garments were appalling; he much preferred her in foamy white. But the dark, curling hair and alabaster skin were exactly as he remembered, and so were those soulful eyes, with secrets lurking in their silvery depths.

"Lord Garrick?"

Realizing she'd asked a question, he apologized for his inattention. "You were saying?"

"Is there any chance Mrs. Bruce would have me back?"

"Doubtful. She cherishes her grudges." Watching her perfect teeth worry at her delectable lower lip, he asked, "Where have you been living?"

"In a room over a tallow chandler's shop."

"*Mio Dio*," he moaned. "Don't you know young ladyships aren't supposed to stay alone in lodgings?"

"But I'm not."

"Not a ladyship?"

"Not alone," she corrected, a hint of mischief creeping into her voice. "Xanthe is with me."

"A cat is *not* a proper chaperone," he informed her sternly.

"No one will ever know. Unless you tell."

"I'll make a bargain with you. Silence in exchange for truth." Was it fear he saw in her face, or merely confusion? He couldn't decide. "Jenny believes you're an impostress."

"Do you?"

"I'll make up my mind after you've provided more information about yourself."

"*Mi dy liooar.*" The words emerged as a sigh of resignation. "All right then. Long, long ago, my father's forbears acquired—most likely seized—barony lands and a fortress on the eastern cliffs of the isle. As the years passed, the Cashins turned their fort into a castle and built up their fortune from—well, from an enterprise we Manx have always referred to as 'trading'."

"Smuggling," he interjected, "would be the English term."

"My great-grandfather, a proud and ambitious man, was jealous of the Earl of Derby's power and prestige—in those days, the Stanleys were hereditary Lords of Man. So he visited London to get an earldom of his own from the second King George. He sought out influential courtiers and offered them expensive gifts and generous loans."

"Bribes," Garrick translated.

"The islanders weren't greatly impressed by his elevation to the British peerage, but a rich Liverpool merchant certainly was. His daughter married my grandfather, the first Lord Ballacraine's heir—she left me her pearls. Theirs was a marriage of convenience, not a happy one. When my father came of age, he too was encouraged to wed an heiress. But he fell in love with my mother and married her in spite of his parents' strong opposition. Our people call him Mad Jack Cashin because he renounced a fortune to follow his heart."

"Will you follow your grandparents' example, or that of your parents? Jenny says you've come to London hunting a rich husband."

Her anger resurfaced with a splash of petulance. "She *does* have a busy tongue!" Without answering his question, she went on, "Kerron and Kitty and I were educated at home, very expensively. My brother was tutored in Greek and Latin; we girls had our English governess. My sister had a drawing master as well. She's a most talented artist."

"Which studies did you excel in?" Garrick inquired.

"Dancing," she replied. "And deportment."

"Are the others older or younger than you?"

"They're five years older, and twins."

"Curious that you alone were chosen to ornament London society."

"Oh, that was decided long ago. Kerr must manage the estate in Father's absence, and Kitty wasn't well enough to travel. And for some reason, the family has always believed that I might achieve a brilliant match. My grandmother disapproved of the plan—and of what she called my worldliness— for she was a deeply religious woman. And could afford to be, having so much money of her own."

No adventuress, Garrick concluded, would relate the family history in such detail, or so critically. She was a genuine Cashin, as honest as she was beautiful. "I was wrong to listen to Jenny's foolishness," he said contritely. "Somehow I must make amends for all the difficulty I've caused you, Lady Lavinia."

"Your apology is sufficient, my lord. I prefer not to place myself under an obligation to a—a stranger."

"A gentleman, you mean." When she removed a few pennies from her drawstring purse and shoved them across the table, Garrick said, "You can't pay for food you haven't eaten." He shifted the toast rack closer to her plate and gave an encouraging nod. She reached for a slice. "That's better."

He couldn't guess her age. Her innocent air and ignorance of decorum signified youthfulness, but her composure and caution lent her a maturity far beyond her years. Resuming his interrogation, he asked, "How old are you?"

"That's no business of yours, my lord."

Young enough to be sensitive about it. "No need to use my title. You aren't my social inferior, so a simple 'sir' will suffice. There's your first lesson in how to get on in society. You couldn't ask for a more experienced instructor than your obedient servant, or one more eager to assist you."

Regarding him warily, she said, "I'll not have you meddling in my affairs, *sir*. You've done quite enough—creating great unpleasantness for me." She seized her reticule and climbed to her feet.

"I'll walk you to your lodging."

"That won't be necessary."

"In a neighborhood like this, it is entirely necessary." By the time Garrick had added a shilling to the pennies she'd scattered on the table and grabbed his hat, the lady had escaped.

The brighter light outside the coffeehouse dazed him momentarily. He shaded his eyes, looking up and down the street.

Lady Lavinia's dark-clad figure moved purposefully toward the opera house. Garrick broke into a run, oblivious to the glares from more sedate pedestrians.

She turned the corner; so did he, and approached the oasis of trees marking the palatial premises of Carlton House, where the Prince of Wales resided. He'd nearly caught up to her when she changed direction again and darted down a narrow alley. A wagon was turning around in the small space, blocking her progress. One of the coal men, his leather apron blackened by dust, shifted the iron cover over the hole in the ground. He whistled to the horse and his wagon rolled forward, leaving behind a few stray lumps.

Lady Lavinia Cashin bent down to gather up as many of them as she could hold. "Why won't you leave me alone?" she wailed when Garrick joined her.

Because she was so lost and lovely; it was as simple and basic as that. Ignoring her repeated protests, he accompanied her to the tallow chandler's establishment at the end of the street. Burdened by her small hoard of fuel, she had difficulty opening the door.

When he performed the service for her, her eyes misted. "I don't *want* you or need you," she said, her breath coming in little gasps. "You always make trouble, and I've had all I can bear."

The lush, drooping mouth tempted Garrick. Draining a seldom-tapped source of willpower, he repressed an urge to kiss it. Instead, he found his handkerchief and dabbed at her cheeks.

"Your bad luck is about to change. Take me to your room, Lavinia." Already they had moved well beyond formality. He'd watched her weep, and now she was letting him dry her tears.

Together they climbed three flights of stairs to a sparsely furnished garret room without windows, only a skylight. The furry lump that was curled on the low trundle bed stirred and opened tawny feline eyes.

"Never in my continental travels did I live so rough at this," Garrick commented with a harshness born of guilt.

"It's the best I could find for only three shillings a week." She dropped her coal into the empty scuttle near the hearth. Washing her sooty hands in the basin, she wiped them with a ragged cloth. "I've seen one place far more wretched."

"Lavinia," he groaned, "you terrify me. You're ruining yourself, and I'm wholly responsible."

She gazed up at him with wide, uncomprehending eyes.

Meaning to shake some sense into her, he gripped her shoulders. But he pulled her toward him until he felt her breasts pressing against his chest. And he kissed her. For a very long time. And all the while, his hands moved downward, learning the rest of her shape—a long and slender waist, gently flaring hips.

The emotions she roused in him were intense, yet also frighteningly pure. He wanted to know the body in his arms, yes, but also her intangibles—heart and mind and spirit. She intoxicated him, this mysterious earl's daughter who dressed in peasant garb yet owned costly clothes, came from a castle but lodged in a hovel.

Her pliant lips had parted for him, but when his

tongue touched hers, she backed away. Her face was adorably bemused, and her voice was uneven when she said, "You *are* a devil. That's what the maid called you the day we met."

He smiled at the memory. "You were the most beautiful, exotic creature I'd ever seen, and I wanted to carry you off to beautiful and exotic places." Curling his arm around her, he made her sit with him on the bed. "I'm going to show you Venice— as near to paradise as I shall ever get. I own a *palazzo* there, on the Grand Canal."

The cat rubbed her head against his sleeve, as if warning him that he couldn't say such things to someone he scarcely knew. Seeing that Lavinia was still pressing her fingers against her mouth, he guessed, "You've not had many kisses." And was fiercely glad.

"Never from a lord," she said faintly.

"My empty title impresses you?" He realized the full force of his infatuation when he heard himself ask, "How much money must a suitor have, to win you?"

"At least five thousand pounds. A year."

"*Che peccato.* At the moment, I've got no more than five hundred—if that."

"Oh." The single syllable was charged with dismay. "I thought you must be wealthy."

He wouldn't lie to her. "Wish I were."

"*Cha nee eshyn ta red beg echey ta boght, agh eshyn ta geearree ny smoo,*" she said ruefully. " 'Tis not the one with little who feels poor, but the one who desires more—that's what Father always says."

Because there was something refreshingly dubious about this girl, he couldn't resist probing further. "If I had that five thousand a year, would I get you with or without benefit of clergy?"

"I intend to be a wife, Lord Garrick, not a whore."

"If your primary object is getting a man's money, the distinction seems irrelevent."

"Not to me. Or my family." She bowed her black head, avoiding his gaze. "By the time Father returns—"

"And where is he, exactly?"

"He's gone away—over the water—and I don't know when he'll be back. Before he does, I shall have a husband." She turned imploring eyes upon him. "If you truly wish to be helpful, Lord Garrick, introduce me to the richest bachelor you know."

"That, *cara mia*, is asking too much."

He was disturbed to learn that she aspired to the sort of passionless, mercenary union he'd been so desperate to avoid. Why, he wondered as a spasm of regret squeezed his heart, did she have to be as unobtainable as she was attractive? He might be able to help her, but it was painfully clear that he could never have her.

Frances would no doubt welcome the companionship of this charming creature. Unlike Jenny, she was the ideal chaperone, eminently respectable and relentlessly social. And Garrick, a born opportunist, instantly found a benefit to himself in the arrangement he envisioned. By escorting the ladies to concerts and balls and theatrical performances, he'd probably manage to meet Lord Everdon again. The baron might bar his door, but he couldn't hide behind it forever.

"No lady is better qualified to sponsor you than

my cousin Mrs. Radstock. I'll present you to her today—if you truly want to meet a man of fortune."

"More than anything."

"More than this?" His arm crept around her waist, drawing her near.

"Yes," Lavinia whispered, just before his mouth covered hers.

His kisses, she thought, were magical. He wasn't a devil after all. He was a wizard—a charmer, casting a spell with lips and hands. His power over her senses and her will astonished her. Other men had looked at her with admiration, but none had ever touched her this way—or made her feel like this. Lord Garrick's lovemaking roused in her the same helpless fascination she experienced whenever a storm swept down from the heights of Mount Snaefell.

Desperate to save herself before it was too late, she shoved his chest, pushing him away from her. "I really shouldn't go with you," she said breathlessly, knowing she really had no other choice. Fevered kisses and an indecent proposal did not justify a refusal, given her circumstances.

"To Italy? Or St. James's Square?"

"Anywhere," she whispered. He was so handsome and daring, and she hadn't wanted to him stop. "I'm afraid of you."

His face changed, and with a new harshness he said, "Don't be—you'll get no more kisses from me. However, I shall insist upon one chaste, congratulatory peck when you wed that rich gentleman of your dreams."

Disdain dripped from every word, acid burning holes in her heart.

"Pack up your things," he advised her. "I'll carry your trunk downstairs and hail a hackney."

During their journey, his expressive face was a mask, stiff and impassive, and the wicked fire in his eyes had died out. Lavinia missed his sunlit smile. Wedged between them, separating them, was the woven willow fisherman's creel in which Xanthe travelled.

She regretted telling him about her plan to make a marriage of convenience—a necessity that seemed particularly distasteful to her now, in the uncertain aftermath of those kisses. Yet she longed to confide still more. He couldn't hate her if he knew her reasons, if she explained that the Cashin coffers were entirely empty and had been so for a very long time. And made him understand that she had a duty to rescue her father, a prisoner of the Crown.

The ruthless and ambitious first Lord Ballacraine had beggared himself to get his title and forced his reluctant heir into that match with the merchant's heiress. The second earl, proud and dictatorial, had resented his countess for holding the purse strings. She had outlived him, and with her religious fervor and craving for dominance, she'd been no less a tyrant. In the year since her death, she had continued to rule her family—from the grave. Her last will and testament bestowed the bulk of her fortune upon the Catholic charity she'd founded, and placed stringent conditions on the bequests to her elder grandchildren. Kerron's legacy was supposed to build a shrine to the Holy Virgin. Kitty's dowry would be paid out only if she entered a convent. Lavinia had been left portionless, receiving only the pearl bracelet.

Her trepidation increased as the conveyance bumped over the cobblestones paving St. James's Square. Lord Garrick's touch was chillingly impersonal when he assisted her down from the vehicle. A footman admitted them to a vestibule of breathtaking splendor, paved with marble.

Studying the silk-hung walls and gilded furnishings, Lavinia knew she'd stepped into a rarified world, one of unimaginable wealth and exquisite taste. With Lord Garrick's assistance, she removed her pet from the cage, then followed him up the graceful, curved staircase. He ushered her into a sunny sitting room occupied by an auburn-haired lady with a newspaper.

"Francesca, allow me to present Lady Lavinia Cashin."

Rising, Mrs. Radstock removed her gold-rimmed reading spectacles. "I'm pleased to make your ladyship's acquaintance, and I trust my cousin has apologized for his atrocious behavior. I never doubted he'd find you or that he would bring you here, so a guest chamber has already been prepared."

With her arms full of cat, Lavinia was unable to accept the hand held out to her. She managed an impromptu curtsy.

The lady reached out to stroke Xanthe's head. "And who is this? Two guests—how delightful! Garry, make yourself useful and take the cat down to the kitchen for a saucer of milk."

"Will she come to me?" he asked Lavinia.

"I don't know." She was surprised and not altogether pleased when Xanthe went willingly into his arms, without a protest—exactly as she'd done herself, she remembered in mortification.

Her hostess showed her to a spacious room with cheery chintz curtains, pale damask chairs, and a folding Chinese screen with silk-embroidered panels. The tented rosewood bed, Lavinia's fourth one since coming to London, promised to be the most comfortable of all.

"I'm glad to have company just now. My husband is in Naples on a diplomatic posting, as Garry probably explained."

He hadn't. He'd been too busy torturing her with passionate kisses and ambiguous offers of protection.

She was unsettled by what she saw in the mirror. Her hair was mussed, and several loose curls dangled upon her brow. A streak of soot marked one cheek, and Xanthe's white hairs were visible against the darker background of her gown.

"I'll send Celeste with some washing water," Mrs. Radstock said with an understanding smile. "And Alfred will soon be here with your trunk. As soon as you feel ready, join Garry and me, so we can drink a toast of welcome."

She felt miserably dishonest. This extravagantly hospitable woman would be sympathetic, but she would never agree to serve as social sponsor to a debtor's daughter. Lavinia's concern over the necessary deception turned into panic when she learned that Lord Garrick also lived in this house. She, too, had been duped.

He was dangerous, a potential threat to her campaign to ensure her family's survival. Each time his arms closed around her and his mouth joined with hers, she felt as free as she did when roaming her island's rocky coastline or riding across its heathery hills. For a few glorious minutes today, she'd been a wild, untamed creature again, rather than the cool-headed aristocratic lady her expectant family had trained her to be.

For it was financial security she sought, not romantic fulfillment. She needed a man of substance and of honor, one whose intentions were matrimonial.

Chapter 5

⌒⌒〰⌒⌒

The Grecian Coffee House was a crowded and busy place early in the day. Daniel Webb, ignored by the harried waiter, looked for acquaintances among the diners. His interested gaze drifted past rumpled literary gentlemen and humble scribes to linger enviously on a party of barristers from the Middle Temple. All were robed in black silk and wore white wigs with neat rolls of side curls and twin tails at the back.

Not a one of them, he reflected bitterly, would deign to accept his brief. His lack of prestige forced him to seek out young, unproven barristers whose expertise came cheaply.

The server, passing him again without pausing, rushed over to the barristers' table and inquired respectfully, "Do your worships desire anything more?"

Webb, too proud to remain, left the coffee room. He hadn't come seeking sustenance, but to gather scraps of gossip about bar and bench.

The route he followed back to his chambers took

him along the Strand, past the shop of a peruke
maker who catered to the legal profession. The full-
bottomed wigs displayed in the window added to
his sense of ill usage. If his parents had been gen-
tlefolk, he might be a barrister now—perhaps even
a judge. Hampered by his humble origins, too poor
to read law at the Inns of Court, he would never
acquire the coveted wig and silken gown.

Yet by becoming an attorney, he'd achieved a
great deal more than anyone had expected of an
actor's son. His father had died young. Success on
the stage had eluded his widowed mother. As a
boy, Daniel had augmented her meager salary by
picking pockets at Bartholomew Fair. Discovering
that he'd been cheated of his fair portion of the profits, he'd retaliated against his older accomplice and
their fence by laying information against them. Both
had been tried, convicted, and transported to Botany Bay. At an early age, he'd been impressed by
the power and effectiveness of the law.

Eventually his mother's luck had improved. She
received a summons from the Theatre Royal at
Drury Lane, and soon thereafter gained a generous
and influential protector who provided her with an
income and a house and arranged for young Daniel
to attend the famous Bluecoat School.

Standing outside his timber-framed residence in
Stanhope Street was the newly fledged barrister
who had proved his merits while handling a recent
criminal case. Shaw was exactly the man he needed.

"How fortunate that you've come," he declared,
smiling benevolently upon the younger man.

"Present your brief to someone else," Shaw retorted. "I've sullied my hands with your dirty work

one time too many, Webb. Besides, my fee is in arrears."

"You were paid."

Sheer outrage briefly deprived the other gentleman of speech. "You promised a bonus if the jury acquitted your client—which they did, little though he deserved it."

"Didn't he? There was a dearth of incriminating evidence. The prosecutor failed to produce a single believable witness. And our rogue was a most convincing liar; he gave an impressive performance at the Old Bailey."

"I surmise that you've not yet persuaded your estimable perjurer to part with his ill-gotten gains. How long does it take to melt down so many pieces of hallmarked silver with the owner's crest engraved upon it? Robbery is a crime, Webb. Fourteen years in New South Wales might have given him a better understanding of right and wrong."

Webb regarded the earnest young barrister from his superior height. Removing his purse, he plucked from it a five-pound note, which he handed to Shaw. "Step inside, now, and hear me out. I've got a most intriguing case to lay before you, a nobleman arrested for debt."

"Did you lead the bailiffs to his door yourself, as in the Dimsworthy affair?" asked the barrister in a voice of loathing.

"Let's not argue that point again."

"I'd rather go briefless than accept another one of yours."

Said Webb firmly, "If you refuse to assist me with the Ballacraine matter, I shan't pay you another penny."

Shaw, cowed by this threat, trailed him to the door. Its brass knocker and the square plaque bearing Webb's name and occupation both wanted polishing, and he cursed his housekeeper's negligence.

His chambers, located on the lower floor of the rambling house, consisted of a compact office and library, and a shabby parlor for the reception of clients. Webb's living quarters were situated on the second level. He rented one wing to theatrical performers, who complained regularly about cracked windowpanes, falling plaster, and smoking chimneys. His clerk resided on the premises, as did the cook-housekeeper. He couldn't guess the whereabouts of the former, but at this hour the latter would be making her daily pilgrimage to Clare Market.

He fully intended to seek a more reputable and impressive address, preferably in the environs of Westminster Hall. He regarded his location as an impediment, despite its proximity to the criminal court at the Old Bailey and also to the Inns of Court, where barristers and serjeants congregated.

He searched through the documents cluttering his desk for the ones pertaining to Lord Ballacraine. Shaw grudgingly studied the particulars and asked a few questions before he departed.

With no pressing task to fill the morning, Webb diligently plowed through the hills of papers until a shuffling tread in the passageway heralded his clerk's return. "Will!" he bellowed.

The young man sauntered into the office, penknife in one hand and a letter in the other. "Somebody's servant brought this. It's for that Ballacraine chap." Carelessly he tossed a square of folded paper onto the desktop, then picked his protruding front teeth with the knife point.

"Where the devil have you been?"

"Tavern," Will mumbled.

"You aren't supposed to leave without my permission."

"You weren't here to ask."

The rascal would make a fine attorney, Webb acknowledged, provided he finished the five-year apprenticeship. "Take these away," he commanded, shoving a stack of pages across the desk. "I've already sorted them by client name. Begin drafting solicitations for payment."

Webb waited until Will was out of the way before he examined the letter. With great care he pried up the disk of red sealing wax and spread out the single sheet. The heading startled him—when had Lady Lavinia Cashin transferred from Charing Cross to St. James's Square? Provincial she might be, but she was spectacularly clever to have established herself among London's elite so quickly. Her current hostess and chaperone was some woman called Radstock, wife of a diplomat and cousin to the Duke of Halford.

An Armitage of Langtree. The duke, Webb knew perfectly well, was the elder son of his mother's longtime protector.

Scanning each succeeding paragraph, he discovered that Lady Lavinia would attend an evening concert at the Hanover Square Rooms on Saturday. He lingered over her description of the clothes and jewels she planned to wear, then refolded the note. Then he searched for a stick of red wax, held it to a candle flame, and used a single molten drop to reseal the letter. No one could possible guess that it had been opened.

"Will!" he shouted once more. "I want you!"

"Voilà." The French maid released a long black ringlet she'd trained around her finger. "This new style suits you. Ah, but you are fortunate to have *un profil parfait, un visage charmant."*

Lavinia had hoped to wear hair powder, for the very first time, but Frances Radstock had gently opposed her. What she saw reflected by her mirror compensated for the disappointment. Celeste had teased and fluffed out the shorter curls clustered at her temples, creating a fashionable fullness. The candlelight struck fire from the ruby-studded combs and added a sheen to her bodice of cream satin. She fingered one of the lace butterflies sewn to her ballgown's gauzy overskirt.

She'd inserted each of the ruby drops into her earlobes and was reaching for the heirloom necklace when her chaperone swept into the room, expertly coiffed and powdered, with emerald bracelets sparkling at her wrists.

"Garry grows impatient."

"I'm ready," Lavinia answered, fastening the clasp. On her way to the door, she paused by the tufted bench where Xanthe reclined.

"Don't you dare touch that animal!"

With playful disobedience, she tickled the cat's furry chin. *"T'ou uss litcheragh agglagh.* Lazy thing, she'll lie here sleeping till I return."

Lord Garrick waited for them in the hall, dressed all in black and sporting a snowy cravat and shirt frills. He, too, had visited the powdering closet.

The stark whiteness of his hair, neatly tied behind with a black silk bow, made his eyes look particularly dark and intense.

Lavinia descended the curving stairway at a cautious pace, unaccustomed to her narrow shoes and hazardous heels. How he'd mock her if she landed in a heap at his feet!

"I do believe you've lied to us, Lady Lavinia. It's inconceivable that you've come to us from a tiny island rather than a grand European court."

"You mustn't flirt with her, Garry," Frances reproved him.

Lavinia accepted his proffered arm and let him lead her out of the house. The lamps affixed to the waiting coach cast their golden light across the sharp planes of his unsmiling face.

The clatter of horses' hooves and the metal-edged carriage wheels impeded conversation during the journey. Nevertheless, Frances pointed out an edifice, saying, "St. George's is the most fashionable church in all London. On the morning of my wedding, crowds gathered along both sides of the street to view the procession of carriages."

Lavinia leaned forward to study the church's shadowy outline and imagined herself passing beneath that columned portico as the bride of a wealthy man. Sinking back against the velvet cushions, she avoided Lord Garrick's sardonic gaze.

The concert hall was located on the eastern side of Hanover Square. Its principal room was elborately decorated with Italianate frescoes and filled with fashionable persons. Lavinia was impressed by the rich brocade coats and satin breeches worn by the gentlemen, and the magnificence of their ladies' gowns. Male and female heads were uniformly white, for everyone else wore wig or powder. She turned accusing eyes upon her chaperone.

Said Frances, in a soothing voice, "Sometimes being conspicuous is a good thing."

An unshakeable awareness that she wasn't quite what she must pretend to be sapped her confidence. Although she possessed the outward trappings of an aristocratic female—costly clothing, heirloom jewelry—she felt out of place in this elegant company.

"The musicians have just started tuning their instruments, so we've a little time to circulate," Frances said knowledgeably. "No royals are here tonight, but you'll meet them soon enough. Let me introduce you to some of my particular friends— you'll feel more comfortable when you can associate names with faces. Ah, there's someone I know quite well—the Marquis of Newbold."

He was even taller than Lord Garrick Armitage. Bowing over her gloved hand, he expressed the hope that she would enjoy the music.

"When Herr Haydn lived in London, Newbold was one of his patrons," Frances volunteered. "But he's too modest to mention it."

"I was privileged to know him," the marquis responded, "and never failed to attend his concerts. What instrument do you play, Lady Lavinia?"

"None," she answered candidly. "But I do enjoy singing, with or without my sister's accompaniment."

"Her ladyship is an accomplished dancer," Frances added. "I had a Frenchman come to the house to show her all the latest steps, and he was most favorably impressed."

For the duration of the orchestral program, Lavinia's fears of saying the wrong thing or appearing gauche were in abeyance. But she failed to enjoy the German composer's symphony because she was constantly comparing the splendor of her surroundings with the squalor of the King's Bench prison.

For her father's sake, she had to mimic the appearance and manners of all these lords and ladies, just as *lhondhoo* imitated the calls of other birds. Like the blackbird, she was seeking the shiniest, most juice-filled berry on the vine—rather, the wealthiest husband she could get.

Her father had fondly bestowed avian nicknames upon all his children. Kerron, sharp-eyed and clever as a falcon, had been rechristened *Shirragh*. Gentle, wrenlike Kitty was *Drean*. Somewhere at Castle Cashin hung a watercolor of the three birds perched together on the battlements. Lavinia wished she'd brought it with her to England, as a remembrance of those who would benefit most from her marriage.

Garrick, after several attempts, succeeded in cornering Lady Everdon, who told him nervously, "*Monseigneur* my husband prefers that I keep away from you."

"But he's not here to object, is he? I'd hoped to meet you both again—our conversation in the foyer of Covent Garden theatre was regrettably brief."

"He spends the evening at his club—*je vous assure*, he does not go for the gaming. That pastime he has given up, for fear of losing our daughters' dowries."

"I hadn't guessed he was such a devoted father."
Wryly, Garrick added, "Not in my experience."

"What do you want from him?" she asked fearfully.

"The chance to test his famous talent for card play. I'm not interested in winning money. We can wager counters, or pins, or buttons."

"To return to his former habits, for even a single night—*ce n'est pas possible*. He doesn't care to see you again, ever."

"But you and I know better. Don't we?"

She stared at him, aghast. *"Vraiment*, you are much mistaken." Turning, she walked swiftly away from him, heels tapping on the parquet floor.

The gossips, Garrick supposed, had witnessed this latest snub. Throughout the evening, people stared him down as if daring him to approach, or edged away when he passed near them.

He was joined by his one friend, Oliver Parfitt, who grumbled, "Devil of a dull affair. Time to bolt, I'm thinking."

"Prawn, in which gentlemen's club would I be likely to find Lord Everdon?"

"White's, almost certainly. What d'you want him for? A fearsome grim character—no fun in him at all."

"Care to accompany me, or does a certain fair widow wait for you?"

Prawn's plump cheeks puffed out in a grin. "Jenny needs a restful night—for a change. Aye, I'm with you, Garry."

Frances accepted his excuses with complaisance and resumed her dialogue with Lord Newbold.

Lavinia raised her angelic face and surprised him

by saying sympathetically, "I don't wonder at your leaving. Everyone is being shamelessly rude to you, apart from Mr. Parfitt and the Frenchwoman. And that lady in blue keeps looking over here, as though she might like to speak with you."

"Only because she craves news of my brother," said Garrick. "Last winter she bore his daughter—unbeknownst to her husband, who assumes the child is his. That shocks you, does it? Well, Francesca is a paragon of marital fidelity. She probably neglected to inform you that many wives take a lover after producing the requisite son and heir. I advise you to learn all the rules of a game before trying to play, *bellissima*."

Her eyes were bottomless wells of reproach. "I would never—"

"You can't be certain. Your desires lie dormant now. But I predict they'll one day erupt and spill forth like lava from that great volcano at Naples."

"Coming, Garry?" called Prawn.

On his way across the room, Garrick looked back at Lavinia. Poor girl, now Newbold was chatting her up. An utter bore, William Shandos, forever droning on about music. Lavinia might be a mercenary little schemer, but she didn't deserve so dull a mate as the stiff and pedantic peer. She was too vital a girl to be interested in a man like that, no matter how rich.

Chapter 6

Not one of the gentlemen Garrick found at White's Club in St. James's Street was politically or socially prominent. A majority of the lords and great landowners, freed from their duties by a Parliamentary recess, had deserted the capital.

He and Prawn made their way to the upper floor, pausing on the half-landing to adjust their cravats at the gilt-framed looking glass. Portraits of present and former members lined the walls, and Garrick directed a baleful stare at the painted image of the late Duke of Halford, clad in the ermine-banded robes he'd worn at the king's coronation. The artist had been unable to soften or eliminate the hauteur he remembered so well. Presumably, the duke hadn't considered the Reynolds canvas sufficiently flattering. A vain man, he'd been quick to discard anything that failed to satisfy him, whether a costly work of art or a wayward son.

Proceeding to the card room, they found several elderly whist players gathered around a baize-topped table. A younger party was engaged in a livelier, far noisier game of hazard, and each roll of the dice was greeted with a groan of dismay or a shout of triumph. Garrick disapproved of their boisterous behavior and their choice of game—one that depended upon sheer, unpredictable luck. He preferred piquet or cassino, which required the skillful selection of a card, caution, and an ability to calculate the odds.

"Crabs again," moaned one unlucky fellow, striking his palm against his forehead. "May the devil take back his blasted bones. They're no use to me."

The young amateurs earned Prawn's scorn as well. "Young fools." Hailing a waiter, he called, "Fresh pack here!" After paying out the card money, he suggested to Garrick that they find a quieter room for a civilized game of *vingt-et-un*, and they retreated to a small library redolent of old leather and brass polish and tobacco.

Seated by the fireplace, smoking a long-stemmed clay pipe, was Lord Everdon. He and Garrick exchanged glances but no greeting. Outwardly, the baron was indifferent to his presence.

"Go on, Everdon," said one of his companions. "Explain why you remain so attached to our enemy, whose citizens clamored for the blood of their king and queen."

"Englishman I may be by birth," Lord Everdon answered wearily, "but France is my adopted country. Had any of you seen my *château* in the Vendée, you might better understand the sorrow I felt on leaving. I rejoice to learn that so many revolutionaries have fallen victim to their own foul instrument. Of the twenty-one men recently guillotined at Paris, seventeen voted for their king's murder."

Prawn joined in the conversation. "Did not Louis also receive a fitting judgment? He plundered his nation's treasury to buy diamonds for his Austrian queen."

A rotund gentleman lounging on the sofa sat up abruptly. "White's is a Tory club, Parfitt. If you've got a taste for Jacobins, step across the street to Brooks's. That's where you'll find Charles Fox and his radical followers."

"Are you perchance referring to the diamond necklace affair, sir?" asked Everdon in his gravelly voice. "That villainess Madame de la Motte made false claims at her trial. I assure you that neither the king nor the queen cared to possess it. Monsieur Bohmer, the court jeweller, wanted two million francs, and no royal house in Europe could afford to pay so much. Six hundred and forty-seven stones were used to make the *esclavage*, some of them the size of partridge eggs. A magnificent disaster."

"I say, Garry, didn't that uncle of yours buy the thing?"

Prawn's query made Garrick the focus of all eyes.

"Not exactly," he replied. "Monsieur de la Motte, who stole the necklace, disassembled it and sold the best bits to several London jewelers. Uncle Bardy purchased a dozen stones from Siberry of Bond Street, for my Aunt Anna."

Garrick watched Everdon place his pipe on the mantel. It was like gazing at an older version of himself reflected by a faulty mirror. The baron's hard, antagonistic eyes matched his in shape and color, and he recognized that sharply defined bone structure, with the long, deeply cleft chin. A difficult face to shave, as he well knew—too many angles and hollows.

Did no one else notice the likeness that was so obvious to him? In appearance, if not temperament, he resembled his father.

Emboldened by resentment, he addressed the man who had sired him. "When Prawn and I have played out this hand, Lord Everdon, I should like to test your legendary skill. *Vingt-et-un* or *casino* or piquet, whatever game you prefer."

Drawing himself up to his full height, the baron responded coldly, "I no longer play, and when I did I was always careful to avoid sharpers such as you." He scanned the company. "Gentlemen, I propose that Garrick Armitage's name be stricken from the membership roster. Ours is a gentleman's club, not a gambling den."

"Strong language, Everdon," said Prawn. "No rule bars professionals; the only prohibition is against men who are proven cheaters. Which, I can assure you, Garry is not!" His round eyes darted from face to face, daring anyone to contradict his assertion.

"Armitage has never been accused of dishonesty," conceded the large man sprawled across the sofa. "Not in his card play. However, in his dealings with the Halsey heiress. . . ."

"I was unaware," Garrick said dispassionately, "that my personal affairs were the club's concern."

"You make them so, sirrah," barked Everdon.

"Have a care, my lord," he warned. "If my past crimes are grounds for expulsion, so should yours be."

The baron's lined and sallow face was terrible to

behold, and his wasted body shook with rage. "Out of my sight," he commanded in a voice of pure loathing. "Send for the porter—I want this villain flung into the street. Member or not, he shan't remain while I'm here!"

Everdon's cronies gathered around, pleading with him to relent, trying to calm him.

Garrick, inwardly raging, marched out of the room.

"You should've stayed," Prawn said. "No one can order you out of your own club!"

"What was I supposed to do?" he wondered as they descended the stair. "Challenge him to a duel?"

"You're entitled to seek satisfaction. He questioned your honor."

"He's old enough to be my father."

"He's a madman. A hypocrite, too, even if only half the stories about him are true."

"I suspect they all are," said Garrick.

In England and abroad, he'd heard the tales of Everdon's enormous wagers at the gaming tables, his intrigues and debauchery at foreign courts, the duels with irate husbands. In Paris, Garrick's besotted mother had succumbed to his lordship's insidious charm, and after casually seducing her, he'd callously abandoned her.

They were irrevocably bound, he and the disreputable baron, by their shared blood and a festering secret. Whether or not they possessed the same gift for card play, he had yet to determine.

"We should find ourselves a faro bank," Prawn suggested. "I know of a place in King Street, across from Willis's Rooms."

"A hell?"

His friend shrugged. "The play's fair enough, for those who recognize the usual tricks and feints. But I pity the young country pigeons just arrived in London fresh for plucking."

The establishment Prawn took him to corresponded with his expectations, which weren't very high. The antithesis of White's, thought Garrick on entering the shabby salon. Tapers were missing from the sconces; the carpet was stained and charred. The middle-aged proprietress wore too much rouge and too few undergarments—her scarlet garters showed through her transparent muslin skirt. She had beady eyes, black as the star-shaped patches she wore to hide the pits left on her face by the smallpox. Her dealer looked shifty and greedy. Their clientele consisted of the most desperate and the most hardened gamesters. And yet he felt more at ease here than in the more reputable, exclusive club in St. James's.

Moving directly to the faro table, he and Prawn each accepted a *livret* of thirteen cards, and four figured cards needed for multiple wagers. The dealer counted and shuffled a fresh deck, then presented it to Garrick for the cut. Exhibiting the bottom card to the players, he laid it face up on the table and announced the stake.

"Gentlemen, place your bets."

Garrick watched through narrowed eyes while cards were drawn off the top of the stack, one at a time. The dealer called out each one before alternately placing it on his right side—the bank's—or to left, for the punters. At the conclusion of every draw, he either received payment or shoved a *rou-*

leau of guineas across the green cloth to a successful punter. The croupier hovered nearby, studying the gamesters' faces and hands, lest they cheat the bank with a falsely cocked card.

Garrick knew he had an even chance at winning his first stake; thereafter, the odds would favor the bank. In the beginning, he bet heavily. After the dealer ran through half the deck, he felt far enough ahead of the bank's tally to risk still more. He left the faro table richer by two hundred guineas. Not bad—actually, quite good. *Molto buono.*

When he went to the adjoining room to sample the supper laid out there, a servant gave him a chipped plate. The food selection was ordinary at best. Accustomed to the luxuries of European casinos and the elegance of Lady Buckinghamshire's popular salon in St. James's Square, he couldn't help being critical.

If this gaming house belonged to him, he'd refurbish it from garret to cellar. Hangings and rugs could be attractive without being expensive. It needed bright chandeliers and *torchères* blazing with candles—the darker an establishment, the more he doubted the honesty of the personnel. He'd have a room for billiards, very much in vogue now. It might be wise to devote an entire chamber exclusively to hazard and roulette, so the card players wouldn't be distracted by the constant click of the dice and the ball endlessly revolving in the wheel. And he'd want a faro bank, of course, for that would ensure a tidy profit.

Purely as a mental exercise, he calculated the probable cost of his hypothetical venture. A thousand pounds should cover the rent and renovation of a modest house in the environs of St. James's, and first-quarter's wages for the servants and cook, as well as providing two decent suppers between midnight and morning. His dealer could have a share of the profits, and he'd let the croupiers keep all the card money as their perquisite.

Growing ever more enamoured of the plan, he considered possible sources of funding. He never borrowed money, nor did he want a partner. The most logical means of financing his enterprise, he decided, would be to win that thousand quid at play from his fellow gamesters—and future customers.

He sought out Prawn, whose face glowed pink from an excess of port, and announced, "I'm going to open my own gaming house."

"Are you boozy?" his friend asked.

"I never drink strong spirits when I'm playing. Who could possibly be better suited to running this sort of place than I?"

"No one," Prawn answered staunchly. "But you'd never be able to recover your reputation, and your brother won't like it."

"I couldn't care less about Edward's opinion. Nor do I mind if I create a scandal—that will ensure my success," Garrick said blithely. "Consider Lady Buckinghamshire, my cousin's near neighbor. Scurrilous tales about her house appear in the papers every week; it's commonly described as a den of iniquity—which makes it even *more* popular. Everyone goes there, from the Prince of Wales on down."

He was so hot to revenge himself against Everdon that he'd do everything in his power to stir the coals of gossip. There could be no finer, more perfect reprisal than steeping himself in infamy, while at the same time emulating his father's notoriety. The baron's outrage would know no bounds when he learned that his unacknowledged bastard labored in a gaming house, and lived there. And to add to his torture, Garrick would publicly proclaim their relationship

Money—he had to get some, and quickly. Burning with determination, he made his way back to the faro table.

Exhausted and stiff from hours of maintaining perfect posture, Lavinia pressed her aching back against the softness of the velvet carriage seat. She peeled off her tight kid gloves and confessed her longing to remove the constricting satin shoes.

"We'll soon be home," Frances consoled her. Stifling a yawn, she added, "I shall fall asleep if John doesn't pick up the pace. I can't understand how Garry manages to keep awake and active so late into the night. Drinking and gaming and—and whatever else he does."

"Why did so many people shun him?" Lavinia wondered.

"Because he cried off from an engagement, which a gentleman does at his peril—especially when his reputation is already suspect."

"He must have had a reason," she persisted.

"Very likely he did, though he never explained it to me. My cousin is entirely ruled by his whims, and I'm afraid he rarely considers the possible consequences of his actions."

At the bottom of Swallow Street, the coachman made an abrupt turn onto Piccadilly—far too sharply, for the vehicle bumped over the curb, jolting its passengers. It came to a sudden stop.

"Hit 'im again, harder!" a man shouted. "Knock the bugger out!"

Frances pressed her face against the window. "Footpads!"

The pane on Lavinia's side shattered, showering her with broken glass. A greasy, unshaven face filled the gap.

"What have you done to my driver?" Frances demanded.

"Me friend put 'im right to sleep. And if you lot don't give up your jewels all nice and easy-like, I'll do the same to you."

Chapter 7

F rances stripped the bracelets from her wrists. "Do as he says," she advised Lavinia, and delivered them to the thief without protest. He bobbed his head, dropping the emeralds into his coat pocket.

Sick with regret, Lavinia unclasped her ruby necklace. Before she could surrender it, the nervous horses plunged forward, and the carriage swayed.

"Hold 'em still, blockhead!" the man shouted.

"That's what I'm tryin' to do." This anguished reply was followed by curses and the renewed stamping of hooves.

While the robber's attention was elsewhere, Lavinia shoved her treasure into the crevice where the seat-back joined the bench.

His head turned back, and he frowned at her. "Be quick there—we ain't got all night." As she placed an eardrop into his open palm, he said approvingly, "That's a good lass. Now the other one. And them fancy baubles in your hair."

In her haste, she lost hold of the ruby-studded

comb she'd withdrawn, and it fell into her lap. The metal prongs were sharp, like tiny knives. Seizing it, she stabbed the robber's outstretched hand, and his startled gasp became a howl of pain as she drove her weapon deeper into his flesh.

"Bitch—you'll pay for that!" He wrenched open the carriage door and dragged her out. She could see the driver lying sprawled in the gutter, unconscious.

With balled fists, she hammered at her captor's and used her pointed shoe to deliver a cruel kick to his kneecap. Cursing, he retaliated, shoving her toward the vehicle. As her back slammed against the rear wheel, she screamed in agony.

"Shut up, damn you," he grunted, his face contorted with fury. When his wounded hand closed around her neck, she felt the sticky dampness of his blood. "That necklace—where's it gone to?"

He was distracted by his accomplice, who leaped down from the box, waving the coachman's gold-laced hat. "Look sharp—the watch is coming! Best run for it while we can."

Lavinia's attacker released her so abruptly that her legs buckled. She doubled over, struggling to recover her breath, and saw gold flashing in a gap between the cobbles—her lost earring.

Frances climbed out of the carriage. "Oh, my dear, what has that villain done? Your bodice is soaked with blood!"

"His," Lavinia panted.

The night watchman arrived on the scene, lantern in hand. Profoundly shocked by Lavinia's blood-stained gown, he tried to calm the restive coach horses. After she gave a halting account of her ordeal, he asked, "Did they seize any valuables?"

"My bracelets," said Frances. Producing her vinaigrette, she held it beneath her coachman's nose.

When his senses returned, he moaned about pain in his head. Finally, he managed a few coherent words. "Where's me hat? Did those ruffians take it?"

"You shall have another," Frances assured him. "Can you describe the man who struck you?"

"Never even saw him," he stated helplessly. "I'd just slowed to make the turn when he crawled up the side and onto the box, and coshed me head with a truncheon."

Said the watchman, "Likely them fellows crawled out of a rookery in Tothill Fields—wretched, low taverns they is, crammed with robbers and murderers and scum. They must've been chasing your coach all the way from Hanover Square, ma'am. Disgraceful," he declared, bushy eyebrows meeting over his bulbous nose. "What's to become of us when there's so many criminals and too few night patrols? If I had a shilling piece for every time someone cried 'Stop thief!' I could live in high style the rest of my days. These be perilous times, ladies, perilous times indeed."

Garrick, returning to his cousin's house at an advanced hour, was amazed to find her waiting up. With mounting horror, he listened to her description of the robbery.

"Lavinia defended herself with a hair comb, and when the footpad pulled her out of the carriage, she kicked and shrieked like a Billingsgate fishwife. I don't know what would have happened if that watchman hadn't come to our aid." Frances shuddered.

"Where is she now?" he asked.

"In her bed—asleep, I hope. I made her drink warm milk with a drop of laudanum in it. I'm thoroughly in awe of her; she was so brave—and afterwards, so calm and quiet. Until we were safely home, that is. I couldn't tell whether the loss of my emeralds or the damage to her ballgown made her weep so much. Celeste washed the blood from her neck and rubbed lotion into her poor back. I'm afraid she'll have a nasty bruise."

Crossing to the cellaret, Garrick took out a bottle of cognac. "I was wrong to leave you."

"You couldn't forsee what might happen. I suppose I should have asked William Shandos to escort us home, but it never occurred to me that it would be necessary."

Garrick sipped from his glass, studying his cousin's weary face. "You were the object of Lord Newbold's attentions for a long time before you wed Radstock. D'you mean to pair your protegée with your cast-off marquis?"

"Well, I did consider Halford—briefly. But Madelina Fowler seems to be his *grande passion*, and I doubt he would wed anyone else, not even a girl as beautiful as Lavinia. It must have been providence that brought Newbold to the concert room. You can't deny the merits of the match. He is thoroughly respectable, free of any entanglement, and his fortune is immense. And she'd make a magnificent marchioness."

The prospect was unsettling.

"I do, however, mean to put Halford to good

use—and Langtree. How many marriages have been made at a country house gathering? If Lavinia and William spend time together in a more relaxed setting, I believe their acquaintance might well develop into affection."

"A time-honored matchmaker's trick," Garrick acknowledged. "The poor bachelor, isolated from society, is more vulnerable to attack. After lulling him into a false sense of well-being, his stalker moves in for the kill."

"Your metaphors are too bloodthirsty."

"I still bear the scars from my last skirmish," he reminded her.

He parted from her and went up to his bechamber, which was decorated with souvenirs of his travels. Pieces of hardened lava from an excursion to Pompeii were lined upon the mantel alongside seashells he'd collected from the beach at Capri and the gilt *maschere* he'd worn the previous winter in Venice, during *Carnevale*. His well-thumbed editions of *Hoyle's Rules* and the *Racing Calendar* lay on a table; several journals devoted to horse breeding and farriery were piled on a hassock.

Combing the hated powder out of his hair, he damned himself to hell and back. If he hadn't rushed away to White's, Frances would still have her emeralds, and he could have saved Lavinia from a mauling. Although he hadn't been a witness, he shared his cousin's admiration of the resourcefulness and valor she'd displayed—remarkable for a girl of wealth and privilege. He recalled other occasions when Lavinia Cashin had surprised him— pawning a pearl bracelet, grovelling for coals in the street. That ambitious smuggler who'd bought himself an earldom would've been proud of his spirited great-granddaughter.

The next morning he was roused by church bells calling the parishioners of St. James's to worship. When his valet arrived with a steaming bowl of shaving water, he reluctantly vacated his comfortable bed and wandered into his dressing room. Carlo, lacking the frosty reserve of an English-born servant, recounted all the gossip circulating below-stairs as he draped a linen towel around Garrick's neck and lathered his cheeks with the brush.

"*Banditi* attacking ladies in a carriage! Is common in Roma or Napoli. Not in London, with lamps lining the streets and a constable at every corner."

Garrick put on the shirt he was given and straightened his arms so the valet could fasten the sleeves. He wound a cravat about his throat and secured it with a pin.

Carlo produced a russet waistcoat with horn buttons, then displayed two coats. "*Nero o marrone?*"

"The black. No, the brown. *Benissimo.*"

Head pounding from hunger and lack of sleep, he ambled down the staircase to the breakfast room. Lavinia stood by the window. Last night's tight ringlets had been brushed away, and her black hair hung loosely over her shoulders and down her back. Her simple morning gown was block-printed with sweet williams and forget-me-nots, and parted at the front to reveal a white-work petticoat. A broad blue silk sash circled her slender waist.

Her eyelids drooped, and her gaze was slightly vacant from the opiate she'd taken. Garrick could imagine her in his bed, giving him that same drowsy and welcoming smile. Its effect was too powerful for his peace of mind. He'd wanted her from the moment he'd met her in Cork Street, before he'd learned why she had come to London. And even though he knew her for a fortune hunter, his desire for her still ran strong.

He retreated behind a flimsy *façade* of neutrality. "Have you rung the service bell?" he asked.

She nodded. "The footman is supposed to bring a pot of chocolate and some bread. He seemed rather afraid of me."

"The servants are convinced that you carry a stiletto on your person at all times."

Her pale lips parted, and waves of soft laughter burst forth as she moved to the table; it had already been laid with the Radstock breakfast service, which had an oak leaf and acorn design. When Garrick pulled out a chair for her, she thanked him with another of those heart-wrenching smiles.

"Francesca says you acquitted yourself most courageously last night."

"I was terrified," she confessed. As always, her candor was striking—and entirely too endearing.

The footman arrived with a tray of food, followed by Selwyn and the chocolate pot, which he set down in front of Lavinia. Her simple request for sustenance had brought forth a rack of toast, slices of plum cake, and hot crumpets. Garrick noted that she winced as she passed him the butter dish.

"Are you terribly sore?"

"I've had my share of bumps and bruises tumbling off Fannag, my pony. I don't always manage to stay in the saddle when we're jumping over walls and water."

"Ever been out hunting?"

She shook her head regretfully. "We've no foxes on our island. But at home, I went riding every day."

It occurred to Garrick that if only he spent more time in her company, the more he would notice her chief faults—shallowness and greed and calculation—and the quicker he could break free of her spell. This was his thinking when he said, "I'll ask Francesca to loan you her hack, and I can take you to Hyde Park. Once you feel up to it," he added, recalling her infirmity.

"I've nothing suitable to wear. The seamstress measured me for a habit, but I never collected it from her." Setting down her cup, she said forthrightly, "If the bill is more than ten guineas, I shan't be able to pay. That's all the money I've got."

Garrick rolled his eyes. "Why can't people blessed with riches ever seem to manage them? Ask your father's solicitor for an advance on your allowance."

"I couldn't possibly."

Laughing at her dismay, he said, "Then give those guineas to me, and I'll be your banker. As for that riding habit—don't bother paying for it now. Tell the seamstress you'll settle with her next quarter day."

If only it were that simple, thought Lavinia. She couldn't admit that she received no allowance and never had done, or refute his assumption that she came from a wealthy family. It was possible to deceive, she'd discovered, without even telling lies.

Her long separation from her father had made her long to visit the prison again, but so far she'd been unable to escape her vigilant and concerned chaperone. One sunny afternoon, she persuaded a reluctant Frances to let her walk around the square. As she completed one circuit and began another, she formed and rejected plots. If she dared to slip away to Southwark, how could she explain her absence?

She'd almost reached the northern side of the square again when Garrick came around the corner of King Street. He waved, and she crossed the cobbles to meet him by the central fountain, which was enclosed by an iron railing. A lock of blond hair had escaped the ribbon at his nape, and his unbuttoned coat hung lower on one side, weighted down by the contents of his pocket. He regarded her with bloodshot eyes, and she noticed pale whiskers sprouting above his mouth and along his jaw.

"You look dreadful," Lavinia informed him.

"Busy night," he responded cheerfully, "and successful." He took a fistful of gold coins from his coat. "Yours."

Confused, she asked, "What do you mean?"

"Return on your investment. I staked your ten guineas in a card game and won forty more." He flashed a triumphant smile.

"But you might have lost them all!" And what a disaster for her, if he had done.

"Oh, ye of little faith," he chided. "Here." He thrust more coins at her.

"But they belong to you," she reasoned. "You won them."

"For you."

What to him was a lark was for her nothing short of salvation. Although she couldn't tell him that, she did say, "You've done me an enormous favor, Lord Garrick. I hardly know how to thank you or repay it."

"No need for that," he said carelessly. "Now go and pay off that mantua maker, and get that habit of yours so we can go riding in the park together—tomorrow. Don't feel like sitting on a horse today. I celebrated by drinking too much of Prawn Parfitt's punch, a lethal concoction. Can't remember much about what happened after that."

Lavinia was torn. "Your cousin mightn't like my going to Miss Fallowfield's shop on my own."

"Run along, *bellissima*. I'll tell Francesca where you've gone, and why."

Lavinia cast one more grateful glance upon him and did as he suggested. In Manx and then again in English, she heartily blessed Lord Garrick Armitage and his extraordinary luck with the cards.

Chapter 8

"I 've spoken to the turnkey already," Lavinia explained to her father. "Your transfer to the State House is arranged."

"At a cost of two shillings and sixpence a week? I can't afford it."

With a beatific smile, she presented the money she'd brought him, tied up in her handkerchief.

When he unwrapped the gold, he reminded her, "You were supposed to keep these guineas for yourself, Lhondhoo."

"Don't worry, I've got many more. Lord Garrick Armitage, a very clever gamester, wagered the ten I had—and quadrupled them."

Consternation creased his brow. "I cannot be comfortable knowing that you're beholden to this man I've never met."

"I'm not beholden," she insisted before returning to the topic of greater concern. "You can pay to have food and wine delivered from the shops outside the prison, and plenty of coals."

When they paused to observe a boisterous game

of skittles, he nodded to a pair of onlookers.
"Friends of mine," he explained. "The man in the
brown coat is an author; he shares his book collection with the rest of us. The fellow smoking the pipe
used to be in the army. We meet daily here in the
yard or at the tavern or the coffeehouse. I've encountered any number of professional men—bank-
rupt merchants, churchmen, even a lawyer or two."

Tugging his sleeve, Lavinia pointed to the sharp-
featured man staring at them from the other side of
the enclosure. "Who is he? He knows Mr. Webb,
and I saw him the last time I visited."

"Stoney Bowes, the greatest rogue in the King's
Bench. When his wife, the Countess of Strathmore,
decided on a separation, he kidnapped her and as-
saulted her and kept her prisoner. She succeeded in
divorcing him, but because his legal fees beggared
him, he's now suing her for support and mainte-
nance. He lodges in the Marshal's House with some
woman he seduced—a prisoner's daughter—who's
borne him several children. She and their brats and
his dogs look half starved, but Bowes never misses
his dinner."

"I don't like the way he looks at me," she declared.

"If he tries to land one of his filthy hands on you,
I'll murder him," her father blustered.

"And then they'll cart you off to Newgate
Prison," she warned him, "which is far worse than
this one."

He escorted her to the prison gate, where they
met Daniel Webb on his way in. Lavinia told both
gentlemen about her invitation to spend Christmas
at the Duke of Halford's Oxfordshire estate. Her fa-

ther sought his attorney's opinion before giving his consent.

Said Webb, "The Armitage connection could be a useful one, my lord. And Langtree is a magnificent house."

"Then you shall go, Lhondhoo," he decided.

"Promise me you'll take exercise in the fresh air whenever the weather permits. Winter is coming, so you must have a flannel waistcoat—I can make one before I leave town. Mr. Webb, will you bring it to him?"

Nodding, the attorney replied, "With an outbreak of typhus on the common side of the prison, all inhabitants should guard their health."

Typhus, Lavinia reflected as she passed through the courtyard, was a virulent disease, almost inevitably fatal. She was relieved that her father would soon be moving to the State House, where he would be at a safe distance from the contagion.

As usual, the lobby was crowded, and her eyes watered from the pungent odor of unwashed humanity. Searching for her handkerchief, she remembered that she'd given it away with the guineas.

"Leaving so soon, Miss Cashin?"

Mr. Bowes had followed her. To escape him, she tried pushing her way past the impenetrable wall of bodies. People cursed, and a little girl with a goblin face pinched her arm.

Moving in closer, her pursuer drawled, "My Janey is away—if you come up to my room, I can show you many fine objects. One in particular will please you very much indeed." He placed his hand over his crotch.

Disgusted by the man's crudeness, Lavinia shoved through the throng.

"You'll be back," she heard Mr. Bowes shout above the buzz of voices. "And here I'll be, a-waiting for you!"

Garrick had chosen to bring Lavinia to Hyde Park in the morning, and he was thankful. At a more fashionable hour, hordes of bucks would have clustered around her—she looked so superb on horseback. Much to his relief, the bridle paths crisscrossing the vast acreage were deserted.

The starched neck ruffles of her white chemisette frothed up delightfully between the lapels of her burgundy jacket, so tightly boned at the waist that he wondered how she could draw breath. The long skirt of her habit flowed like a river of wine, cascading nearly to the ground.

"Stop fidgeting," he told her when she adjusted the position of her high-crowned hat for the third time.

"This silly feather keeps tickling my ear. I'm surprised there's no one else here, the air is so pleasant and mild for November. My birthday is usually cold and damp."

He was curious to know her age, but none of his teasing or cajolery had persuaded her to reveal it. "The park is livelier in spring and summer. During the season, hordes of people stroll the footpaths, and the carriageways are clogged. The Prince of Wales swans about, ogling the most voluptuous ladies or presiding at military reviews."

"I don't care about seeing soldiers, or even a prince," she stated, "but I would like a brisk gallop and some stone walls to leap over. A sedate walk isn't my idea of invigorating exercise."

Garrick's black-and-white horse, Magpie, jerked his head up and down as if agreeing with her. "You must curb your impatience till you're in Oxfordshire. I'll take you foxhunting, for at this time of year, Edward is out with his hounds three days out of seven."

Although he'd never much liked spending time at Langtree, he looked forward to the Christmastide revelries. No man was required to be saintly when within range of a mistletoe ball.

His piebald and the chestnut hack ambled companionably through drifts of fallen leaves. Another couple was wandering through the grove on foot. When the young woman noticed Garrick, she turned to her companion and spoke urgently, then spun around and hurriedly changed direction. Her cloak had opened, giving him a brief glimpse of a rounded belly.

"Londoners can be so rude," Lavinia commented.

"That lady has good reason to avoid me," he responded grimly. "When I knew her, she was Miss Halsey—the girl I almost married. The man is her husband."

"Did you see, she's—"

"With child," he supplied. "In a promising situation."

"You broke her heart. That's what Mrs. Bruce told me."

"Some hearts are too fragile. Serena was only nineteen, too young to be sure of her feelings or to correctly interpret mine."

Lavinia's chin came up, and her eyes flashed silver sparks.

"Ah, the shocking truth comes out! Today you turn nineteen."

Flushing, she said, "I don't understand what was so dreadful about your breaking the engagement."

"I had the reputation—well-earned, I should add—of being rather a rake. My drinking and gaming and foreign upbringing were bad enough, but the wenching made me notorious. The popular version is that I took advantage of Miss Halsey during our betrothal and, after having my evil way with her, discarded her most cruelly." Chilled by Lavinia's gray glance, he said, "Untrue. I didn't want her maidenhead, but her money. Or so I thought till I came to my senses."

"There's no reason a mutual affection can't blossom in a marriage of convenience."

"Very pretty," he sneered. "Are you girls brought up to believe such nonsense? I'm fonder of Magpie than I ever was of Serena Halsey. In saving us both from a disastrous and unhappy marriage, I brought about my own ruin. They called me reprobate, fortune hunter, jilt. The tradesmen who gleefully extended credit during my betrothal to an heiress sent their bills as soon as they heard I'd ended it. I pawned my possessions to pay my debts, retaining only my clothes and two friends: Prawn Parfitt and Francesca. My sanctimonious brother, who was seducing another man's wife at the time, informed me that I had a duty to leave England. So I did—gladly."

When they returned to St. James's Square, Lavinia thanked him politely for the outing. This was her special day, and instead of entertaining her with pleasantries, he'd gifted her with tales of his sordid past.

Frances came gliding out of her drawing room. "Lavinia," she said brightly, "I'm so glad you've returned. A visitor has come, and he wishes to felicitate you."

Garrick went with them, unbidden, and witnessed Lord Newbold's reaction to Lavinia in her burgundy riding habit. The thin lips parted; the skimpy brows shot upward in a spectacle of admiration that nettled him more than he would have thought possible. But he detected no telltale light in the lady's face, to his relief. And then he grew annoyed with himself for noticing—and caring.

On balance, Lavinia Cashin was not exactly marchioness material. Yes, she was beautiful, but beauty in a wife was not necessarily a desirable commodity; it might attract too many admirers for a husband's comfort. Her origins might be acceptable to a pedigreed peer of the realm, but they were hardly impressive. Moreover, Newbold, dull as ditchwater himself, would surely regard her keen intelligence as a defect. And her cause wasn't helped by the fact that her father, who ought to be here supervising her social debut, had hared off in a most eccentric fashion.

If offered a wager on the likelihood of a match between the avaricious islander and the monied nobleman, Garrick would lay the longest of odds against it.

Chapter 9

⟨᪥⟩

The letter reached Lavinia late one afternoon, while Garrick was teaching her the rudiments of piquet.

"For your ladyship."

She took it from the footman's silver tray. Although there was no writing on the cover as confirmation, she felt sure it had come from her father or else his attorney.

"Open it," said Garrick.

"Later. I'm still waiting for you to declare your points."

"Quint minor." To illustrate, he spread his twelve cards across the marquetry tabletop. "Knave, ten, nine, eight, and seven—fifteen points. I add four more with this sequence of hearts, plus three for my three tens. Fifteen and seven makes twenty-two. Had I won thirty-eight points, I'd have repique."

Lavinia stared helplessly at her own array of cards. "We've just begun, and already I'm muddled. I'm starting to think Grandmother was right—she said all games of chance were wicked. We weren't allowed to keep cards in the house."

"You accuse me of undermining your morals by teaching you how to play piquet?"

"No, of giving me a headache," she retorted.

"*Che peccato.* I intended to teach you faro as well. I'm going to need a croupier when I open my gaming house, and a female one would certainly attract the punters."

"You're being ridiculous."

"*Niente affatto, sto dicendo sul serio, dolcezza mia.*"

"What does that mean?"

"I'm perfectly serious, my sweet." Under the table, his foot insinuated itself between her slippers, then brushed her ankle.

The brief contact made Lavinia's flesh tingle; the endearment caused her pulse to race. Thoroughly discomfitted, she reached for her letter. The paper was of poor quality and the masculine writing, unfamiliar.

"A *billet doux* from a lovelorn swain?"

Ignoring his taunt, she studied the scrawled message.

Dear Lady,

By surrendering the rubies in your possession, you can prevent a scandal ruinous to yourself and to your parent. His misfortunes and place of residence will be revealed if you fail to comply. My next communication will direct you to a meeting place—you will appear at the designated time or suffer greatly.

There was no signature.

The strapping footman had returned to the sitting

room to light the candles in the sconces. Trying to keep panic out of her voice, she asked, "Alfred, did you see the person who delivered my letter?"

" 'Twas a young ragamuffin, my lady, in tattered coat and dirty breeches," the servant answered before making his exit.

No boy had composed the chilling lines.

Garrick finished laying out a vertical row of cards. "Does your mysterious lover seek an assignation?"

Lavinia responded with a weak smile. Moving to the fireplace, she thrust the incriminating paper among the reddest, hottest coals. Its edges browned, then blackened and crumpled into ash.

"Must be a tradesman's bill—I've burned plenty of them myself. Another one will follow."

"I pray not," she said fervently.

Her father, she knew, lived among hardened and unscrupulous persons, and spent many an evening in the prison alehouse. Under the influence of drink, or in an effort to prove that he was an earl, he might have described the Ballacraine jewels to his cronies. Any inmate of the King's Bench—or any visitor— could have overheard him. He'd known beforehand that she would wear his heirlooms to the Hanover Square concert; it was possible he had mentioned that as well. Which meant that there could be a connection between the robbery attempt and her threatening letter.

Mr. Bowes, with his bloodshot eyes and croaking voice, was the very model of a villain. Could he be the anonymous writer? He'd abducted his own wife, seduced a prisoner's daughter, and consorted with prostitutes. Easy to believe he was acquainted with ruffians living outside the prison walls—and capable of arranging for them to attack a carriage at night.

"Done!" Garrick crowed triumphantly, completing his solitary game. He looked at Lavinia, who stood at fireside wearing a hunted expression. "What's amiss?"

Instanly she abandoned her dejected pose. "I've decided that it might not be wise to take my rubies to Langtree. Highwaymen, I've heard, lie in wait along the roads."

"Fear not. I travel with a pair of loaded pistols."

Her smile was faint. "I wish there were a safe, well-guarded place where I could keep Father's gems."

"Hand them over to his attorney. Better yet, to a reputable jeweler. My family has always relied on Siberry of Bond Street." He deserted the card table, saying, "Fetch your treasures, *dolcezza*, and we'll deliver them to him now."

While strolling the streets of Mayfair at his side, Lavinia amused Garrick by peering nervously down the alleys and mews, and casting wary glances at every pedestrian along the way.

"There's a knife blade concealed in the shaft of my cane," he informed her. "If any footpad dares to accost us, I'll make him regret it."

"You carry a swordstick," she marveled, "and travel with pistols. Have you ever used them?"

"When I lived abroad." Her brows arched in amazement, and he added, "Your weapon of choice, I believe, is a spiked hair ornament."

Her perfunctory laugh told him she was distressed by his reference to her recent ordeal. He resolved never to speak of it again, unless by her choice.

Mr. Siberry was counting his collection of enamelled snuffboxes when they entered the shop. "Lord Garrick!" he cried in pleased recognition. "How fortunate that you've stopped by. One of my artisans has fashioned a jade cravat pin—when when he showed it to me, I knew it would suit your taste exactly." After he'd run his experienced eyes over Lavinia, assessing her quality, he inquired, "How may I assist you this afternoon?"

Garrick set the leather case on the counter. "The contents belong to Lady Lavinia; she's the one who requires your services."

The jeweler looked inside, then picked up the necklace to examine it more closely. "This must have an interesting history. I'd say the mounts are the work of an Italian goldsmith, before the middle of the last century. Did a member of your ladyship's family acquire these rubies on the Continent?"

"My great-grandfather purchased them in London," Lavinia answered.

Garrick toyed with one of the hair combs. "Label the case as Lady Lavinia's property, and place it in your vault with my Uncle Bardy's bits and pieces. As for your fee—"

"There is none," Siberry assured him. "The Hydes and Armitages have long been my clients, and I'm happy to perform this small service without charge. I will safeguard your gems, my lady, and when you wish to wear them again, I shall clean them before restoring them to you. Now, my lord, let me find that jade pin I mentioned." He bent to open the drawer of a wooden cabinet; then his frizzed head bobbed up. "Here 'tis."

When he had studied the item, Garrick sought Lavinia's opinion. "What do you think?"

The plumes in her bonnet fluttered as she shook her head. "You're the one who'll be wearing it."

"It might be useful for pinning my hunting stock," he decided, "and the color will complement my green riding coat. Yes, Siberry, I'll take it."

The shopkeeper placed the purchase in a small leather box embossed with a gold design. "Does Sir Bardolph Hyde have plans to visit town?"

"He said nothing about it during Newmarket Meeting."

The jeweler quirked his bushy brows. "He kept the French queen's diamonds, didn't he?"

"Most definitely. I would imagine he has them at Monkwood still."

"I well remember the day he bought them from me. Nearly two dozen, the largest weighing all of ten carats. I made a collar for Lady Hyde to wear on state occasions, and a grand thing it was."

"Too grand for my Aunt Anna," Garrick commented. "She wore it but once, when her portrait was made."

"The most splendid ornament I ever produced," Siberry confided to Lavinia. "It saddens me to think of it shut away in a case or a drawer, never to be seen."

Despite the swift and visible approach of night, Bond Street was still bustling. Garrick led Lavinia to the print seller's window exhibiting Mr. Gillray's popular caricatures of notable and notorious Londoners. He knew she would appreciate the humorous scenes, even though she wasn't acquainted with the individuals they depicted.

"The thin, pointy-nosed gentleman is Mr. Pitt," he explained. "And the fat, glowering chap with the thick black eyebrows is Charles James Fox, the Opposition leader."

"The French Republicans in this drawing look quite savage, don't they?"

Garrick spied a shadowy figure lurking in an upper window. "There's the artist himself—he lodges with Hannah Humphrey, the owner of the shop. Mustn't linger, or he'll stick you in his next etching." Hooking his arm through hers, he drew her away from the window.

"And have you ever appeared in one of them?" she asked, smiling.

"On several occasions. Last time, Gillray placed me at a hazard table—a rare lapse in accuracy. I'd just given up dicing."

Her lovely, laughing face roused complicated emotions. He wanted to kiss those upcurved lips and caress the glowing cheek, fill his hands with her ebony curls. To tell her how foolish she was to let a craving for money rule her life. She must have a heart—if he put his hand over her breast, he'd feel it beating beneath that pretty coral-colored jacket she wore.

No, no, no, he warned himself.

Her face changed, becoming serious. "Lord Garrick," she said softly, "I must thank you for being so kind—introducing me to your Cousin Frances, winning all those guineas, taking me to Mr. Siberry's. It's quite clear that you don't like me very much." Her gray eyes were shadowed by pain. "And I think you disapprove of me, too."

He didn't want to like her at all, but how could he help it? She was so damned beautiful, and charming, and—he could no longer maintain his feigned indifference. "You're mistaken," he heard himself say. "In fact, I've grown rather fond of you."

"Enough to be my friend?" she asked.

"I think so." Friend, lover, suitor—whatever she allowed him to be.

They walked the rest of the way to St. James's Square in silence, and all the while he wondered how soon he would regret what he'd said to her.

"Where *have* the two of you been all this time?" Frances wondered when they entered the house. "Lavinia, we've got an evening engagement. You'll have to make ready as quickly as you can."

Garrick watched Lavinia scurry up the stairs. "Hope she doesn't need her rubies—we've left them with Siberry."

"So that's where you went. No matter, she can borrow my pearls. Garry," Frances said rapturously, "I've received the most encouraging letter!"

"Is Radstock on his way home to you?"

"How I wish! No, it's from William."

He gave a curt, mirthless laugh. "If you want a *cicisbeo*, surely you can do better than Newbold."

"Don't be slanderous. Last week, when he offered us his concert tickets, it wasn't to please me. Tonight he's taking us to the theatre." She pressed her hands together. "Promising, don't you agree?"

"If you say so."

"I shouldn't have any difficulty persuading him

to join us at Langtree. Of course, I must also include another gentleman and possibly a lady, the better to cloak our machinations."

"*Your* machinations," he said pointedly. "I wouldn't wager a ha'penny on the chance that my brother will permit you to fill his house with your company."

"Much you know—he's already given his consent. Mind you, we mustn't say anything to Lavinia; it wouldn't be kind to raise her hopes too high. But I'll stake my gold-tipped riding crop against your halfpenny piece that she's Lady Newbold within the year."

Never had he been offered a more disagreeable challenge. Unclenching his teeth, Garrick muttered, "Done."

Part II

She is a woman, therefore may be wooed;
She is a woman, therefore may be won;
She is Lavinia, therefore must be loved.

William Shakespeare
Titus Andronicus, act II, scene 1

Chapter 10

Oxfordshire, December 1793

"We're quite close now," Frances said. "I always feel I'm home when I cross the Thames at Caversham. No more than a mile separates us from a cup of tea and a seat by the fire."

"You're eager to be out, aren't you?" Lavinia asked the caged Xanthe. Tawny eyes peered back at her through a gap in the willow basket. "Not much longer."

The carriage left the high road for a narrower lane, and Lavinia was unable to see over the tall boundary hedges. Garrick's dock-tailed piebald surged past, and she heard him command the coachman to halt.

After dismounting, he came and opened the door on her side, letting in a blast of frigid air. "Step out and have a look," he invited.

"She'll have many weeks to study the local scenery," Frances objected. "Why stop when we're so very close?"

But Lavinia had already accepted the hand he held out to her.

121

His fair hair was wind-whipped; his cheeks, reddened. Nestled among the folds of his muslin cravat was the jade-studded pin he'd recently purchased. His green riding coat, a masterpiece of tailoring, was molded to his broad shoulders, and leather riding breeches fitted his muscled thighs and calves like a second skin.

He led her to a break in the hedge. "Langtree," he said, his breath emerging in wispy clouds.

In the distance, at the end of a long avenue of trees, sat a large, red brick house with projecting wings and numerous chimney stacks. Gazing at the outstretched *façade*, she said, "It's very grand, your home."

"Never a home to me," he said, his face as bleak as the skies above them. When the piebald ambled over to crop the few windblown leaves left on the branches, he reached for the bridle.

"Why not?" she wondered.

"Perhaps I'll tell you—some winter night when we've run out of more interesting matters to discuss." Moving to his horse, he placed his foot in the stirrup and swung himself aboard. "*A presto, bellissima*," he called as Magpie pushed through the gap, and at once they charged across the open ground at a breakneck pace.

"He's as reckless in the saddle as out of it," Frances declared as she and Lavinia completed the final leg of their journey. "He flies at any obstacle, regardless of the height, and has muddied a score of coats by leaping a puddle instead of riding round it." She shivered beneath the carriage blanket as they rolled down the avenue of leafless elms.

A few minutes later, while Frances gave orders

to the liveried footmen swarming around them, Lavinia admired the intricate diamond patterns in the Tudor brickwork. Together they passed beneath the arched doorway and entered a great hall, panelled in wood from floor to ceiling and decorated with an array of weaponry and antlers of various sizes.

An astonishingly large dog lumbered forward, jowls quivering. Lavinia froze, fearing she would be mauled, and Xanthe hissed and spat, claws scraping at her cage.

"Charlemagne, come to heel!" his master commanded sternly.

With comical abruptness, the oversized creature halted, then obediently returned to the Duke of Halford.

Not at all handsome, thought Lavinia, disappointed by her host's plain, ordinary face and lack of inches. His hair was auburn, fluffed out at the sides and tied into a tail at his nape.

Xanthe let out a frustrated mewl.

"What are you carrying in the basket?" asked the duke.

"My cat."

"Ah, no wonder Charlemagne forgot himself." The dog, hearing his name, sprang forward and was ordered away again. The duke kissed his cousin's cheek. "And where is Garry?"

"Galloping about the countryside," said Frances.

"He rode from London?" The gingery brows came together in a frown.

"To protect us from highwaymen—so he said. It must have been a jest. I suspect he didn't want to be confined in a carriage with a pair of chattering females."

Ascending the oaken staircase, Lavinia glanced down at Charlemagne, whose massive paws rested on the bottom step, and resolved never to let Xanthe roam the house.

Hard to believe that Langtree was nearly as old as her home, for decay and neglect had never been allowed to mar this magnificence. The floorboards shone from regular polishing, and none of the carpets was threadbare. Despite their great age, the upholstery and tapestries retained their colors. This antique grandeur was sadly absent from Castle Cashin.

The chamber allotted to her held a bed curtained with cheerful crimson damask. Beckoning her to one of several windows, Frances said, "The view of the park is particularly fine in the morning. You can see the statue of Old Father Thames on the lawn, and the fern house."

Lavinia carried her pet over to the casement. She could also see the river, which ran close to the house, and a revolving mill wheel.

"I hope you'll enjoy your stay here," said Frances.

"I'm sure I shall," she replied.

"If there's anything you want or need, you have only to ask Halford's servants. Oh, and I must encourage you make use of the bathing chamber, one of the nicest features of the house. My uncle was a staunch believer in the medicinal qualities of cold-water immersion—less hardy mortals prefer it heated. Nothing is more relaxing, especially after a journey. I shall instruct the staff to prepare a bath, if you like."

A maidservant, after unpacking Lavinia's things and putting them away for her, led her down a back staircase to a room walled with blue and white Dutch tiles. There was an oval-shaped opening in the floor, larger than the basin of a fountain and many times as deep.

Dipping her fingers into the water, she found it surprisingly warm. "What is the source of it?" she wondered.

"The skies, my lady." The girl placed a folded linen towel on the marble bench. "The rain pipes all round the house drain into lead cisterns. In the next room is a great copper boiler, and after the water's been heated, it's pumped straight into the bath."

The servant departed, and Lavinia stripped down to her shift. Armed with a ball of floral-scented soap, she proceded down the stone steps. It was like stepping into the sea, only the water was warm— and still. Accustomed to the usual horrors of bathing—the long wait for cans of heated water, the haste to finish before it cooled—she gloried in this marvelous invention. She could even wash her hair with ease.

The wet cambric clung to her flesh, outlining her breasts. Richer food and a more sedate style of living had improved her figure, although the thinness of her arms made her thankful that fashion dictated long sleeves. As for her legs—it was some consolation, knowing she'd never have to expose them. Removing one's nightdress, her mother had declared, was not essential to the fulfillment of the marital obligation.

Her own wedding night, she feared, would be a long time coming. The only offers she'd received had been illicit ones—from an amorous Lord Garrick, which had tempted her more than she liked to remember, and from the disgusting Mr. Bowes, whom she preferred to forget.

She emerged from the bath to put on fresh undergarments and gown, then rubbed her wet head with a towel. Thoroughly refreshed and deliciously clean, she left the bathing chamber.

A figure emerged from the shadowy stairwell, its hand darting out to capture her skirt.

"Lord Garrick!"

"Quiet," he croaked. His green coat was draped across his shoulders, its left sleeve hanging loose and empty. "Don't raise an alarm."

"You've hurt your arm," she fretted. "And your head." Reaching up, she touched the scrape upon his brow and tried to brush away the mud that marked his cheek.

"Magpie refused a ditch, and I went over without him."

"You need a doctor."

His laugh made him wince. "Old Peyton? He'd only tip his brandy flask down my throat. I've already dosed myself with that excellent medicine, at the Drover's Rest. The farrier happened to be in the taproom, and he looked me over. No bones broken, he says." Plucking at her muslin overdress, he murmured, "White. So lovely, dressed in white."

"Are you tipsy?" she asked suspiciously.

He bent his head and inhaled deeply. "You smell nice and—and soapy."

"You're *drunk!*"

"Probably. You have that effect on me, *carissima.*"

His exploring lips were more warming than the bathwater. Her soap's lingering scent was over-

powered by the masculine aromas of leather and
horse and mud.

She pressed her body close to his, and he deepened his kiss. Until that moment, she hadn't realized the extent of her loneliness or guessed that in
his awkward and partial embrace she would find
both comfort and contentment.

All along, she'd fought to save herself for a myth-
ical, monied suitor. Garrick Armitage was a real
man, broken and brandy-flavored, skilled at rous-
ing her emotions.

He gave a moan of pain or longing, or a combination. "I vowed I wouldn't do that again."

"S'aashogh dy ghialdyn," she recited, "ash ny sasse
dy yarrood. It's easy to promise, but easier to forget."

"And you don't mind?"

"I like it," she confessed.

They gazed at each other with heightened awareness, saying nothing.

He was the one who broke the silence, saying
cheerfully, "This may turn out to be the most interesting Christmas I've ever spent at Langtree—if I
live to see it, for Carlo will doubtless murder me
for ruining this coat. I can't expect a state funeral,
dolcezza, but don't let them schedule it on a hunting
day, or no one in the district will attend."

A world without Garrick Armitage—unimaginable.

Unbearable.

Garrick was moderately sober when he took his
customary place at the dining room table, but his
sprained arm ached like hell. An inability to wield a
knife forced him to limit his choice of food to those

items he didn't have to cut, and therefore he had to
let a mouthwatering platter of roast beef pass him
by. He welcomed the arrival of the fish course and
sated his hunger with half a boiled carp and scal-
loped oysters that were elegantly served in a shell.

Horses were the one few interests he and his
brother shared. After they had discussed the management of their stud at Moulton in Suffolk, Garrick
commented, "Fling is looking well. My favorite
hunter," he explained to Lavinia, seated across the
table. "Bred for racing, but he has a greater talent
for taking jumps. I'll find a lady's saddle for you,
and you can exercise him. I won't be able to do it
for a while."

"You are an equestrienne, Lady Lavinia?" the
duke inquired.

Before she could reply, Garrick said, "When I
took her to Hyde Park, she complained that the
pace was too slow. I told her that if she wanted a
good run, she could help us chase our foxes."

"Females don't ride with the Langtree hunt,
Garry, you know that."

"Don't be so damned stuffy. After all, you make
an exception for the Peyton woman."

"Her husband is our whipper-in."

"I suspect it's because you chaps are afraid of her.
I am myself."

Said Lavinia hastily, "I'll be content if I can hack
around the estate on your horse, Lord Garrick."

Her tact impressed him, for he believed that she
desperately wanted to follow the hounds and was
disappointed by Edward's edict.

After the presentation of the cheese and fruit,
Frances led Lavinia away, and Garrick found him-

self alone with his half-sibling. He listened absently to criticisms of his foolhardiness—tumbling off Magpie, encouraging young ladies to hunt. But it wasn't long before Edward posed the expected question.

"Have you seen Madelina?"

"At social functions, but our discourse hasn't run very deep."

Edward removed the port decanter from its silver coaster and poured a large measure into his glass. "And how fares my daughter?"

"I've no news of her."

"She's delicate, you know, like her mother. Madelina nearly died during the birth. She'll never bear another child."

"I'm so sorry, Edward." His sympathy was sincere, but it seemed dreadfully inadequate. His poor brother's life was doomed by his passion for another man's wife.

"When she recovered from the confinement, I urged her to leave Fowler. She begged me to give her up, to forget her. Though I cannot do that, to spare her feelings I came to Langtree."

"You did the right thing," Garrick said, plucking a glazed fig from the centerpiece. More accustomed to receiving advice than giving it, he was nonetheless moved to say, "You ought to marry, and sire sons."

Edward shook his head. "Impossible."

"It's your duty."

"In the eyes of the church and the law, you are my father's legitimate son. The stipulation in his will doesn't alter the succession; it merely prevents me from assigning property to you during my lifetime or granting you an allowance. You're my heir presumptive, Garry—everything I possess will be yours."

"No offense, but I don't want any of it. I'm not a true Armitage. Why are you so determined to preserve your bachelorhood?"

"If Mr. Fowler divorces his wife or predeceases her, she'll be the next Duchess of Halford."

"But you've just admitted she's barren."

"And I'm responsible. We paid a heavy price for our illicit love. But someday, somehow, we shall be united. I couldn't go on living if I didn't believe that."

Garrick's pity was swept away by a wave of irritation. He wanted a nephew—a whole string of them—to save him from being saddled with Langtree and all the other uncomfortable trappings that came with the family title. Even in earliest childhood, long before he'd known the truth of his paternity, he'd felt out of place; in later years, he'd been repeatedly exiled. He'd never been happy here, never could be. Though the duke and duchess were dead and gone, their strife had polluted every inch of the house.

But no argument or reasoning he could offer would persuade the besotted Edward to marry. *In verità*, Garrick was discovering how passion for a particular female could alter a chap's perspective and affect his logic.

"Frances," said Edward glumly, "wants me to spend the season in town. She's made a list of all the aristocratic young ladies being presented to society."

"She did the same for me once, but they were all

heiresses. Lineage was of no great importance."

"She has high hopes for her latest candidate."

"Is there one?" Garrick leaned forward. "Who?"

"I'd better leave it to Frances to tell you."

"Give me a hint, then, so I can work it out for myself. Anyone I know?"

Edward bobbed his frizzled head.

"Beautiful?"

" 'Passably pretty' was our cousin's description. What's more, she has a large dowry—and speaks fluent Italian."

That was enough to provide Garrick with the answer. "Caroline Rogers." He drained his glass in a single gulp. "Radstock is a subtle fellow. When he invited me to stay with him in Naples, I never guessed I was supposed to offer for his by-blow."

"Not so bad a match for you. Just think—money, Italy—"

"Bastardy. *O, mio Dio,*" he groaned.

"That won't have occurred to the Radstocks," his brother pointed out. "They don't know you're Everdon's son."

They'd find out. He intended to disclose his relationship with the baron as soon as his gaming house was established and successful.

Climbing to his feet, Edward said, "Shall we join the ladies?"

In the candlelit drawing room, they found Frances with a book, spectacles perched on her nose. Lavinia, on the settee, was making friends with Charlemagne.

Garrick joined her there. Rubbing the dog's muzzle, he assured her, "I'll get you onto the hunting field, never fear. Edward doesn't have the only pack of foxhounds in the district." Next time, he mused, he'd press his lips against that throbbing pulse point on her white neck.

"Your brother and your cousin are very much alike—similar hair, and eyes, and height. Yet I've seen no resemblance between him and you," Lavinia said.

"I daresay I'm a changeling," he responded, which made her smile. He wished he could tell her why he exhibited none of the Armitage traits or temperament, but this was not the time or place. Subsiding into silence, he continued to take note of all her most kissable places.

Above the prison yard, the black sky was clouded and starless. Daniel Webb had emerged from the noisy taproom after the gates had been closed and locked, which greatly disturbed him.

Said his drinking companion, pausing to scratch an itch beneath his wig, "My girl will have my guts for garters, staying here so late."

"Your cronies were so boisterous that I missed hearing the visitors' bell."

"Come with me; Janey'll find a pallet for you."

Webb had no intention of spending the night with Bowes and his doxy and their ragged children and the pack of filthy dogs they kept. "My other client, Lord Ballacraine, can put me up—he now lodges in the State House."

Stoney Bowes glowered at him. "And so would I, if that bitch Lady Strathmore would supply the funds for't. Jack Cashin may call himself earl, but his money will run out long before his case is tried. That daughter of his will whore for him yet—the day will come when she spreads her legs to put food on his table and coals in his grate."

"Keep a civil tongue in your head," Webb advised, disgusted by the image Bowes had conjured. "Have you anymore information for me?"

"Maybe yes, maybe no," the debtor sneered. "I'm thinking I deserve a reward. I've got a nice one all picked out, too—Cashin's daughter."

"Go to the devil, Bowes."

Webb strode angrily across the yard, rubbing his hands together to warm them. His skin was cracked and chapped—he'd mislaid his gloves. Or his clerk had stolen them; it had happened before. But he couldn't sack Will. The lad knew far too much about his confidential dealings with moneylenders and bailiffs and thieves.

And with the grasping, degenerate Bowes, who lusted for Lady Lavinia Cashin. Her beauty was an asset too valuable to barter, and Daniel Webb would let no man despoil her—she was destined for greater things than becoming a prisoner's trollop. All his plans for the future depended on her getting a husband with great wealth and political influence, whose patronage would remove Webb from the sordid underworld in which he operated.

Chapter 11

Reaching up, Lavinia placed the evergreen bough on the mantelshelf. "On Christmas Eve," she told Garrick, "Kerron and I drive Fannag and the *car-sleod* to a nearby glen to gather holly branches. Kitty ties them into clusters with red ribbons, just as I've done." She collected the crimson berries that had fallen and tossed them into the flames. Stepping back, she asked, "What do you think?"

"*Magnifico*," he answered lazily. A hassock propped up his feet, and an embroidered cushion supported his head. A purring Xanthe lay contentedly in his lap. His attire was as informal as his pose; he hadn't bothered to wear a coat since his riding accident.

He meant to exploit his infirmity as long as possible, for it was a way to ensure Lavinia's constant attendance. With great energy and enthusiasm she'd kept him amused—describing her life on the island, resuming her study of piquet and his other favorite card games: *vingt-et-un*, cassino, even faro.

She'd played the harpsichord for him—or tried to, and her unspectacular performance had thrown them both into hysterics.

"So many books and maps," she commented, her gaze roaming the library, "and all belonging to one person. Your brother's quite learned, but in a different way from mine."

"How so?"

"The duke has closed himself off from the world to pursue scholarship, yet to him it's just a hobby. With Kerr, it's a passion. And he's so eager to visit the places he's read about—Greece and Italy especially."

"Why doesn't he?"

"First he wants to earn his degree at Cambridge." Yapping hounds and shouting voices drew her to the window. "They're ready to depart," she reported.

"I deplore the new fashion of waiting till mid-morning to begin the chase." Garrick's forefinger traced Xanthe's pointed ear. "I prefer to set out at daybreak."

"The doctor gave you leave to ride again. Why aren't you going with them?"

Because she wasn't allowed, it was that simple. "I'm conserving my strength for the Boxing Day outing." He shifted Xanthe to the hassock and joined Lavinia, who was still staring curiously at the busy scene on the front lawn.

Edward, mounted on a showy black horse, sported a bright scarlet coat with the Langtree hunt insignia. The other huntsmen copied their ducal patron's costume, and the lone female wore a bright red habit.

"Dr. Peyton's wife. She's Jenny Bruce's sister." Looking at the wistful face beside him, Garrick said, "I know a less exclusive hunt that you could join. If you're daring enough to wear men's clothes," he added, "and don't mind leaving the house before sunrise. My friends start early and finish before breakfast—you could get back to Langtree without ever being missed. Have you ever ridden astride?"

"On the sly."

"A lass after my own heart. I'll have to get you some breeches and a shirt and hat. Carlo is narrow in the shoulders; one of his coats might serve."

"I've got an old one of Kerr's." She clutched a fistful of curls. "What about my hair?"

"Tie it back in a queue to keep it out of the way. You won't be concealing your sex—can't be done— but you'll want to make yourself less conspicuous."

"What about boots?"

"I can borrow a pair." Crossing to a bookcase, he took down a heavy quarto volume and ripped out a blank page. "Let me have one of your slippers."

"Why should I?"

"I need to know the size of your foot."

Her indecision showed in her pursed lips and downcast eyes. "You'll peek at my ankle."

"No, I won't. I prefer kisses."

"Oh, very well." Peeling off her shoe, she presented it to him.

He took it over and sat at the *secrétaire*, plunged a quill into the inkpot, and, with a single, swift stroke, traced the sole. "Such a tiny, aristocratic foot."

She in leaned close, near enough for him to breathe in her scent. And to count her eyelashes—

so many of them, it would take forever. He was at leisure, but there was something else he wanted to try.

Using his sound arm as a crook, he pulled her onto his lap.

After a swift kiss, he whispered, "You gave me leave."

She responded with an outraged squeak. "Did not!"

"When I said I prefer kissing, you replied, 'Very well.' Sounded like permission to me."

His lips found hers again and forced them to open. This time, his kiss was long-drawn and more intense. Lavinia felt his darting tongue; it sparked curious sensations. Her hands crept up, quite involuntarily, and curved themselves over his broad shoulders. And then she made the mistake of thinking rather than only feeling.

Face flushed, she scrambled away from him, safely out of reach. His eyes glinted. A shaft of sunlight burnished his golden hair—a haloed devil, or else an outcast angel. She couldn't decide which.

"Don't go," he begged. "Things were just getting interesting."

"I've got to finish the decorations," she answered unsteadily, determined to remove herself from temptation. "I'm going to pick more ivy."

He was bored, she told herself as she tugged at the vigorous vines twining up the outside of the fern house, a Gothic-styled garden building. Garrick flirted with her to enliven his idle hours; she couldn't assume that it signified a deep affection. Actions meant nothing unless accompanied by words. And if words should ever be spoken—most unlikely, she cautioned herself; it was too remote a prospect to worry over.

She'd hoped to be distracted from thoughts of Garrick by the Christmas Eve merriment, but the celebrations were more muted than at Castle Cashin and too restrained for her taste. To be sure, a Yule log was carried into the Great Hall and a bowl of wine punch appeared, but neither could brighten her dimmed spirits. Nostalgia for holidays past increased her despondency. Nor could she forget that tonight her father was separated from his loved ones and surrounded by prison walls, or the anxiety that those at home must be feeling on his behalf, and hers. And she knew that everyone she missed so keenly longed to hear news of her engagement.

The closing paragraph of her mother's latest letter had offered advice about how to attract a gentleman without appearing too bold or money-hungry. Lavinia might have been amused by her parent's naïve assumption that gentle manners and a modest style of dress would result in a marriage proposal, had she not been so depressed by it. The man she liked best had no fortune.

The duke, staid and serious, offered her a silver goblet filled to the rim. "How do you honor this night on your island, Lady Lavinia?" he asked.

"After dark, the mummers and the carolers visit, and the boy with the darkest hair is invited to cross our threshhold and bless us. Then we drink toasts with homebrewed ale, and we sing together."

"Sing for us now," Garrick suggested. "A Manx carol."

A desire to perpetuate her familiar ritual bolstered Lavinia's courage. She sang first in her native Gaelic.

> *"Ollick ghennal erriu as blein feer vie,*
> *Seihll as slaynt d'an clane lught-thie,*
> *Bea as gennallys eu bio rycheilley,*
> *Shee as graih eddyr mraane as deiney."*

Then, for the benefit of her audience, she repeated the English version.

> *"A merry Christmas on ye*
> *Long life and health to the whole family,*
> *Life and merriment living together,*
> *Peace and love 'twixt women and men."*

Her performance won her many compliments. Garrick cornered her and said, "I particularly liked the last line."

"There's more to the song," she confessed. "I left out the part wishing everyone plenty of bread and cheese and potatoes and herrings in the coming year."

"You Manx are a race both prosaic and whimsical. From all you've told me about the island, I gather you're preoccupied with farming and fishing. Yet you believe in mermaids and little green men, and beauteous dancing witches. As much as I admire your practicality, your romantic sensibility appeals to me even more."

He'd trapped her under a kissing ball of mistletoe and holly. Hopping out of his way would be undignified, she decided, accepting her fate. She lifted her face and received a hearty buss. For him, it was merely a bit of harmless holiday revelry, but it left her wanting so much more.

The next morning, she accompanied the Armitage family to their parish church, a short walk from the house. Seated in the ducal pew, which was sumptuously appointed with velvet cushions and padded kneelers, Lavinia thought of the more primitive church of St. Maughold, where her mother and the twins would receive the sacrament from Mr. Cubbon. Her father, she felt sure, was attending service in the King's Bench.

In the afternoon, Frances distributed the Christmas letters that had arrived in the post.

The duke was more bemused than flattered to receive so many greetings. "I'm barely acquainted with most of these ladies and gentlemen," he complained, breaking another wax seal. "Why should they write to me or care whether I mean to spend the season in town?"

"Because you're a duke," said Frances, "and unwed. They've all got daughters. Garry, a letter here for you—with a Bury St. Edmunds postmark."

"That will be Uncle Bardy," he guessed, "inviting me to Monkwood."

Lavinia assumed a great interest in Xanthe's padded paws. She examined each one carefully, trying to hide her fear that he might go, and her sorrow that the postbag held nothing for her.

"Here, Lavinia, this one's yours, forwarded from London."

Her nameless blackmailer's crude scrawl destroyed her eagerness to open the square of folded paper. Garrick had gravitated to her side, so she pushed it into her pocket hole.

He picked up the watercolor of Castle Cashin, which she'd brought downstairs to show him. "Very imposing. I gather it has a long and rich history."

"Quite an eventful one," Lavinia replied. "It served as a lookout point in ancient days, when the Norse raiding parties came to the island. Later, it was a military fortification, and then it became a residence. During the Civil War, when the Roundheads invaded the island, it sheltered Manx Royalists. A cannon used during the siege sits in our stableyard."

"Which side won the battle?"

Shamefaced, she admitted, "My ancestor surrendered to the Commonwealth forces. Manxmen, and Cashins in particular, care less about English affairs than their own comfort and prosperity. They profited equally during the Commonwealth and after the Restoration."

"And enriched themselves trading contraband."

She pointed out the east tower to him and said, "According to family legend, my great-grandfather used to sit by this window and watch for the return of his smuggling vessels."

With dismaying perception, he said, "You're sorry to spend this Christmas away from your family, aren't you? I've spent more holidays apart from my relations than with them."

"Where were you last year?"

"At my *palazzo* in Venice. I miss it almost as much as you do Castle Cashin." His finger flicked at the tears along the paper's edge. "These will worsen if the picture isn't set in a frame. I'll order the estate carpenter to make one—my New Year's gift to you."

"I've no present to give you."

"*Non importa.*" Lowering his voice to a confidential murmur, he said, "All I want is your company on the hunting field tomorrow."

"I'll be there," she promised.

"You've got to be up and dressed before dawn," he reminded her, "so you should retire early tonight. And unless you wish to scandalize your chambermaid, don't let her turn down the bed."

Lavinia did as he suggested, and shortly after dinner she went upstairs to her room. While the maid helped her remove her garments, she pretended to be extraordinarily weary.

"I shall probably sleep later than usual," she said as a precaution. "You needn't bring my morning tea—when I want you, I'll ring the bell."

"As you wish, my lady."

Mindful of Garrick's cryptic warning, Lavinia added dismissively, "That will be all, thank you."

The girl curtsied and withdrew.

The instant the door closed behind her, Lavinia rushed to the bed and swept back the crimson curtains. Xanthe gazed up at her with secretive eyes as she seized the counterpane and pulled it back. Tucked among the pillows was a bundle—shirt, gray flannel waistcoat, riding breeches, boots, and a triangular cocked hat. Impressed by Garrick's ingenuity and awed by his daring, she hid everything under the bed and climbed into it.

Lavinia was awake and fully dressed—the clothes fit her almost perfectly—by the time Garrick tapped on her door. When she stepped out into the corridor, he grinned, presumably at her altered appearance, then handed her a bun. On the way down the back staircase, she tore off pieces and crammed them into her mouth.

They crept into the stable, and the sweet scent of hay reminded Lavinia of the *soalt* loft where she and the twins had so often gathered to confide their troubles and dreams. "We'll lead the horses out as quietly as we can," Garrick told her, "to the avenue. Then I'll come back for the saddles." He put her in charge of the bay hunter and went to fetch his piebald gelding.

Fling endeared himself to her by standing calmly as she slipped the bridle over his elegant head. His forelock and mane were black; his brow was marked with a white star. She'd succeeded in placing the saddle on his back when Garrick, having finished his preparations, came over to assist her.

His eyes roamed the length of her body. "Those boots don't pinch?"

"They're fine."

"I got them from a stableboy. The rest of the things were mine and came from a box in the attic. But I neglected to provide you with a neckcloth." He produced his cambric handkerchief, crisp from recent laundering. "Hold up your chin." He wound the material around her neck, loosely knotting it. Then he straightened her hat and tucked a stray curl underneath.

"You look a bit more like a chap—or as close to one as I can make you." His gaze lingered on her bosom.

Her face flamed. Sweet kisses she could accept;

lascivious glances were an entirely different matter. She bent over to adjust the tiny brass buckle at her knee but straightened quickly when she realized she'd exposed her bottom. He laughed softly, wickedly, *mooidjean* that he was.

She fitted her left foot into the stirrup iron. Gripping the animal's withers for support, she swung her right leg over his back. Once seated, she marvelled at how comfortable she felt, perfectly balanced in the center of her horse rather than perched precariously behind the two curved pommels of a sidesaddle.

"You've ridden Fling around the park, so you already know he's just an oversized rocking horse," said Garrick. "There's no bad temper in him, and he'll get you over anything, be it water or timber or hedge. Won't you, my good fellow?" He ran his hand along the chestnut muzzle.

They took the road that led to Caversham and Reading, and had gone no more than two miles when they came to an inn. It was larger and more sprawling than Boayl Fea in Maughold parish, which Lavinia knew so well and had often visited.

"The Drover's Rest. It offers lodging and stabling to travelers. At night, the taproom is as busy as a London public house, and the barkeep knows all the best gossip."

Lavinia hadn't imagined that such a great number of people would be up and about in the semi-darkness. Exuberant without being disorderly, the crowd was formed by several distinct and recognizable types: laboring men mounted on sturdy cobs, prosperous farmers with well-tended hacks, and boys astride their ponies. On the periphery stood a motley group identified by Garrick as foot followers.

"The Langtree hunt won't permit them. The longer the run, the greater their difficulty keeping pace."

Quizzical glances and some ill-concealed grins told Lavinia that her sex was no secret, but her fear that she'd be a target of malice or derision faded before the hounds were unleashed.

"We're hunting with a mixed pack today," Garrick observed, "more dog hounds than bitches. Eight couple—that should serve."

"Who's the owner?"

"Nearly every man present, saving myself. They aren't kennel-bred and raised all together like the Langtree hounds. Be still, Magpie," he said as his piebald danced about.

Although Fling maintained his composure, he signalled his interest in the proceedings by flicking his ears forward and back.

The chief huntsman, clutching a battered horn, approached them. "Happy to see you among us again, Lord Garry. When were you last out for a Boxing Day meet?"

"Three years ago."

"So long as that? A sure sign of age, when a twelvemonth passes like a day. What kind of hunting did you find in those foreign places you visited?"

"None at all, to my regret."

"Hmph," the other man responded in patent disgust. "No wonder you've come back."

"How lies the scent this morning?"

"Tolerable well, my lord, near breast high, and

the wind is blowing out of the west. Conditions have been poor since the leaves dropped off the trees, but in open ground we should have some fine runs. Not too foggy or too frosty, neither. Ours is well-foxed country; we'll not have trouble finding.'' He directed a sharp, speculative glance at Lavinia before riding on.

"You need to keep up with the hounds," Garrick instructed her, "and stay on your horse as best you can. If I give you an order in the field, you must obey without question or protest. Is that clear?"

She nodded.

"Take this." He held out his riding whip. "If you choose to ride through a gate instead of leap it, use the crook of the handle to lift the latch. I'll stay as close to you as I can. Just remember—hunting is a simple matter of fear and balance. Master your fear and maintain your balance, and you'll come to no harm."

"I'll try," she answered, her throat dry from mounting excitement.

"Hark forrard!" called the master. The huntsman and the two whippers-in guided the hounds to the adjacent meadow.

The proprietor of the Drover's Rest and his wife watched the hunt move away. Their youngest children, too small to ride or follow on foot, capered about the muddy yard.

The hounds fanned out in all directions, sniffing among fallen leaves in the adjacent orchard and nosing tufts of grass. The whippers-in herded them together with shouted commands and rebukes, calling each animal by his or her name. The hunt was travelling through a field when the dogs started to form a line.

"Have at 'im!"

In response to the call, they surged forward more swiftly still, paws scarcely striking the ground.

"They've found!" Garrick applied his heels to the piebald's flanks.

Lavinia copied him and sent Fling bolting after Magpie.

The hounds ran mute, hunting their line in unified silence. Suddenly they broke into full cry. Lavinia could now see the fox dashing well ahead of the baying pack, ears flattened and tail flying behind like a bushy pennant. When he slipped through a break in the hedge, the hounds followed. Fling approached this first obstacle with assurance and carried her over quickly, soaring effortlessly. He ran like the racehorse he was, neck and legs stretched out, hooves cutting up the turf. Lavinia pressed her legs tight against his sides and crouched lower in the saddle. The cold wind in her face was invigorating, and the exuberance of the chase was like nothing she'd experienced.

The huntsman's horn screeched out a pattern of sounds, two staccato blasts succeeded by two longer ones. The hounds, gaining on their prey, pushed him on toward a millstream. The fox darted into a reed bed at the edge of the weir and swam out to the water gate. Scrambling up its edge, he trotted across to safety with all the elegance and precision of a circus ropewalker.

His clever escape was first applauded and then bemoaned by the hunters. The hounds splashed among the spiky cattails, vocal in their dissatisfaction.

"They've lost him?" Lavinia asked Garrick.

"For the moment," he said, his cheerfulness unimpaired. "He's probably heading for an old covert in the woods. To get there, we'll have to ride farther downstream to the bridge. The hounds will cast again as soon as they reach the other bank."

"I'm glad he got away," she confided, overlooking the fact that his elimination was the desired result of their outing.

"The foxes hereabouts are wily as the devil himself. Ask any farmer who's lost his hens to them."

One overeager hound dove into the water, paddling furiously. "Back to me," the huntsman shouted, "back to me!"

The pace of the hunt was more leisurely after the river crossing, for the pack was slow to pick up a fresh line of scent. Fling pulled far ahead of the stocky cobs and plough horses plodding through the miller's fallow field, and Lavinia felt confident enough to let him gallop on a looser rein.

Daunted by a five-barred gate in their path, she debated whether or not to stop and open it with the whip Garrick had provided. Determination to win his respect won out. She rode straight for it, her heart in her mouth. Fling tucked up his legs and showed Magpie the way, springing over and landing smoothly on the other side.

The hounds resumed their high-pitched baying.

"Hard forrard!" screeched the huntsman, blasting away on his horn. "Onto 'im!"

The canines charged into the covert, a woodland carpeted with bracken. The fox made a surprising move and unexpectedly reversed direction, but his daring was his undoing. The skirters, who ran wide of the pack, cut him off in a thicket. The others circled intently.

The huntsman dismounted. He marched into the gorse and seized the trapped beast, gripping its neck. The fox squirmed helplessly, lips drawn back from his fangs, as he was presented to the slavering hounds.

Chapter 12

Lavinia would not witness the kill. When the fox was flung to the dogs, she averted her eyes but heard their snapping and snarling as they fought for a share of the spoils. She sincerely mourned the brave, rust-colored creature.

"And so ends the chase," she commented sorrowfully.

Garrick climbed down from the saddle. "If not for the reward, the hounds wouldn't be so eager for the next run. These lads follow the custom of their fathers and grandfathers. Set out early, ride as far as the first fox takes them, and return to the inn to feast and recount the morning's sport."

The huntsman walked over and presented the fox's tail to Garrick. "We've agreed that the brush should go to your lordship's friend. A souvenir of her first—that is to say, *his* first ride with us." With a knowing wink, he concluded, "A bold rider to hounds, very bold indeed."

"On my friend's behalf, I thank you." Garrick carried the offering to Lavinia, saying, "A rare honor."

"What shall I do with it?" she wondered, unwilling to touch the grisly object, yet reluctant to forfeit the goodwill of the men who had bestowed it.

Evidently aware of her dilemma, he tucked the tail into his coat pocket. "With your permission, I'll add it to the trophies in the gun room at Langtree."

He gave her cheek a light and playful pinch, much as Kerr might have done. But there was nothing brotherly in the way his hand rested on her thigh after he'd helped her back into the saddle, which made her leg tingle all the way to the toes of her borrowed boot.

The victorious party pointed their horses toward the Drover's Rest, eager for the celebratory breakfast. Garrick and Lavinia brought up the rear of the procession.

"Do you regret coming along with me?" he asked, for she'd been very quiet since the murderous conclusion of the hunt.

"*Atreih*, I feel bad for the fox. But I greatly enjoyed the ride, more than anything I've done since coming to England."

He grinned. "How I wish I might tell the chaps it was a ladyship who condescended to join them this morning."

"It wasn't condescension," she protested. "Class distinctions might matter here, but they aren't so important at home, where aristocrats are a rarity. When the twins and I were younger, our only playfellows were the children of Manx crofters and fisherfolk. Our grandfather was a lord and held himself aloof, but we felt no superiority. Quite the contrary—because we were confined to the schoolroom with our tutor and governess, we envied those who could be outdoors all the day long."

"Then, in its own way, your upbringing must have been as unconventional as mine. I detested Eton, that miserable kennel for pedigreed pups, so much that I ran away. To her credit, my mother let me accompany her on her travels. We settled in Venice but made regular visits to Rome and Spa and Paris."

"Your father didn't travel with her to the Continent?"

Garrick hesitated before replying. "My parents were estranged. The duke was willing to support my mother, provided she stayed out of England. He gave her the money to buy the *palazzo*. He covered her gaming debts and dressmakers' bills, and he paid the stipend to the poor chaplain who had the thankless job of educating me. At her death, he insisted that I return to Langtree. He—and Edward—swiftly discovered that my vagabonding had spoiled me entirely."

By the time they arrived at the inn, the other hunters had already gone inside. Leaving Lavinia with the horses, Garrick entered through the kitchen door and successfully cajoled the cook into surrendering a portion of the feast.

The innkeeper's wife wrapped the food herself. "Roasted breasts of chicken, cheese tarts, and muffins," she said, bundling these items into a linen cloth. "If you want some of my husband's home-brewed, you can take that firkin."

The other woman flung up her hands. "I was savin' that to make the rarebit."

"The tapster can draw more."

Grumbled the cook, "His lordship ought to sit down at table with the others and take his breakfast like a Christian."

Said her mistress, "He can't, not if he wants to keep that lass of his away from a group as unruly as that one will be after a few rounds of drink."

"What lass?" Garrick asked innocently.

"The one a-waiting for you in our stableyard."

He cocked his head at her. "What a tragedy, that so fine and fair a woman should lose her eyesight, and in the very prime of life."

"Oh, get along with you." She gave him the food and the jug. "Save the roguish talk for your sweetheart."

Garrick took Lavinia to a coppice he knew, a pleasantly pastoral spot to enjoy their meal. While they ate, Lavinia questioned him about Venice. Answering her, he wished—not for the first time—that he could take her there. He wanted her to see his fine *palazzo* and experience the holy silence of the many churches, each one uniquely beautiful. And every night they could dance together at a *ridotto* or one of the many *balli in maschera*.

"I envy you the exciting life you've led," she said. Her silvery eyes shone back at him as she brushed back the short, wispy curls that had escaped the ribbon to frame her glowing cheeks. She wore her boyish garb with the same flair she did her muslins and silks and satins, and he espcially liked the way those breeches revealed the contours of her lithe and slender legs.

Desire for her burned him like fever. He yearned to possess her, to press her lovely body onto the grass and teach her all about passion. At the same time, he knew he could not seduce her. The circumstances of his birth had been the first link in an endless chain of scandal; he'd spent years adding to its length. He wouldn't shackle an innocent girl with his shame and drag her to perdition along with him. He had to remember that she had expectations rather than experience.

Raised in the lap of luxury, pampered all her life—how could he possibly convince her to marry him? And if she accepted him, he certainly wouldn't be able to provide the comforts and security she'd always known. Hell, he didn't even have a home to keep her in.

Look—but don't touch, he warned himself, even as his hand moved to her cheek, so smooth and warm, exquisitely sculpted. Her beauty had attracted him first, and everything else about her had thoroughly mangled his emotions.

She gazed back at him uncertainly.

"You say you envy me. But could you be happy living as I've always done?" he wondered. "Recklessly, without regard for what other people might think or say."

"You're a man," she responded, "so it's easier for you to do as you please. For a woman it's more difficult."

"And you've drastically limited your options—you're waiting for someone who has five thousand pounds a year. What you need, Lavinia Cashin, is a man who'll give you five thousand *kisses* a year and show you pleasures you've never even imagined."

The press of his mouth made her head tip back, so he supported it with one hand. The other untucked the shirt—his shirt. The contact with her bare flesh was searing; she couldn't have felt more fiery if lava had flowed in her veins.

She murmured a protest. "You must not—I won't let you."

"What's the harm," he asked, "if we both enjoy it?"

"None, for you. You're a player of games, a risk-taker. I'm not. Nor am I free to follow my impulses—or my heart."

He placed his hand upon her bare breast. "I rejoice to know that you've got one."

Again he kissed her, forcing her lips apart. When he continued to fondle her, she sighed and arched her back. He welcomed this sign of his mastery over her, until he realized he could not contain his raging need indefinitely.

"No more," she pleaded. "Garrick, don't make me want what I cannot have."

What did she mean? That she actually cared for him?

He wasn't sure what he should say. Impossible, he realized, to bare the secret of his soul to one who had such firm control over her emotions. Yet if he didn't do it soon, he would lose her.

Releasing her, he bounded to his feet and moved through the densely clustered saplings to the edge of the coppice. When he came to a maturing oak with a sturdy trunk, he took out the hoof pick he carried and used it to peel away the outer layer of bark.

"What are you doing?" Lavinia called.

"Carving our initials. I want a memorial to this morning and to what we both felt when I held you and touched you." He gouged the soft wood, imprinting upon it all his joy and torment. The oak would live a century more at least, proclaiming his great and glorious hope that he could win the unattainable Lavinia Cashin.

As the old year slipped away, Lavinia grew increasingly troubled about Garrick's surreptitious advances. In private, he exerted soft and appealing persuasions, whereas in the presence of the duke and Frances, he teased and tormented her mercilessly. If his intentions were honorable, she warned herself, he wouldn't court her so furtively.

On New Year's Day, he returned her watercolor, protected by glass and enclosed in a wooden frame. She thanked him politely, battling the urge to kiss him, for that would only lead to more trouble.

Later that week, the expected company appeared on the scene. Lavinia was aware of a burst of ill feeling when Jenny Bruce emerged from Mr. Parfitt's carriage, remembering all too well that Garrick had once sought the widow's favors.

Jenny, in a fetching violet travelling dress, spurned her escort's ready hand and tottered over to the duke on her high heels. "So kind of Your Grace to ask me to Langtree! I vow, I've never been more delighted to receive an invitation."

Halford, visibly discomfitted by her enthusiasm, replied with characteristic stiffness, "My cousin sent it, ma'am."

Lavinia was quick to perceive that Jenny had designs upon the duke. Her lover—evidently the amiable Mr. Parfitt continued to hold that title—was greeting Frances and missed the brilliant smile his mistress bestowed upon their host.

Darkness was falling when the chaise bearing Lord Newbold and his valet drove down the avenue of towering elms. Lavinia missed his arrival; she was involved in a daring game of hazard with Garrick, in which they wagered vast and entirely fictitious amounts of money.

That night at dinner, the duke turned to her and expressed the hope that she was enjoying her visit to Langtree.

"Indeed I am," she responded absently, aware that Garrick was signalling the footman for more claret. He'd already taken two glasses, and they hadn't yet finished the first course.

The duke then began questioning the marquis about his property in Northamptonshire, where he'd spent Christmas. "And besides your principal seat, what holdings have you?"

"A manor house in Sussex. And property in the borough of Kensington."

"Those rents must be substantial. And your family is well?"

Lord Newbold inclined his dark head. "My four sisters remain at home with my mother. Neville is now a Fellow at Oxford, and the two youngest boys are at Eton."

"Seven siblings!" Lavinia marvelled. Eight children, counting Newbold—her father would have called that a litter.

With a glance in her direction, the duke said, "This lady comes from the Isle of Man. I used to think Atholl was the only peer with a connection to the place, before I knew there was a Lord Ballacraine. He's travelling on the Continent now."

Although Lavinia had never said so, this was the assumption made by the Armitages. She'd never bothered to refute it.

The marquis was saying, "Lady Lavinia's naturalness is one of her greatest charms. All parents should dispatch their girls to that marvelous island instead of shutting them up in academies where they are tutored in gossip and silliness."

"You should hear her sing in the ancient language of her people. Delightful."

The gentlemen, she reflected, were talking *about* her rather than conversing *with* her. The manners of the English aristocracy were most perplexing. During a formal meal, it was considered bad form to address the person seated on the other side of the table, so she could only sit there mutely and contribute nothing. At Langtree, decorum ruled.

Laughter erupted from the other end in response to a remark Garrick had made to Jenny Bruce.

"You're most ungallant to say such things!" the lady cried out. "Dear Mr. Parfitt, I rely on you to champion me. Challenge Garry to a duel."

"Wouldn't think of it," the portly gentleman replied. "He's by far the better shot. Besides, he's quite right; you've displayed a most prodigious appetite of late. Two pieces of Twelfth Night cake!"

Cheeks pink, Jenny stared down at her empty plate.

Garrick endured an hour in the company of the other gentlemen, consuming his usual amount of port. He was impatient to move into the drawing room, where Lavinia was ensconced. As soon as he entered, Frances approached him and drew him aside.

"I've a request to make," she told him.

"Whatever it is, consider it done," he answered carelessly.

"I know you don't much approve of Lavinia—no, don't try to deny it, for I've noticed your tendency to avoid her. But for as long as William is with us, I want you to pay more attention to her. I'm not asking you to throw yourself at her feet," she said quickly, "or toy with her affection. But it would be most helpful if you'd show an interest in her."

"You want me to rouse Newbold's jealousy," he said flatly.

"Yes," she admitted. "But in a subtle fashion; you mustn't be too blatant about it."

She was giving him permission to do exactly what he wished, to pay court to Lavinia. He looked over at her, standing by the harpsichord with Newbold. In her watered silk gown the color of harebells, she was the very picture of elegance, a different creature entirely from the madcap in masculine dress whom he'd taken to the Boxing Day hunt. Her hair, exquisitely coiffed, shone like black satin in the candlelight. The marquis was droning to her about a composer he admired. Garrick couldn't imagine that she was interested in the subject; her polite smile looked fixed.

Newbold's knowledge of Lavinia was limited to social settings—concert rooms and theatre boxes. He'd never seen Lavinia on horseback or shown her which card to play in piquet. He hadn't traced the shape of her foot or arranged the framing of her castle watercolor. And he certainly had not kissed her—and never would, Garrick vowed.

The nobleman was outrageously rich and patently enchanted, but money and admiration were all he had to offer her.

Non è abbastanza, dolcezza, he warned silently. Not enough for a girl like you.

"I don't know what I *can* do," Frances complained to Lavinia, plucking at the knot of ribbons at the neck of her morning robe. "I'm not concerned that Halford is interested in her. Jenny possesses none of the qualities he admires—a lively wit, graceful manners—and is much too frivolous to suit him."

"Mrs. Bruce flirts with all the gentlemen," Lavinia pointed out.

Frances added pithily, "Except Oliver Parfitt, who must have paid for the expensive gowns she's been showing off all week. Colonel Bruce didn't leave her enough to buy them, I assure you. Foolish creature, her wits have deserted her if she seriously hopes to become mistress of Langtree." Her burst of annoyance was broken off by Celeste's arrival.

"Madame, *je regrette—mais* Madame Bruce has a great need of you. She has been fainting and sickening, *une tel maladie!*"

Lavinia went with Frances to Jenny's bedchamber. They found her bent over the washbasin, dabbing at her face with a towel; she'd splashed water on her diaphanous nightgown.

"I'm so sorry you're unwell," said Frances. "Is there anything I can do?"

"Oh, no, there's nothing the matter with me," the

widow declared. "I intend to go down to—breakfast." The very word brought on an attack of queasiness. She sat down abruptly.

"I've not heard of illness among the servants, but—"

Jenny's shoulders slumped. "What's the use pretending?" Splaying a hand across her abdomen, she said dully, "I know these symptoms."

Lavinia heard Frances gasp. "Can it be you mean, Mr. Parfitt's?"

"Yes. And I hate him for it!" Jenny pounded the chair arm with her balled fist.

"You mustn't excite yourself," Frances cautioned. "Lavinia, bring me the lavender essence from her dressing table, and the water pitcher. And a cloth. Lie down, Jenny, and let me bathe your temples."

Lavinia, a fascinated observer of the drama unfolding, was relieved that Garrick had not fathered Jenny's child.

Frances led her to the bed. "You'll have to tell him."

"He might abandon me."

"But he's devoted to you."

"I can't face him. Someone else must do it—anyone. You. Or Garry."

"That might be better," Frances acknowledged. "He's a friend to you both. And I'm sure he'll make Mr. Parfitt understand it's his duty to make you an offer."

"Marriage?" Jenny wailed, struggling to sit up.

"Surely it's what you want?"

"No. Yes." Apparently overwhelmed by indecision, she fell back against the pillow. "I hoped to be a duchess. Or a marchioness. Anything but plain

Mrs. Parfitt. Oliver has money, but it's a constant struggle persuading him to spend it on *me*. Hateful, selfish man!"

Garrick shook his head regretfully when his cousin disclosed Jenny's condition. "Little idiot," he muttered.

"Will Mr. Parfitt marry her?"

"Devil if I know," he answered bluntly. "Question is, do I inform Prawn of his impending fatherhood when he's sober or while he's drunk?"

In an uncharacteristic show of distress, his cousin clenched her hands together. "Garry, the tragedy of it! She doesn't love him."

"She wasn't especially fond of Colonel Bruce, either."

Frances sighed. "Unfair, that I should have no children and mind so much, and she's *enceinte*—for the second time—and doesn't want to be."

Fate was indeed harsh, giving a self-centered, careless creature like Jenny the one thing that selfless, caring Frances longed to have. "Don't reproach yourself, Francesca *mia*."

"I can't even be a mother to my husband's daughter," she continued forlornly. "He believed it was kinder to keep her at school or hidden away in Italy—and I suppose he knew best. Tell me, Garry, what did you think of Caroline Rogers when you met her in Naples? Radstock is eager to know your opinion of her."

"I can't think why, because at the time, I was profuse in my compliments." *Dio*, she was ready to play her hand. With Lavinia and Lord Newbold sequestered at Langtree, her matchmaking zeal was running rampant. Before she could pursue the unwelcome topic, Garrick told her he needed to locate the expectant father without delay.

His indolent crony was reluctant to stroll the river walk with him. Shaking out the lace at his wrists, Prawn asked, "Why should we exert ourselves trudging about the wilderness when we'd both rather play cards?"

"Exercise will sharpen our wits."

His friend laughed. "I don't want yours any sharper."

"You'd rather be as lazy and useless as Charlemagne here? This brute needs a good run," Garrick pointed out.

Hearing his name, the great mastiff rose and wagged his tail.

"Oh, very well," said Prawn. "I'll join you."

Once outdoors, the dog chose not to run but merely ambled behind the two gentlemen and kept close to the riverbank, sniffing out the burrows of otters and water rats.

Garrick walked slowly, tempering his long stride out of consideration for his shorter companion. Prawn's notion of country attire, he thought in amusement, was formed by fashion rather than experience—he was more appropriately dressed for a Bond Street strut than a walk down the muddy, tree-lined path beside the Thames.

The water mill's great wheel revolved unceasingly; ducks bobbed in the backwater, diving for food. Garrick spied a rowing skiff beached on the small island, a favorite escape during his turbulent boyhood.

Overcoming his reluctance to embroil himself in another chap's private affairs, he began, "D'you recall how we teased Jenny about her appetite on Twelfth Night?''

"Yes, and damned cross she was about it."

"There's a reason. She's carrying your child."

Prawn came to a standstill. "Bollocks! One of your jests, Garry?" he asked, almost pleadingly.

Garrick shook his head.

"How far along is she?"

"No idea. But I gather that a timely proposal would relieve her mind."

Prawn thrust his hands deep into his coat pockets. "I'm damned fond of her. But I've never regarded the connection as permanent."

"Are you opposed to a marriage?"

"I suppose not. If that's what she wants." The round eyes stared vacantly at the opposite bank.

"You could have the wedding here. But you'd need to go to London for a license."

"You'll support me to the altar?"

"Most definitely."

Prawn turned to Garrick. "I hope I won't lose your respect when I relinquish my freedom."

"Not at all. A highly respectable state, matrimony." Cheerfully he added, "After you sweep Jenny off her tiny feet, you and I can sit down to that game of piquet."

Not exactly a match made in heaven, he reflected. But there was no reason why it shouldn't prosper as well as any other. For himself, he foresaw a union that could be better and richer in every way, based on deep affection and compelling need and a raging, yet enduring, passion. Now that he'd come to realize exactly what he wanted, he was eager to tell Lavinia.

* * *

"She's entirely too pale. Apply a *soupçon* of rouge to her cheeks," Frances advised Lavinia as they prepared a listless Jenny for her nuptials.

"I don't know how," Lavinia confessed. "Perhaps you should do it."

Seated glumly before her looking glass, swelling waist confined by a tightly laced corset, Jenny moaned, "How shall I ever face my sister? She'll guess why I'm rushing to the altar."

"She'll be most impressed." The sharp voice indicated that Frances had wearied of her role as comforter. "Halford's giving you away, and you've got Lady Lavinia for your bridesmaid."

"And Oliver will be glaring at me all through the homily." With difficulty, Jenny drew a breath. "I vow, I've quite lost patience with him. He stayed in town two days longer than he told me he would, and since returning, he's spent more time with Garry than with me. They sit up together all night playing piquet, and he's lost nearly every game. He said his luck deserted him when he got engaged."

Lavinia interjected, "Lord Garrick told him it would come back as soon as he becomes a husband."

"I know Oliver blames me for this, so unfair. It takes two to make a brat."

In the library, Garrick was fortifying the doleful bridegroom with liberal doses of wine. His own feelings on this occasion were chaotic. Ever since the emotional and highly revealing interlude with Lavinia in the coppice, and throughout his friend's engagement, matrimony had become the focus of his thoughts.

Lavinia did indeed possess a heart; time and familiarity had convinced him of that, and he was determined to conquer it. Ordinarily he would develop his strategy with care and precision, but the presence of a rival forced him to take swift and decisive action.

Caressing the tapered bowl of his wineglass with his thumb and index finger, Garrick catalogued the evidence of Lord Newbold's serious intentions. Persistent questions about the Cashin family and their castle. His willingness to partner Lavinia in a game of whist within hours of admitting his aversion to card play. A curious reluctance to make his dutiful return to London and the House of Lords.

He didn't envy Lavinia her choices. A dull but wealthy nobleman who could assure her of the comfortable, easy life she'd always known. Or a roving gamester, a byword for scandal, driven by his desire to get revenge on his natural father.

"Don't let Parfitt drink any more," Lord Newbold advised him, "or he won't make it beyond the nave without falling."

Edward joined them, an open prayer book in his hand. "I've been reading the marriage service. Beautiful language, isn't it?"

Every man in the room, Garrick reflected, had marriage on his mind. Edward, pining for Madelina Fowler, whom he would wed if she were free. Prawn, about to marry his pregnant mistress. Newbold, the unwitting victim of a matchmaking scheme. And himself.

The guests fitted into a single church pew: Frances and Lord Newbold, Dr. and Mrs. Peyton.

Lavinia, accustomed to the lighthearted nuptial

celebrations for Manx relations and friends, considered this company too solemn. Standing before the altar, she stole a glance at Garrick, looking particularly splendid in a bronze dress coat and dark breeches, his golden hair confined by a broad satin bow. He, too, appeared thoughtful and was paying remarkably close attention to the parson for a man of his lively and careless disposition.

Mr. Parfitt recited his vows in a grim monotone. The brightly rouged Jenny panted her responses. Lavinia was envious. She wished she were the bride—with a tall and blond and smiling gentleman at her side.

As everyone bowed their heads for the final matrimonial blessing, Garrick's eyes locked with Lavinia's. A hard knot deep within her chest rapidly dissolved and, with it, her carefully cultivated detachment. The longing she read in his face told her that her feelings were reciprocated.

At the conclusion of the brief ceremony, Mr. and Mrs. Parfitt were escorted to their wedding breakfast by the duke. Their fate firmly sealed, they relaxed visibly.

Lavinia had never had less appetite for food or drink. Throughout the meal, her stomach felt decidedly fluttery, she couldn't steady her voice, and her hands shook so much that she could barely raise her glass in the succession of toasts to the newly wedded couple.

When the party transferred to the drawing room, Garrick held back and prevented her from going with the others.

He took her hand and twined her fingers with his. "You dream of being a bride. What sort of fellow will make you a happy one, I wonder?"

Her senses whirled, from an excess of champagne and her awareness of him. "I'm not sure."

"The marquis isn't the man for you, not even if he were twice as rich. He wants a simpleminded, overbred poppet, not a girl as bright and lively as you, with so much *brio*. He'll never understand that you'd rather run than walk, loll on the floor instead of perch primly on a settee. You're happier riding cross-country at dawn to meet the hounds than listening to a pair of opera singers warble a duet."

"Are you saying I'm not refined enough to wed a lord?"

"Not *that* lord. Newbold doesn't cuddle with you or kiss you. He won't fill your days—and nights—with passion and adventure. But I can."

"I don't want a lover. I need a husband."

"Let me be both, *dolcezza*." His hand clenched on hers. "Marry me." Swiftly he added, "You won't regret it."

"But you probably would. I'm very expensive." This was one of his teases; it had to be. He'd also drunk too much champagne.

"My gaming house is going to very profitable. And my trainer thinks my racehorses will do very well this year. As for a settlement—I've won six hundred pounds from Prawn; I can let you have that much straightaway. After we're married, I'll sit down with your father's attorney to discuss a more formal arrangement."

Her heart raced at this proof of his seriousness, yet she felt compelled to ask, "Are you quite sure? I thought your engagement had turned you against marriage."

"I've never objected to the institution," he replied. "I was waiting to find the right girl." He turned his voice into a caress. "I admired you from the moment I met you in Cork Street. I know you so well now, and I've learned we both crave excitement. I believe we shall find it—together. Most of all, I treasure your honesty."

Lavinia flinched. "Perhaps you don't know me as well as you think." Laughter wafted from the drawing room. "We'll be missed," she said nervously, moving away from him.

"You haven't given me an answer."

Turning back, she said simply, regretfully, "I can't. Not yet. I need time to—to consider. I didn't expect this. I feared you were only trifling with me."

"Feared?" Garrick repeated, relieved by this clue to the feelings she was guarding so carefully.

She placed her fingers over his lips, as if to silence him.

Even if she hadn't actually accepted him, that intimate gesture had also betrayed her feelings. Garrick followed her into the corridor, convinced that his fate was sealed.

They rejoined the company in the other room. Frances, at the harpsichord, was playing a minuet so the groom and bride could dance together. As soon as Lavinia entered the room, Lord Newbold claimed her hand—the very one that had reached out to Garrick so tenderly. He watched her dip and glide, skirts swaying as she followed the stately figures. She curtsied to her partner, her face faintly troubled and her manner subdued. Garrick, disturbed by her gravity, hoped his rejoicing hadn't been premature.

Chapter 13

Descending from his post chaise, Daniel Webb was taken aback by his familiarity with his surroundings. Although he'd never gazed upon Langtree's famed *façade*, he knew it well—an aquatint of the house hung in his chambers. As a lad, listening to the Duke of Halford's descriptions, he'd absorbed every detail. Now, through Lady Lavinia Cashin, he'd gained access to this most hallowed place.

The porter left him to wait in the great hall. Chilled from the drive, he inched closer to the hearth. While warming his hands, he examined the many swords and maces and shields on display.

An auburn-haired lady soon arrived, saying, "Lady Lavinia braved this horrid cold wind to go riding, Mr. Webb."

This had to be Mrs. Radstock, the late duke's niece. She rather resembled him. "Could she be sent for?" he asked. "I've come on a matter of considerable urgency."

"Not bad news, I hope? Oh, dear," she mur-

170

mured at his nod. "Then I shall send one of Halford's grooms to bring her back."

After conferring with the porter, who then disappeared, she asked Webb, "Will you take tea, or do you prefer wine or brandy?"

"Tea would be most agreeable, ma'am." His head still ached and his eyes burned from the spirits he'd consumed the previous night at a Tothill Fields tavern.

She took him into the library, impressively grand, with an array of ancestral portraits and many valuable books. A footman in livery brought the tray, and the lady poured two cups, handing one to Webb.

He mentioned his acquaintance with her uncle, if not the exact circumstances through which they'd met.

"I was a pet of his," she told him. "He had no daughters."

"You wed a gentleman in the diplomatic service, I believe." The duke, he recalled, hadn't approved her choice. "I daresay you've seen much of the world."

"Not lately. The war with France has curtailed my travels but not my husband's." She paused for a sip. "The Earl of Ballacraine has been away quite a long time. When will he return to England?"

"Possibly in the spring, though I cannot say with any degree of certainty."

She returned her cup to its saucer. "If you are in regular contact, you might inform him that his daughter has attracted a highly eligible suitor."

Asked Webb hopefully, "His Grace of Halford?"

"Dear me, no. My cousin admires Lady Lavinia,

but matrimony is not his object. I was referring to the Marquis of Newbold.''

A marquis. Not bad, not bad at all—so long as he had more than the title to recommend him. Arranging his face in sober lines, he said, ''As the earl's legal representative, I feel it my duty to review the pertinent facts about a prospective son-in-law. Is this nobleman worthy of her ladyship, in your opinion?''

''My acquaintance with Newbold is a long-standing one, and I can attest to his honorable character and many sterling qualities.''

''And his fortune?'' he probed.

''The Shandos wealth derives from London properties and extensive holdings in Northamptonshire and Sussex.''

Well done, he silently commended the girl. Rarely did a penniless nobody from a godforsaken island become the bride of a rich and respected marquis. He deserved praise also, for discovering her and realizing how useful she could be. Eager to know more, he added, ''The marquis is not, I trust, one of those wild-eyed Jacobins, a follower of Mr. Fox and his ilk?''

Mrs. Radstock laughed. ''Most certainly not. Newbold's allegiance belongs to Mr. Pitt and the Tory government. I wouldn't be at all surprised to see him occupy a ministerial position one day.''

Better and better.

He learned a great deal about Lord Newbold by the time Lady Lavinia arrived, clearly disturbed by the summons. As soon as Mrs. Radstock left the room, she asked him breathlessly, ''Why hasn't Father written to me?''

"My lady, perhaps you ought to sit down."

Her face went ashen, but she didn't take his advice. "*Och*, what has happened? Tell me!"

"His lordship has succumbed to a malady not uncommon to those confined in the King's Bench."

"Typhus? *Agh Livrey shin veigh olk*," she whispered, "may the Lord have mercy. Has he seen a doctor? Is he in danger of—" She failed to complete the question. "You must take me back to London, Mr. Webb."

He hadn't expected that response. "For what purpose?"

"Father needs me! He's trapped in that dreadful place, surrounded by sickness and—and death, with no one to care for him. I need to be with him."

"And endanger your own health? He doesn't want you to do that—he warned me to keep you away. He asks only that you find some way to pay off his debts, as speedily as possible."

She stared at him helplessly. "How? I've no hope of getting two hundred pounds."

"Three hundred," he corrected her.

"Is there no word from Liverpool about the wool cloth?"

"Regrettably, that matter remains unresolved. His lordship's factor has informed me that the cargo has not been released by His Majesty's Customs. Cannot your friend Mrs. Radstock lend you the sum?"

"She'd ask why I need it, and I promised Father that I wouldn't tell anyone the truth—I gave my word."

"You could say that you need the money to pay duty on his impounded shipment. It's a plausible explanation." He could see that it found no favor with her. "Matrimony has always been an option," he pointed out.

"I know. And I have received a proposal," she admitted, "although I haven't yet given an answer."

"Then you ought to accept," he advised her, "without delay. In the meantime, I shall see that a physician attends the earl. And I can arrange to have a letter delivered to him, if you wish to write."

"Yes, of course I do—thank you." She flew to the desk and sat down to compose a hasty missive. As she scratched away with her pen, Webb inspected the many Armitage faces upon the wall.

Without even bothering to seal her note, she handed it to him. Her gray eyes were tearful; her delicate chin quivered. "I am most grateful to you, sir. For coming here to tell me, and for anything you're able to do on my father's behalf. I mean to get the money, as quickly as I can."

"I have great faith that you will succeed," he told her. "And so does his lordship."

Exiting the library, he met a fair-haired gentleman in a voluminous greatcoat on his way down the oaken staircase.

"You, sir, are Lord Ballacraine's attorney?" he asked Webb in a voice of surprise.

"Solicitor," Webb corrected, preferring the newly fashionable term.

"I expected you to be some gray and dessicated old codger, like the ones who serve the Armitage family."

Although this tall, broad-shouldered fellow looked nothing like his sire, he definitely possessed the late duke's air of supreme self-assurance. A keen intelligence flickered in his brown eyes, as piercing as any of the daggers adorning the wall.

"The earl," said Webb, "is most appreciative of your cousin's kindnesses to his daughter. He was highly gratified when Your Grace invited her to Langtree."

After a harsh laugh, the young man said, "You mistake me for my exalted brother, the duke. I'm Garrick Armitage."

The younger son—the one disliked by his father. "Pray excuse the error, my lord." He bowed.

"No need to toady; I'm the black sheep of the family. And I assure you I don't require assistance from a limb of the law. *Scusa,* I should've used your term—solicitor."

An unmistakable snub. His lordship's initial choice of words had been most uncomplimentary, yet not entirely inaccurrate, Webb acknowledged to himself. Facing up to the unpleasant truth only added to his dismay. He retreated to his post chaise, which was standing in the drive, and regretted that this first visit to Langtree had concluded with his mortification.

Garrick found Lavinia in the library. She sat on a bench by the window, fingers twisted together in her lap.

"Care to go driving with me?" he asked, inserting his hands into a pair of leather gloves. "Edward has loaned me his phaeton. I'm off to Reading to post a letter to Nick Cattermole, my trainer."

"I've already been out. I should go up and change." In her rush to escape, she nearly tripped on the trailing hem of her burgundy skirt.

He gripped her shoulder to steady her. "Not so fast."

Garrick recognized Lavinia's stricken expression; it revived memories of other desperate people he'd seen. Most memorably, a young gentleman who lost all at a Parisian roulette wheel, and shot himself. And that other fellow, beggared by the dice, who flung himself into a Venetian canal. But his beloved was made of stronger stuff, as she'd proved many times. No need to lock the gun room, or keep her away from the river walk.

"Did Newbold propose during your ride?"

"No."

"Something has alarmed you. Was it that attorney?"

"Yes, only I can't talk about it," she said miserably. "Besides, it's complicated, and we might be interrupted."

"Then we'll hide ourselves in the fern house. It's the most private place I know." Their passage through the Great Hall went unnoticed by the porter, who dozed in his chair by the fireside.

"What about your journey to Reading?" she asked.

"My letter will keep. It may have to—from the look of the sky, there's going to be snow later. Take them back to the stables," he called to the groom who stood waiting with the horses and carriage. "I've changed my mind."

Garrick held Lavinia's hand as they crossed the lawn. "Our future looks bright, *dolcezza mia*," he said in an attempt to cheer her. "This year, the odds favor the Armitage Stud at Newmarket, for the field has been less crowded ever since the Steward warned the Prince of Wales away. I and my fellow members of the Jockey Club had to banish His Royal Highness's riders from the course after one was caught cheating." Striding past the weathered stone statue, he commented, "Father Thames could use a cloak—he's freezing, poor chap."

He took her to the ornamental building of glass and brick and flint, and they passed beneath the Gothic arch. The interior was cool and moist, an ideal atmosphere for the profusion of ferns cascading down rock-faced walls.

"You haven't listened to a word I've said," Garrick accused. "Now tell me what's troubling you. Something to do with money?"

"Yes," she answered baldly.

"You've exceeded your allowance again," he guessed, "and that attorney came to scold you."

"Worse than that—by far." She drew a long, agonized breath before saying, "A shipment of wool cloth produced at my father's mill was seized by the Customs officers at Liverpool. The duty has to be paid at once. I need two—three hundred pounds. And I'd do just about anything to get it," she declared, "short of theft or murder."

Innate gallantry warred with his hunger to possess. He had money enough; he could give it to her. But that would win him nothing save her gratitude, and he needed so much more. Here was a gamble he couldn't resist.

"If you marry me," he said, "you'll have that six hundred I promised I'd settle on you. More, when I get it."

"But if I accept you now, you might think I married you because of the money."

"And you might suppose I'm marrying you because I want to get you into bed. Lavinia, we've got the rest of our lives to convince each other it's not so. Say yes. I've tried to be patient, to give you time to be sure. But we both know we belong together."

When he opened his arms, she came to him and laid her cheek upon his chest. "Will you seek the duke's permission?" she asked, her voice muffled by his waistcoat.

"Not necessary. In fact, I'd rather present him—and Francesca—with a *fait accompli*. We can elope. I've no reputation to lose, and after we're wed, yours will be unassailable." Warming to his impulsive plan, he continued, "We'll slip away to the Drover's Rest tonight and set out for Gretna Green at dawn."

"But that's so far away! I can't possibly travel to Scotland; I have to take care of Father—of Father's business."

"Leave everything to the lawyer—what's his name?"

"Mr. Webb."

"I'll send Carlo to London. He can deliver the money."

Lavinia was torn by her conflicting desires. She wanted to be Garrick's wife, for marriage would end her long and lonely struggle, and she desperately needed someone strong to share her burdens. But he valued her honesty—he'd said so the first time he proposed. Not only had she deceived him, she'd just lied about why she needed his money. Her father expected her to pay his debts, and to do that she must marry. But to run away while he was so very ill, and to withhold the facts of her family's poverty and expectations from her bridegroom seemed equally wrong.

Here, in Garrick's embrace, she felt secure. Here she would always be happy. He was the man she loved and desired, the only one she could possibly wed. As he'd said, she had a lifetime in which to atone for her sins.

"I'll go with you," she said.

He captured her face between his palms, forcing her to look at him. "I cannot pretend with you." His voice was ragged with emotion; his eyes were wild. "Be warned, I cannot easily travel beside you for so many days and nights, and keep my distance. I'm no saint. I've waited so long—*sposina mia*. My little wife. For that, I hope, is what you will become, this very night."

His kiss lured her into an oasis of temptation, rich with promise.

Daniel Webb listened glumly to the menials who had taken refuge in the taproom of the inn. His scowl deepened with each description of hazardous, snow-glazed roads and bitter, bone-chilling winds. The Drover's Rest, much to his annoyance, was short of rooms. He had to share a bedchamber—and a bed—with another traveller stranded by the inclement weather. The best room was assigned to a lord, some highly regarded personage whose valet, a swarthy foreigner, had claimed the full attention of the landlady and her harried staff.

He lifted his tankard to swallow the dregs. The hostler could probably tell him whether the turnpike would be passable in the morning. Country folk had a gift for prognosticating the weather.

Several inches of snow coated the innyard, he discovered, and the flakes fell fast and thick. Voices from the stable caught his attention. A pair of riders—a man and a woman—were dismounting, their clothes and their horses white with snow.

"They've not travelled far," said the man, "but they'll want a good rubdown."

"Aye, m'lord," the hostler replied. " 'Tis colder'n a spinster's arse. Down dogs! Down, I say!"

Excited foxhounds swarmed around the lady, noses pointing at the basket she carried. A dark shawl shrouded her figure and concealed the lower part of her face.

Webb stepped behind an overgrown box hedge. He'd been the target of his lordship's sarcasm once that day, and he preferred to avoid a second encounter.

The landlord came hurrying out with a lantern. "The wife was afeared the storm would keep you away. But I told her, if Lord Garry sets his mind on coming, come he will."

"Has Carlo got a fire going in my room?"

"And your lordship's supper's all laid out. Come in by the back door, so none will see you."

Lord Garrick place an arm around his companion. As she looked up at him, her black cowl slipped—revealing Lady Lavinia Cashin's cameo profile.

Webb thought he'd dissuaded her from going to London; obviously, she had prevailed upon Lord Garrick to take her. But the way they looked at each other, and the absence of a chaperone or maid, roused his suspicions.

He waited impatiently until they entered the inn

before following—at a discreet distance—to make certain they were sleeping in separate chambers. He lurked under the hall stair, hiding in the shadows. After they reached the upper floor, he peeked out— and saw them going into the same room. The door closed; he heard the scrape of a bolt being drawn.

In frustration, he pounded a fist against the wall, drawing quizzical glances from the occupants of the taproom.

Just when matters had seemed to be moving in the direction most favorable to him, he'd discovered Lady Lavinia's unreliability and duplicity. Her innocent ways had deceived him into thinking her pure as the snow piling up outside. Never had he guessed that she was a cockish wench, or even knew what a prick was. She was supposed to be helping him rise in the world, not holding him down. Oh, he'd pay her back for her tricks—and that lover of hers as well!

His ambitions would not, he swore, be thwarted by that pair of randy young aristocrats having a shag up in the best bedchamber.

Chapter 14

An attractive setting for seduction, Garrick reflected as he gazed around a cosy room lit by glowing candles. Xanthe, drawn by the heat of a crackling wood fire, sat down and stared into the flames.

Lavinia spread her damp shawl over a Windsor chair and began to unbutton her habit jacket. She glanced over at him, looking very young and decidedly frightened.

Going to the table, he placed a selection of candied fruit on a plate. "Here," he said, presenting it to her. "You might feel more brave if you take some food. I noticed that you ate very little of your dinner."

"You were staring at me."

"I was counting the hours till we'd be alone together."

She picked up a sugared plum and perched on the oak settle. Garrick joined her, wineglass in hand. He stretched his legs out, feeling thoroughly optimistic about the future.

Fueled by animosity, he'd returned to England intent on tormenting his father. And then he'd kissed a black-haired beauty, a typically careless and impulsive act that had changed the course of his life. His initial infatuation had been a distraction, and over time he'd focused his attention more on Lavinia and less on Lord Everdon. Because of her, the dreaded visit to Langtree had turned into a peaceful interlude of discovery about himself and what he wanted in a wife. He didn't much regret the postponement of his vengeance, or mind that the six hundred pounds wouldn't be invested in his gaming house. He knew how to get more.

The bracket clock on the mantel chimed a dozen times. Lavinia's black head bobbed up. "I fell asleep."

Gently he brushed away the grains of sugar from her lips. "Come to bed," he invited. The change in her face made him say soothingly, "Don't be alarmed or afraid. Your first time will give you more pleasure than pain."

"How—how many times will there be?"

He pressed a kiss on the fluttering pulse in her neck. "None tonight, if you aren't ready."

"I am," she declared. "I love you, and I know we'll soon be wed."

Her simple statement revealed to him her innocence and the depth of her trust—gifts more precious than any others he would ever receive. He was her first love, and her first lover. No heartbreak or disappointment inhibited her or embittered her, or made her wary. She was virginal in every possible sense of the word, and he was thankful.

He began the pleasant business of undressing her.

He took away the lawn chemisette and untied the tapes of her riding skirt, letting it sink to the floor. Underneath, he found a white shift and thick woollen petticoat, and he stopped there—for the present. He couldn't go too fast, for he fed on the anticipation. Next, he withdrew her ivory hair combs and placed them on a blanket chest. She climbed onto the bed unaided and watched him remove his own garments. The curious appraisal from those wide gray eyes was singularly arousing. To conceal the evidence of his desire, he left his shirt on.

"Am I supposed to do anything?" she asked when he joined her.

"Kiss me."

She did it so tentatively that he had to laugh. "You can do better."

And indeed she did. She was generous by nature, and giving, and wanted so much to please. Her questing mouth explored his face and neck, moving the length of his shoulder. Soon she was pushing his shirt out of her way, baring the length of his body. Iron-hard, almost insensible with desire for her, he could no longer hold back. Now certain that she would welcome it, he removed her shift.

She had the softest skin imaginable, as smooth and pale as polished marble. Her breasts were deliciously formed; their rosy tips puckered under his tongue. His caressing hands traced the curves of her hips and thighs, and found her delicate, feathery curls. As his fingers delved into her opening, she gasped her surprise. He lingered there, stroking the sensitive secret bud, and became more desperate with each of her sighs.

Gently parting her legs, he eased his rigid flesh

into the tender place he had made ready for him. She tensed, as he knew she would. Pressing on, he muffled her cry with his kiss.

The rapturous sensation of being fully joined was excruciating. His heart raced and his head hummed. Each stroke brought him ever nearer and nearer to the brink—he wanted to fall over, he wanted to hold back. But he was lost in her now, moaning with his release. A calm engulfed him, and he was at peace.

Lavinia stared up at him, eyes wide with wonder. "Are you all right?"

Breathless as he was, he managed a laugh. "Never better. And you?"

Her answer came as a kiss.

Slowly he detached himself from her. "Then you won't mind very much if we do it again sometime?"

"You're teasing me—even in bed." She smiled back at him.

"The best place for it," he declared. "I'll bring you some wine."

Before filling a glass, he turned his gaze back to the bed. Lavinia was sitting up now, her dusky hair streaming over her body in a long, tangled mass. Never had she looked more lovely to him than she did in the aftermath of their lovemaking, visibly moved by her new knowledge of him—and herself.

Lavinia couldn't dredge up any sense of shame. Her discomfort had been fleeting, and her joy was immense. Her love for Garrick raged more fiercely than an island storm; it was more pure than the remotest mountain spring. He'd kissed and touched her; he had opened her up and poured himself into her. She had held him, in her arms and deep inside her body.

She reached up to take the glass he offered. His tawny hair had slipped loose from the narrow ribbon at his nape, and a few stray locks hung about his face. Disheveled as he was, half dressed, he was more attractive even than the modish lord who frequented the clubs and gaming houses of London.

"You must think I exaggerated when I said you would feel pleasure," he said. "But you shall understand—soon, I hope."

"When will I know if there's to be a child?"

"Not before the time of your next monthly courses." He borrowed her glass and sipped the wine. "No one has yet borne an infant of my making."

She couldn't bear to think about him lying with his other women; it made her feel queasy and wretched.

His hand found hers. "Our children, when we have them, will bear the Armitage name. And yet I'm not, as you and all the world believe, an Armitage myself. Only Edward is the Duke of Halford's true son. I'm a bastard, fathered by an English baron my mother knew in Paris. I would've told you before now, but it's not the sort of thing one casually inserts into a conversation."

After a moment of bemused silence, Lavinia asked, "Does it bother you?"

"Not the fact of it. In a way, my illegitimacy has been more a blessing than a curse, because I had to become self-sufficient. The duke, knowing my mother had cuckolded him with Lord Everdon, tolerated me, but he didn't feel that I was entitled to a legacy. Most people assume I was cut out of the will because I displeased him—Francesca among them. She isn't aware that we aren't actually cousins, by blood. Besides you, only Edward and Uncle Bardy know I'm baseborn—and Lord Everdon, my true father. He wants nothing to do with me."

Lavinia detected frustration in his clenched jaw.

"And you really don't mind not being an Armitage?"

"What I minded was the way my relatives kept throwing heiresses in my path. When I realized my engagement to Serena Halsey was a mistake, I did what I believed to be the honorable thing, giving it up. I'll never live down the scandal. I wouldn't care about the damage to my name, either, if not for you."

"You mustn't worry on my account," she told him. His revelation could not alter her feelings for him, and she'd always known about his blemished reputation.

After the many months of keeping her own secrets, she ached to unburden herself to Garrick. He deserved to know that his money would settle her father's debts, and she needed to enlist his support for her family. And yet, she didn't want to rupture this exhilarating new intimacy with such problematic confessions.

He gave her an off-center smile. "I've bared my soul to you; now it's your turn. Go ahead," he prompted. "Tell me something shocking about yourself."

After a momentary hesitation, she smiled. "I'm not a virgin."

Laughing softly, he carried her fingers to his lips.

When he'd kissed each one, he turned over her hand and placed his mouth upon her wrist.

"That tickles."

"You seem to like it." He pulled her closer.

It felt so right, so perfect, to lie beside him. Tipsy from the combined effects of his lovemaking and the wine, she let her eyelids fall. The last thing she felt was his hand on her forehead, brushing back her curls.

When Lavinia woke, she found herself alone in the bed, wrapped in a quilt. Xanthe slumbered on the armchair closest to the hearth. Searching for Garrick, she saw his lean figure silhouetted at the window. He'd shed his shirt.

Drowsily, she asked, "Does the snow still fall?"

"I'm afraid so."

Pulling the quilt around her, she went over to the window. Large flakes whirled outside, tossed by a steady wind, and those that hit the glass panes stuck there.

"Past two o'clock," he mumured. "We're supposed to depart by six. Time enough for the storm to subside."

The fire burned less vigorously, but there was light enough for her to see that his arms and chest and long limbs were covered with pale golden down. A fine line of hair extended down his flat belly to form a thicker patch near the part of him that was so fascinating and new to her.

She reached out and put her arm around his waist. The contact made her shiver, for the air had chilled his skin. "You'll take cold if you don't come back to bed."

He turned to her. "Already you are a most devoted little wife—*sposina mia*." His fingers rested briefly on her throat before sliding down to her collarbone. "And more desirable than you can possibly know."

His caresses grew bolder, eliciting the most delicious responses throughout her entire body. His mouth took in the tip of her breast; his tongue lapped at the nipple. Every inch of her tingled with awareness, and even though the quilt slipped to the ground, she felt warm all over. His hand slid between her thighs, softly stroking. His thumb grazed her inner flesh—her legs buckled and she felt dizzy, as if she might faint. She flushed all over, and her breath came in erratic bursts.

"What are you doing to me?" she wondered.

"Making you want me again."

They returned to the curtained bed and lay down together. His hardness pressed against her, seeking to fill her. As her fingers curled around the firm flesh, he murmured incoherently, desperately. She understood what he felt, for he'd already taught her an entirely new definition of need. The wanting, the desiring—it was pain and delight mixed together.

He slid into her, his heat joining with her heat. His body moved, rising and falling; each time, she arched upward to meet him. Daring to open her eyes, she saw that his reflected her own wondrous anticipation. Whatever waited just over the horizon of their mutual desire, she wanted to find it.

With a powerful, perfectly timed stroke, he plunged her into a bath of fire and ice. She burned; she shivered. She clutched at him, her fingers digging into his sweat-slick flesh, holding him as she dissolved into little flames and tiny shards.

He cried out, shuddered, and was still.

When she was able, she said shakily, "It can't be proper for me to enjoy this."

Garrick rolled over to face her, grinning. "To hell with propriety. Life is far more exciting without it."

He said nothing else for a long while, but just when she thought he'd drifted off to sleep, he took her hand and placed it over his heart. She could feel it pumping, and she watched his chest move as he filled and emptied his lungs.

"Garrick, will it always be this nice?"

"Even nicer," he answered. "You'll see. Try to sleep now."

Obediently, she closed her eyes and wandered into the realm of unconsciousness.

Chapter 15

⟨~~⟩

"Where will we sleep tonight?" Lavinia asked Garrick while they dressed.

"At an inn along the Great North Road," he answered, surveying the snowy scene from the window. "Under ideal conditions, the journey to the border takes the better part of a week." He smoothed the ruffles at his cuffs, saying, "Your travels with me are just beginning, *dolcezza*. Once we're wed, I'm carrying you off to Venice. With luck, and a fast ship, we'll be there in time for *Carnevale*."

Her face was rueful. "How can we travel abroad when there's a war?"

"War be damned. I want to take you to my *palazzo*. I'll tour you around in my state gondola and show you all the wonders. We could even be back in England in time for Newmarket First Meeting, to watch my horses run. If any of 'em win, the purse will help to fund my gaming house. All the most wealthy and titled punters in the kingdom will flock to us. What a grand time we'll have, swanning about in our Italian silks and satins, receiving our guests—making our fortune."

191

She looked dubious.

Before she could respond, he said, "I might not have five thousand pounds a year, not yet, but I'll support you in style. Faro is all the rage, and—"

A knock at the door interrupted him.

"*Perdoni*, milord," came Carlo's muffled voice from the corridor.

Garrick said, "I must find out what arrangements he's made for our journey." Leaving Lavinia to finish her preparations, he exited the bedchamber.

His valet's doleful aspect was unencouraging.

"What's the state of the roads?"

"*Spiacente*, milord. The man of the stable says you must wait to travel by carriage."

"*Quanto tempo?*"

The Italian shrugged. "Another day, *forse*."

Garrick's temper flared. With a fluency certain to command Carlo's respect, he let the curses fly.

Remaining at the Drover's Rest indefinitely was too risky to contemplate. If their tryst should become known, Lavinia would be as notorious as he was. The landlord and his wife were discreet and trustworthy, but the Drover's Rest was too close to Langtree for comfort.

"Have that hostler saddle Magpie, so I can take her ladyship back to the house before she's missed."

He rejoined Lavinia, who was ready to depart. When she heard about the sudden change of plan, her eager expectancy was replaced by alarm. Seeking to calm her, he said, "If flight to the border is impossible, we'll marry elsewhere. I think I'd better go to my Uncle Bardy in Suffolk to see if he'll help us. Holding the ceremony at Monkwood Hall would be more respectable than an anonymous chapel in town."

"But I'd feel so odd staying at Langtree without you," she protested, placing a hand on his arm. "Garrick, can't we tell the duke and your cousin that we wish to be wed?"

He shook his head. "It would do more harm than good. Edward will lecture; Francesca will plead. I'm expected to marry Radstock's ward, and you're supposed to become Newbold's marchioness."

He kissed her forehead, where the curls clustered so temptingly. "I can't imagine that your relatives will be any more pleased than mine."

"Surprised, I'm sure, but not displeased," she said quietly. "They'll be exceedingly grateful when they learn you gave me the money."

"Money?" he repeated blankly. Then he remembered—three hundred pounds to pay the import fees on her father's manufactured goods.

Always in a tangle over finances, he thought smiling upon her indulgently. He'd have to teach her how to manage her resources, whatever they might be. He didn't know the amount of her allowance or the size of her dowry. The earl owned a mill, so they could be substantial—a prospect that made him uneasy. People would assume that his motive for marriage was the same as it had been three years previously. He'd take a penniless bride over a rich one, for he'd had a surfeit of heiresses.

Crossing to his baggage, he searched for the leather pouch containing his cash. "You can have the three hundred now—and your bride gift as well." He handed her a folded piece of Venetian brocade secured with one of his cravat pins.

"Jeeagh er shen!" she cried when she looked inside. "Are these the same diamond earrings you gave Mrs. Bruce?"

"And stole from her. You should have them—after all, they brought us together." He wrapped the jewels and some banknotes in the cloth and tucked the small bundle into Xanthe's basket. He poked her velvety pink nose, saying, "Guard it well, *micia mia.*"

Buffeted by a rough and bitter wind, they rode across the snow-encrusted landscape on Magpie, the leggy piebald. Lavinia, perched in front of Garrick, balanced Xanthe's cage on her lap. When they passed the coppice, he pointed out the tree decorated with their initials.

He carried her as near to the house as he dared, and unstrapped her valise from the horse's back. "You can return through the door we left by," he said. "When we set out, I didn't envision this moment—I was looking forward to a lifetime of nights like the one we've shared." Her white face peered up at him, hooded by the dark shawl. He kissed her chilled nose playfully.

"Take me with you—don't leave me," she begged him.

"You've seen the road to Reading, and the others are probably worse. Lavinia, for your sake, I'm thinking before acting. So go inside," he urged her, "before I can change my mind."

"Be careful," she said.

He laughed. "Too late for that, *sposina mia.*"

When would she see him again? Watching him ride away, she wondered how long she must wait till she could be the wife he already called her. The postponement of their wedding forced her to prolong her many deceptions, and now she regretted not telling Garrick about her debtor father, her derelict home, her nonexistent marriage portion.

She returned to the room she hadn't expected to see again. When she had released Xanthe from the creel, she sat down on the bed with her doubly precious bundle. Staring at the glittering gems and the roll of banknotes, she recalled a maxim from her youth.

"Te ny share dy ve boght as onneragh na dy ve berchagh as breagagh," she murmured.

Better to be poor and honest than to be rich and lying.

"What do you mean, he's *gone?*"

"That's what his letter says—he wrote it from the King's Arms at Maidenhead. He's on his way to Monkwood Hall to stay with your uncle." Frances snipped a woollen thread from the skein Lavinia held for her.

"Garry's rudeness is appalling! He fills the house to the rafters with his friends, then dashes off without a by-your-leave. And still we're stuck with all these people—"

Jenny Parfitt entered in the midst of this outburst. Filling an awkward lull, Frances said mildly, "Garry has left us; he's paying a duty visit to Sir Bardolph Hyde. Lavinia, I'm ready for my blue worsted, if you've got it." Reaching again for her scissors, she suggested to the duke, "Why not ask Newbold to ride with you in Garry's stead?"

"I shall." With a ceremonious bow to each of the three ladies, he strode out of the parlor.

Jenny, looking distinctly unwell, dropped onto a sofa. "Are all our gentlemen out of sorts today? Oliver has been grumbling at me without ceasing."

"Newbold appears to be in a happy frame of mind," said Frances. "He glides about as though borne upon a cloud of joy."

Jenny Parfitt eyed Lavinia, saying sourly, "Best snap him up, my lady, and quickly. The marquis will be a generous husband, I daresay—far more generous than mine has turned."

Overlooking the comment about Newbold, she answered, "Mr. Parfitt dotes upon you, ma'am."

"Only in company. If you could hear the horrid things he says when we're alone together! Just this morning he told me I can't order a new gown for the masquerade at Brandenburgh House next month; he says I'll be 'puffing up' for months to come. He's almost as beastly as Lord Everdon."

Garrick's natural father. Lavinia involuntarily dropped her hands, but at a protest from Frances, she held up the skein. "Why do you dislike him?" she asked Jenny.

"Because he's a monster. I know all about him; he's my son's guardian. He used to be the most disreputable rake in all Europe."

"And a legendary gamester," Frances elaborated. "I'm reluctant to attend a masquerade without a male escort, so I hope Garry doesn't linger at Monkwood."

She'd have to do without, thought Lavinia, for he'd be married by then—and honeymooning in Venice, if he had his way.

Thinking of Garrick, she radiated with happiness. Could no one see the change in her? Were they not blinded by her glow? She'd slept very little, yet she was brimming with life and love and hope. She had three hundred pounds, and soon her father would be free. She was engaged to marry a dashing adventurer. For the first time, she'd experienced passion and the rewards of desire fulfilled.

Frances looked over the rims of her spectacles. "You should go as an Italian lady, your hair is so dark—a Shakespeare heroine. Juliet or Beatrice. My cousin gave me some beautiful masks, the sort the Venetians wear at their *Carnevale.*"

Said Jenny glumly, "Everyone will recognize my costume. If Oliver won't let me have a new one, I'll go as a shepherdess. Again." On this despondent note, she left the room.

"She grows more peevish by the day," Frances said, threading her embroidery needle. "Yes, it's definitely time for our house party to break up. Halford wants to be a hermit again. We need to have our dresses made for the Anspachs' party. Newbold is anxious to take his seat in the House of Lords. I wonder if I might persuade him to escort us to the masquerade?"

Lavinia didn't care what the marquis did or didn't do. Her interest lay elsewhere—with her lover, plowing along snowy highways on his solitary journey to Suffolk.

"I hoped my Christmas letter might bring you to Monkwood," Sir Bardolph Hyde greeted Garrick. Short and stocky, he favored countryman's attire that matched his country pursuits. "I'm eager to hear your strategies for Newmarket Spring Meeting."

"My five-year-old will try for the Hundred Guineas," Garrick replied. "And we also expect to run for the Gold Cup."

"How does Cattermole rate your chances?"

"Haven't seen him yet. I came here first."

The baronet threw back his head and laughed aloud. "I could ask for no greater proof of your devotion to me! Come along, my boy, and I'll show you where I've sown my winter rye."

An acolyte of Mr. Coke of Norfolk, he had implemented several modern agricultural innovations and was eager to indoctrinate Garrick, who listened politely to the instructive discourse. All the while, he wondered what his lass from the Manx hills would think of these flat fields and neat, hedgebound pastures. A windmill pumped water away from the low-lying land; the village houses were quaint, decorated with pargetted plaster and topped with thatch. The wood from which the estate took its name was extensive enough to require a forester.

Garrick's great-grandfather, a Restoration courtier, had acquired Monkwood. His grandfather, cousin and confidant of Queen Anne, had built up the family fortune, wisely selling off his shares in the South Sea Company before the bubble burst. With the arrival of the Hanoverians, the Hydes had retired from court life to devote themselves to agriculture and horse breeding.

"And I have followed that tradition," said the baronet as he showed off the newly renovated stable block.

"The Armitages became rabid Jacobites," Garrick commented. "Devotion to lost causes is a family trait. Edward actually believes Mrs. Fowler will someday be his duchess."

"Armitage men are ever unlucky in love."

"Everdon blood also carries a curse." In a few terse sentences, he described his encounters with the baron.

"He ordered you out of your own club? The audacity! Had you told me of your desire to meet him, Garry, I would've dissuaded you."

"You couldn't," he answered frankly. "I was determined to know the man who ruined my mother's life."

"My dear boy, 'twas the Duke of Halford who did that. He introduced her to his world but never taught her how to survive in it." The baronet drew a long sigh, then said, "We must concern ourselves with the present—and your future. For unless you reform yourself, you'll end up as jaded and embittered as Everdon."

Garrick braved his uncle's disapproving eye. "I'm getting married," he blurted.

The old man was stunned into silence. Then he asked, almost fearfully, "To whom?"

"Lady Lavinia Cashin, daughter of the Earl of Ballacraine and a Manxwoman. Tumbled into love the first time I clapped eyes on her."

Once again, strong emotion deprived his uncle of speech. "My dear boy—oh, this is happy news indeed! When's the wedding?"

Garrick released a gusty sigh. "If only I knew. It's all so tiresome. Francesca has been matchmaking with a vengeance. She means to pair Lavinia with a wealthy marquis and stick me with Radstock's ward. To stave off family opposition, we decided to elope. And then the snowstorm interfered."

"Why do something so rash, so unnecessary? Get yourself a special license and be married here."

"I'd like nothing better," said Garrick, greatly relieved.

"It's settled, then. Let's go in and drink a toast to your bride, shall we?"

The red-brick manor house was less grand than Langtree and a great deal cosier. Following his uncle through the ground-floor chambers, Garrick recalled his Aunt Anna, a cheerful, motherly soul whose untimely passing he deeply mourned. Her print room reminded him of how he'd stirred the glue pot while she cut out all the portraits and swags and borders from sheets of engravings purchased in London.

In his uncle's study, carved wooden mouldings in the Grinling Gibbons style framed sporting pictures by Wootton and Stubbs—a visual history of the Hyde racehorses and their riders. Over the mantel was a formal portrait of the late Lady Hyde, her neck encircled by the necklace made from Marie Antoinette's fabled diamonds. No one but a doting husband would have claimed that the magnificent bauble suited the plain-featured woman.

"Siberry, the jeweler, was asking me about Aunt Anna's collar," he said, accepting a wineglass and a long-stemmed clay pipe. "That night at White's, Everdon referred to the diamond necklace intrigue. Was he really the French queen's lover?"

"Only he can tell you that, and I doubt he would. But he was most certainly a favorite of hers—and of many other females."

"I don't imagine he treated his other victims any

worse than he did my mother. I'm at a loss to understand why she let him seduce her."

Sir Bardolph tamped the tobacco into the bowl of his pipe. "You must understand, Garry, she suffered a severe disappointment shortly after Edward's birth. After Halford was assured of his precious heir, he began flaunting a mistress—Mrs. Webb, one of Drury Lane's lesser actresses. The newspapers printed salacious innuendo and crude cartoons, showing him in his ducal coronet entangled in a spider's web. When my sister confronted him with his infidelity, he flew into a rage, then packed her off to France with your aunt and me."

"He wanted her out of the way," said Garrick sourly.

"She was in a vulnerable state when she met Everdon—and was so enthralled that she was more delighted than dismayed to learn that she would bear his child. She told the duke, thinking he would divorce her, leaving her free to marry Everdon. Who, of course, had no such honorable intention."

Garrick drew on his pipe. Exhaling a smoky cloud, he asked, "Why did the duke conceal her indiscretion?"

"For Edward's sake. By taking responsibility for the second pregnancy, he avoided any dispute—or gossip—about his heir's paternity. By the time you were born at Cherbourg, Everdon had turned his back on your mother, and she'd decided that your aunt and I should have you. But Halford wouldn't permit it; he believed people would grow suspicious. He had no sympathy for our childlessness."

Garrick hadn't known about the Hydes' desire to adopt him. If Uncle Bardy and Aunt Anna had raised him there at Monkwood, his life would have been unimaginably different. "I've told Lavinia I'm Everdon's son," he said. "It makes no difference to her."

"I'm guessing she's a beauty."

He beamed. "I'll let you decide that for yourself."

That evening, they dined together on roasted hare trussed like a chicken and smothered in onion sauce. While carving, Garrick pondered whether or not he'd like living in Suffolk. Very probably, he would grow bored with nothing to do but manage his stud and watch his glorious Lavinia dwindle into a country matron. He much preferred his gaming-house scheme, which promised excitement and adventure, and a satisfying unpredictability.

"I knew you'd give up your wild ways when you found the right sort of lass." Puffing out his chest, the baronet added, disastrously, "Within a year of your wedding day, the price of seed corn will be of greater import to you than a lucrative wager—you mark my words!"

Chapter 16

London, January 1794

"Father is leaving the prison *today?*" Lavinia repeated, staring at Daniel Webb.

"As soon as his creditors were paid, the insolvency charge was withdrawn," he replied casually. "All that remains to be settled is my fee. My clerk has provided an accounting."

Lavinia accepted the paper he held out to her. The total was staggering. "A hundred pounds! How can Father owe you so much, when his case was never brought to trial?"

Slowly, as if explaining to a child, he said, "Regardless of whether I go into court, I incur expenses on a client's behalf. Many letters were posted to the bank in Liverpool and to the Customs House. Mr. Shaw prepared affadavits. I paid entrance money to the gatekeeper of the King's Bench on many occasions. The cost of my journey into Oxfordshire must be reimbursed—post chaise, lodging, food. And the doctor submitted his bill to me."

At Langtree, when he'd said three hundred

pounds would be required, he'd neglected to tell her that one third would belong to him.

"You don't contest the charges?"

Lavinia's protests died on her lips. "No, sir, I do not."

"I've got bills of my own to settle," he continued, "So, I'd appreciate an immediate payment."

"Yes—of course."

She left the parlor and soon returned with a pair of fifty-pound notes. Determined to get her money's worth out of him, she asked about the process of obtaining a special license for a marriage.

"One can be purchased from Doctors' Commons, in the Archbishop of Canterbury's office. The cost is five pounds, and the document remains in effect for three months after being issued." With a smile, he presented his card to her. "Should Lord Newbold require additional information, give him this. I will happily assist him in every possible way."

"It's nothing to do with him," she said quickly. "I plan to marry Lord Garrick Armitage—in secret."

"The Duke of Halford's brother?" He frowned. "I gather you've not told him about your parent's recent—difficulties."

"I will, when he returns from Suffolk."

"I should think his lordship will be astonished, perhaps even angry. Will he stand by you?"

"He loves me," she replied, "so he will understand. But I can't expect that of Mrs. Radstock. I've explained to her that my father must return to London to recuperate from an illness—which is perfectly true." Extending her hand, she said, "I'm most grateful for everything you've done for us, Mr.

Webb." His fingers felt cold against hers, and she couldn't shake the feeling that she'd displeased him.

Webb was exceedingly cross with her, so much so that he failed to take pleasure from his highly profitable dealings with the Cashins.

The reckless little slut and her cocksure lover were wrecking his dreams. A runaway marriage— nothing could be more disastrous for him!

Lathered horses and a post chaise were standing in front of the Radstock house. His wrath increased when he saw the foreign manservant and his long-limbed, fair-haired master.

Damned scoundrel, why couldn't he have stayed in the country, out of the way?

"Mr. Webb, we meet again," Lord Garrick hailed him. "You're a dedicated member of the legal profession, it appears. Are you as devoted to all your clients as you are to Lady Lavinia Cashin?"

Quite the jealous lover, thought Webb, as he bowed. "Lord Garrick. I hadn't heard that you were in town."

"I've just arrived. My cousin wrote to tell me that Lord Ballacraine was expected back sometime this week. I'm most eager to meet him."

"And to ask his blessing?" Lowering his voice to a confidential murmur, he said, "I am aware of your lordship's clandestine engagement. The joyous reunion of father and daughter will take place this very day, and due to some pressing business I shall be unable to share in it. Lady Lavinia will not, I hope, go to meet the earl without her chaperone— or yourself. By so doing she might imperil herself and her reputation. You will appreciate my concerns, I feel sure."

Garrick did. "I thank you for the warning and can assure you that she won't be alone."

He entered the house and paused in the black-and-white paved hall to remove his round-brimmed hat and leather gloves. Xanthe was rubbing her head against the bottom banister rail.

"*Micia mia*," he said as he ran his hand across her arching spine. "Where's your mistress?"

At the top of the stair, he met his cousin. She carried a small medicine bottle in one hand, a spoon and glass in the other. "Garry—what brings you back to London?"

"Your last letter—and my desire to meet the earl," he told her, without elaboration. "Have you given up my room to him?"

"Oh, no. Because Lord Ballacraine is in poor health, he's to stay in Radstock's chamber. I fear he may require nursing—he's had a fever, so I've made up a decoction of Peruvian bark. I'm on my way to the housekeeper's room for some distilled lavender water."

He did not detain her. On his way down the corridor, he met Lavinia coming out of the sitting room.

"You're here!" she cried in amazement. Her black hair was tucked under one of her large plumed hats, and she wore a russet walking gown.

"Going out? Not till you've kissed me."

She did, with furtive haste.

"Properly," he added. "Your Xanthe gave me a warmer greeting than that. Haven't you missed me?"

She gave him a chastening look. "I did—so very much. But your cousin might see us, or a servant.

Garrick, the most wonderful news! Father has returned."

"I know; your lawyer told me. Where are you off to in such haste?"

"The chemist's. To purchase some Peruvian bark."

"Francesca's got some, I saw the bottle."

"It—it might not be enough," she faltered.

With the attorney's warning fresh in his mind, Garrick said, "I'll take you."

"I'd rather you didn't. I'm—I've an appointment with Mr. Webb, at his chambers. I may be away for some time," she said, brushing past him.

But Webb had made plain his inability to devote himself to the Cashins today. Lavinia, always so candid, had told him a falsehood—two of them. She intended to join her father, wherever he was, and she meant to go by herself. If she didn't want his company, he wouldn't impose himself—but as her lawyer had implied, the wharves were no place for a beautiful woman to wander. Garrick had a responsibility to follow her and to make sure she came to no harm.

He watched from the front door until she'd turned the corner of York Street. Setting out in pursuit, he maintained a cautious distance. Lavinia crossed over Piccadilly to the coach stand, claiming the first hackney in the queue, but Garrick was too far away to hear when she told the jarvey her destination. Flinging out his arm, he flagged down a sedan chair headed for St. James's Street.

"Keep close to that hackney, wherever it may go," he told the bearers. When they gave him dubious looks, he pointed out, "You've got four legs between you, same as the horse. And you're a damned sight healthier."

"Gawd help us," muttered one chairman, scratching his cheek. "He's one o' them crackbrained nobs. We'll end with split shins."

"I'll make it worth your while." Garrick climbed into the compartment. The window panels were grimed and streaked, but he was able to make out Lavinia's conveyance.

His carriers, correctly judging that haste was more important than providing a smooth ride, loped along Swallow Street, moving in the direction of Whitehall. As he travelled down Parliament Street, he admired Westminster Abbey's soaring towers until the chairmen made an abrupt turn. They carried him across Westminster Bridge to Southwark, a region of slums, gaols, madhouses, hospitals, and burying grounds. Fumes rose in great smoky clouds from the borough's breweries and distilleries.

Garrick supposed that Lavinia was bound for St. Saviour's, the largest of London's docks. At the roundabout where Westminster Bridge Road united with four other thoroughfares, her hackney unexpectedly veered onto the Borough Road—a clue that her destination was in fact the George Inn, the terminus for coaches arriving from the southern ports of England.

The whip-scarred horse slowed, and the vehicle edged in close to the spiked walls of the King's Bench Prison. Lavinia stepped out and exchanged a few words with her jarvey, presumably asking him to wait.

Garrick pounded his ungloved fist on the roof of

his chair. His bearers set it down with a jarring thud.

"Not many folk rush to get *here*," commented the one in front.

"Ain't much custom for us at this end of Lunnon," whined the other.

Garrick paid double the fare and hurried after Lavinia. He assumed she'd come in search of that Webb chap—evidently a member of the disreputable fraternity known as gaol lawyers, whose clients were confined for debt and other petty offences.

At the prison entrance, a portly, red-faced man shuffled forward to meet him. "Your phiz is a fresh one to me, sir. What's your business?"

"Where will I find Attorney Webb?"

"He's come and gone already. Settled with the clerk o' the papers so 'is biggest gaolbird could be let out o' the cage—'im we calls the Earl o' King's Bench."

A fearsome possibility forced Garrick to ask, "What's his name?"

"Jack Cashin. Lives in the State House, 'e does, just like a real lord, and dresses near as fine as you. 'Twas 'is daughter walked in just before ye. Ye're welcome to 'ave a look round, sir, so long's you get out when the visitors' bell rings."

Reeling from his discovery, Garrick entered a small forecourt surrounded by dwellings and offices. Lavinia, conspicuous in her russet gown, moved swiftly toward a second gateway.

"Lavinia!" he shouted.

She turned around, and he saw his own outrage and astonishment mirrored in her face. "*Och*, Garrick—why did you have to come?" she wailed.

"To see the Earl of Ballacraine," he sneered. "Apparently it wasn't the Channel your father crossed, but the Thames." Fury swelled within him until he thought he was going to explode with it. "By hell and all the devils, Lavinia, why didn't you *tell* me?"

His thundering voice attracted the attention of a scrawny, sharp-nosed individual lurking beside a rain barrel. "Good sir," he drawled, "you must not bluster at our Miss Cashin."

Garrick advised the intruder to mind his own business.

The fellow's greasy, grasping fingers closed around Lavinia's wrist. "Come to fetch your papa, my pretty? I'll take you in."

"I know the way, Mr. Bowes."

Connecting the surname with the face, Garrick said, "Stoney Bowes. Last time we met, you were using weighted dice. Were you sent here as a felon or a debtor?"

The man's ugly face twisted in a scowl. "Bugger off, you bloody sod."

"If we weren't in the presence of a lady, I'd—" Garrick looked around and saw Lavinia passing through the gate. Forgetting the foul-mouthed Bowes, he resumed his chase.

His first impression of the prison yard was that it most resembled a riotous fairground.

He saw some men chatting up a gaudy prostitute. Scruffy children ran about, hiding behind the fruit and vegetable barrows. Women studied the wares on display in a butcher's window. A large party emerged from the coffeehouse, in merry spirits, and moved toward the skittles alley. King's Bench, Garrick realized, was a microcosm of that larger but no less crowded and busy world beyond its walls.

He approached Lavinia, who scanned the throng with anxious eyes. "Here he comes," she said in relief.

Garrick saw a gentleman moving in their direction. His black hair, frosted with gray, was pulled back in a bushy tail. Although his coat and breeches were well made, the cravat was yellowed from poor laundering, and his shoes lacked buckles. A boy at his side supported a small trunk on his shoulder.

When the earl embraced his daughter, his first words were muffled, and hers were inaudible.

"You look so much better than I expected," Garrick heard her say. "But I'm sending for a physician the instant I get you to St. James's Square."

"No need," her father interrupted. "I've naught but a trifling cold." Frowning to see a stranger at her side, he asked, "*Quoi eshyn*, Lhondhoo?"

"Lord Garrick Armitage. Mrs. Radstock's cousin."

He addressed another singsong question to her in their island language, to which she replied with a brief "*Ta.*" Her face, tense and watchful, turned to Garrick. "I've told him we may trust you not to expose what we've managed to conceal."

She sought reassurance herself. From a need to inflict punishment, he didn't give it. "We can discuss that later."

"Has Mr. Webb paid my garnish money?" asked the earl.

"The clerk discharged you—you're free to go." She sounded as if she couldn't quite believe that what she said was true.

Tossing a shilling to the lad, Garrick took charge

of the box. Arm in arm, father and daughter made their way through the inner and outer gates to the lobby.

" 'Ere comes our madman," the turnkey announced to the loiterers. "Oh, but won't we miss 'aving your lordship about the place. You must be sure to pay us a visit now and again, dressed up in your earl's robes."

The Cashins ignored the taunts. Lavinia, head high and cheeks as ruddy as her gown, guided her parent to the waiting hackney.

Garrick's weary mind was buzzing with questions, and he had difficulty absorbing the incredible truth. His exhaustion, physical and mental, added to his sense of unreality. He'd spent the better part of the day traveling from Suffolk to London. His frame had been rattled to bits during his mad dash across town in the sedan chair. And now he'd learned—in a most unpleasant fashion—that his promised bride, whose very honesty had won his heart, was a liar of outrageous proportions.

When they had crowded into the carriage, the jarvey applied his whip to the horse's bony rump.

Garrick felt sick whenever he glanced at Lavinia's regretful, guilty face. Of all the many disappointments he'd sustained—and survived—during a trouble-plagued life, this had to be the worst. Unless, he thought morosely, other terrible revelations awaited him.

Chapter 17

Lavinia, nerves on edge, kept dropping her father's belongings as she transferred them from his gaping trunk to the tall chest of drawers. Carrying the last of his shirts, she paused at the foot of the massive four-poster and asked, *"Cre'naght ta shiu?"*

"G'aase ny share as ny stroshey dagh laa."

Getting stronger and better every day—and she was glad of it. *"S'mie lhiam."*

He tickled Xanthe's ear, saying drowsily, "I've not the slightest symptom of a fever, Lhondhoo, and I can't think why the physician dosed me with that foul mixture. It was merely a cold I had, not typhus—Webb was mistaken. I've not seen him lately to ask how you got the money to pay Onslow and all those other tradesmen. Large sums rarely fall into one's hands so conveniently."

She'd expected an inquiry into the source of her funds and had prepared a candid but incomplete answer. "I did something you probably wouldn't like—or approve of. But our long nightmare is over,

213

and you're at liberty now, so I don't regret anything."

She hadn't decided when or how to declare her engagement. This was not the moment—he was dozing now, with Xanthe sharing his pillow. She went to the corridor and followed it to Garrick's chamber, knowing she had much to explain to her enraged lover.

Carlo was there, laying out several pairs of leather gloves on a tabletop. "Milady wishes to speak to milord?" he asked politely. "I bring him." He disappeared into the adjoining room.

She heard a brief dialogue in Italian, after which Garrick emerged. "I'd be most obliged, Carlo, if you would locate a bottle of brandy. But don't return with it too quickly—*capisce ciò che dico?*"

"*Sì.*" The manservant made himself scarce.

"Step into my tiring-room," Garrick said to Lavinia.

Not an invitation—a command. She obeyed. He turned the dressing-table chair around and made her sit in it.

"Let us begin at the beginning. When, exactly, did your father become a guest of the King's Bench warden?"

Lavinia knitted her fingers together. "The bailiffs arrested him the day I met you."

"*Mio Dio,*" he muttered.

"He owed a great deal of money to a silk merchant," she went on, "who found out we'd come from the Isle of Man—a haven for delinquent debtors. Father was prevented from settling his bill, and all the rest of them, because his woollen cloth was seized by the Customs officers in Liverpool, as I told you. He couldn't even pay his bail. Because no one in London could confirm his identity to the court, he was presumed to be an imposter. He wouldn't let me stay at the prison and take care of him. For the first month, he was alone in a miserable, dirty hovel. After you won that forty guineas by staking my ten, he moved to a State House room."

"Why did you keep it from me?"

"You were the last person I could turn to—so contemptuous, always mocking me."

"Not at Langtree."

She bowed her head. "No, not then. But Father forbade me to reveal the truth, so I never did, not even to you." She wound one of her long curls around her finger. "I nearly broke my promise after Mr. Webb told me my father had contracted the typhus—that's why Mr. Webb traveled to Oxfordshire. I feared Father might die in that hateful place."

"You agreed to marry me," he said harshly, "so you could rescue him. You sacrificed yourself—and your maidenhead—for three hundred quid. I do hope you enjoyed yourself a little during those fleeting moments when you weren't thinking so hard about how to get my money."

A man in love would never speak such hard, unkind words. Lavinia's throat felt painfully dry, but she couldn't swallow. She could barely breathe.

She'd told her father she had no regrets. Now, confronted by a righteously outraged Garrick, she was sick from shame. He accused her of bartering her innocence; he believed her motive for marriage had been entirely mercenary. And he didn't yet know about the greater tragedy of her family's poverty. Should she tell him, or would that make him hate her even more?

"Lies and pretense and duplicity—a firm foundation for a marriage." He took her chin, tipping her face upward. "To think that all this time I've been kissing a stranger, falling in love with someone I couldn't really know. A baron's bastard and a debtor's daughter. We were better matched than I realized. Well, I may not be a rich man, but you'll not starve, *sposina*. Trust me, your gowns will never be more than a year or two out of fashion."

His kiss was a blow; his mouth was cruel and punishing.

She pushed him away from her so hard that they both lost their balance. She recovered, but he backed into a tall cabinet, dislodging a box on the top shelf. It tumbled down, spilling white hair powder all over his head and his clothes.

"I don't want to be your wife," she said crossly. How could she marry a man who despised her so much? She'd gambled with her heart and her virginity, losing all—to him. And now he'd even robbed her of her pride.

She recognized that intense and calculating stare. He might have been seated at a baize-covered table, the cards fanned out in his hand, searching for an opponent's weakness. "Don't fight me, Lavinia. I hold the trump card, and if you force my hand, I'll play it. If I tell your father that we shared a room at the Drover's Rest, we'll be wed by sundown tomorrow."

Lavinia had responded to Garrick's threats as he might have expected—and perhaps deserved. He'd roused her defiance, but he doubted it would last. She couldn't refuse him. His honor was at stake along with hers. He'd been falsely accused of debauching one young lady and deserting her, and he wasn't about to lay himself open to that charge a second time. He had seduced Lavinia—he must marry her.

With no time to get the powder out of his hair, he was forced to complete the tedious ritual, much to his valet's amazement. When he presented himself in his cousin's drawing room, he discovered that he was not the only man with a white head.

"I invited William to dine with us," Frances announced cheerfully.

"I did not anticipate being so long away," Lord Ballacraine was telling the marquis. With a glance at Garrick, he said, "My daughter says you are an experienced traveller, sir."

With heavy irony, Garrick replied, "I'm happy to say the discomforts you've lately suffered are entirely alien to me."

Said Newbold, "I look forward to hearing about your experiences, Lord Ballacraine."

Lavinia, wearing a gown of darkest blue with pleated frills at the neckline and cuffs, stood behind her father's chair. She placed a hand on his shoulder and said, "Father mustn't talk too much or tire himself. He's quite weak from his illness."

Only Garrick—and the earl himself—could appreciate her efforts to deflect queries about his sojourn in foreign lands. Listening to her clever fabrications and evasions, he wondered how he could ever trust her again. Her skill for deception was unparalleled. Had she felt any affection for him, or had she always been acting? Not in bed, he reminded himself. There—but only there—he'd been sure of her feelings.

After dinner, while Frances was entertaining the marquis and Lavinia with her newest piece of music, Garrick cornered the guest. He'd never imagined a situation so trying. He resented this man, the chief cause of his misfortune, and was in no mood to be conciliating. However, this was his future father-in-law, and if he said all that was on his mind, he'd make a very bad impression.

"Lord Ballacraine," he said stiffly, "I have proposed marriage to Lavinia."

The earl's eyes, darker than his daughter's, assessed him. Then he said, *sotto voce*, "Will you make her happy?"

"I wasn't aware that was a consideration," he retorted. "Did you not bring her to London to secure an impressive title, and a fortune to match?"

"Neither one can enrich a life devoid of love. I'm blessed with a better wife than I deserve, an heir to be proud of, and two fine girls. Yes, I had hopes that Lavinia would marry advantageously. But I'll not deny her the same freedom of choice that I demanded for myself so many years ago."

This was promising, although he suspected that the outwardly resigned parent favored Newbold— a marquis with a vast fortune must appear as a godsend to a man who had so recently walked out of a debtors' prison. "You give your consent?"

"It's Lavinia's consent that you require," Lord Ballacraine pointed out gravely.

She joined them, and after a brief, unfriendly look

at Garrick, told her father, "Lord Newbold wishes to know the history of Castle Cashin."

"Then he shall hear it. Lhondhoo, I believe this gentleman has something to tell you."

When the earl left them together, Garrick muttered, "He has no objections to our marriage. I didn't even have to mention how you lied to get your three hundred pounds, or explain how we passed our time at the Drover's Rest."

His sarcasm washed the pink from her cheeks and dimmed the light in her eyes. "I will *not* wed you."

"You were not so reluctant during the storm, when I promised you a future filled with passion and excitement."

"Marriage," she said repressively, "is a serious matter, not some madcap adventure."

"Ours could be. *Shall* be," he declared. "For I'm determined to make an honest woman of you, *dolcezza*. In every sense of the word."

Chapter 18

Swathed in emerald satin, the top half of her face concealed by a silver mask, Lavinia wandered through the Great Gallery of Brandenburgh House. Her escort, draped in a plain black domino that accentuated his height, was stating his disapproval of their hostess.

"She constantly seeks admiration of her beauty and supposed charm. And she's far too eager to display her histrionic talents. Whenever she pens a new play, its heroine is a glorified version of herself."

Lord Newbold's carping couldn't spoil Lavinia's first masquerade. Her pleasure would have been more complete, however, if her father had made the journey to the Anspachs' Hammersmith villa—and Garrick had stayed home.

She was clothed in satin and lace he'd purchased during his travels—at her chaperone's suggestion, she was costumed as a Venetian noblewoman of the Renaissance. Frances had also fished those endlessly troublesome diamond earrings out of Lavinia's jewel case, insisting that she wear them. Their giver had made no comment, but his smirk on first seeing her had been infuriating. She would have to return them to him—tonight.

His domino, as vibrantly scarlet as a Catholic cardinal's robe, made him easy to spot. A gilded *papier-mâché* mask concealed his entire face; the beaky nose and sharply pointed chin were gross exaggerations of the features underneath.

His dancing partner, a blowsy, thick-waisted shepherdess, was certain to recognize the diamonds, having briefly possessed them. Jenny Parfitt's husband, sporting a jockey's silk shirt and tight-fitting breeches, stood on the sidelines drinking champagne and talking with Frances, elegant in a sultana's turban and gauzy Turkish draperies.

Lavinia had already counted half a dozen Queen Elizabeths. Second in popularity to the Virgin Queen was her unfortunate cousin, Mary, Queen of Scots. Henry the Eighth was forever popping into view with one or another of his six wives. Many of the guests personified Greek and Roman deities, wearing classical robes that exposed their limbs. Gypsies pounded their tambourines, adding to the cacophony and drowning out the orchestra.

"All these Tudors and Elizabethans look as uncomfortable as they deserve to be, hopping about that way," Newbold commented. "A most indecorous gathering. Judging by the accents, many of the guests are French *emigrés*. I shall encourage Frances to take you away before the midnight unmasking."

Lavinia regretted that he hadn't entered into the spirit of the entertainment. "I should like to see the king's sons."

"You won't—not their faces. Members of the royal family never remove their masks at these affairs, or so I've been informed."

Frances had warned Lavinia that some gentlemen attended masques for the sole purpose of approaching females; anonymity permitted a greater degree of license. Lavinia didn't expect Newbold to make advances, for his mode of courtship was formal and restrained. He never snatched kisses, and he never clasped her hand unless required by the stately *minuet de la cour.* He spoke eloquently only when discussing a favorite piece of music or a notably gifted musician or a political development.

Instinctively, she knew that he was on the verge of making her an offer. She hoped he would not. Despite his many desirable attributes—such as steadiness and reliability—she couldn't spend her life with him. His placidity made her miss Garrick's lighthearted, needle-witted banter. And his attentive presence was no consolation for Garrick's every barbed word and sardonic glance, those constant and painful reminders that she'd forfeited his respect—and his love.

No longer a virgin, she was doomed to remain a spinster and a burden on her family. Her father, whom she'd convinced of her unwillingness to become Lady Garrick Armitage, would soon be taking her home.

"What makes you so pensive?" Newbold inquired.

"Do I seem so? I was remembering that I shall leave London before long."

"I think it best that you return to your island— for a visit. In future, I daresay, marital duties and responsibilities will keep you tied to this country."

He implied that her destiny lay in England, possibly with him. She knew better, but because he'd spoken hypothetically, she needn't offer up a denial. If she became his marchioness, she'd be restricted from travelling back and forth to her homeland. For the first time, she realized that this highly desirable marriage, the only one that could safeguard the people and the place most dear to her, would also separate her from them.

Just as well, she consoled herself, that her stained honor prevented her from ever accepting him.

"I wanted to dress as a woman," a genial young naval officer confided, presenting Lavinia with a glass of champagne—her third.

"What prevented you?" she asked.

"Couldn't find shoes large enough to fit. And when I tried squeezing myself into a corset, it wouldn't go round my middle. M'father says I'm too plump." His hand, as white as a maiden's, stroked the bulging flesh beneath his dimpled chin. "You don't think so, do you, m'dear?"

"Not at all," she answered, with more civility than truth.

He bestowed a brilliant and undeniably appealing smile upon her. "After the unmasking, I'll take you in to supper. That'll make my brother Willy jealous. I can see enough of your face to guess you're prettier than that actress he's got for a mistress." His appreciative azure eyes focused on her square-cut neckline.

Lavinia prepared herself for trouble when a tall,

scarlet-draped figure in a gold mask approached. "I've been looking for you."

The young sea captain pouted. "Go to perdition, Master Devil! Ah, but that's where you've come from, isn't it? Well, m'dear, I shall see you again at midnight. Tried to damn the devil himself," he murmured, "must tell my brother Willy."

Garrick took away Lavinia's glass, saying, "I've come at Francesca's behest. She commanded me to detach you from the prince."

"What prince?"

"Wales. Your hearty sailor lad is heir to England's throne. Much to the nation's—and the king's—dismay."

"*Agh atreih*," she said contritely. "During the dance, when he looked down the front of my gown, I deliberately trod upon his toes."

Garrick responded with a waterfall of a laugh, which started on a high note and descended to a low, gurgling chuckle. "He's a thorough pest, and such a *poseur*. Mad about uniforms—he clamors to join an army regiment."

"So he told me. He borrowed the officer's coat from his brother Willy."

"The Duke of Clarence. *Cose da pazzi*, what's that chap wearing the horns going to do next?"

He referred to a particularly uninhibited reveller dressed as Actaeon, who had deserted his Diana and was loping up and down the length of the gallery. He aimed his antlers at the massive, gold-framed looking glass and butted so forcefully that it shattered on contact.

An uproar ensued, altering the tone of the ball. The noise level rose significantly; the laughter grew more raucous. When the music and dancing resumed, the participants cavorted with wild abandon.

A blackamoor bussed and nuzzled a chalk-faced Columbine, leaving streaks of inky paint upon her stark white cheek and rounded breasts. Searching out a new victim, he lurched toward Lavinia, at which point Garrick towed her out of the room.

Her head was full of bubbles, and her joints and muscles refused to work properly. A perilous substance, champagne, and disastrously potent. She allowed Garrick to guide her along a broad passage— a tunnel of tall windows—where potted palms and citrus trees grew in tubs. As they raced along the glass-enclosed corridor, she breathed the intoxicating scent of orange blossom.

He paused and plucked a lemon. "Catch," he challenged, tossing it to her.

She missed. The yellow fruit hit the marble-paved floor, rolling between two massive planters. When he reclaimed her hand, she asked muzzily, "Where are we going?"

"To see Elizabeth's theatre."

She knew she shouldn't follow him but couldn't arrive at the reason.

He took her inside the small pavilion at the far end of the hall. Two chandeliers cast shimmering light over a small auditorium. There were three rows of low-backed wooden benches and four raised compartments with armchairs upholstered in blue. Garrick led Lavinia to the largest and most splendid one.

"The Margrave's box," he explained. "When the

Prince of Wales attends plays at Brandenburgh House, this is where he sits."

She ran her hand over the velvet that covered the throne-like chair. "Our host must spend a fortune supporting his wife's whims."

"Oh, he does, and he's stupendously rich. They've formed their own acting company; it includes their French friends, and Elizabeth's sons by her first husband. Lord Craven divorced her years ago, but he's dead now. Lady Buckinghamshire, manageress of the faro bank in St. James's Square, performs here, the fattest of all the Queen Elizabeths."

"She keeps a gaming house, yet is received by society?"

"You won't meet her at court," he admitted, "or in any of the most exclusive mansions. There are levels, you see. Francesca and Lord Newbold belong to the upper echelon, who make the rules and live by the rules. The next lot includes people who have a title or riches, or both, but are tainted by scandal or some other deficiency. The Anspachs. Lady Buck. Prawn Parfitt. Lord Everdon. Me. We stopped following the rules long ago."

Lavinia mulled this over.

His dark eyes gleamed through the holes in his gilded mask. He removed it, saying, "You are one of us. You've frequented a debtors' prison. Went hunting foxes in man's attire. You shared your lover's bed."

His body pressed up against hers with intent, strong and solid, and her knees buckled as he bore her down to the carpet, luxuriously plush and cushioning. He pried off her silver half-mask, breaking the string in his haste. "Sorry," he rasped. "I need to see your face."

His mouth merged with hers and he kissed her with the hunger of a starving man. Famished for physical contact, Lavinia joined in the feast. Then his tongue flickered along her neck, moved down to her bared breasts, and charted slow, deliberate circles around each nipple.

When he pushed up her satin skirt, she made no effort to prevent him. He touched that most private part of her and separated her sensitive outer folds, seeking the tender bud where her most intense sensations resided. His skilled fingers brought her to the edge of ecstasy, then pushed her over. Falling, she cried out his name.

Shaken to her core, she dared to open her eyes. He was smiling down at her. "You take my breath away," she gasped.

"Perhaps you're laced too tight. I'd be happy to loosen your stays, *dolcezza mia.*"

"No!" she protested.

"You are never more lovely than during your pleasure. Here you make me soft." He placed a hand over his pounding heart, then shifted it downward. "And here you make me hard."

By giving in to this seduction, she would prove herself the whore he believed her to be. Once more he'd taken advantage of her body's weakness, and she was shamed by her susceptibility.

"You want me, too; it shows in your eyes. They flash brighter than those diamonds."

She climbed unsteadily to her feet and unhooked the earrings, declaring in a high, strained voice, "I don't want them." She flung the jewels at his chest and added, "And I don't want *you*. I'm going home, where I belong—and I'm glad of it."

"Then why do you weep?" he asked.

Holding the broken mask to her tear-streaked face, she left Garrick lying in a pool of scarlet silk and unrelieved desire.

After he tucked the discarded diamonds into his money pouch, he replaced his own disguise. By the time he reached the long conservatory, Lavinia was a blur of emerald satin moving toward the French double doors. He didn't think she would return to the Great Gallery in her disheveled state. He knew the house quite well and was confident that he could intercept her before she reached the tiring-room set aside for female guests.

He'd gone as far as the door when his path was blocked by a diminutive lady wearing a nun's habit. Several times during the evening she'd approached, as though intending to speak, but had always retreated.

"*Monseigneur* Garrick?"

A Frenchwoman—there were so many here. "How did you know me?"

"No false face can hide your resemblance to *mon mari*."

His head came up; his spine stiffened. "And is your husband present, Lady Everdon?"

She shook her wimpled head. "He seldom goes out; he does not want to meet you again. The night of your *contretemps* at the club, he came home with *le diable* in him. You—what is the word? You goated him."

"Goaded," Garrick corrected.

"His *paternité* is to remain a secret. He insists

upon it. And I, too, hope you will keep silent—for the sake of our daughters."

His half-sisters. Insatiably curious, he said, "Tell me their names, their ages."

"Marie is sixteen; Henriette is younger by two years."

They didn't know they had a brother. Why that hurt so much, he wasn't sure.

"*Un scandale dans la famille* spares no one," Lady Everdon continued. "Please remember, *monseigneur, les innocents* will be the most wounded."

Her plaintive words echoed in his mind even after she left him.

In order to gain all he sought—from Everdon, from his stubbornly resistant Lavinia—he would cause much suffering. By enacting vengeance against his father, he might destroy his half-sisters' lives. Seducing a reluctant female into marriage, he acknowledged, would be a callous act, ultimately unsatisfying. Bad enough that he'd roused Lavinia's fury—he didn't want to make her hate him.

Rejected by his ladylove and, by proxy, by his father, he entered the salon where sat Lady Buckinghamshire presided at a faro table. Prawn Parfitt stood before her, anxiously awaiting the turn of a card. Colonel Hanger, noted for his lewd jests, played piquet with the Prince of Wales.

This was exactly where he belonged; he'd got that right. But his imagination balked when he tried to fit Lavinia into this rowdy and disreputable scene. Not such a pleasing picture after all. In fact, it was downright alarming.

Chapter 19

Isle of Man, March 1794

"**I** want to hear more about the masquerade ball."

Lavinia took the potato from her sister and with her knife pared away the mottled brown skin. "I danced with the Prince of Wales," she said airily, "and drank champagne, and ate my supper from a golden dish."

Kitty sighed. "It sounds like a scene from a fairy tale. What else happened?"

Lavinia recoiled at a flash of memory—flame-red silk and emerald satin, her sighs and her shame. "Nothing," she said.

"Is the Marquis of Newbold handsome?"

"Not precisely."

"Dark or fair?"

"His hair is dark," she answered. "He's exceedingly tall—awkwardly so. But he dresses well and has splendid manners."

Wrinkling her nose, Kitty commented, "I hoped you would be courted by a man as handsome as you are lovely. Will you marry him?"

"I don't see how I can. He never asked."

"Another lord courted you, Father said, but you never speak of him."

Lavinia's heart clenched. "That match wasn't suitable."

"But he proposed to you—didn't he?"

She admitted, "We discussed marriage."

Many times. But Garrick hadn't mentioned it at the masquerade, and none of his words that night could be construed as a renewed offer of matrimony. He lusted for her. He'd exploited her body's ready responses, as a prelude to other intimacies. But he also regarded her as a lying, money-grubbing schemer. If he'd expressed forgiveness before demonstrating his desire, she would not have left him and returned to her island.

As if tossing away her cares, she dropped the diced potatoes into the kettle that hung over the fire. Here, she could learn to live without him, without his love. Somehow, someday. Castle Cashin was a comfortably safe distance from her predatory lover and her supposed suitor. She hadn't brought a fortune with her, but she had a pair of capable hands and a boundless supply of energy. She'd sowed oats with her brother, collected eggs, fed the horses. Unhampered by etiquette, she could race up and down the staircase, or muck about in the stableyard. She didn't miss the more sedate manners imposed on her in England, where she'd consorted with lords and ladies, a duke—even a royal prince.

Nor did she miss the stifling elegance of Frances Radstock's house, or Langtree's oppressive splendors. She preferred her beloved home despite the shabbiness she tried to remedy—mending faded curtains and re-stuffing flattened, threadbare cushions.

She and her sister wore simple dresses several seasons old, cut from the same bolt. The humble, homespun garment felt better against her skin than the costly, diaphanous creations Garrick so admired—London gowns, Kitty reverently called them.

Lavinia found some comfort in her sister's blooming cheeks, although her cough persisted, and she was thin. The doctor still recommended the curative waters of Bath or Bristol Hot Wells, but with less urgency than he'd done the previous year.

"Your health seems much improved," Lavinia commented. "Mother must be dosing you with yarrow every day."

"I do feel stronger, as though I could march to the top of Mount Snaefell and run all the way down."

"You'd best not try!"

Kitty laughed. "Dr. Christian says if I keep from taking cold, I might make the journey to England by summertime. Just think, Lhondhoo, I could be your bridesmaid!"

"I told you, I'm not engaged. To anyone."

"You will be," Kitty predicted.

Their brother, Kerron, strolled past the kitchen table and paused by Lavinia's chair to say, "I'm bound for Dreeym Freoaie to look over the property. Shall I saddle Fannag for you?"

"Go with him," Kitty urged her. "I'll mind the stew."

Kerr's mount, like Lavinia's Manx pony, was prized more for his stamina than his looks. These horses were entirely different from those she'd known while in England. As they crossed a landscape quite unlike that of Oxfordshire, she described her ride on Fling.

Kerron's grave expression softened while he listened to her lively reminiscences of the chase. "If a miracle occurs and I get to England, I'll have to give foxhunting a try."

Eventually they reached the deserted farmstead of Dreeym Freoiae, so named for the thickets of heather covering the ridge.

"I like this place," said Lavinia during her brother's careful inspection. "Has a tenant been found?"

Kerr bestowed one of his keen, hawkish glances. "*Cha nel foast.* Not yet—though it will probably be occupied before summer. Nothing's settled, so I shan't say more. The house and farm buildings are in good repair overall, but the roofs want new slates."

They returned home a different way, which took them past the mill, no longer in operation, and Boayl Fea, the crossroads tavern.

"*Jeeagh*—look, there's Ellin Fayle," said Lavinia. "We must stop, for I've not seen her since I returned."

He was agreeable, and they left their horses in the lane. The girl working in the garden came to meet them, a basket of cabbages balanced on her hip.

"How is your grandmother, Ellin?"

"Very well, my lady, *gur eh mie ue.* Come inside and see for yourself."

Growing up fast, Lavinia observed, and very nearly a woman. Ellin's green eyes sparkled; her soft brown hair flowed down her back in waves.

The Cashins followed her into the stone dwelling. The *thie mooar* was similar to that of other houses, but held many more tables and benches and chairs. Henry Fayle and his wife Marriot sat before the granite-faced *chiollagh*, polishing tankards. Kerr, addressing them in Manx, requested a mugful of ale.

Lavinia and Ellin went to the spinning wheel. The elderly woman ceased pulling flax from her distaff and cocked her silvered head. "Who has come?"

"The young lord and his sister," the girl replied. "Lady Lavinia."

Atreih, Lavinia mourned, the Widow Moore couldn't see how pretty her granddaughter had become. For she was blind, and had been since anyone could remember. Her face was lined and careworn, its sightless eyes clouded by age.

Lavinia knelt down beside her. "You must have heard I was in London."

The delicate hands reached out to feel her face. "I hope the great people in the city admired you as much as you deserve, my lady. I remember well how the late countess boasted of your beauty."

She smiled, unable to imagine her toplofty grandmother deigning to converse with a lowly commoner. "You've cause to be proud of your Ellin's looks."

The girl bowed her head, blushing rosily.

Said Mrs. Moore, "A great help to me, she is. Turned fifteen now."

"As old as that?" Kerr commented.

"Is our young lord there? It's sorry we are that the earl's mill is no more. The taproom was busier when the weavers were so near."

"It couldn't be saved," he told her soberly. "British Customs officers refuse to let our woollens into their country." He picked up a web of unbleached cloth produced from the widow's thread. "There's a market for linen—especially of such quality as this. My father and I hope to acquire machinery for the retting and scutching of flax, and to divert the millstream to make a bleaching dub. But," he concluded regretfully, "it would be a costly undertaking."

Mrs. Moore nodded her understanding.

Lavinia and Kerr left the house, with Ellin trotting behind like an eager puppy.

"My lord," she said breathlessly, "I've a favor to beg."

Smiling down at her, Kerr asked, "What is it?"

"I read to my grandmother while she spins, and I've got all the way through her English Bible several times, and Uncle Henry's Manx one. And both versions of the prayer book." She hesitated, then plunged on, "I wondered if I might borrow one of your books, *my saillu*—if you please. I'd be careful with it."

"*Ta*, of course you may. What book do you want?" When she failed to answer, he said, "Perhaps you should come to the castle and make the selection yourself."

Ellin's gratitude shone in her bright eyes. "*Gur eh mie eu!*"

"*Failt erriu*," he responded casually.

Said Lavinia, when they resumed their homeward journey, "You've made a friend for life."

"An appealing child. Let's hope she'll grow up to spin thread as fine as her grandmother can."

"Ellin is no longer a child, Kerr."

"She looks it."

"She's surprisingly well-spoken and mannerly, for a girl whose uncle keeps a house of rest. And Mrs. Moore—she works at her wheel, yet dresses and speaks like a gentlewoman." These discrepancies puzzled Lavinia.

Despite the many exertions of her day, she was slow to drop off to sleep that night. Xanthe, who commonly shared her bed, was missing. Her pet had been twitchy of late, inclined to prowl at odd hours.

Lavinia's restless mind recalled the brief visit to Boayl Fea. She compared Ellin Fayle's sweet and gentle grandmother to her own, the spoiled daughter of a Liverpool merchant, an unwilling partner in the marriage of convenience that had soured her. A chilling presence in Lavinia's early life, she'd dressed in black at all times and always carried her rosary. Father Louis, the only Catholic priest in the island, had been her confessor and confidant. Never had she courted her son's or her grandchildren's affection, but she'd demanded their obedience to her will.

There were, thought Lavinia, several sorts of loving, and they brought either gladness or sorrow. Her grandmother's religious fanaticism had impoverished the family. Her parents' mutual devotion had supported them through many a crisis. Her love for Garrick Armitage had carried her to the heights of joy, before plunging her to the depths of despair. Her feelings for him had survived his fury and even his disdain. But she couldn't wed him if he wouldn't love her back.

What if, she asked herself, there were a simpler, calmer sort of love to be discovered?

Lord Newbold required a wife, and—even more important—he respected and admired Lavinia. Dazzled by Garrick's blazing personality, she'd overlooked the quiet nobleman's attributes. Could a man so civilized, so dispassionate, save her from remorse and help her forget her disappointment? And a lover who was bold and daring, reckless and adventurous—in and out of bed?

She was no longer a virgin. Would Lord Newbold be able to tell? She wasn't sure about that, but she knew someone who could tell her—Calybrid Teare, the *ben-obbee.* The people of the parish went to her for charms and curses, and information of the sort a well-bred girl dared not even ask of the doctor.

A cat's anguished squall rose above the murmur of the sea.

Lavinia pulled the pillow over her head. Poor Xanthe. She could sympathize, knowing exactly how it felt to be preyed upon and ravished by a ruthless and aggressive tom.

The ladies of the household were carding wool when the earl stormed into the *thie mooar* and flung his copy of the *Manx Mercury* onto the table.

"Here's a pretty piece of news for you," he declared. "Females always welcome a description of a wedding."

"Whose wedding?" asked his wife.

"His Grace the Duke of Atholl. John Murray, this island's illustrious—and neglectful—governor."

Lavinia reached for the newspaper, scanning it

for the item. "He wed Lady MacLeod, a widow. And a Scotswoman."

"A curse upon him," said the earl viciously, "and all his clan. *Dy jinnagh y Jouyl lesh eh-hene as ooilley yn doogys echey*—there, I've said it in Manx to make it stick. When the Atholls transferred their Lordship of Man to the British government, they lined their own pockets and beggared the rest of us."

Smiling up at him, Lavinia said, "I remember the first rhyme we ever learned from you. Babes unborn will rue the day—"

"That our Isle of Man was sold away," Kerr and Kitty chanted with her.

"I found a letter waiting for you at the receiving office, Lhondhoo, with a London postmark."

Lavinia recognized Frances Radstock's precise, ladylike handwriting.

"My dear Lavinia," she read aloud, "I shall begin with a complaint, for you have not been as regular a correspondent as I expected when you left town. My friend Lord Newbold calls daily to ask whether I have received word of your return. Not even the prospect of a splendidly refurbished Drury Lane theatre or the brilliance of the Italian opera can cure his dejection." Lavinia paused. "I don't think the rest would interest you."

Her siblings exchanged a knowing look.

"The marquis is pining for our Lhondhoo," said Kerr.

"He's lovelorn," added Kitty. "You'd better hurry back to England, before he expires of a broken heart."

"When I go," Lavinia replied, "it will be for Father's sake. He's stuck with one spinster daughter already—what a terrible misfortune it would be, having a pair of them!"

Kitty retaliated by tossing a handful of wool. "Wretch! Just wait, one day I'll be married. My husband will be *Vanninagh dooie*—a native Manxman. I don't want one of your prim and proper English lords!"

"No, you'd rather be wed to your doctor," her twin teased.

"Lhondhoo," said their father solemnly, "you know you can stay here with us. But if you decide to go—for whatever reason—I'll pay your passage back to England. Just remember, this time the choice is entirely yours."

When he placed a consoling arm around her shoulders, she asked, "Do you remember the watercolor you made years ago, of Kerr and Kitty and me, as the birds?"

"Shirragh, Drean, and Lhondhoo. Whatever happened to it, I wonder?"

"It hangs in my room," said Kitty. With a happy smile, she said, "I'll bring it to England in the summer, Lhondhoo—as your bride gift."

Part III

Words, vows, gifts, tears,
and love's full sacrifice . . .

William Shakespeare
Troilus and Cressida, act I, scene 2

Chapter 20

Suffolk, April 1794

The horses charging across Moulton Heath stirred the thick fog that hovered over the dewy turf. Holding a spyglass to his eye, Garrick followed their progress. "A marvelous sight, Nick."

His companion, who stood less than five feet tall in his stockings and was lean as a whippet, gave a brisk, businesslike nod. "They'll do, m'lord."

He'd plucked Nick Cattermole from the obscurity of the tackroom, saddling him with the management of the Armitage Stud. His faith in the Yorkshireman had been rewarded by some impressive wins. He couldn't blame his trainer for the failures of the previous racing season, when a batch of spoiled feed had sickened their most promising runners. But nothing short of spectacular success at the upcoming Spring Meeting would repair their reputation in racing circles.

"Folk remember we had a bad run of luck," said Nick. "They dunna know why it happened. Nor care."

"You've nursed them back to health. Double the Stakes looks particularly strong."

"Eh, he's got a fine head and honest eye. And were easy to train, bein' so calm and settled."

Garrick turned and pointed his glass at a bay mare being ridden out of the stable by a baby-faced jockey. "Here's our Con with Play the Trump. Has he achieved a better rapport with her?"

"Not sure." Nick called to the attendant groom, "Lengthen those leathers a couple o' notches. Con's just stretchin' her legs, not racin' her."

Like all riders under Cattermole's tutelage, Con Finbar carried no whip.

"She'd three wins from four starts as a four-year-old," Nick reminded his employer. "I want to see her improve on that record." Shading his eyes from the eastern sun, he asked, "Be your lordship expectin' company? Or be this some spy, set upon us by the competition?"

The chaise coming up the rutted drive halted a short distance from the paddocks. "Uncle Bardy." Garrick moved quickly across ground that was perpetually scarred by his horses' hooves.

A fortnight past, he'd fled Monkwood Hall after he announced the unravelling of his matrimonial plans. He dreaded yet another inquiry from his relative, especially at such an early hour and while his head was still pounding from a long night of drowning his sorrows.

The baronet was making his way to Cambridge. "Couldn't pass Moulton without looking in, Garry. Got your string on the run today," he observed, watching the horses streak across the chalky heath.

"Which will you enter at Newmarket First Meeting?"

"Double the Stakes, Play the Trump, and Ten of Diamonds," Garrick recited.

"Those names will proclaim you the owner as much as the green and white silks. What jockey will try for the Hyde Cup?"

"Con Finbar."

"Your Irish lad? I expected you to use George Gosling. He's been at Moulton forever, since the late duke's time."

"Goosey will keep busy enough," Nick Cattermole interjected. "There be plenty of races to go round."

Smiling, the baronet said, "Now there's a prize you covet, right, Garry? I'll place a bet myself, if you say this is your year to win the Hyde Cup."

"We'll not have as good a chance in future, for I may need to sell our winners to cover expenses. I haven't the infinite resources of the Duke of Bedford or the Prince of Wales."

"Lord Grosvenor is already limiting the size of his stud, I've heard, and I'd be sorry if you had to do the same. The soil of Moulton Heath has long produced sound horses—and many a champion."

It was a troubling topic, one of several Garrick was reluctant to pursue. "Care to share my breakfast?" he asked his uncle. "I was up before dawn and had nothing but strong coffee."

He ushered Sir Bardolph toward his temporary residence, a windmill converted to a folly, which had long served the Dukes of Halford as their racing headquarters.

Abashed by the parlor's disarray, he said, "I granted Carlo a holiday."

A pair of riding boots, a brush, and blacking littered the floor; a carriage whip lay upon the mantelshelf. Arranged haphazardly at the oval table were half a dozen mahogany chairs, each with a different racing scene painted across the broad top rail.

"Quite smart," said Sir Bardolph admiringly. "Are they new?"

"Just delivered from Sheraton's workshop. The decoration was my idea, and Sartorious undertook the commission. You see before you all the winners and jockeys from the Armitage stable. Here's Flying Arrow crossing the finish at Epsom. And Suffolk Belle's famous Newmarket victory."

The old gentleman's gaze moved from the decorated chair backs to the empty decanter. "I'm worried about you, Garry. You've taken your latest loss very badly—and I don't mean on the field."

"I'll win a wife yet," he said bravely. "Lavinia's had plenty of time to come to her senses. So have I." He sank onto one of his intricately painted chairs. "Circumstances forced her to use her wits—and rely on her instincts. Yes, she deceived me, but the earl and his attorney made it impossible for her to do anything else."

"Did you consider my suggestion that you strive to make amends?"

Nodding, he answered, "I've already worked out how I can do it. Lavinia forgot to remove a family heirloom from Siberry's vault. I plan to travel to the Isle of Man on the pretext of returning the Balla-craine rubies. I shall humble myself before her and apologize for—distressing her. She can be married from her home, with all her family there, and you'll see us in Suffolk by First Spring Meeting."

"I can improve upon that plan. Tell her she'll be living at Monkwood." The baronet presented a leather pouch. "And offer her this."

Dio, but it was heavy. Garrick looked inside. Incredulous, he stared at his uncle. "You might've been set upon by highwaymen!"

Sir Bardolph shrugged dismissively. "Most unlikely in this quiet corner of England. Besides, they'd have asked for my money. Nobody expects a man of my years and mien to carry a diamond necklace."

And a grand one it was, Garrick marvelled. Never had he seen stones of such size and brilliance.

Clapping him on the back, his uncle said merrily, "This lady of yours deserves compensation if she agrees to wed so disreputable a chap."

"You're right," he agreed. "I'll set out for London later today to get those jewels from Siberry. And," he added, "to give Francesca my long-delayed explanation of why I *cannot* and shall not be marrying her husband's ward."

Coaches cluttered the turnpike, bearing the aristocracy and gentry to London. The all-important social season would commence at Easter, lasting until Parliament's summer dismissal.

Garrick had departed Moulton in a hopeful frame of mind. Uncle Bardy, meddlesome old goat, had smoothed the rocky path to matrimony. Lavinia could not refuse him, now that he could offer her a proper home and a respectable style of living. It was more necessary to gratify the lady he loved than to open a gaming house and humiliate the father who refused to acknowledge him. Mentally he pounded in the final nail, sealing the coffin of that dead scheme.

The one check on his enthusiasm was uncertainty about how his cousin would receive the news of his intentions. His brother's probable objections no longer concerned him; Edward had eventually calmed down about the Halsey affair. The worst he could do was withdraw his support of the Armitage Stud, and if that happened, Garrick would invite his uncle to become his partner.

London's inhabitants were bustling on this bright spring day. In each smiling face, Garrick read a determination to make the most of the sunshine.

His arrival in St. James's Square caught his cousin unawares. She gave a little cry when he marched into her sitting room.

"Why do you never send messages?" she asked.

"Because I rarely form my plans in advance. A warning would have deprived you of this delightful surprise."

"I've had so many of them this week," she replied. "Your return is the third. First Lavinia returned to town, and then—"

"She's here?"

"In London, yes. Mr. Webb sent for her; she left for his chambers a little while ago."

Lavinia had come back to him. Rejoicing at this unexpected development, Garrick produced his leather pouch. "You shall be the first to see the marvel I've brought from Suffolk." He held up the string of diamonds and dangled it before her eyes.

"Gracious," she breathed. "This must be your Aunt Anna's necklace."

"With diamonds splendid enough for a queen. Marie Antoinette, alas, was never destined to wear them. Try it on."

Unable to resist, she wound it around her neck. After a few moments at the looking glass, she declared, "It would look better with evening dress. Even so, I'm not sure I could carry off such a magnificent piece with the appropriate *élan*. If you loan it to me for the next court ball, I shall try."

"Depends when it is. I've got plans for that bauble."

She turned away from the mirror, saying, "Next month. It coincides with the formal announcement of a betrothal."

"Whose?" asked Garrick absently.

"That's my other happy surprise. William Shandos and Lavinia Cashin are engaged. I've won our wager, Garrick—I'm keeping my gold topped riding whip, and you owe me a halfpenny. Just as I predicted, she'll become Marchioness of Newbold. In June."

After initial disbelief came the realization that this was the greatest calamity of his life. The agony was searing. And to think he'd been about to announce his marriage! Lavinia had returned to London to marry the marquis. *È orribile!* The most horrible thing imaginable. He wanted to tear his hair and curse and rage, but he must suffer in silence.

"Newbold's mother came from Northamptonshire to meet her," Frances told him blithely. "Yesterday, while I was out shopping, he called, and by the time I returned, the deed was done. I stand *in loco parentis,* for the Cashins won't be coming to England for the wedding. How busy I shall be! All the bride clothes to be made, and so many other arrangements. I'm undecided about what gentleman should give Lavinia away. I thought perhaps Halford. Or you."

"I'll be in Newmarket in June," he managed to say.

"Well, you'll have to miss a day or two of the racing, for there wouldn't even *be* a marriage if you hadn't asked me to find her a husband."

Now he felt physically ill. When she returned his diamond necklace, he wondered what the devil he was supposed to do with it. If the strand were just a bit longer, he could use it to strangle himself.

Desperation had often driven Lavinia to the attorney's Stanhope Street house, but not today. Not even his sullen clerk could sink her buoyant spirits. Her engagement to the marquis had imposed peace of mind.

Before accepting him, she'd confessed a prior attachment—without revealing the gentleman's name or any details. He'd responded with an understanding smile, and assured her she needn't apologize for her youthful follies. Then he had kissed her—gently, ungracefully. His raptures about her charm and beauty had touched her vanity and restored her self-worth, and she'd forgotten all about his fortune. She wanted to love him and was confident that one day she would.

Garrick was away in Suffolk, conveniently out of sight if never completely out of mind. Sometimes she tried to imagine his reaction to her betrothal.

Fortunately, she consoled herself, he wasn't there to cut up her heart with his sharp tongue and barbed words. And after the racing was over, perhaps he would resume his travels on the Continent. As long as she didn't have to face him again, all would be well.

The clerk shuffled into the anteroom where she waited, mumbling that his employer would receive her now. Curious to know why she'd been summoned, she entered the attorney's office.

Daniel Webb beamed upon her like a schoolmaster whose pet pupil had pleased him well. "I received your message." Placing a chair opposite his cluttered desk, he invited her to sit. "When is the wedding to be?"

"June is Lord Newbold's preference."

"I hoped it might be sooner."

She couldn't imagine what difference it made to him. And she didn't much want the date moved forward. "I am content with his lordship's decision."

Webb made a steeple of his hands. "You intrigue me, my lady, and have done ever since Solomon the moneylender mentioned a Manx earl, deep in debt, and his lovely daughter. I hastened to Cork Street to have a look, and the moment I laid eyes upon you, I shared your father's optimism that you could achieve a brilliant marriage. I knew you would prove most valuable to me."

Confused, she said, "I don't understand."

"After leaving your house that day, I informed the silk merchant that he would not be receiving the payment he demanded. He behaved exactly as merchants always do—and swore out a complaint against your father. The bailiffs were sent to make the arrest, and as a result of my deliberate mismanagement of that court proceeding at Westminster, he was sent to prison."

Lavinia sat immobile in her chair. Her father's trusted advisor had brought about his ruin. "You contributed to our misfortunes? For what reason?"

"I wanted to gain influence over you, to make you my puppet. I knew you had a set of rubies, so I hired that pair of bunglers who attacked Mrs. Radstock's carriage. Later, I sent anonymous letters, thinking I could frighten you into surrendering your jewels. My first misjudgment," he acknowledged wryly.

"But that wasn't your handwriting on the notes I received," she said.

"Actually, it was. You didn't recognize it as mine because Will, my clerk, takes care of all my correspondence—he writes a clearer hand. Off you went to Langtree, and like your father, I expected an engagement to be the result. When I visited you there, I exaggerated the serverity of his illness in order to hasten your marriage, never guessing you'd take up whoring to pay off his debts."

"I didn't!" she defended herself.

"I received quite a different impression at the Drover's Rest. Yes, that's where I stopped to wait out the snowstorm. You arrived with Lord Garrick, and he took you to an upstairs room."

"We were eloping—we intended to be wed."

"And I prevented it," he said, smiling at her. "I encouraged his lordship to follow you to the King's Bench, where he discovered the dreadful secret you'd kept from him. A highly successful tactic."

The room grew smaller and smaller around her, while the man on the other side of the desk assumed the terrifying proportions of a malevolent giant. She climbed to her feet. "Whatever you want from me, you'll never get it."

"I believe I shall. Sit down, my lady; I'm not finished. I mean to strike a bargain with you. If you refuse, I'll feel compelled to divulge certain unsavory facts to Lord Newbold—to begin with, your father's poverty and imprisonment. Followed by the details of your assignation with your lover. I hardly think the marquis will approve of your exploits in the bed of a notorious rake and libertine."

"*Mooidjean*," she muttered. He was a complete blackguard. Her loathing boiled over in an angry outburst. "You are despicable!" When she rushed toward the door, he blocked her escape.

"You'd be wise to hear me out, for my demands are not unreasonable. My discretion is yours—for a price."

"I haven't got any money—you know that. Better than anyone," she added bitterly.

"I can negotiate a large marriage settlement, which will be mutually advantageous. But even more important than money, I need Lord Newbold's patronage. I aspire to become his chief solicitor. And, in due course, to embark upon a political career. He sits in the House of Lords and controls two boroughs sending a member to Parliament."

"You must be mad," said Lavinia scornfully.

"So says the future marchioness," he retorted, "who spread her legs to save her pauper father from debtors' prison. You, my lady, are an inspiration." He kissed his hand to her.

She sought for some way to achieve victory in the midst of this appalling defeat. He'd used her like a marionette, but she intended to pull his strings just once, for her family's benefit.

"I'll do my best to assist you, but I require more than your silence, Mr. Webb. When you draw up my marriage contract, it must include a stipulation that the marquis will provide Father with an annuity. One thousand pounds per annum."

After digesting her counterproposal, he said grudgingly, "I shall try. But I warn you, the representative of a dowerless bride has very little influence."

Lavinia left the room feeling thoroughly defiled. Why had she ever left Castle Cashin? Genteel destitution was preferable to the empty triumph of her engagement. No longer did it give her peace of mind; all her joy was gone.

In the parlor, she encountered a black-robed gentleman who approached her. "Lady Lavinia, is something amiss?" He cupped her elbow with his palm.

The concerned face beneath the horsehair wig belonged to Mr. Shaw, the young barrister Webb had engaged to plead her father's case in the Court of King's Bench. Assuming he'd been party to the attorney's conspiracies, she jerked away from him, snapping, "Let me go."

"What outrage has Webb committed now?"

"Don't you know?" She enlightened him about the attorney's campaign to secure employment from Lord Newbold. After a cathartic condemnation of the attorney's character and morals, she asked, "Are you aware that he is in league with footpads?"

"Oh, yes. He spends his evenings in the Rib of Adam, a flash house in Tothill Fields, fraternizing with housebreakers and fences and swindlers. When they're careless or unlucky enough to get caught, he makes me defend them. He also preys on insolvent merchants. After he advises them to declare bankruptcy, he takes possession of their goods at a reduced cost. And then he sells—at a profit."

"Is that legal?"

"It isn't *illegal*. His interest in your father's case made me suspect an ulterior motive. Robbery and blackmail," the barrister muttered. "What an excellent politician he'll make. One day his sins will catch up with him—I couldn't sleep nights if I didn't believe that."

The gentle April sunshine failed to warm Lavinia as she made her way to the Radstock carriage. During her drive back to St. James's Square, she stared dully at all the yellow daffodils and golden primroses in the parks, looking less bright now than the last time she'd seen them.

The ordeal in Stanhope Street had drained her of all emotion. Or she believed, until Frances cheerfully announced her cousin Garrick's return from Suffolk.

Garrick had no intention of offering his best wishes for Lavinia's future happiness. He lacked her great talent for lying.

He managed to get through an interminable dinner without making a scene. She ate almost nothing, he noticed—even less than he did. It would have pleased him to think that he might be the reason, but she scarcely glanced his way. Something else had caused her distraction, and he could tell it wasn't feigned.

He spent a solitary half hour with a brandy bottle, sorely tempted to drink up the lot and numb his fevered mind and anguished heart. But an over-powering desire to be with his tormentor drew him to his cousin's sitting room. Frances, wearing her spectacles, studied a gazette. Lavinia stared down at the open book on her lap, as if committing it to memory, but she never once turned a page.

Breaking a long silence, he inquired, "Where's Xanthe, your faithful companion?"

"At Castle Cashin. A Manx tomcat took a fancy to her and left her in no condition to travel."

Garrick longed to brush that drooping side curl away from her cheek, to place his finger at the corner of her luscious mouth and create a smile. He sat down at the card table and placed his deck of cards on inlaid wood. "What d'you say to a game of piquet?"

"I'm out of practice."

"Then I'll tell your fortune instead."

"I don't believe you can."

"Come over here and I'll prove it."

Curiosity must brought her to him, because she sat down and watched him shuffle. He made three cuts before laying out a row of nine cards, face up, on the marquetry table.

He frowned.

"If you mean to foretell a death or some other terrible thing, I'd rather not hear it."

"No, no. I find no sign of death." He placed his finger on the first card. "The nine of diamonds represents a vagabond, one who will cause you much vexation." Moving down the line, he pointed out the next card. "The queen of spades stands for corruption, and an attempt on your virtue by a handsome man. The king of diamonds indicates that he's obstinate and vengeful, and of fair complexion."

"You're making this up," she said, her voice laden with distrust. "Aren't you?"

He braved her accusing glare. "I wish to heaven I were."

"The next card has hearts on it—that must signify love," she said hopefully.

"A nine of hearts promises great wealth and grandeur, and the esteem of all who know you. Unfortunately, the nine of spades comes next; therefore, your good luck will be shadowed by disappointment. And here's a ten of clubs. A mixed card, signifying riches from an unexpected source, and the loss of a friendship."

She was hanging on his every word now, eyes wide with fascination. "And the seven of clubs?"

"Further assurances of a brilliant future and exquisite bliss," he told her sourly. "And last of all, the two of hearts. It predicts overall success and good fortune, but you may have to wait for it."

"That's not so bad," she said in relief.

"Certainly not. Your early encounters with the troublesome, lustful, vengeance-minded, fair-haired vagabond are followed by wealth and grandeur. And after a slight disappointment, you get more riches and achieve perfect bliss. We should all be so lucky."

Damn, damn, damn. The devil was in his cards tonight.

Said Lavinia, "This has been a most interesting—and eventful—day. If you'll both excuse me, I shall go up to—go to my room."

She felt self-conscious about mentioning "bed" in his presence—now that was encouraging. The pulse in her swanlike neck fluttered erratically; sadness shadowed her silvery eyes. Garrick realized he was entirely mad, and hopelessly besotted with her, when he took these for signs that she wasn't yet irrevocably lost to him.

Chapter 21

O n Easter Monday, Lavinia and her chaperone accompanied the marquis to the opening of the newly rebuilt Theatre Royal in Drury Lane. Aristocratic and fashionable Londoners swarmed in the foyer, eager to view architect Henry Holland's latest masterpiece. She clutched Lord Newbold's arm, fearful of being separated, and he responded with a startled glance.

She excused her action by saying, "All these people make me nervous."

"A great crush," he agreed, leading her on toward the box seats.

From the safety of their private enclosure, Lavinia admired the theatre's lofty dome. Intricate gilt and plaster decorations and the crimson hangings formed a suitably rich setting for the ladies' gowns and jewels, and the gentlemen's equally lavish evening suits.

"Has the magnificence of our surroundings awed you into silence?" asked Frances.

"I'm counting the chandeliers," Lavinia confessed. "Two dozen—so far."

Said their escort, "The place is cavernous. No player, not even Kemble or a Siddons, can overcome its size. They'll be inaudible."

She wondered if Garrick, familiar with the great theatres of Paris and Vienna and Rome, would be impressed by Drury Lane's glory.

Without ever revealing his opinion of her engagement, he'd scurried back to Newmarket for the Craven Meeting. One of his horses had run today, and she wished him success and a handsome purse. She bore him no ill will. If he believed her engagement was motivated by greed, so be it. At least it would protect him from the malicious attorney. For if Daniel Webb should ever make good his threat and reveal what had happened at the inn, all the worst rumors about Garrick's character would be confirmed, sealing his reputation as a debaucher.

A reverent hush descended when the elegant Miss Farren claimed the stage. In her sweetly pitched voice, she recited a prologue composed in honor of this great occasion, alluding to theatre's many new marvels. Her declamation was followed by the lowering of the iron curtain. A man struck it with a hammer, demonstrating its strength and solidity, and boasted of its ability to withstand fire. The playgoers cheered and applauded enthusiastically.

The curtain rose, and the approving roar increased in volume. On one part of the stage stood a grove of trees, encircling a statue of Shakespeare. Elsewhere, a cascade of real water tumbled down artificial rocks and spilled into a large pool, and a boatman rowed himself back and forth across it.

"A charming tableau," murmured Frances, echoing the comments of the other occupants of their box.

After the thrilling prelude, Lavinia's expectations for the rest of the entertainment were extremely high. Why, she asked her companions, was a green baize carpet lying across the front of the stage?

"It shows us that the play is a tragedy," Newbold explained.

"But everyone knows it's *Macbeth*. I've seen placards posted round the town, and it's printed on the playbill you bought from the orange girl."

"The tradition is an established one."

A sudden rumble of thunder made Lavinia jump. Lightning flashed, and three crones appeared, reciting their incantation.

John Philip Kemble, a stately and eloquent Macbeth, was matched by his sister Sarah Siddons, a majestic Lady Macbeth. Lavinia admired the famous actress's queenly bearing and classically aquiline features. The thick, dark braids wound about her head were covered by a veil that fluttered with each dramatic utterance.

"False face must hide what false heart doth know," Mr. Kemble declaimed at the conclusion of the first act.

"I can't remember when I've witnessed so stirring a performance," Frances commented during the interval. "A pity that Garry is missing it." She turned her head to converse with a female friend across the low partition dividing the boxes.

In an undertone, the marquis said to Lavinia, "Armitage is far happier with his horses, and all the harl—and the females who loiter in Newmarket during the racing."

Lavinia waved her fan, seeking to cool her heated cheeks. Was Garrick chasing loose women? She shouldn't care what he did, for it was disloyal—positively wicked—to be affected by him.

Regarding Lord Newbold's austere profile, she resolved anew to forget her troubled past with her former lover. This man would become her husband at St. George's Church, in June. Although she knew exactly what would occur on her wedding night, and despite Calybrid Teare's advice about how to behave, she dreaded it. Most essential of all, the Manx charmer had warned, she must give the marquis no reason to think that she enjoyed the experience. Genteel virgins were supposed to shrink and weep, and then give in—dutifully.

"Did you sit for your portrait today?" Newbold asked, and she inclined her head. "I trust the experience isn't as tiresome as you expected."

"It isn't easy to keep still hour after hour," she acknowleged. "But Mr. Hoppner entertains me by gossiping about the royals he's painted—the Prince of Wales and all the princesses."

"I did consider having Romney do it, but he charges thirty guineas for a three-quarter length, which seems excessive."

She couldn't imagine why one someone so rich would quibble over a difference of five guineas.

"Nor can I regard him as a society painter. He mixes with the likes of Lady Hamilton, and that Anspach creature."

"But the Margravine is also sitting for Mr. Hoppner," Lavinia told him. "We met today as I was leaving his house. She invited me to attend her summer theatricals."

"I hope you declined. Hers is not an acquaintance we can cultivate. Divorcing Lord Craven and living with the Margrave before their marriage was bad enough. That monstrous spectacle of a masquerade was further proof of her shamelessless. In future, you shall be treated to the finest quality of acting and singing, here at Drury Lane and Covent Garden, and at the opera house. The deplorable fashion for private theatricals will not last, any more than the mania for private gaming houses."

His criticism was a fresh reminder of Garrick and his comments about rules—during that mortifying interlude in the Anspachs' theatre. She was relieved when Newbold changed the subject.

"This morning I received a curious communication from your father's attorney. I cannot approve of his attempt to deal with me directly; he should have contacted my solicitors about altering the provisions of our marriage contract."

Daniel Webb regarded his own interests as paramount. Could he be trusted to promote her family's welfare? Perhaps she ought to plead their case herself.

"My father has suffered financial reverses," she began, "from bad harvests and the downfall of the woollen trade. He cannot contribute much to my marriage portion."

"My dear Lavinia, the size of your dowry is immaterial," Newbold said with quiet conviction. "One advantage of great wealth is the freedom to choose a bride for her beauty and her good breeding."

She could have let the discussion end there. But filial duty compelled her to add, "Father wishes to make improvements to his estate, his mill. My brother's university education has been delayed. And my sister's physician insists that she visit a spa. Mr. Webb knows this and will negotiate on their behalf as well as mine."

"These matters are not to be decided between us," Newbold interjected. "My solicitors will assuredly advise against any settlement or annuity or allowance for my in-laws. As they should do," he added dampingly. "To give away large sums of money outright would significantly reduce my capital. I'm responsible for my widowed mother and seven brothers and sisters. But my chief duty as head of the family is conserving my fortune and properties for my heir. And all future generations."

Lavinia felt the blood draining from her face and fingertips and toes. No settlement—no annuity—no allowance. Newbold, preoccupied with the security of individuals not yet born, cared nothing for the needs of living people.

"Naturally," he went on, "I shall permit you to send presents to your relatives on suitable occasions—birthdays, and at Christmas. You may be as generous as you please."

"Your lordship is kind." What else could she say?

If the magnificent theatre suddenly went up in flames all around her, she couldn't be more alarmed. His decree had laid waste to her most cherished dream.

Newbold was fond of her, but that fondness did not extend to her family. Garrick would have supported them, she thought sadly, if it cost him his last gold guinea. He'd have done anything for her, during that brief, glorious time when she'd possessed his love.

"I trust you understand my position," said the marquis calmly.

"Nothing you said is unreasonable," she answered with forced composure. *Atreih*, it was unexpected—and so unfortunate.

"Your devotion to your family does you credit. But remember—in future, your loyalty will belong to the Shandos family and our interests. You must distance yourself from your island and its ways. As my marchioness, you will hold a prominent position in English society, and any little oddities will cause comment. Which would, I imagine, be distressing for you."

For him also, that was abundantly clear. Rules, she thought bleakly. Garrick *had* warned her.

The play resumed. Watching Lady Macbeth stride up and down the stage, shrieking and shuddering, Lavinia heartily envied her facility for imposing her will and venting her frustrations. Spectacles of scenery and stagecraft failed to move her. Witches dancing on a heath, the lavish banquet, a smoking cauldron, kingly apparitions—none seemed as real or as horrible as the tragedy she was living.

Overwhelmed by her emotions, she whispered to Frances, "I need air—I'm withdrawing."

"Shall I come?"

Lavinia shook her head, preferring to go alone. "I'll not be long."

Rising from her seat, she received yet another mildly disapproving stare from Newbold. She hoped he'd outgrow the habit.

The box lobby was deserted but for the pair of

orange sellers whispering in a corner. She sat down upon a giltwood chair and peeled off her pinching kid gloves. From the auditorium came muffled music—martial trumpets and drums. She eased her feet out of the tight shoes and leaned down to rub her cramped toes. The orange girls' mouths gaped in amazement.

They'd be far more surprised if they knew that she, in all her satin and lace, would gladly exchange places with them. Bartering fruit in a theatre seemed less distasteful than bartering her favors to a husband so he would increase her allowance.

If she couldn't supply money to her family, they would lose Castle Cashin.

If she failed to satisfy Daniel Webb, he would destroy her.

Her soul cried out to Garrick. She longed to feel his solid arms and comforting embrace. But he couldn't help her out of this difficulty, even if he wanted to.

False face must hide what false heart doth know.

The remembered phrase jarred her conscience. She'd shown her false face to Garrick one time too many, and he believed her heart was equally untrustworthy.

Beyond bustling Newmarket, the Radstock travelling carriage crossed into Suffolk, the shire Lavinia had never expected to see and least wished to be in.

The fields were immense, broader and flatter than any she'd seen. The thatched cottages were whitewashed, their walls decorated with intricate plasterwork.

"Pargetting, it's called," Frances told her. "That's Moulton Heath on the left. All the horses you see are Garry's. And Halford's."

Some of the animals were walking; others moved at a slow, graceful gallop. They bore no saddles. Green cloths covered their backs, and the youthful riders sported matching caps with a pale band—the Armitage colors, Frances explained. A man on a pony trailed after the group, shouting instructions.

"There's no point stopping; Garry will be at the morning horse auction. And I assured William that you wouldn't come in contact with the rougher elements of the racing profession."

Their route to Monkwood Hall followed the Kennet River southward, to a terrain that was gently rolling and more wooded.

"I've not attended First Spring Meeting since my girlhood," Frances confided.

"Do ladies attend the races?" she asked. Lord Newbold had reacted to the news of their plans with one of his stony looks.

"They did when I was young. You mustn't worry about William. He was cross because he's stuck in London, listening to lawyers argue over settlements and jointures by day and suffering through dull political speeches all night."

Although Lavinia found much to like in Sir Bardolph Hyde, she quailed at his hard, penetrating scrutiny when he commented on her engagement. His nephew, she perceived, had confided in him— surely he wasn't privy to all the details of that night at the Drover's Rest? But no, his face and manner gave no indication that he regarded her as a fallen woman.

Frances was rapturously informing their host that the village was as charming as she remembered, and the house a delightful combination of elegance and comfort.

"My carriage is at your disposal," he declared, "whenever you care to watch Garry's horses run. Although he resides at Moulton, he often turns up, for he stables one of his hacks here—no room for both at his racing box. I shouldn't be surprised if he dined with us this evening."

Lavinia was spared. Garrick did not put in an appearance at dinner, but his name popped up with disturbing regularity as her chaperone and the baronet exchanged tales of his youthful exploits. Sir Bardolph told how his nephew had caught a greased pig at Bury fair and accidentally shot the Monkwood gamekeeper with his bow and arrow. Frances countered with a description of Garrick's first Langtree ball and the havoc he'd created by letting a pet rabbit loose among the dancers.

In the morning, a landau carried the ladies to Newmarket and its racecourse. The baronet, well-informed about his nephew's entries, told them what to expect.

"Double the Stakes will compete against other six-year-olds, and the odds favor him. Still, Roving Minstrel shows remarkable speed and is ridden by an ambitious jockey. I pray Garry's horse has the stamina and the pace to hold them off. Goosey—his rider—has sweated and purged himself all week in preparation. He's become such a wraith, he'll have to carry extra weight."

The majority of racegoers, Lavinia noted, were gentlemen, many of whom congregated at the bet-

ting post. When the race began, Sir Bardolph joined
the Duke of Halford at the rope near the finish line,
leaving the ladies in possession of his open carriage.
Lavinia sat rigidly upright, squinting at the distant
track. Frances was armed with a pair of opera
glasses.

The horses came tearing along the stretch, their
hooves churning the alley of smooth grass. Lavinia
saw George Gosling's green silk shirt and cream
vest—he was holding his lead. The cheers intensi-
fied.

"It's Double the Stakes," screeched a red-faced
man.

"Bugger 'im," his companion moaned. "My
money's on Roving Minstrel. C'mon, you big bastard, ride for 'ell!"

Just the sort of language Lord Newbold would
deplore. Bugger *him*, thought Lavinia. She had no
idea what it meant, but it adequately expressed her
rebelliousness.

"He'll win, he'll do it," Frances muttered. "Oh,
yes—oh, a *very* fine run!"

The gentlemen moved as a mass to the betting
post to settle with their bookmakers.

"I wish I'd made a wager," said Frances regretfully. "I shouldn't be surprised if Garry bet hundreds of pounds on the outcome."

"A thousand," Sir Bardolph, returning to the landau, informed her. "And the odds were five to
one—he pockets five times that."

And the money had come to him in an instant,
Lavinia marvelled. "How much does the jockey
get?"

"Three guineas per race," the baronet answered.

"And a prize from the grateful owner. I'm off to make sure old Goosey passes his weigh-in."

"Well, Lavinia," said Frances, "how do you like this sport of kings and Hydes and Armitages?"

She liked it very well.

On the following day, Sir Bardolph made sure they arrived at the racing ground even earlier, to get a better viewing place. Spying his nephew, he waved him over to the landau.

"Were you buying at the morning's auction?" he asked.

Garrick nodded. "A yearling sired by Handsome Ned. Legs like a stork. I outbid the Duke of Bedford."

"And did Play the Trump have a fair outing on the heath this morning?"

"She's in a mood to run, says Con. Old Tattersall certainly liked the look of her. But everyone buzzes about Delia's Delight, and the odds are shortening."

The baronet grinned. "Before the afternoon is out, you'll have won enough to take her off Gormley's hands."

"I wonder. Six wins in six starts."

"Then it's time she learned how to take a loss."

Garrick threw back his head and laughed, long and loud.

But his mirth was merely a shield, hiding the misery that dwelled in his soul. How much longer, he wondered, must he endure Lavinia's presence? Meeting her here at Newmarket was more than he could bear.

She was a visible reminder of what might have been. As his bride, she would have shared in every victory earned by his horses and jockeys. He'd have looked to her for consolation at his losses. She'd be living with him at Moulton, standing at his side as he watched the morning gallops over the heath. And in the evening, she'd join him in his bed.

Dio, but she was a beauty. Midnight hair and dawn-gray eyes. And that face—the one he covered with kisses in his dreams.

Scowling, he turned his back on her. He walked over to the makeshift gaming tables—evens and odds, faro, hazard—all operated by rogues and sharpers who offered marked cards and weighted dice to the unwary punters. Moving on to the betting post, Garrick joined a motley crowd. Peers and gentlemen in carriages and on horseback were surrounded by stablehands and jockeys, all of them calling out wagers to the bookmakers. The din was deafening.

With studied nonchalance, he read the names of the horses listed in chalk on the blackleg's slate, and considered the odds. "Two thousand, Play the Trump," he decided. "To win."

"Arr," the bookmaker confirmed, noting the amount.

Today he was more nervous than yesterday, and determined not to let it show. He'd wagered twice as much as he should've done, and he blamed Lavinia. He wanted to win great sums—not that she would be impressed, for she'd soon have access to Newbold's vast wealth.

"They're off!"

He hurried through a sea of surging bodies to the winning post, edging himself into a gap between a gig and a phaeton to watch the finish. He was in view of the steward's box, a small wooden hut raised on wheels.

He glanced over his shoulder at Lavinia, seated in his uncle's carriage. She was peering through his cousin's opera glasses, and her worried face gave him pause. What was happening on the field?

He surged against the ropes, leaning over for a view of the oncoming thoroughbreds. The bay mare decked out in his colors was hemmed in on all sides, unable to break out of the cluster. "Skirt them, Con," he muttered.

"Sir, move back," the marshall chided, brandishing a whip. "Keep the way clear, the horses are comin'."

"Gawd, lookit the gray!" a spectator marvelled. "She's got the lead now—there'll be no catching her."

Garrick could envision the scene without seeing it. The onlookers' shouts told him that the outcome was already decided.

The leader flew past, a pale streak—now Delia's Delight could boast seven wins in seven starts. Play the Trump was the third horse to finish.

Garrick's hands clenched the rope barrier until he felt the rough hemp cutting into his flesh. Two thousand, gone in a flash. He couldn't expect a victory in every race—perhaps luck would favor him tomorrow. His greatest regret was that Lavinia had witnessed his defeat, and he was about to confront her pity. Or, even worse, her scorn.

Chapter 22

That night, Garrick dined at Monkwood Hall, and during the meal he regaled his uncle with gossip heard at the auction and in a meeting of the Jockey Club. Frances, whose taste ran to society news, exhibited her innate politeness by pretending to be interested. Lavinia listened avidly, hanging on his every word. Although she was a fresh convert to the religion of horse racing, her questions were intelligent and her comments astute. Garrick gave curt replies—and hated himself for it.

His relations thwarted his desperate flight back to Moulton, insisting that he stay to complete a foursome for whist. When they cut cards to choose partners, he drew Lavinia.

He was fully prepared to finesse his way through the game, making up for her lack of experience. To his surprise, she recalled the tactics he'd taught her during their stay at Langtree. She consistently led with her strongest suit. She played her trumps with confidence. When in doubt, she followed his lead, enabling him to played his king, queen, and knave to advantage. Blessed with diamonds, he trumped their adversaries, ensuring a win.

A second, more challenging game ended in victory for his cousin and his uncle. The third and deciding contest was the hardest fought. The leading suit was clubs; Garrick had few of them. He threw out his strong suit—diamonds again—to no avail. Lavinia, confused by his stratagems, floundered. Failing to play her sequence properly, she was soundly trumped.

Afterward, she apologized, humbly accepting responsibility for their defeat.

"Not the first loss I've suffered this day," he responded carelessly.

"I'm so sorry about Play the Trump."

Garrick shrugged. "Many great horses aren't true stayers. She didn't have the pace to hold off Delia's Delight. Young Con tried too hard; he couldn't get the best out of her. He'll do better tomorrow when he runs for the Hyde Cup."

Her hand vanished into pocket slit of her muslin gown and brought out some banknotes. "I've got twenty pounds to give you."

"Whatever for?"

"I want to wager it on your horse," she said earnestly.

Probably all the cash she possessed, he thought, knowing her inability to manage her funds. And she was staking it on his untried horse, without any knowledge of the odds. This ridiculously optimistic gesture revived his belief that she was and would ever be the only girl for him.

"You might lose it," he warned.

"If you don't place the bet for me, I'll do it my-self," she countered.

"Oh, very well," he said.

Riding back to Moulton, Garrick nursed his frustration over the dark-haired, secretive beauty who had turned his life upside down. Deceitful, greedy, inconstant—and he loved her still. Always would.

From the outset of their acquaintance, she'd desired a rich marriage. Her motive had always mystified him, but never more so than now. Her father was free from prison, the debts were paid, and she could marry whomever she pleased. She'd accepted Newbold, and not because she was madly in love with him. Why, then, had she done it?

Throughout a troubled, restless night, he reviewed and rejected a variety of wild and impossible schemes to save her from a deplorable fate.

Abducting her and dragging her across the border for a Gretna Green wedding would effectively rupture her engagement. If he were the utter rogue everyone believed him, he'd inform Newbold that the future marchioness was not as pure as she should be. Destroying a lady's reputation was cruel and boorish, so not even worth considering. Asking for his cousin's help was a flawed stratagem; she wasn't likely to help him sabotage her brilliant achievement in matchmaking.

In the morning, he arrived in Newmarket with his retinue of horses, jockeys, grooms, and trainer. He went directly to the White Hart, where he met Prawn Parfitt. A story circulating in the coffee room cast doubt on the integrity of Garrick's youngest jockey; he feigned indifference, but inwardly he seethed.

Shortly after noon, the racing began. He and Edward watched the early heats to see which animals might be worth adding to the Armitage stud, then went to their own paddock. Not many spectators—a bad omen.

A bowlegged groom was leading Ten of Diamonds up and down the enclosure. Gaunt and ungainly, the black horse had a quirky, shuffling walk.

A bystander at the rail commented to his companion, "They say when he runs, he's steady as can be."

"But is he swift? I go by the rule 'If it walks well, it'll gallop well.' Don't think much of the rider, either. Let's have a look at Don't Tell the Wife."

Nick Cattermole, overhearing this remark, screwed up his leathery face. "I s'pose you've heard what they're saying 'bout our Con, that he threw his race yesterday."

"We've heard," Edward said bitterly. "So has every man in Newmarket."

"One good thing's come of it, Your Grace. Old Goosey, always so jealous of that lad, stands up for him. Now he's throwing out hints on how to manage the race."

Garrick went over to the riders. Con, cradling his pigskin saddle as he sat on an upturned crate, listened carefully to the bowlegged veteran.

"Stay calm," Goosey instructed, "and your horse will be also. Ride your race as it develops. And when time comes t'move up, do't gradual-like. Keep him on the bit and don't let him run too free, else he'll lose his speed too soon. You want t'make a *late* charge. So when you come at the Dip, take it fast as you can. And don't never look round at t'others; you'll unbalance your horse. If you must, turn only your head, not your whole body."

"Enough, Goosey," Garrick interrupted. "Con knows the ways of that great shuffling beast better than any of us. We must trust them both to ride the best race they can."

The cherub-faced lad in the green-and-white silk shirt stood up. "We will, m'lord. You can depend on that."

The bell rang out.

"Time for that saddle," Nick called to Con.

The older jockey confided to Garrick, "The fellows made sport of him in the boozer yesternight. He took it more serious than he should've done. High-strung, and too sensitive to slights—he wants toughening. But that lad's a right'un, ne'er doubt it, m'lord."

"I don't. Come along, Edward; let's seek out the blackleg and make our bets."

The long odds on Ten of Diamonds gave him pause.

"Seven to one," the leg repeated, not even glancing at his slate.

The punters hadn't liked the animal's configuration or the jockey's recent loss. Nevertheless, Garrick placed Lavinia's twenty quid on his horse as instructed, then wagered a thousand for his own benefit. Edward shook his head at him and did not bet.

The premier lords of the sport had gathered for the running of the Hyde Cup—Derby, Grosvenor, Bedford. Sir Charles Bunbury, mounted on a handsome hack, conversed with Edward and Sir Bardolph. Frances and Lavinia sat in the landau, surveying the crowd through their opera glasses. They weren't the only ladies in attendance, but they were by far the most attractive. His cousin's partiality was evident; her green habit was embellished with white ribbons. Lavinia wore the burgundy one he knew so well—intimately, in fact.

He belonged with the other desperate punters and anxious owners hovering near the finishing post.

Nick Cattermole was already there. He chewed the inside of his cheek, then muttered, "Canna do nowt but wait. The answer lies in Con's hands and head. And in Ten's hooves."

"Diamonds were ever my lucky cards," Garrick declared.

But the gemstones, he remembered, were associated with unlucky incidents. The earrings had brought trouble to him and to Lavinia. She'd worn them but once, after she'd jilted him, at the masquerade ball—when he had offended her, and she had flung them at him in anger.

And he'd learned of her betrothal to Newbold on the same day he'd recieved his Aunt Anna's necklace.

Diamonds, he thought glumly, did not always bring him good fortune.

"The horses are moving." Edward had trained his spyglass on the field. "I can't see them well; they're too far off."

A loss, Garrick tried to persuade himself, would not be a complete disaster. He could easily repay Lavinia's twenty pounds. Ten of Diamonds was starting his career; so was Con Finbar. They would have other opportunities to shine.

"A promising start," his brother reported. "But they've got three more miles of turf to cover."

When the spyglass was offered to him, Garrick held it to his eye. Green cap, black horse—in fourth place. A good position, so long as they didn't lose ground to the others crowding in from behind.

Con shook his reins, and Ten lengthened his stride to move up on the leaders. Stretching out his neck still more, he passed them by. The only one ahead of him now was Don't Tell the Wife.

Garrick lowered the glass. The front pair were dead even as they headed down the Dip.

"Ride on, ride on," Nick said through gritted teeth. "Give him his head—there's a good lad. Ah, you've got by them—they canna catch you now!"

The trainer's excitement was drowned by the sound of thunder as the black horse hurtled past, followed by the favorite and the rest of the field. As soon as the last racer reached the finishing post, spectators and horsemen stormed onto the course.

Garrick nearly fell over, Edward and Nick were pounding his back so hard. Excited voices buzzed all around him; every face wore a grin.

Dazed, he stared down at his trainer. "We've won. By God, we've done it!"

As the enormity of his achievement sank in, he grinned from ear to ear. The Hyde Cup was coming back to the family that had given and named it all those years ago. In addition to prize money, the return on his wager was enormous.

After the Clerk of the Course confirmed the win, the presentation of the prize took place. Sir Bardolph, his face pink with pride and glee, offered hearty congratulations.

"A great victory, Garry! Your Ten of Diamonds is a splendid beast."

"Bred and born and reared at Moulton," Garrick asserted. "Which makes this win even richer." He accepted the bulging purse from his uncle—five hundred guineas felt nice and heavy—and gave it to Edward.

"And, of course, the Hyde Cup."

At a gesture from the baronet, Lavinia stepped forward with the trophy, a masterpiece of silversmithing outshone by her eyes. When she passed it to him, their hands touched. He heard a smattering of applause and a few cheers.

"Give t'lady a buss, m'lud!" cried Goosey.

He bent down and brushed his lips against her cheekbone. "I'm luckier in racing than in love," he told her under his breath. "*Sposina mia.*"

She made no response to his covert endearment, the cruel, coldhearted little witch. He wanted to shout to the crowd that she belonged to him, was more precious to him than the gold coins and his silver cup.

But all he could do was grin and nod, and spout witticisms to his friends. And make himself as drunk as it was possible to be.

"Early in June," Lord Newbold informed Frances and Lavinia. "That, I have determined, is the most advantageous time for the marriage to be solemnized."

"I'd hoped it might be sooner," commented Frances, studying her *Ladies' Pocket Repository.* "Three weeks from now! If you'd but acquire the license, you needn't wait so long."

"I've been extremely busy with this investigation the House of Lords has mounted. We're attempting to discover which organizations here in London are promoting seditious practices." With an apologetic smile for Lavinia, the marquis said, "I mustn't reveal all I know. But rest assured that I and my fellow peers will never permit anarchy to rise up here, as it did in France."

Lavinia didn't mind that the marquis was so preoccupied with his Parliamentary duties. She had a great deal on her mind, too.

"Well, don't overlook the queen's ball," said Frances. "Garry can't escort us; he's not received at court. Even if he were, he wouldn't care to miss the Epsom races."

"You may depend on me to put in an appearance. I am most eager to present the future Marchioness of Newbold to Her Majesty."

When he consulted his timepiece, Frances teased, "Are you so impatient to return to Westminster and that secret committee of yours?"

"I said nothing about being on a committee," Newbold said firmly. "Secret or otherwise. Not a single word."

"Don't assume I'm ignorant about how these matters are conducted. The House of Commons has just completed its investigation, and you can't deny that it was performed surreptitiously."

They entered into a civil debate upon procedure. Lavinia watched their faces, trying to make sense of what they said.

Drawing himself up to his full height, the marquis said, "You've turned out to be an alarmingly opinionated female. When you were younger, you never disagreed with me."

"Free speaking is a privilege that comes with maturity," Frances declared. "As a girl, I was careful to conceal my views for fear of displeasing eligible gentlemen."

He laughed. "How devious you ladies can be! My dear Lavinia, are you waiting till the matrimonial knot is tied to show your true colors?"

Lavinia struggled to come up with a reply and failed.

Said Frances cheerily, "It matters not, Newbold. Trust me, it would be very dull if you knew everything about your spouse at the outset of the marriage." Again she studied her almanac. "Such a short time until the queen's ball. I must remember to have Siberry clean my garnets. Lavinia, you'll want to get your jewels back."

Newbold cleared his throat, then announced, "It is my intention to purchase a suitable parure for my bride. Unfortunately, my time has been entirely taken up with this sedition inquiry."

Lavinia raised her head. "I've got the Ballacraine rubies."

"Your father's property," he reminded her, "not yours to keep. You should have something of your own. The trinkets my father gave my mother are her private possessions, and they will go to my sisters. You'll have to tell me exactly what you would like; that will save time." He came over to her and took possession of her hand. "I cannot stay any longer, so we must resume this discussion another day."

She hoped he might kiss her cheek, but as usual

it was her fingers he saluted. Nonetheless, the gesture drew a sentimental sigh from Frances.

When he was gone, she said, "How fortunate you are; the days leading to my wedding were filled with strife and opposition. My family preferred Newbold—he was very near to proposing, I believe, when I tumbled into love with Radstock. Nobody expected such a sophisticated and dashing man to wed a clergyman's daughter. At the time we became acquainted, his mistress had just borne him a daughter."

"That must have been painful for you."

Frances nodded. "Extremely. But he broke off with Mrs. Rogers and pensioned her off, and I was so relieved that I wept all over him. Radstock used all his diplomatic skills on my parents, vowing to be faithful to me till death, and in the end I was permitted to marry him. But up to the moment my father delivered me to St. George's Church, I feared that the ceremony might be stopped."

"What happened to your husband's daughter?" Lavinia wondered.

"She's Radstock's ward and will have half his fortune."

The girl Garrick had said he was supposed to marry.

"He sent her to one of the best boarding schools," Frances continued, "and took her with him on his posting to Naples." Lowering her voice to a conspiratorial murmur, she added, "My husband and I—and Halford—agree that Caroline is the perfect match for Garry."

"How—interesting." And disheartening.

"While we stayed at Monkwood, my cousin and

I had the most curious conversation. He said he wished he'd behaved differently to a young woman he met last year, and I'm certain she was the one he meant. He spent some time in Naples before he returned to England."

Unable to sit still any longer, Lavinia moved to the window overlooking the square. "Such a sunny day. I'm going to walk to Bond Street, to Mr. Siberry's, and get my rubies."

"Don't be too long—you've got a fitting this afternoon."

So many fittings and sittings by day, and parties and operas and plays at night. She was impatient to begin her married life. After the wedding, she and Newbold would travel to his Sussex manor, close enough to London that he could attend the House of Lords as necessary. Neither Garrick nor Daniel Webb would be able to penetrate her sanctuary and disturb her peace.

Earlier in the day, she'd received a letter from the attorney, boasting of success in negotiating her pin money. The Shandos side had offered five hundred per annum; he'd countered with a request for double that amount. They had agreed upon seven hundred. Webb pointed out that she could expect an increase in her allowance as soon as she provided her husband with a son and heir.

A broodmare, that's what she would become. Well-tended, closely guarded. Occasionally displayed for public admiration, then guided back to her stable. She knew her master would treat her kindly, but he expected her to obey him, to serve him.

During her walk to the jeweler's shop, she re-

membered the adventures Garrick had promised—
a honey-month in his Venetian villa, masked revels,
gaming houses. A life without rules, enriched by
mutual passion.

When she explained to the owlish Mr. Siberry
why she'd come, he said briskly, "Yes, yes, your
ladyship's rubies. I'll have them cleaned immediately and shall deliver them to St. James's Square
myself. Let me make a note of it, so I do not forget."

While he was occupied, Lavinia noticed the open
case he'd left on the counter. Its specially fitted compartments held a complete suite—necklace, eardrops, twin brooches, a pair of bracelets, and a tiara.
All were set with large blue gemstones and tiny diamonds.

Mr. Siberry turned back and caught her staring
at them with undisguised admiration.

"Quite a collection, eh? I accepted it in lieu of
payment. If I can't dispose of the entire set, I shall
break it up and reassemble the sapphires in more
fashionable settings. But the necessary labor and
materials would cut into my profit."

"How much does it cost?" she inquired.

"Twelve hundred pounds."

"Lord Newbold wishes me to have a parure of
my own," she mused. "But he might think the price
too high."

"He'll not find such a bargain at Mr. Rundell's,"
Siberry informed her. "The Shandos family have
seldom made lavish purchases, I know—only the
occasional snuffbox, or a set of apostle spoons for a
christening gift. But the marquis is marrying a
young lady with excellent taste, and he'll likely
loosen his purse strings, eh? If I could gain him as

a regular customer, I might be inclined to reduce the price. Would that make a difference?"

"I've no idea," she said candidly. "I'm very ill-informed about finance."

He lifted the necklace from the case. "Fit for a marchioness, isn't it? This large pendant stone detaches, you see. A most elegant size and shape, and every stone flashes blue fire." Loosening the catch, he presented it to Lavinia.

As she stared at the ornament filling her palm, a bold and desperate plan came to life in her mind.

Chapter 23

If Newbold purchased jewelry for her, it would be her private property.

"These matching brooches can be worn as shoulder clips, you see," Mr. Siberry continued, pinning them to her dress. "Try the necklace also, and the tiara."

She did as he suggested, then accepted the mirror he offered.

"I'd let them go for a thousand, perhaps. They become you so well."

In his eagerness to make the sale, the shopkeeper was flattering her. The cold, cobalt-blue stones made her eyes look dead and her complexion wan. Lavinia didn't care; she didn't need them for her own adornment. She would put them to a far better use.

Removing each piece, she said calmly, "I shall speak with Lord Newbold. And I'd be most grateful if you could hold this set until I know his answer."

"My pleasure." He went to open the door for her, bowing low as she left the shop.

She wanted the sapphires. If she got them, she could sell off the individual pieces or their stones and gold—and use the proceeds to support her family. Daniel Webb had involved himself in nefarious dealings with jewel thieves, and was probably acquainted with smiths who removed gems from their settings and melted down the precious metal.

How would she explain the disappearance of Newbold's gift? A robbery, she decided. Webb could arrange one—he'd done it before. London crawled with footpads, and aristocrats were fair game.

Her conscience began to stir. Unchaste, dishonest, scheming—oh, yes, she thought bleakly, a splendid marchioness she would make. She balked at another deception. If only Newbold had granted her father that annuity. . . .

She returned to St. James's Square and gave Frances an enthusiastic description of the sapphires she'd seen at Mr. Siberry's shop. Exactly as she'd hoped, her chaperone sat down to pen an entreaty to his lordship, advising him to hasten to Bond Street.

At the appointed hour, the dressmaker arrived with Lavinia's court gown, a copy in blue of the white one she'd worn the night she'd met her marquis. Some of the lacy butterflies salvaged from the ruined garment were stitched to the gauzy overskirt of Miss Fallowfield's newest creation.

Lavinia stood stiffly while the seamstress pinned lace cuffs to each of her sleeves, and Frances gushed about the parure.

"You *must* have it for the queen's ball," she declared. "Nothing could be more perfect than sapphires. The dark blue will complement the lighter color of your bodice and underskirt."

She required Lavinia to practice walking about the room and gave hints on how to manage the bell-like hoop and the long train, *de rigueur* for a court appearance.

All that day and into the night, Lavinia's thoughts constantly returned to the jewels. One thousand pounds. Suppose Newbold considered the price too steep? Tossing and turning in her bed, she fretted over his frugality. Yet her appearance was a matter of great importance to him, and he might be tempted by such a grand parure.

When she joined Frances for breakfast, she found Garrick seated with her at the breakfast table. His cousin wore a dismayed expression, and no wonder, thought Lavinia. He looked dreadful. Strands of yellow hair hung about his flushed face. His neckcloth was poorly tied, and dark stains marred his broadcloth coat.

"Lady Lavinia," he croaked. "The beauteous bride-to-be."

"Pay no mind to anything he says," Frances advised her. "He's thoroughly drunk."

He placed his elbow on the table and rested his chin in his palm. "Brought me luck at Newmarket, the pair of you. Better be there for Second Spring Meeting."

"You'll have to manage without us. Very likely that will be the week of Lavinia's wedding."

"The joyous day approacheth." Garrick passed a hand over his face, flinching when he came in contact with bristles. "Want a shave. Where's Carlo?"

"In your room, unpacking."

Lavinia's mouth dropped. "He's staying here?"

"So he says."

"Breaking my journey to Epsom," he mumbled. "Stopped with Prawn last night. Went to a gaming hell. I won five hundred—maybe more. Celebrated."

"Here, take your cup," said Frances. "And don't spill coffee on the cloth." Turning to Lavinia, she said, "I'm going to Bond Street to have a look at your sapphires,"

Garrick glanced up. "Sapphires?"

"At Siberry's. Lavinia chose them yesterday."

"Diamonds, that's what she ought to have. I've got some—great 'normous ones."

"Finish your coffee," Frances commanded. "My apologies, Lavinia, for abandoning you to such a pitiful object. I'd be most grateful if you'd refill my cousin's cup; I don't trust him to manage for himself."

When they were alone, Garrick narrowed his eyes at Lavinia. "You want sa-sapphires? You can have 'em. For a kiss."

"Don't be absurd. I've no desire to kiss you."

"Liar."

She glared at him. "You might as well call me slut and jilt, and be done."

He pressed his fingers against his forehead. "Stop ranting—it makes my head hurt."

"Drinking too much makes it hurt." It broke her heart to see him in this shameful state, and she wondered if she might be the cause. *Cha nel*, she argued to herself, she couldn't be blamed for his lack of self-control.

"Got something to tell you—trying to remember

it." The effort made him frown. "Right. 'He that marrieth for wealth sells his liberty.' Or she. P'raps I'll have Siberry engrave it on a gold collar; you can wear it round your neck."

"Why can't you be civil and wish me happiness?"

"Because I don't," he answered with a fierce look. "If you marry that walking rent-roll, I want you to be miserable. You'll deserve it." He lurched out of his chair, tipping over the oak-patterned china cup. "Blast and damn! Frances will skewer me."

She didn't know whether to laugh or cry. "Oh, do be careful," she cautioned as he gripped the Sheraton sideboard for support. She had visions of the whole thing pitching over on him.

"Soon's I'm shaved, it's off to Siberry's. You're going to get a fine bride gift, *dolcezza*. Something to remember me by," he added mockingly.

"Here are your ladyship's rubies, well cleaned." The jeweler presented the case to Lavinia. "And Mrs. Radstock's garnets, which she brought when she came to the shop this morning. I'm glad to know that you decided to have the sapphires, but I can't say how long they'll be available. For Lord Garrick is also desirous of purchasing the parure, I don't know for whom. He didn't ask the price, nor did I inquire about the recipient."

"It might be me," Lavinia confessed.

Siberry's white brows shot up, making him look like a startled owl. "Well, then. If you really want the jewels, my lady, I can make certain that you receive them."

Now it was her turn to be surprised. "How?"

"If Lord Garrick returns, I shall inform him that

the set costs but five hundred pounds. And I'll tell Lord Newbold the same. Each will consider the cost extremely low for so magnificent an ornament. By allowing both to make the purchase at half the price, I'm assured of the one thousand I require, and of my profit. Thus your ladyship receives a handsome present from two gentlemen, with neither of them the wiser."

Lavinia digested this. No suggestive overtones had flavored his proposition. He'd presented it matter-of-factly, as if this kind of deceptive transaction were customary.

Marvelling at his oddly liberal notions of client service, she said, "Someone might find out."

"Never from me. I'm practiced in these little deceits. For instance, after a certain lady lost a valuable brooch in a card game, I made up an indentical one of paste gems so her lord wouldn't know. Just last week, one gentleman purchased a pair of fine gold bracelets, asking me to send one to his opera dancer and the other to his bride. I name no names! I'm as trustworthy—and as silent—as a confessor."

"What if Lord Garrick commits to buying the sapphires but Lord Newbold doesn't? Or the other way round?"

"In that instance, I would declare—most regretfully—that I'd quoted the lower price in error." He smiled encouragingly. "You want the parure; why should you not have it? Permit me to arrange everything, my lady, and it shall be yours."

The serpent tempting Eve in Eden could not have been more persuasive.

She was fond of Newbold and she loved Garrick. But neither of them was as devoted to her, or as reliant upon her, as her parents and Kerron and Kitty. For them, she was willing to risk anything.

Alerted by the thud of the brass door knocker, Garrick leaned expectantly and precariously over the stair rail. The footman was receiving another delivery. People had arrived hourly, bringing new gowns and hats for Lavinia, books and invitations for Frances. Everything but the item he awaited so impatiently.

"For 'er ladyship, from Siberry's." The courier presented a flat parcel to the servant.

"I'll take it, Alfred," said Garrick, making a hurried descent.

"Very good, my lord," the footman responded, relinquishing it to him.

He carried it to the hall table and fumbled for his penknife. Cutting the string, he removed the paper wrapping and stared down at the leather case.

He must have been mad or drunk—or both—when he'd returned to the jeweler's shop yesterday. *Something to remember me by.*

The words had sounded well enough when he'd uttered them so harshly to Lavinia, and later when he'd repeated them to Siberry. Now their very finality haunted him.

He raised the lid to view the gems. Tucked within the semicircle of the tiara was a card engraved with a crest—an unfamiliar one. Turning it over, he found an inscription.

My dear Lavinia,

It would please me well to have you wear these ornaments at your presentation to Her Majesty the

queen this evening. I have great hopes of attending,
but undoubtedly I shall arrive late.
Your devoted servant,
Newbold

Right gift—wrong giver. The jeweler had made a mistake.

Perplexed, he read the note again.

Then he carried the case upstairs, to Lavinia's bedchamber. The door stood ajar, and boldly he walked in.

The room had not been empty for long. The tapers affixed to the dressing table were lit, and their flames fluttered. A blue satin evening frock, elaborately embellished with lacy butterflies, lay in readiness on the bed. He placed the case beside it. Then he walked to the other side and pulled the curtain across to conceal his presence.

It wasn't long before he heard Lavinia enter, closing the door behind her. She moved quietly, from bureau to dressing table and back again. He watched her remove her afternoon gown and drape it over the top of the embroidered screen. When she turned toward the bed, she noticed the case. Opening it, she found Newbold's card.

Garrick whisked the curtain aside.

With a gasp of alarm, she dropped the case. Jewels spilled out of their compartments—necklace and brooches and bracelets. "You shouldn't be here!"

"Don't worry, I'm in no mood to ravish you." He came around to gather up the fallen pieces. The tiara had landed near her feet, upside down. "Put them on," he ordered her. "Unlike Newbold, I won't see you wearing them at the ball. Go ahead. For me." When he tried to set the jewel-studded crescent on her head, she batted his hand aside.

"Don't," she begged.

Ignoring her protest, he placed the heavy necklace around her neck, slipped the bracelets onto her fragile wrists, and hung the earrings from her earlobes. Carefully, he pinned one of the brooches to her chemise, puckering the filmy lawn.

"Aren't you going to thank me for the fine present I've given you? Or are you saving all your gratitude for Newbold? I'd like to know why *his* card was enclosed with *my* purchase. Give me the truth, Lavinia. The complete truth."

"Mr. Siberry duped you and Newbold both," she told him, her voice distant and dead. "I let him, because I wanted the sapphires."

"*Dio*, but you are the greediest, most damnably acquisitive female I've ever known. And the most fiendishly calculating. I'd have pawned my very soul for you. But my love wasn't enough; you craved Newbold's fortune. And now that you've nearly got it, you cheat me for a parcel of jewels your marquis can better afford. I applaud your consistency, *carissima*."

She hung her head. "*B'egin dou*," she murmured. "I had to do it. I want nothing for myself, and never did. Not Newbold's money or these horrid sapphires. But I had to help my family."

Here, thought Lavinia, was her chance to relieve herself of her suffocating guilt. He couldn't possibly think any worse of her than he did already.

"We're paupers, the lot of us. Great-grandfather squandered his fortune to buy his title. My grandmother left hers to Catholic charities. Father received no inheritance, only the estate. Castle Cashin—it sounds so grand, but it's nearly a ruin. Our crofters barely eke out a living from their farms; the harvests have been dreadful, and rents are low. The woollen mill closed down." Relieved and ashamed, she sank wearily onto a bench. "There's the truth you wanted, Garrick. I'm penniless. And a liar and a cheat."

"An adventuress," he muttered. "Exactly what Jenny suspected." With a humorless laugh, he added, "I always knew you were the girl for me."

"All these months I wanted to confide in you— but I didn't dare, not even when you asked me to marry you." It seemed so long ago, that time when he had wanted her for his wife. Across a chasm created by her own deceit, she gazed up at him. "My family expects me—and the man I marry—to support them."

"You gave me up because I lacked riches?"

She shook her head. "After you learned Father was in the King's Bench, I lost your trust, your respect—your affection. I couldn't wed you, knowing how much you despised me. All I wanted was to return to the island with Father. So I did. And while I was there, I toiled in the fields and cooked meals and helped with the livestock. But I couldn't make my sister well again. Or give my brother a university education. Or ensure that my parents can keep their home. And I was so lonely—that's why I decided I should marry Newbold, if he ever asked. He did, as soon as I came back to London. And then everything went wrong, because I found out that Mr. Webb had conspired against me and used me."

Lavinia told him about the attorney's role in her father's arrest, and his attempt to steal the Ballacraine rubies. "He hired the footpads who attacked your cousin and me. He sent letters—anonymously—demanding that I give up the rubies. You were with me when I received the first one."

"That note you burned? Yes, I remember—and after it came, you handed your heirloom over to Siberry for safekeeping."

"Daniel Webb visited Langtree and told me Father was ill, to hasten my marriage to a rich and powerful man. You were the one who had proposed—the only one I wished to wed. Mr. Webb was at the Drover's Rest on the night you and I were—eloping. He knew we shared a room. To prevent our marriage, he sent you to the King's Bench on the day of Father's release."

"*Un perfetto mascalzone*," said Garrick through gritted teeth. "A complete scoundrel."

"Now he's blackmailing me again. If I don't persuade the marquis to employ him and help him enter politics, he'll reveal that you were my lover. The only decent thing he's ever done was to try and negotiate an annuity for Father in my marriage settlement. But Newbold was not as generous or as malleable as we hoped. I hoped to have a happy marriage—but it can never be an honest one." She fingered the heavy sapphire pendant. "Mr. Siberry claimed that he could sell the parure to both you and Newbold, with each paying half the price. I'm planning to sell all these jewels and give the money to my family." Tears coursed down her cheeks, and when he tried to brush them away, she averted her face.

"And I botched the scheme by opening the case. I'm glad of it. Lavinia, do you love the marquis? Does he love you?"

"I'm fond of him. But I suspect that his admiration of me far exceeds his affection." She looked up at Garrick. "You don't admire me, do you?"

"Not at the moment, not particularly." He continued, quietly yet firmly, "But I love you. Nothing you've ever done—or could do—will change that. Ah, you mustn't weep, *mia amata. Sono il tuo schiavo.* I am your slave." Fiercely, he pulled her into his embrace.

This was her homecoming, after a lengthy and arduous exile. She exulted when his body, solid and strong, strained against her. Need, raw and rough, made her quake.

His mouth hovered over hers. "Will I ever learn all of your secrets? I daresay you're holding back a few more, just to tantalize me. Or torture me."

"I can't remember." Her head whirled; her stays felt entirely too tight and confining. He must have sensed it, for his fingers tugged at the ribbons, freeing her. Reckless man, he meant to have her, here and now.

He flung off his coat, clawed his neckcloth.

"The maid!" she cried. "When she comes to dress me for the ball, she'll find you here."

"That would simplify things," he said, breathing heavily. "Caught in *flagrante delicto*—the libertine and the fraud." He crossed to the door and turned the key. "There—you're safe from prying eyes. But not from me."

He dragged her over to the bed. With a vengeful sweep of his arm, he knocked the magnificent butterfly ballgown onto the floor and said, "You'll not be needing this, not tonight."

Chapter 24

The peaceful aftermath of lovemaking was shattered by an insistent tapping on the door. Lavinia, thrown into panic, rolled out of Garrick's embrace.

"*C'est moi,*" Celeste called.

He held a finger to his lips, whispering, "Don't answer."

"You are there, Lady Lavinia?" The French-woman tried the handle. "*Mon Dieu!*" Her hurried footsteps faded along the corridor.

"Quickly, fetch my clothes," Garrick instructed.

Lavinia left the bed to collect his shirt and coat and breeches. "What are you going to do?" she asked.

"Hide," he said matter-of-factly. "Pretend you've fallen ill; tell her you feel faint."

"It's no pretense," she hissed.

Laughing, he brushed damp curls from her brow. "Be very careful what you say." Clutching his garments, he retreated beneath the bedskirt.

She tried to smooth out the rumpled covers before crawling under them. Soon she heard voices approaching—Celeste had brought Frances.

And a key.

They were letting themselves in when she realized that she still wore the blasted sapphires. No time to remove them all, but with trembling fingers she unhooked the brooch from her chemise and dropped it over the edge of the bed.

Frances was dressed for the evening, her lemon satin gown billowing over a court hoop and her hair perfectly coiffed and powdered. "My dear!" she exclaimed. "What's the matter?"

"I feel so weak. When I began to dress, a faintness came over me. I had to lie down." She made a feeble attempt to rise.

"No, don't get up," said Frances.

"But the queen—the ball!" A cool hand felt her cheek; another reached for her wrist.

"You cannot possibly go. Why, you're burning with fever, and your pulse is racing."

Little wonder, thought Lavinia, with a lover lurking under her bed. Nervously, she chewed her lip as Celeste bent over to rescue the ballgown from the floor—and the sapphire brooch.

"I know how disappointed you are, but there will be other royal balls," Frances assured her. She unclasped the bracelets and gently removed the earrings and necklace, replacing everything in the case.

"You'll go, won't you, and give my apologies to Lord Newbold? I want to know what Her Majesty wears, and all the princesses."

"I don't feel right about deserting you. Celeste, bring a cold compress and a cordial for her ladyship, *s'il vous plaît*." Fluffing the pillow, Frances asked, "Have you perchance seen my cousin? Oh, I'm sorry, did I jostle you?"

"No," Lavinia managed to say.

"I think he must have spent all last night at Lady Buckinghamshire's gaming salon."

Garrick, lying naked under the bed, listened to his cousin's fretful commentary. This scene, he thought wryly, was nearly worthy of a Moliére farce, except there was more desperation than hilarity about it. He tried not to move or breathe, or do anything that could reveal his presence. Dust clung to the bed frame and the floorboards, and he was terrified that he might start sneezing.

He could forgive Lavinia for all she'd done, after hearing her heart-wrenching confession. Now all his wrath was focused on that rogue of a lawyer. He'd make Daniel Webb pay for all his meddling and manipulations. But a blackmailer could be a dangerous adversary.

Months ago, he'd warned Lavinia about the hazards of playing society's games without first learning all the rules.

His mother had suffered from her extramarital liaison with Everdon. His brother, Edward, yearned for his Mrs. Fowler. Now Garrick was in love with a girl whose wedding was imminent.

Impossible, he thought, to discreetly withdraw from Lavinia's life until she had fulfilled her duty to her husband and produced the requisite male heir—the thought of her sleeping with the marquis revolted him. And if Garrick himself ever got her with child, their situation would be even more unendurable. By law, any offspring of his would be a Shandos; Newbold would be the acknowledged father. He was the unwanted product of adultery, and he hated to think that history might repeat itself, that another man might raise—and resent—his son or daughter. He was no Everdon, embittered and detached. His love for Lavinia was too strong; his connection to their children would be equally strong.

He understood now why she'd accepted Newbold, and could see that she might have difficulty breaking the engagement. But she had to. The strain of deception had worn her down; he could see that. Could she survive a lifetime of it? He knew he couldn't.

His cousin and her French maid were still ministering to the supposed invalid. He heard a familiar clink as a stopper was replaced in a crystal decanter.

"If you insist, I shall attend the ball," Frances said reluctantly. "Celeste, we must soon depart—I can't manage my headress and train without your help. Meet me below, with my velvet evening cloak."

"*Oui, madame.*"

After the servant withdrew, she said softly, "As a woman of the world, I am aware of one possible reason for your collapse. Engaged couples sometimes become carried away and impatient. You may tell me if it's necessary to advance the date of your wedding."

Lavinia quickly replied, "Oh, no—the only time we were alone was when Lord Newbold proposed. In your sitting room."

"Don't be offended," Frances soothed her. "I'm responsible for you, so I had to ask. I never really imagined that William was the sort to seduce his betrothed."

Garrick grimaced. *He* was exactly that sort.

"My coach will be waiting; I must leave you now. Try to sleep—I'll leave orders that you're not to be disturbed."

Garrick didn't leave his hiding place until Lavinia, standing at the window, reported that the carriage had rolled out of the square. No longer flushed, her face was as white as her shift.

"We're safely out of that tangle," he declared thankfully.

"How can you say so? I've never been so mortified!" As he towed her back to the bed, she asked, "What are you doing?"

"Making the most of an opportunity, *dolcezza*." His hand closed over her breast and stroked it in a seductive rhythm. Tugging up her garment, he exposed her legs, and spanned his fingers across her thigh. "I want you, Lavinia. Say you want me, too."

Her eyes were great pools of molten silver. "So much," she whispered. "More than is wise. Or safe."

He removed the shift, laying bare her snowy bosom, and flicked his tongue over each cresting nipple. "Never shall I get enough of you," he declared. When he found her soft and moistening flesh, her whole body quivered.

Lavinia revelled in his attentions. Growing ever more frantic with desire, she responded with eager caresses and hungry kisses. He was oh, so wicked to touch her there.

And there.

He hovered over her, pinning back her arms, spreading her legs apart, and she raised her hips to meet his most welcome intrusion. As his hardness eased into her, she caught her breath in joyful anticipation of the wondrous act of love.

She wrapped herself around him. Their mouths locked, and their ecstatic murmurs mingled. His tongue darted in and out between her lips, copying the steady thrusts of his flesh.

Then it came, all at once, their mutual, soul-shattering release.

"You are mine," he panted, "and I am yours."

"Son dy bragh as dy bragh. Forever and ever." The vow was forged from pure need.

"Let's run away. To Gretna. To Venice. To Monkwood."

"To Castle Cashin?"

Her wistful question startled her. Some powerful force seemed to be drawing her back to her island. She felt the need to be home again but wasn't sure why.

"Anywhere you wish to go." He separated himself from her. "But until I can put a stop to Webb, we mustn't do anything rash."

That made her smile. "What could be more rash that what we've been doing? I'll go to Daniel Webb tomorrow, and tell him—"

"No," he objected.

"He won't dare to harm me; he depends on my goodwill."

"As I see it, the boot is entirely on the other foot. You won't meet that blackguard."

"But I have the power to ruin him," she persisted. "The barrister, Mr. Shaw, accused him of terrible crimes."

They continued to argue while he dressed. But Garrick was implacable.

"Do I have your word that you'll keep away from Webb?'' he persisted.

Atreih, he would accept only one answer. So she gave it.

Chapter 25

He had chosen the most notorious flash house in Tothill Fields for the assignation. Its raucous taproom, social center of the criminal underworld, was crowded. At this season, the daylight was slow to fade, and those who conducted their business in the darkness had gathered here to wait.

Daniel Webb recognized each of the petty thieves, footpads, forgers, and scruffy prostitutes. A long-limbed highwayman in mask and cloak occupied a dim corner. His companion, a constable, probably received hush money from the tavern's proprietor, for a silent conspiracy existed between certain unscrupulous officials of the law and those who defied it.

The Rib of Adam provided its customers with cheap rum and geneva and brandy. A hidden passageway led to a gaming den. Located throughout the building were secret compartments for the concealment of stolen goods. Persons requiring a swift exit could use the upper floor casement that opened onto the roof. Robberies occurred here with regularity, and more than one murder had contributed to the Rib's foul reputation. It also functioned as a brothel; a bed could be hired for a few hours or an entire night.

A coarse, amply rouged female wiped the bar with a rag that looked none too clean. "Wot toddy d'yer fancy tonight?" she asked.

"No drink for me," he said tersely. "I'm meeting a lady."

"Hmph," she grunted back at him. "Takin' 'er up to yer reg'lar room fer some rumpy-pumpy?"

"What I do with her is no business of yours."

The woman's mouth hung slack, and her red-veined eyes bulged. "Cor! A leddy indeed, too foine fer the loikes o' *you*."

He turned. Even with her remarkable beauty curtained by a length of figured lace, Lady Lavinia was unmistakably a creature who had strayed here from a more refined world. Every rogue and moll in the room would know to the halfpenny the worth of her flowered muslin dress, her kid gloves, and her silver shoe buckles.

A whoremaster and a bawd were already making ribald comments, and both the constable and the highwayman stared at her.

Webb led her to the stair, saying, "I've taken a chamber where we may talk without being overheard."

They went to a room as familiar to him as the ones in his own house. He had spent countless hours sitting in the Windsor chair, holding court with criminals. He knew every lump in the mattress, and how it wobbled beneath the weight of two bodies.

His guest pulled back her veil. "I couldn't slip out of the house until Mrs. Radstock left for the opera," she said. "I'm sure you must wonder why I requested this meeting."

He liked her best when she was nervous; it was proof of his power over her. "Do not look so distressed. If a problem has arisen, we shall overcome it."

"I've changed my mind about marrying the Marquis of Newbold. I can't do it," she declared.

"But you will," he insisted. "I'm sorry if becoming Lady Newbold is distasteful. You can comfort yourself with your seven hundred quid a year in pin money, and all the clothes and jewels and carriages and houses you'll be getting." When she bowed her head, he asked, "Still pining for that gamester? He abandoned you quick enough when he learned that your father was a gaolbird; evidently your talent for bed-sport wasn't lively enough to hold his interest. Perhaps I ought to inform him that you've lain with half the men in the King's Bench, from Stoney Bowes to the turnkey."

"Garrick won't believe you."

"You stupid girl," he raged, "I won't let you spoil everything. Do you hear?"

"The whole tavern has probably heard," she said with maddening calm. "Mr. Webb, you'll never get very far in politics if you don't govern your tone and manner of speech. It's rude to shout, particularly at a lady."

She was making sport of him, the bitch. "Disdain me at your peril. I'll ruin you."

"After I'm free of my engagement, what harm can you do? I will lose Lord Newbold's favor and Mrs.

Radstock's friendship. They won't have much regard for you, either, when I explain that you were responsible for Father's arrest, and hired footpads to steal from me."

"What about your liaison with Lord Garrick? Surely you don't want your whoring to become public knowledge."

"Be careful how you threaten, Mr. Webb. You blackmailed me, and I can prove it."

Her serene smile was beyond bearing. He stalked over to her, feet pounding the floorboards. "What proof have you got?"

"Your letters."

"You *kept* them?"

"Well, I did burn the first one, but the rest I saved. I hope you won't ask me to return them, because I've already handed them over to Mr. Shaw. The barrister."

Her triumphant expression didn't waver until he raised his hand. When he smashed it against her left cheek, she let out a most satisfying shriek. The power of his blow knocked her head against the panelled wall.

Instantly, the door of the tall cupboard swung open. The masked highwayman stepped out.

"What the devil do you want?"

"Justice. And may your black soul rot in hell!"

Webb stared into the barrel of a pistol. After a sudden, quick flash and an ear-shattering report, a bullet struck his right arm. He screamed as it tore through his flesh, and he dropped to the floor.

"Now, my lord," said an aggrieved voice, "there wasn't s'posed to be no shootin'." The constable came crawling out of the compartment.

"You'll have to write it up in your occurrence book as an accident." Ripping away his mask, Lord Garrick Armitage hurried over to Lady Lavinia. As he pried her hand away from her cheek, he said gently, "Let me see."

Blood oozed down Webb's arm. "Murder!" he groaned. "He tried to murder me."

"Not as I saw it," the officer retorted. "He didn't aim at your head or chest, did he? 'Twas your arm he went for—the one what struck the lady. I mean to say, that's where the pistol was pointin' when it went off accidental-like. Daniel Webb, I must inform you that you're under arrest on a charge of blackmail."

"And assault," Lord Garrick added. *"Serpente!"*

"If this female claims that I blackmailed her," said Webb, flinching as the constable staunched his wound with a handkerchief, "I shall lay a counter-charge of slander."

" 'Tain't slanderous if 'tis proved. We'll see what the magistrate has to say. Get up, Mr. Webb; I'm taking you to the Queen's Square Police Office."

This could not be happening to him. Fired upon—wounded—arrested—what could be worse? Glaring at Lady Lavinia, now supported by her lover, he realized he'd been trapped. She had requested this meeting, and she'd brought her accomplices. Very clever—but the game wasn't ended yet. He had studied the law, and he'd practiced it for many years—and, when it suited his purposes, he had broken it. But always he had managed to evade it.

"Bring the prisoner to the bar," commanded the magistrate.

The constable nudged Daniel Webb. A surgeon had anointed and re-bandaged his wound, and the painful effect of these ministrations showed in his pale, set face. Had he been anyone else, Lavinia might have pitied him.

The chamber was both crowded and poorly ventilated. After the constable had given a pithy account of the events at the Rib of Adam, she'd also given a statement. The heat was stifling, and her battered cheek throbbed. But she had told her story, and the magistrate in his chair and the spectators on the benches had listened attentively.

Now she sat with Garrick and Mr. Shaw, anxiously awaiting Webb's examination.

"Sir, you have listened to these witnesses and heard their accusations against you," the magistrate proceeded. "As an attorney, you are aware that a prisoner suspected of a felonious act cannot retain counsel. I shall leave it to the Crown to make further inquiry into your dealings with known rogues and thieves, as described by Mr. Shaw in some documents he has delivered to me."

Webb turned his head and scanned the courtroom. The barrister returned his baleful stare.

"Writing and sending threatening letters has long been an offense under common law," the magistrate continued. "I've taken down Lady Lavinia Cashin's deposition and examined the evidence she brought forth. This letter, received by her on Christmas Day, is dated but unsigned. 'Dear Lady, Do you think I have forgotten you during your absence from town? If you fail to deliver your rubies unto my hand at an agreed time and place, I shall publicize your parent's arrest and confinement in a debtors' prison.' Did you write these words?"

"I've not seen them, therefore I cannot say."

The magistrate handed the letter to his clerk, who held it up to the attorney.

"The handwriting corresponds to an example of your penmanship submitted by Mr. Shaw. The next item was dictated to a clerk, I gather, but it does bear your signature." Moving his finger across the paper, the magistrate quoted, " 'I require money and employment both, and if you do not provide them, all your secrets shall be exposed. Your reputation as a virtuous female—false though it is—cannot survive. Never forget, I was present when you stopped at the inn with your lover, and I saw you enter his bedchamber. You will pay for my continued discretion, else you will suffer. Daniel Webb, Esquire.' Show him." He thrust the paper at his assistant.

Lavinia had kept her head bowed throughout the reading of Webb's defamatory words.

Everything she'd sought to conceal these many months was revealed: her father's imprisonment for debt, her reliance upon Mr. Webb's silence, his various demands.

"The signature is yours, correct?"

"Appearances can be deceiving. It might have been forged."

"While we're on the subject of false appearances, I am curious about your observation at the inn. Can you say with certainty that the room her ladyship entered with that gentleman was in fact a bedchamber?"

"I assumed so."

"And based on that assumption, you made threats. What sort of room it was, and what might or might not have occurred inside it, are not the subjects of the present inquiry. From her ladyship's account of your dealings, I conclude that you have twice deliberately plotted and carried out blackmail. In the first instance, you violated the Waltham Black Act, for any person who sends an unsigned letter demanding money or other valuable items is guilty of felony without benefit of clergy. Additionally, you made an anonymous threat to accuse other persons of crime—debt, lechery—with a view to extorting money. For that alone, the penalty is seven years' transportation."

Said Daniel Webb, "It is beyond the scope of this court to convict and impose sentence."

The magistrate retorted, "You may not speak, sir, unless to answer my direct question. In your latest letter, you propose to guard her ladyship's secrets in exchange for employment in a nobleman's house—and an unspecified monetary reward. I find it thoroughly reprehensible," he proceeded, "that an attorney would so betray his client's trust as you have done. Moreover, the constable and Lord Garrick Armitage report that you struck this lady. How do you plead to the charge of assault?"

Webb's black head rose. "I did not intend—it was not a premeditated act."

"Not exactly a denial," the magistrate muttered, recording this reply. "Daniel Webb, you are hereby remanded for criminal prosecution and will be confined at Tothill Fields Bridewell until such time as you are removed to the Criminal Court of the Old Bailey to stand your trial." Studying the large clock mounted on the wall, he puffed out his cheeks in a relieved sigh. "Nearly eight. No time to review another case. The court is dismissed till tomorrow morning, ten sharp."

Lavinia climbed to her feet. Her life would change the moment she exited this cramped and airless chamber. Although she couldn't be sure what awaited her on the other side of those doors, she was thankful that the lies and evasions were behind her.

Soon she and Garrick would be equals—penniless outcasts, the adventuress and the rogue. Would their shared disgrace strengthen their bond, she wondered, or destroy it?

Chapter 26

~~~OO~~~

Mr. Shaw, triumphant over the exposure of Daniel Webb's crimes, arrived in St. James's Square early the next morning. A disapproving Selwyn delivered him to Garrick's dressing room.

"I always knew his foul deeds would catch up with him," the barrister declared. "And last night turned out exactly as I hoped. Lady Lavinia is bolder and more brave than I expected, and was most affecting when she gave her testimony. If he'd had the power, that magistrate would have consigned Webb to a dungeon for so cruelly abusing such a lovely creature."

Heedless of the razor in his valet's hands, Garrick whipped his head around to say, "Nevertheless, she will not appear at the Old Bailey."

"I didn't think you'd allow it. Her absence from the Criminal Court isn't likely to affect the outcome. Blackmail cases usually result in acquittal, regardless of whether the victim testifies or not."

"Milord, is time to arrange *cravatta*."

Garrick waved Carlo aside. "Do you mean Webb will go free?"

316

Shaw's eyes glittered. "I shall do my utmost to prevent it. The prosecutor will submit those letters, as well as her ladyship's deposition. You and the constable will describe how he struck her. Even if Webb escapes the blackmail and assault charges, he'll be ruined—that snivelling clerk can tell many a tale of sordid dealings in stolen property."

"Hanging's too good for him, *sporco parassita!* When does his trial take place?"

"Tomorrow morning."

"So soon? *Questo è troppo stretto,*" he complained to Carlo, who had wound the neckcloth too tightly. When it was looser, he continued, "Is there any way to keep Lady Lavinia's name out of the papers?"

"I doubt it," said Shaw frankly. "But she's the wronged party, and public sympathy will be on her side. The journalists are going to aim their barbs at Webb. His rise and fall will provide them with a morality tale—a clever attorney brought down by his own overreaching ambition. Son of an actress, friend to thieves—"

"Webb's mother was an actress?" Garrick interrupted.

The barrister bobbed his head. "At Drury Lane. And his father was an actor."

"*Mio Dio,* not *that* Mrs. Webb!" The attorney's mother—had she been the Duke of Halford's mistress? If not for her, the duchess would not have taken Lord Everdon as a lover—and Garrick would never have been born.

"*Scusi,* milord—*il panciotto.*"

Carlo's insistent voice pulled Garrick out of his incredulous reverie. "*Bene.*" He stood up and extended his arms so the waistcoat could go on.

The barrister also rose. "I'm spending the morning at Webb's chambers, schooling young Will in his testimony. I'll also churn through the rest of the documents; I might find some more damning evidence to hand over to the case prosecutor."

"At what hour tomorrow should I present myself at the Old Bailey?"

"I'll send word as soon as I know myself."

When Carlo finished dressing him, Garrick gave instructions about packing for a journey.

"We leave soon for Epsom and the racing?" asked the valet.

Epsom! All the recent crises had made him forget. *"Non me importa niente,"* he replied. "I'm going to Monkwood."

At the moment, his chief concern was removing Lavinia from town. They would seek refuge with his uncle. In Suffolk, far away from the social chatterers and nosy journalists, they would marry.

He needed to get a special license. And tell Frances of his plans. With a grin at his reflected image, he decided he would also visit Lord Everdon. He wanted to see the face of that crusty old devil when his illegitimate brat asked for a paternal blessing. Would news of a marriage win him the acknowledgment he'd been seeking?

A dark bruise, tender to the touch, had formed on Lavinia's left cheek, and the flesh surrounding it was swollen.

"Does it pain you?" asked the marquis.

She admitted that it did. "And my face feels stiff."

"Struck by your solicitor—it doesn't seem possible! Did it happen in this house?"

Lavinia shook her head. "At a low tavern in Tothill Fields. But I didn't go alone. When Lord Garrick found out I was being blackmailed, he advised me to consult a barrister—and a constable. Mr. Webb was arrested and put in prison. There's going to be a trial."

"I wish you had told me sooner, Lavinia. I am your future husband."

"I couldn't disturb you with my troubles when you were so busy with your Parliamentary committee."

"You'll have to remain in seclusion until your face improves," he told her. "Frances and I will tell everyone that you still suffer from the same indisposition that kept you away from Her Majesty's ball. If necessary, we can postpone the wedding."

Her altered appearance evidently troubled him more than the blow she'd received. But his shallowness made her task easier, for it confirmed the nature of his feelings for her.

Lacing her fingers together, she began her prepared speech. "My lord, I've made many mistakes, more than I care to admit. Some are about to be revealed in open court—Father's misfortunes, his imprisonment for debt. My deposition will be read, as will some letters in which Mr. Webb accuses me of—of indecency."

"I can appreciate your concern, my dear. But no one will believe that charge to be true," he asserted.

But it is, she cried silently. "It might as well be."

"My reputation will be your shield. You've not lived in town so very long; you don't know how temporary these little scandals can be."

"Lord Garrick is still ostracized for something he did three years ago," she reminded him.

"I shall not jilt you, Lavinia. My sense of duty and honor prohibits it."

"Don't you mind that my father spent nearly four months in the King's Bench?"

"I regret only that you both were imposed upon by his attorney. Once you become a Shandos, you will rise above any stigma associated with the Cashin name."

Sadly she studied his lean, unhandsome face. She cared for him, despite his inability to rouse her passions. And therefore she pitied him.

"We have a saying on my island," she told him softly. *"Yn ven aeg ta mee goll dy phoosey, shegin dou fakin staak yn jaagh dy hie yn ayrey voish yn thorran ainyn.* Never marry a woman unless you can see the smoke of her father's chimney from your own barnyard. Our barnyards are too far apart. When we met, you liked me because I seemed unusual. But during our betrothal, you've regarded it as a defect."

"You are young yet, my dear, and with time, my tastes and interests will influence and improve yours."

"I'm nineteen years old, with tastes as fully formed as my character. If your intent is to alter me, you must not marry me."

"Indeed I must," he insisted stubbornly.

Desperate to extricate herself, she said, "It would be wrong, and shameful, for me to wed you. I am so very sorry, but my affections have been won by another man—one who can accept me as I am, with all my faults and—and my bruises."

He drew a ragged breath. "Who is he?" When she failed to answer, he commanded, "Tell me, Lavinia. I want to know the name of this despicable specimen who dares to court an affianced woman. But of course," he said as comprehension dawned. "A man without honor. A jilt—who has taught you his scurvy trick. Good God, that I could be so deceived! I valued you as a creature entirely innocent of intrigue. So many times I've told Frances . . ." He paused. "Does she know? Am I the last to learn that you've played me false with her libertine of a cousin?"

"I didn't!" she protested. "It pains me to disappoint you, and I do not wish to deceive you. Another man claimed my heart—and asked for my hand—before you did. I told you as much, or tried to, the day you proposed to me. I sincerely wished to please you, to be the wife you wanted and deserved. But I can't."

"No, you've made that abundantly clear. You will not think me petty, I hope, when I insist that you return the sapphire parure."

"A servant will bring it down to you." He was too outraged and affronted to listen to any more of her well-rehearsed apology, so she offered her hand in farewell. He refused to take it.

From her bedroom window, she watched him leave with the leather case. Without a backward glance, he climbed into his carriage and drove out of her life.

How would she ever make up the financial loss to Garrick, who could least afford it? He'd paid hundreds of pounds for the sapphires now in New-bold's possession.

Pausing at her dressing table, she dipped the hare's foot into a powder pot and gently dragged it across her discolored cheek. She'd wanted to show her worst face to Newbold, but she hated for Garrick see her injury.

"Lavinia?" Frances peered into the room. "Has Newbold gone? A letter has just arrived for you, express."

When Lavinia saw her mother's neat handwriting, her heart pounded ominously. *Hiarn, jean my ghin orrin,* Lord have mercy . . . Her fingers felt frozen and stiff; she could not use them.

"Open it for me, please. Read it."

Frances unfolded the single sheet. "My dear Lon—Loon—"

"Lhondhoo," she whispered.

" 'Your sister, Kitty, has—' oh, my dear, this is sad news indeed. Perhaps you'd rather read it yourself."

With a violent shake of her head, Lavinia cried, "No! I can't bear to look. *Och,* my poor parents. And Kerron—Kitty was his twin; they were so close and so—"

"But she was alive when this was written. Listen! 'Your sister is desperately ill. By the time you receive this, she may already be delivered into the care of God. Remember us in your prayers, and be assured that she speaks about you with the true and tender love that she has ever shown. She asks that you not delay your wedding, but hopes that on that day you will hold her in your thoughts.' Oh, Lavinia, you poor child."

"I don't feel it yet. I can't feel the loss of her."
Lavinia dashed away her tears. *"Cha jeanym credjal
shen . . .* I will not believe. What day did Mother
write?"

Glancing down at the letter, Frances replied,
"Sunday."

"If there's a chance of seeing her before she—"
She couldn't speak the dreadful word. "I've wanted
so much to be home again; now I know why. *Shegin
dou,* I must travel to the island, fast as I can."

"Newbold will let you have his travelling carriage and horses."

"No, he won't," Lavinia stated baldly. "He's very
displeased with me, for I've—"

"Your first quarrel?" Frances patted her arm. "If
he seems angry about your appearance before the
magistrate, he won't be for very long. I'm sure he'll
fly to your side the instant I inform him of your
sister's illness."

"And I'm just as certain that he won't. I broke the
engagement, and he took back the sapphires."

"Lavinia!"

Knowing what else she had to do, she faced her
startled friend. "I'm not able to marry him—because I love Garrick. There, it's said. I'm sorry I
didn't tell you sooner, but I—oh, it doesn't matter
now," she said in a rush. "I've got to get away, and
quickly. Do you know the schedule for the northern
mail coaches?"

"I've always travelled post, never on the mails.
But I believe there's a coach every evening. Shall I
send a servant to Lombard Street to book a place
for you?"

"Yes, thank you," said Lavinia in relief. "I'll want

the one bound for Liverpool, or possibly Kendal.
From there I can get to Whitehaven and make the
regular Monday evening crossing to Man."

"You told William about your—about Garry?"

"Yes," she replied absently, moving to her ward-
robe.

"All your lovely bride clothes," Frances
mourned. "And the Hoppner portrait."

Lavinia began removing gowns and undergarments.

"Celeste can pack for you."

"No, I need to keep busy, otherwise I shall think,
and remember."

She took the framed watercolor down from its
place on the wall and focussed on Kitty's image.
Jean oo fuirraght rhym? Please wait for me, she
pleaded, there is so much I long to say. For I did
find love with a handsome man, just as you hoped
I would. And I want you to know.

Garrick had come to Lord Everdon's townhouse
direct from Doctors' Commons, where he had purchased the special license. On the way, he'd composed the announcement of his nuptials. Lord
Garrick Armitage of Monkwood Hall and Moulton
Heath—most impressive—married Lady Lavinia
Cashin, daughter of Lord Ballacraine, in a private
ceremony.

He tapped on the door with his walking stick.

"I wish to see Lord Everdon," he announced to
the servant.

"Monsieur has a card?"

"Never carry 'em. Tell his lordship that Mr.—Mr.

Siberry is here," Garrick improvised. If he had to lie his way into this house, so be it.

The footman had just ushered him inside when high-pitched squealing erupted from abovestairs. A pair of young girls dashed down to the hall, one pursuing the other.

"Give back my ribbon, Marie!" The younger, in her early teens, had dark hair and a sweet face, her French mother in miniature.

"You know it's mine, and you never asked to borrow it." The older girl halted. "Behave yourself, Henriette; we've got a visitor." Tall and willowy and blonde, she resembled—Garrick.

These lively, romping lasses were his half-sisters, and he loved them on sight.

"Do you wish to see our papa?" Henriette asked. "He's tending his garden."

"We'll take you to him," offered Marie. In fluent French, she dismissed the footman.

"We haven't many callers," Henriette confided, leading the way to the back of the house. "I wanted to leave *l'académie*, but now that I'm back at home it's dull as anything." She fidgetted with the blue grosgrain ribbon.

"Have you run away from your school?" he asked, grinning. "So did I!"

"*Vraiment?*" Henriette's eyes grew very wide, increasing her resemblance to her mother.

"He's jesting," Marie told her. "Aren't you, *monsieur?*"

"No, it's true. I escaped from Eton in the dead of night, and never went back."

"My parents brought me home," Henriette admitted, as if ashamed of so mundane a removal.

"There was an increase in the school fee, and I'd already learned as much as they could teach me. Marie is clever. I'm the pretty one."

"You shouldn't say such things," Marie reproved. "Especially not to strangers."

Wishing he could refute that description of himself, Garrick followed the girls outside.

Lord Everdon was attaching a vine to an obelisk-shaped *tuteur*. His garden was compact, enclosed by a high brick wall, and very French in design. Pollarded oaks formed a single *allée* leading to a small summer house; a pair of classical statues stood on plinths.

Young Henriette rushed over to her father. "Papa, *un monsieur* is here to see you."

The baron looked around. "Marie, take you sister away. *Immédiatement, s'il te plaît.*"

His elder daughter, surprised by his harshness, obediently took Henriette's hand. "Come, I'll tie up your hair. You may keep my ribbon."

When they disappeared into the house, the baron resumed his task. "I thought you were at Epsom."

"How flattering that you know my habits so well."

"I have nothing to say to you."

"I'm not here for conversation. It's customary, I believe, to inform one's parents of an impending marriage. Oh, don't worry, I'm not asking you to be there. My bride-to-be is Lady Lavinia Cashin."

"Never heard of her."

"You will," Garrick predicted. "At the moment, she's engaged to the Marquis of Newbold. But not for long."

"If you assume I have any interest in this trivia,

you're much mistaken," Everdon said brusquely.

"You've already demonstrated your complete indifference. I've got an uncle who never had a child in his life, and he's a better father to me than you could ever be." Had that dart hit its mark? "I'm used to being ignored, pushed out of the way, forgotten. Like you, the Duke of Halford pretended I didn't exist. He cut me out of his will—you probably didn't know that; few people do. From the day he died, I've lived by my wits."

"You must be quite a witty fellow," said the baron. "Costly horses, modish clothes, vast wagers."

"I manage. There's one question I wish to ask you, and then I shall leave. Did you love my mother?"

Everdon responded with a harsh laugh. "What, do you fancy yourself the product of a *grande passion*? Ours was a sordid little intrigue. She wanted revenge on her duke, and I wanted a bedmate."

Garrick said quietly, "You underestimate her feelings for you."

"Raised her son to be a romantic, did she?" Everdon tucked an errant tendril into place, and sunlight struck his heavy gold signet ring.

"She seldom mentioned your name, until she learned that she was dying. We used to sit together on the balcony of our *palazzo*, looking out over the canal. And she would talk and talk. Mostly about you." He saw the baron wince. "I never understood why she cared so much. You've got no conscience. No heart, either. Rumor says you married your wife for her fortune."

Everdon swung around and looked him full in

the face. "Do you think I could alter my life, mend
the ruinous habits of a lifetime, for a woman I wed
out of convenience?" He followed this revelation
with another. "Susanne and our daughters are gifts
more precious than I deserve."

"And I am your curse," Garrick realized. "An accident. An unwanted reminder of all those drunken
nights and gaming losses. And one sordid little intrigue with an unhappy duchess." He shook his
head. "If I'd sired a son, I would want Lavinia to
know him, and for him to be a brother to our own
children." With a cruel smile, he added, "I recognized Marie as a sister the instant I saw her. Your
little Henriette has my recklessness—you'll want to
keep an eye on her."

"You aren't fit to speak their names!" Everdon
blustered. "Go away—leave us in peace."

"I'm done," Garrick declared. "I've told Lavinia
you're my father, and now you know she'll be my
wife. We'll probably spend the rest of the year in
Venice, though I expect to settle in Suffolk eventually. You don't care a damn what we do, and I tell
you only because I don't want you to be afraid of
meeting me at White's again—or anywhere else.
Good day, my lord."

Should he offer his hand? Best leave well enough
alone, he decided. For once, he'd behaved sensibly,
and with dignity.

The baron rejected him as a son. It was time to
accept it as a fact, and then try to forget. After all,
he had Lavinia's love now, and it wouldn't be long
before he'd have Lavinia herself.

He envied the strength and tenacity of her connection to her family. The Cashins might not rejoice

at the news that he, not Newbold, was her chosen husband, but he hoped they would accept him. And he would make sure they benefitted from the marriage. A portion of any money his horses won at Epsom would find its way to the Isle of Man. After handing over five hundred pounds to Siberry, he hadn't much left, but he'd make a recovery at the gaming tables or the faro bank.

Then a plan came to him, in a flash. He stopped walking.

A pedestrian following behind collided with him. "Sir, are you drunk?" the man asked crossly.

"Not at the moment. But where to go?" he wondered out loud. "Don't want a hell; the cards can't be trusted—likely to be fuzzed."

"Your brain is fuzzed," the fellow retorted. "Talking to yourself like that, you're surely bound for Bedlam."

"Possibly," Garrick replied, not offended in the least. "But madman or not, I can't go to Bedlam yet. I have to visit Lady Buckinghamshire."

Chapter 27

"**Y**our deal, my lord."

When Garrick signalled for a fresh deck, Lady Buckinghamshire, her bulk encased in puce satin, brought it to him herself. "Do you wish for any liquid refreshment?" she inquired. "A glass of chilled champagne, or that Italian wine you like so well?"

"Armitage is drinking Adam's ale tonight," quipped his opponent. "Tell me, does the water bring you luck?"

"You might say that." Garrick avoided spirits because he needed to keep his mind sharp and focused.

His strategy was simple. He would agree to play only those gentlemen who could afford to lose and were willing to redeem their IOUs immediately. They didn't always make the most challenging adversaries, but tonight he couldn't begrudge any victory that came easily.

As his winnings mounted, curious onlookers gathered around the baize-topped table and even placed bets on the outcome of each *partie*. Garrick himself netted a quick thousand wagering on whether he could win his next three deals.

He believed more in the doctrine of chance rather than plain, fallible luck. A knowledge of probabilities helped him cover any of his own weaknesses and exploit those of the men he played. This was no sport or pastime; it was serious business. Every one of the thirty-two cards in play could either contribute to his earnings or deplete them.

Sir Reggie dealt until they both had a dozen cards in hand. He placed the remaining eight facedown on the table, the stock from which they'd replace their discards.

As he counted and sorted, Garrick called, "Discard for carte blanche."

After a careful assessment, Sir Reggie made the three discards to which he was entitled.

Garrick showed his cards and made his discards, taking in two of a desirable suit. "Five cards."

"Equal," Sir Reggie acknowledged.

"Making forty-eight."

"Good."

He began calling his sequences, highest to lowest, and found them good. "Quart to a knave."

"Good."

"Tierce minor."

"Equal."

They played out the hand for points, Garrick throwing out his weakest suits first and guarding his spades. As elder hand, the odds had favored him, and the tricks he lost were trifling. He squeaked out a win, his narrowest yet.

"What, Reg, haven't you given Garry his come-uppance?" asked Prawn Parfitt.

"Nay," Sir Reggie answered, pushing fifty-guinea *rouleaux* across the baize table. "P'raps you should have a go."

"Garry mightn't like that. I know his ploys too well."

"You think so?" Garrick's reply was calculated to entice his rich friend into a game. "Up to now, I've insisted on fifty-guinea stakes. But for you, I'm willing to make it a hundred."

"Too rich for my blood," commented one bystander.

"How long have you been at this?" Prawn asked, taking the chair vacated by the defeated baronet.

"Dunno," Garrick mumbled, rearranging his *rouleaux*. "I got here in the afternoon, and Lady Buck didn't want to let me in so early. So I challenged her to a game." He grinned at his friend, "Took a hundred quid off her while the servants readied the salon for the evening. We drank tea, played some more. She even let me put the candles in all the holders and sconces—I lighted 'em, too."

"Fresh cards here," Prawn called to the waiter. "And a glass of claret. Snuff, Garry?" he asked, placing a silver-ornamented box on the table.

"Thank you, no."

Prawn's style of play and his aptitude put Garrick on his mettle. He went down in the first *partie*, losing with good grace. His crony, emboldened by success where many before him had failed, increased the stakes.

The hours passed. Shuffle, cut, shuffle, deal. Points and sequences were called, tricks taken, vowels exchanged. Garrick started to win consistently and saw the hot glare of desperation in Prawn's bulging eyes.

Many a night he'd toiled at the tables, but never had he cared so passionately about the outcome. This time he was wagering for his Lavinia, and for their future together.

Stacks of guineas and IOUs covered his side of the table; there was scarcely any green baize to play upon. He couldn't estimate the extent of his wealth, it was increasing so rapidly. Maintaining an expression as rigid and blank as a stone, he played with greater caution, conserving his best cards till they could do him the most good. Bewildered by steady losses, Prawn grew extremely careless.

Eventually Garrick noticed that they had drawn an audience, quite a large one. Lady Buckinghamshire occupied a chair, fanning her fat face and bosom; her husband stood beside her. The couple's neighbors denounced them for operating a gaming establishment in aristocratic St. James's Square. Rumor reported that her ladyship slept with a blunderbuss and a pair of pistols, the better to guard her bank.

For once, her ever-popular faro table was deserted. A visibly bored dealer turned cards for a pair of punters, but his eye and the croupier's often wandered in the direction of the piquet contest.

Between one *partie* and the next, Garrick and his friend permitted a footman to replace the guttered candles.

"How long's Armitage been at it?"

"Near ten hours, I should think."

"A thousand pounds says he makes it twelve,"

called out a young duke with a vast fortune.

"Done!" cried a chorus of gentlemen, and Lady Buckinghamshire waddled away to fetch her betting book so the wagers could be recorded.

"If I help you win your thousand," Garrick said, "you may have the honor of taking Prawn's place."

"I'll take it now, if he lets me."

"By all means," Prawn said wearily.

After Garrick had relieved the eager duke of two thousand pounds, he was beseiged by other challengers. The gamesters drew lots for the privilege of sitting down with him.

As the light of a new day peeped through the curtains, Garrick realized he was hungry. He vaguely remembered eating some ham and a few fruit tarts to keep up his strength, and he'd regularly relieved himself of the water he'd consumed. When he'd won a paltry hundred pounds more from a very tipsy Colonel George Hanger, he requested a meal. Lady Buck, whose salon had not been so full all season, offered to serve him whatever he desired.

"Hot coffee, cold roast beef. Some bread and butter."

While he ate, his watchful companions chatted about him in hushed voices. Used cards lay at his feet in heaps, and the floor was littered with scorecards.

"Has he counted his winnings?" someone asked.

Garrick had not, but he guessed the total to be many thousands. His neck was stiff and his body ached from sitting so long in one position, but he believed he could continue for several hours more.

Rubbing the prickles that had sprouted during

the long night, he said absently, *"Mi faccia la barba, per piacere.* Shave. I want a shave." He looked over at his rotund, sleepy-eyed hostess. "I mean to play on, my lady, but first I need a wash and a change of linen. Send someone to my cousin's house to fetch my valet—he's to bring soap and my razor, and a clean shirt."

While waiting for Carlo, he marched up and down the length of the salon to exercise his legs. By the time the Italian arrived, a maidservant had produced a basin of warm water and plenty of towels.

The other gamesters studied Garrick's every move and utterance, as if searching for the secret of his long run of luck and his remarkable endurance.

Prawn was saying, "Lived on the Continent, had a reputation there for wondrous skill. Came back to England to amaze us all." He lifted his glass. "To Garry!"

"Aye, to Garry!"

"Well done, Armitage!"

The size of the crowd waxed and waned. Departing gamesters must have been talking about his feat, for everyone who arrived knew about it already.

"Milord," said Carlo when his work was done, "is something I need to tell. *È molto male.*"

Very bad news. "I won't hear it," Garrick said, shaking his head, "I have to concentrate on my game. Inform my cousin that I mustn't be disturbed, for any reason at all." When the valet made an inarticulate protest, he said savagely, *"Non me ne importa un fico secco.* I don't give a damn. This is too important, *è necessario.*"

He resumed his playing, and acquaintances and

strangers continued arriving at the Buckinghamshire residence to gawk at him. Distracted by whis-
pers and her ladyship's awkward curtsy, he looked
up, frowning.

The Prince of Wales swept into the room, flanked
by Colonel Hanger and Mr. Fox.

"No, no, don't rise, Armitage, play on," the heir
to the throne commanded. "Won't stand on ceremony in this circumstance; it might affect your
wondrous run of luck. Why, the whole town's talking of it!"

"Oh, sir," Lady Buck gushed, "it's the greatest
thing to happen this or any season. We've none of
us been to bed. The guests who were drunk had
time to grow sober, and have now got drunk all
over again!"

Garrick invited the prince to play, knowing that
if he prevailed he wasn't likely to receive his winnings any time soon. His Royal Highness owed
hundreds of thousands of pounds; he was deeply
in debt to architects, artists, upholsterers, tailors,
and shopkeepers.

"I really must participate in this most historic
event," the jovial young royal decided. "I daresay
I'll give him a better game than you did, Georgie!"
he jested to the colonel.

Incredible, Garrick thought, this abrupt transfor-
mation from London's pariah to London's sensation. The prince, he decided, would be his final
opponent. Ascertaining the probabilities and tally-
ing his scores had become wearisome, and as his
fatigue increased, his enthusiasm waned.

And, he remembered, some crisis had occurred at
his cousin's house.

The Prince of Wales did not intend to lose; it was obvious that he'd come to Lady Buck's thinking he could unseat the champion. The fleshy face wore a ludicrously dismayed expression when Garrick seized several tricks in rapid succession.

The Prince slapped an eight of hearts onto the green cloth. Glancing up, he commented, "Thought you'd forsworn the gaming houses, Everdon. Come to try your skill against this chap? Damme, but he's a wizard."

After taking the trick, Garrick glared at his parent and said with cold deliberation, "They say the devil's children have the devil's luck."

With the same calm efficiency he'd used to dispatch aristocrats and commoners, he defeated royalty. But he couldn't stop now, no matter how ready he was. Not with the baron looking on.

The prince handed over his vowels and moved away to speak to Lord Buckinghamshire.

"What brings you to this den of iniquity?" Garrick asked the baron.

Said Everdon, taking possession of the empty chair, "Bravado."

"You mean to challenge me? You've sworn never to play cards again."

"And you want me to break my vow."

Did he? Yes, of course—his great ambition had always been to see that haggard, bony face from exactly this vantage. Across the table.

With a sweep of his hand, he cleared away the cards. "Fresh pack!"

"I'll play one hand only," his father stated firmly. "I'm staking no money. Only this." He slid the gold signet from his finger and placed it on the cloth.

Garrick countered with two *rouleaux* of guineas, even though the ring was worth far less. Siberry wouldn't give more than twenty pounds for the thing, he thought derisively.

Most of the gamesters hovered around the prince now. None of those who remained at the table to watch rated Everdon's chances very high.

"Do you recall your last game?" Garrick asked when they cut the deck.

"With perfect clarity. Ah, your deal. Fortunate for me; I'm sadly out of practice."

A bluff? For all Garrick knew, Everdon and his lady played piquet every night of the week, in the seclusion of their home.

Neither he nor the baron could claim carte blanche. As dealer he was allowed only three discards; from the stock, he took in an eight of diamonds that he needed to complete a sequence. His pulse skittered while he waited for Everdon to declare.

"Four cards."

"What do they make?"

"Making thirty-four."

So he was holding a ten, nine, eight, seven combination. "Not good," Garrick answered with ill-concealed jubilation.

The baron's best sequence turned out to be a tierce major—ace, king, queen—worth a mere three points. Garrick's was *huitième*, for which he received eighteen points. His hand was impossibly, ludicrously strong—the game he'd hoped to win on skill had been decided by sheer luck of the draw.

They proceeded to play their cards. Garrick took eight tricks, Everdon four.

He'd won, quite handily. He had trounced his father.

Everdon presented his gold ring. "This is yours."

"I'll give you a chance to win it back."

"No, you must keep it," the baron insisted. His brown eyes rested on Garrick in a long, significant stare. "My father gave it to me."

Garrick reached for the signet and eased it onto his finger. A perfect fit.

"How much did you win altogether?"

"No idea," Garrick confessed. "Enough, I think." Bounding up from his chair, he declared thankfully, "I'm finished."

Heads turned.

"What's that you say, Armitage?" asked the prince. "No longer playing?"

"Why should he?" Prawn Parfitt asked, laughing. "Shall I help you reckon the total, Garry?"

"I'm really, truly finished—forever," Garrick clarified. "Never again, as long as I live, will I play cards. I swear it on—on my mother's memory." Crossing himself, he added, "May God grant her peace."

"Amen," said the baron under his breath.

Garrick gathered up pieces of paper. *Dio,* how many opponents had he faced? He struggled to add the sums—five thousand, eight hundred, six thousand, thirteen thousand . . .

"Twelve hundred cash, in guinea *rouleaux,*" Prawn reported.

"That makes twenty-six thousand."

"Here's an IOU you've missed, from His Royal Highness. Two fifty."

Garrick grinned. "Lady Buck, you'll have to lend

me that blunderbuss of yours, and the pistols. What a catastrophe if I should be waylaid going to my cousin's house!"

"It's only a few steps," she pointed out, stifling a yawn.

"We'll see you there safely," the prince offered. "Come along, Hanger, Parfitt. Let's form an escort for Lord Garrick, the hardiest gamester in Britain."

"Former gamester," Garrick corrected, stuffing IOUs and rolls of guineas into his coat pockets.

He looked around for his father. But Everdon had silently slipped away, giving him no chance to respond to that long-sought acknowledgment—if that's what it had been.

Surely Lavinia, like the rest of London, knew where and how he'd spent the past night and the morning. He was disappointed that she was not waving from the window or waiting on the doorstep, a witness to his triumphant return.

Selwyn let him into the house. He interrupted the butler's congratulations to ask, "Where are the ladies?"

"Madam is in her sitting room, with the—"

He didn't stay to hear the rest but hurtled up the curving staircase two steps at a time.

"Francesca, Lavinia!"

He found three people in the sitting room, but not the one he wanted.

"Garry," his cousin said in relief. "At last!"

"Edward, did I know you were in town? Mr. Shaw!" He struck his forehead with a fist. "*Mio Dio*, Webb's trial! I was supposed to give my evidence at the Old Bailey. That's what Carlo meant when he—oh, I *am* sorry. I forgot all about it."

Said the barrister, "Mr. Webb was convicted, my lord. He received a sentence of transportation and will spend fourteen years at the penal colony in New South Wales."

"Then why such gloomy faces?" Going to his cousin, he pulled her out of the chair and tried to whirl her around the room.

"Garry, don't. I'm in no mood, and neither will you be when you hear all we've got to tell you."

"Do you expect me to be sorry for that *sporco*, that filth?"

"It's about Lavinia."

He ceased his capering. "Where the devil is she?"

"A letter came for her, an express. Her sister has fallen ill and is not expected to live. At eight o'clock last night, Lavinia left London on the night mail coach to Liverpool."

And that, of course, had been Carlo's bad news.

Mr. Shaw collected his case of briefs. "I've arrived at an inopportune moment. I merely wished you to inform your lordship—and Lady Lavinia—of the judgment against Webb. I shall be happy to discuss the particulars with you at some other time."

"Here." Garrick gave him a handful of guineas. "You'd better spread this around Fleet Street, among the printers. Persuade them to keep her ladyship's name out of their damned papers."

"I'll do what I can." The barrister bowed to the duke and Frances Radstock, and made his exit.

"I'm going after Lavinia," said Garrick.

"What?" his brother erupted.

"Why?" asked his cousin.

"Because she's in trouble, and she'll need me."

"Garry, are you sober?" Frances wondered.

"As a judge. Newbold didn't travel with her, did he?"

"No. She broke off the engagement."

"Good girl," he commended her under his breath.

"Garry, you can't go haring after that chit," Edward stated firmly. "What about Epsom races? And the next Newmarket meeting?"

"You cared nothing about my missing Epsom or Newmarket when you ordered me away to the Continent, did you? After I jilted Serena Halsey, you got rid of me to suit your convenience. Now that I'm going of my own volition, you demand that I stay. *Spiacente*, but I cannot. I lost a mother, and I know how wretched and frightened Lavinia must be right now."

"Garry," Frances interjected, "she said she couldn't marry William because of you. Do you also care for her?"

"More than my life, my honor—my family."

"And all this time you let me think you disliked her. I wish you hadn't deceived me."

The pain he read in his cousin's face cut Garrick to the quick. "Well, so do I. From the day I met Lavinia Cashin, I wanted her, and at Langtree I discovered that she felt the same about me. But by then you were pushing her at Newbold, and then Edward hinted that I was supposed to marry Caroline Rogers, of all people. So Lavinia and I planned to elope, only that accursed lawyer of hers interfered. When I found out her father had been in prison, I gave her hell about it—and before I could patch things up, she left London. When she came back, she accepted Newbold. I was hurt and angry—

drunk as a newt half the time, always ripping her character to shreds. I haven't done much to prove my merits," he admitted. "She's much better acquainted with my faults. No wonder she thought she wanted a fortune instead of a rogue like me." With a lopsided grin, he said, "Now she's getting both."

"How much did you win?" Edward asked, handing him several sealed billets. "All morning, people have been leaving their bank drafts here."

"Twenty-six thousand."

Frances put her hand to her throat. "Oh, Garry."

Garrick glanced at the clock. "I've no time to waste telling that tale. I can't possibly overtake Lavinia now, not even if I go by fast post coach. From what port does she sail?"

"Whitehaven," said his cousin. "She hoped to make the Monday packet boat."

He took her hand, then kissed her powdered cheek. "Am I forgiven, Francesca?"

"Your happiness is what matters most."

"Not mine, Lavinia's," he corrected her. "Carlo will accompany me for only the first stage; then I'll send him to Suffolk. Uncle Bardy knows everything; that's why he gave me Aunt Anna's diamond necklace—he wanted my bride to have it. Where's the license? Can't forget that." His coat pockets bulged with his winnings. Digging deep, he found the paper, crushed and rumpled.

"Garry," said Frances, "Lavinia left behind all the clothes made for her marriage. Take them to her, as my gift—it will save you the expense of replacing them."

"I can afford to." Turning to his brother, he said,

"Send me a report from Epsom. But if anyone wants to buy my horses, tell them I'm not selling after all."

Dio, it was grand to be so rich.

Forced by a becalmed sea to stay the night in busy Whitehaven, Lavinia took a room at the Globe Inn. Her journey had been arduous and fatiguing, for at each of its stops, the mail coach allowed the passengers only half an hour for rest and refreshment. For the first time, she had the leisure to mend her petticoat flounce, which she'd torn somewhere between Litchfield and Liverpool.

"M'lady," called the landlord, "you've a visitor."

A messenger from the castle? She rose, preparing herself for the worst, and the door swung open.

"Garrick!" She was unable to say more, for he pulled her into an embrace tight enough to force all the breath from her lungs.

"*Dolcezza*," he murmured against her neck, "I didn't dream I'd find you here."

"The packet was delayed." She ran her hands across his shoulders, his chest. "I didn't expect you to follow me."

"How could I not, when I heard the news about your sister? I've been so worried—"

"No one here in the town has heard about a—a loss at Castle Cashin," she told him. "Fishing and merchant vessels constantly sail back and forth to Douglas and Ramsey, so if anything so terrible had happened, it would be known—I'm hopeful."

He touched her cheek. "That bruise is fading. But you look exhausted."

"So do you." His eyes were darkly shadowed,

and uncombed hair framed his pale face.

"I can't recall when I last slept in a bed," he admitted. "Not the night you left London, and none of 'em since then."

"You need some food."

"And a bath."

While he ate, Garrick told her what he knew about Daniel Webb's trial. "Although he was convicted of a hanging offense, the court was lenient and spared his life. He'll remain in prison until he can be transported to New South Wales."

The chambermaid supplied a hip bath, then carried up can after can of steaming water to fill it. A Manxman from Peel, she said, had just sat down in the taproom—Lavinia hurried downstairs to find him and learn whatever she could. She returned as Garrick was emerging from his bath, and she handed him a linen towel.

"Keeping company with a naked man—aren't you concerned about what the maid will think? These people must know who you are."

"Yes, but they won't blackmail me like Daniel Webb did. Besides, nothing can damage my reputation more than my involvement in a criminal case and jilting Lord Newbold. I'll never be able to show my face in London again."

"Not this year, perhaps," he said. "But over time, fresh scandals will make yours seem stale. Before I left town, I did something that eclipsed your exploits, so everyone is talking about *me* now."

"What have you done?" she demanded, deeply suspicious.

He shook his head. "I'm too weary to tell you

now—or do much of anything else. Come along to bed, *carissima*."

Lavinia was quick to accept his sensible and most welcome invitation.

Chapter 28

Lavinia, wakened by mewling seagulls, thought at first that she might be at home. Then she noticed her bedmate. "You're here," she said sleepily, nuzzling against his chest. Her hand brushed his hip, and she stroked the smooth, taut skin.

"If you keep that up, *dolcezza*, I'll have to show you why I chased you from one end of England to the other." He rolled over to face her. "What you do to me—make me feel—" He drew a sharp breath. "*Dio*, where were you all my life?"

"I'm here now, that's all that matters," she answered, pressing herself against him.

He responded with a devouring kiss. One hand closed upon her breast; the other slid down her waist and darted between her legs, and with faint, inarticulate moans, she begged for still more.

Their hungry bodies merged. With breathtaking force and speed, he took her to the brink of pleasure, pitching her over its edge and letting her fall alone. And afterward he teased her, pressing in hard, pulling back slowly, on and on.

She stared up at him, lips parted, unable to express all that she felt and needed and hoped. Then the wild rush of sensation returned, sweeping her away, and her ecstatic murmurs blended with his gusty sigh of release.

Unsettling yet comforting were these sudden shifts from despair to delight to delirium. His loving could lighten her darkest moments. It was healing the wounds left by those final, eventful days in London. And it even calmed her fears about the future.

As he held her to his panting chest, she told him, "Whatever happens, I shall bear it. *Myr shegin dy ve, bee eh.* What must be, will be."

"Whenever you have need, you've got my shoulder to lean on, and my hand to clutch."

He kissed her forehead, then flung the quilts aside. "I'll find out when the tide will favor a crossing, and arrange for our luggage to be taken down to the quay."

Garrick brought back good tidings and an armful of newspapers. "We leave within the hour. What's in the basket?"

"Bread and cheese—although if the sea is rough, you might not want it. Even in the best of weather, the sailing can take a full day or more."

They boarded the vessel. Lavinia, unlike the passengers crowding the rail for a last glimpse of England, was content to remain below in the cabin. Garrick passed her the London paper, several days old, keeping the Liverpool edition for himself.

Gripping his forearm, she said, "Garrick, this item refers to Daniel Webb, I'm sure of it. 'A most villainous attorney who imposed upon a young lady in high life will pass the next fourteen years among robbers and muderers.' She looked up. "No mention of his name—or mine."

"That's a mercy. I told Shaw I didn't want your identity known. If ever I require a barrister, he's my man."

"You'd better *not* require one," Lavinia warned him.

The packet, plowing into open sea, began to pitch and roll. Lavinia, who seemed impervious, reached into her valise and took out a deck of cards.

"Where'd you get that?" Garrick asked.

"A fellow traveller on the mail coach offered it to me when he got off at Warrington. I thought I might play patience to pass the time, but if you like, we can play piquet."

"At the moment, I'd rather read."

Eventually he'd have to tell her he'd never play again, and about the fortune he'd won. But it would be crass and inconsiderate to mention such things now, when she had more important concerns. This was no time to speak of a wedding, either—their arrival at Castle Cashin might well coincide with a funeral.

Glancing over his paper, he watched her shuffle the cards. She became absorbed in her solitary game, brow furrowed in concentration as she played out her sequences. This unexpected enthusiasm for cards just when he'd forsworn them made him regret all those lessons he'd given her at Langtree.

When he suggested they seek fresher air up on the deck, Lavinia wrapped herself in her great brown shawl. It looked identical to the ones worn by the Manx countrywomen gathered at the opposite end of the cabin, chattering away in their native tongue.

For a long time, Garrick and Lavinia watched the porpoises darting up from the waves and diving down again. When he raised his hand to shade his eyes from the sun's glare, she noticed and commented on his ring.

"You never used to wear it."

"I received it after you left London. From my father. He staked it in a card game, but I like to think he wanted me to have it." Plunging a hand into his coat pocket, he removed his octavo edition of Hoyle. "Partly as a result of Lord Everdon's influence, I've ended my career as a gamester. I'm going to be as straitlaced as that grandmother of yours, the one who wouldn't have cards in the house." The wind was tossing her black curls about, and he captured one in his hand. "I don't much want to spend the greater part of my life staring at a handful of hearts, diamonds, clubs, and spades. Not when there are better, more interesting things to do. Would those sailors be greatly shocked if I kissed you?"

"I don't care." She gave him an inviting smile. After he pressed his mouth to hers, briefly, she asked, "What about your racehorses?"

"Those I'll keep. But for the time being, they're Nick Cattermole's responsibility."

Said Lavinia pensively, "You could've bought yourself a lovely thoroughbred with the money I've cost you. Three hundred pounds to get Father out of the King's Bench. Five hundred for those wretched sapphires. And now Newbold's got them."

"Just as well," Garrick replied lightly. "They didn't suit you at all. You should have diamonds, and nothing but."

"There will be no court balls for me," she replied. "But I don't mind."

Staring down at the scarred, leather-bound book he said, "I'm not sorry about losing this, either. It's no longer any use to me."

He pitched it over the rail. For a little while it floated, bobbing on the waves, but then the vessel's powerful wake pulled it under the water and out of sight.

"That's Maughold Head," Lavinia told Garrick excitedly. "And there's Castle Cashin, near the cliffs."

She gazed lovingly at the familiar cluster of hills, with majestic Snaefell rising highest of all. As the packet boat tacked slowly southward along the rugged coast, she named each rock and inlet to Garrick. Port Mooar, where fishing smacks awaited the summer return of the herring. Gob ny Garvain and its ancient fort. The shingle beach at Port Cornaa, and the river valley that sliced its way inland to her father's abandoned mill.

Garrick, impressed by the broad sweep of Douglas Bay, likened it to Naples. Beyond St. Mary's Rock lay the entrance of the narrow harbor, with steep precipices on either side.

"Dangerous to navigate," Lavinia told him, "especially at night. That tumbledown tower and its lantern are all that's left of the old Douglas light; it was destroyed by a storm nearly eight years ago. The entire herring fleet was washed upon the rocks. Many lives were lost, and families ruined."

"Why wasn't it repaired?"

"Because the British government is reluctant to spend any of the surplus revenues it receives from the island. The Duke of Atholl might persuade them, but he seldom bestirs himself on our behalf. You'll not be long on Man before you learn how little we love the English, or our governor."

After the boat weighed anchor, Customs officers boarded for a perfunctory search. Lavinia was glad to see the postmaster, as reliable a source of local news as the publisher of the *Manx Mercury*. Everyone in the island traveled to Douglas to collect their letters, bringing him their gossip.

"The earl hasn't visited the town this fortnight," he informed her. "There's a letter waiting for him, sent from Liverpool."

From his factor, Lavinia guessed, or else his banker.

When she expressed her desire to get home as quickly as possible, he said, "I'll mention the extreme urgency of your situation to the Customs officers. Is there anything more I can do to assist you?"

"We need a carriage and enough Manx currency to cover the fare."

The inspectors did not ask to look inside Lavinia's or Garrick's baggage, and they were escorted off the packet and onto the ferry ahead of the other passengers. The postmaster met them at the end of the pier, with a chaise and horses.

As they were driving along the crooked streets,

Garrick counted out the coins Lavinia had received in exchange for his English money. "You gave that man a pound, didn't you? He's overpaid, by three shillings and sixpence."

"He hasn't. Fourteen of our pence make up a shilling, rather than twelve. And a Manx pound is equal to seventeen shillings, one and a half pence in English money."

"I already like this island of yours," he responded. "My money will go farther."

Darkness and the poor state of the roads made their journey a slow one, even though the distance from Douglas to the castle was but a few miles. Lavinia felt more fearful with each familiar landmark they passed, and her tense fingers crumpled the letter from Liverpool. Her sister, that serene and soothing presence, might already be gone, and even though her mind was trying to accept it, her aching heart was unprepared for the loss. "Laxey Bridge," she whispered. Looking at Garrick, she admitted, "I'm afraid."

"I know."

"Kitty is so dear, and good, and talented. I wanted her see London and wear fine gowns and attend plays and concerts." She bowed her head. "I was the one who did all those things—and couldn't even enjoy them. And I disgraced myself past redemption."

"No, you didn't," he replied. "Now give me that letter, before you crush it entirely."

Just beyond Dhoon village, the driver turned off the main road into a lane barely wide enough for the vehicle to pass. Its surface was uneven, and the constant jolting and bumping added to Lavinia's anxiety. Garrick held her tightly, offering silent comfort—for what exactly, neither of them knew.

"Boayl Fea," she said soon after they crossed another bridge. Warm light streamed from the windows of the Place of Rest. Home to Ellin Fayle, who borrowed books from Kerron and read them to her blind grandmother.

Then, farther on, she saw the castle, crowning the headland with its battlements and square towers. The winding drive was rocky, and the sides of the carriage brushed against overgrown clumps of heather and gorse.

"Give the driver his shilling," she told Garrick as they came to a standstill.

She leaped out of the vehicle and ran to the door—locked. Gasping and weeping, she pounded it with her fist.

A gruff male voice asked, "*Quoi shen ec y dorrys?*"

"Kerron!" she called.

"*Nee uss t'ayn*, Lhondhoo?" He slipped the bolt, and the door swung open. "*Shee bannee me!*"

"Kitty—oh, tell me, have I come to late to see her?"

"She's already gone to sleep." Peering out into the darkness, her brother asked, "Who's that with you?"

"Lord Garrick Armitage," she said over her shoulder as she went up the stairs.

She entered her sister's room quietly and approached the bed. Kitty's brown hair had been shorn, and her face looked small and white and pinched. Her eyelids fluttered, opening halfway. "Mother?"

"It's Lhondhoo."

"*Och*," sighed Kitty.

"I didn't mean to wake you," said Lavinia regretfully. "Go back to sleep."

"Light—I want to see you."

She took a rushlight holder down from the mantel, lit it on a glowing coal, then carried it over to the bed.

"Why did you come back?" asked Kitty in a feeble voice.

"To be with you." But there was another reason. "*Cha daink me ermy hoshaight ayns Sostyn.* I didn't prosper in England."

Her sister began to fuss with the wispy curls peeking from beneath her white nightcap. Following the direction of her stare, Lavinia turned. "Is he your marquis?" Kitty asked.

"I'm Garrick Armitage."

When he came over to her bedside, Kitty removed her hand from Lavinia's and held it out to him. "*Urley.*"

"What did she say?" he asked Lavinia.

"Eagle."

"A name for you," Kitty said faintly. "My sister will explain."

"Father calls us his flock of birds. Kitty is Drean, Manx for wren. Kerr is Shirragh, the falcon. I'm Lhondhoo."

"Blackbird," her sister whispered.

"No more talking. You need your rest." Lavinia leaned over to kiss the pale cheek, then led Garrick into the drafty corridor where her parents and brother had gathered.

He looked on as Lady Ballacraine embraced her

daughter. Silvery eyes like Lavinia's, he marvelled, and the same milky complexion.

"Dear child," she was saying, "I'm sorry to give you a fright. I wrote to you when we feared the worst, before Kitty's fever broke."

"I sensed that something was the matter before I knew what it was," Lavinia told her parents. "And in London, everything had gone wrong—Mr. Webb made trouble, I broke my engagement to Lord New-bold." She lost her struggle to hold back the tears.

Said Lady Ballacraine, "If you don't get some rest, you'll be ill yourself." Before leading her daughter away, she added, "Lord Garrick, my son will show you to a spare chamber. I apologize for its deficiencies—as you can see, we don't live in state here at Castle Cashin."

"In my travels across Italy," he said, "I've slept in monasteries and stables, and even in an olive grove. Your spare bedchamber will not offend me."

"Italy?" Kerron repeated. "You'll have to tell me about that."

Lord Ballacraine, frowning over the letter Garrick had given him, muttered, "The terms are generous. Better than we expected."

"From Standish?" his son asked.

The earl nodded. "He wants an answer soon. In a fortnight, he'll be here."

Garrick, reluctant to pry into the Cashins' private matters, waited patiently for one of them to remember his presence.

Lavinia's brother ran a hand through his dark hair. "He'd better not force us to vacate immediately. We won't go until Kitty can be moved."

"He was ever a heartless bully, and I don't suppose having money has changed him."

Turning stormy eyes upon Garrick, the young lord told him, "A gentleman from Liverpool has made an offer on the castle. Lhondhoo has returned just in time to be evicted with the rest of us."

Chapter 29

Yesterday in England, Garrick had been worth twenty-six thousand, two hundred and fifty pounds. This morning, due solely to geography, his fortune had swelled to more than thirty thousand.

He parted the thick and dusty length of brocade that curtained his window, eager for a closer view of the spectacular expanse of mountains he'd seen from the deck of the packet boat. To his regret, low, scudding clouds obscured the highland scenery, and he had to be contented with a ragged meadow of odd brown sheep.

No servant came to wait upon him. Using the chilled water in the washbasin, he washed and shaved himself. He clothed himself in a plain coat and riding leathers, trusting that this casual attire was appropriate for a guest in a decayed Manx castle.

The cheerful sound of girlish laughter lured him down the hall to Lady Kitty's room. Lavinia sat perched on the bed with Xanthe on her lap, amused by the antics of four kittens scrambling across her sister's patchwork quilt.

A younger girl scooped up the ones that ventured too close to the edge. She gazed up at him with bright green eyes, then gave him a winning smile. A long brown braid fell to her waist, and she wore a peasant's wool gown.

"Come in and meet Ellin Fayle," said Lavinia, "from Crowcreen. We're letting her choose one of Xanthe's kits." The tears of last night were gone, and she seemed perfectly happy.

Rubbing the watchful mother cat's rounded head, he said, "*Micia mia,* you've increased the population of the tailless."

The smallest of the kittens hopped toward Ellin, and she picked it up. "This one."

"Are you sure you want to take the runt of the litter?" Lavinia asked. "All the others have nicer markings—the little one is mottled."

"Mottle—that's what I'll call her." The girl cuddled the tiny creature. "When will she be weaned?"

"Not for some weeks yet," Kitty answered weakly. "But you may visit her as often as you like."

Ellin's smile was blissful. "A cat for my very own. Someday I'll have a pup as well."

"And then you'll want a lamb. And a foal, too," teased Lavinia. Handing Xanthe to her sister, she said, "I must see that our guest gets his breakfast."

On the way down the stairs, Garrick hooked his arm around her waist and forced her to stop. He looked her over, taking in the plain wool gown and long linen apron. This was a new Lavinia, and she enchanted him no less than she had in her silk and satin. Before he could prove it with a kiss, she slipped away from him and continued down the staircase.

The spacious kitchen smelled of burning turf and was dominated by its vast stone hearth. "You'll find a similar *chiollagh* in every house, large or small," Lavinia informed him.

An old woman kneaded dough at a table near the hearth. In response to a few sentences of unintelligible Manx, she left her bread to rise and began piling oatcakes on a platter. Lavinia brewed the tea herself.

"Joney cooks for us, and her daughter is a maid of all work. Their husbands care for the horses and the sheep, and work the farm. And catch the fish."

"S'goan ta'n skeddan ec y tra t'ayn," commented Joney in a glum voice.

"The herrings are scarce just now, she says. Joney, Lord Garrick Armitage comes from London. *Cha nel Gailck erbey echey,* so you must remember to speak English."

"Va, dy jarroo. Himself has been asking for you."

Turning to Garrick, Lavinia said, "After I see Father, I'll take you up into the hills, and we can ride over to Port Mooar to look for seals."

Before going to the east tower, she stopped in her room to retrieve her jewel case. She found her father seated at his desk, going over his accounts.

Closing a ledger, he asked her, "How did you find your sister this morning?"

"Quiet," she answered candidly, "but in fine spirits."

"Dr. Christian doubts she'll ever completely regain her strength, her heart and lungs are so much weakened. Did she say anything to you about Dreeym Freoaie?"

Heather Ridge—the deserted farmstead Kerron had taken her to during her last visit. "No," she replied.

"Soon it will be our home, Lhondhoo."

"You're giving up the castle." It didn't seem possible.

"I have many reasons for doing so. Kitty will benefit from the change; the air on the ridge is not so damp as it is here by the sea. And your mother says she'll like having a smaller house, with a larger garden."

"When did you decide this?" she asked.

"After I returned from England, Kerron and I began to explore the possibility of producing linen cloth instead of wool. I wrote to a factor in Liverpool, seeking potential investors. He suggested that I contact a manufacturer, a native Manxman who intends to return to the island. Extraordinarily wealthy. He doesn't care to be our partner; he wants to live here in the castle and will pay handsomely for the privilege. The lease runs for a period of seven years, and I retain all my baronial rights."

"But I was engaged to Lord Newbold," she said. "You must have known that we wouldn't let you lose the castle."

"I was unable to reconcile myself to becoming wholly dependent on a son-in-law. You've no cause to regret jilting your marquis, Lhondhoo. I fancy you'll do better without him."

"He's certainly better off without me," she acknowledged. She placed the leather case on the desktop. "I won't need your rubies again, so I'm returning them."

"*Agh*—so you were able to get them back again?"

"Quite easily. I went to Mr. Siberry, who—" She interrupted herself, recalling his ignorance. "After Mr. Webb tried to steal them, I took them to a jeweler for safekeeping. What did you think I'd done with them?"

"Sold them or pawned them, to pay off my debts."

"But you told me not to." She was unprepared for his confusion.

"You said I would disapprove of what you had to do to get me out of the King's Bench, so naturally I assumed—" His eyes bored into her. "*Insh dou*, where *did* you get that three hundred pounds?"

"From Lord—" She hesitated. "It was given to me by a gentleman I know."

"As a loan?"

"*Cha nel*, for he offered to settle it on me. But I suppose it was actually a gift."

"Lhondhoo," he said grimly, "no man in his right mind gives hundreds of pounds to a beautiful woman, unless he has certain expectations."

"It wasn't like that—it wasn't *supposed* to be. His intentions were honorable, but we didn't know Daniel Webb was spying on us, and—" She stopped herself again, before she revealed too much.

After an awful moment of comprehension, her father seized his graying head between his hands. "*Och*, Lhondhoo. Your virtue, unlike the rubies, was irreplaceable—and infinitely more precious."

His implication pierced her to the heart. To her infinite sorrow, she could not honestly refute it. She had no virtue left to defend. She'd lain with Garrick, believing herself to be his future wife. That admission would not absolve her, because she'd accepted a large sum of money immediately afterward, which she had used but not repaid. She wasn't married to him now, or even engaged—not quite. These facts condemned her.

Her father's agony was a terrible thing to see. Just when she should be his comforter, she'd compounded his worries. The closure of the mill, Kitty's illness, giving up his ancestral castle to a tenant—it was more than any man should have to bear all at once. And now this, the discovery of her secret shame.

"That *mooidjean* Webb! Throwing me into prison, trying to steal from us. And forcing you to ruin yourself. What was his motive?"

"Greed. Ambition. He believed he could prosper through my marriage to Lord Newbold."

Rising from his desk, he went to the window from which the first Earl of Ballacraine had watched the return of his smuggling vessels. "I don't reproach you. How can I question your choices, when I was the cause—and the beneficiary? I can only pray that you won't suffer any more than you've already done."

Blinking back tears, she said, "I don't want Mother and Kerron and Kitty to find out. They couldn't possibly understand, for they never saw that prison. Or met Daniel Webb."

"What about Lord Garrick? If you care for him, and he for you, you should not conceal the truth."

"He knows everything about me," Lavinia declared. "I keep no secrets from Garrick. Nor ever shall again."

During more than a week of living among the close-knit Cashins, Garrick had seen firsthand the pleasures and the frustrations of family life. Their interactions were unreserved; they spoke their minds so freely and frankly that he wondered how Lavinia had become so successful a deceiver. And she must have felt very idle when in London, because here she was constantly busy—helping Joney pare potatoes, weeding her mother's garden, sewing linen shirts for her brother and father, nursing her sister.

If he proposed to her today, he mused while mucking out the horse boxes, they could call in Vicar Cubbon to preside over their wedding. Garrick wanted the family to carry a happy memory from this home to their next one. And after a long delay, he was impatient to claim his bride.

He was currying tangles out of Fannag's mane when the earl came marching into the stable and said sternly, "Lord Garrick, put down that comb. An honored guest, laboring like a groom—this is unacceptable."

Without interrupting his task, Garrick replied, "I enjoy it. I've got horses of my own, and I often tend them myself."

Lord Ballacraine seemed agitated. "I wish to discuss a confidential matter with you; it concerns my daughter Lavinia. And that dissipated, degenerate blackguard, Lord Newbold."

Garrick lifted his head, staring at the earl across the pony's broad back. "I must admit that I'm no friend of the most noble marquis, but I've never heard him described in such terms as you've just used."

"You needn't pretend with me; my eyes have been opened. I am fully aware that his honorable reputation is all a sham. He seduced my daughter."

"What?"

"She didn't name the fellow. But who else could afford to make her a *present* of three hundred pounds? Even if he offered her marriage, it doesn't excuse his crime."

"*Mio Dio,*" Garrick muttered, finding himself in a singularly awkward position. Stepping out from behind the animal, he faced the troubled father. "Newbold never laid a finger on Lavinia. And trust me, it wasn't *his* money she used to get you out of prison."

"Then you know where she got it?"

"From me. But it didn't happen the way you think," he said quickly, for the earl had taken an aggressive step forward. "We were nearly married— and would be now, if not for that damned attorney of yours. If she'd told me he was blackmailing her, I'd have dealt with him myself and saved us all the indignity of that trial."

The other man's hands clenched themselves into fists. "At this moment, I don't greatly care about what happened in London, or why," he declared. "Lhondhoo is my sole consideration. A man who violates a Manxwoman's chastity must be brought to justice. I warn you, our law is extremely harsh."

Garrick began to feel uneasy. He wondered what dire and primitive punishment would be imposed upon him. Mutilation? Death?

He listened careully as Lord Ballacraine quoted the appropriate—and alarming—statute. By the time the recitation was finished, his son had intruded upon them.

"Going riding?" Garrick asked, relieved by the diversion and desperate to escape the righteously wrathful earl.

"*Cha nel*," Kerron replied. "I'm off to Dreeym Freoaie to repair the roof—the house is about as watertight as a herring net. Care to have a go at pounding slates? I assured Lhondhoo I won't let you break your neck."

Having just learned that his neck was already at risk, Garrick could think of no reason to refuse. He went out into the haggard and helped Kerr load the farm cart, then brought Fannag over to be harnessed. They set out across the bumpy, twisting lane, and along the way, he answered questions about Rome and Naples.

"I dream of one day treading the paths known to Virgil," the younger man said, "and seeing cities built by the Caesars."

"You will."

Kerr looked dubious. "I'd count myself lucky to get as far as Cambridge."

"You'll do that, too," Garrick assured him.

Scattered across a low ridge, within sight of the sea, were a house, stable, cowhouse with a barn loft, and pigsty, all made of gray stone. Garrick, having previously visited this farm where the Cashins would soon be living, understood why they had chosen it. Their castle might be impressive from the outside, but it was also damned uncomfortable within.

He carried bundles of slates up the ladder, and Kerr set and nailed them. While working, they talked only as necessary, but when they halted to eat oakcakes and swill ale, they returned to the mutually fascinating topic of Italy.

"A house in Venice?" said Kerr, greatly impressed. "I wonder you ever left it. If I were able to live abroad—" He broke off and pointed at a pair of figures in the distance. "Look—Ellin Fayle, with Calybrid Teare, the *ben-obbee*. You'll often see them gathering herbs that grow wild in the fields."

"Young Ellin lives nearby, doesn't she?"

"At Boayl Fea, near the mill."

"I suspect she'll like having easier access to your books after you move. She's a great reader."

Kerron grinned. "I'll let her have the *Aeneid* next; that'll keep her occupied. Although I suppose it might be rather dry and dull for her blind grandmother."

Had he failed to notice how the pretty girl worshipped him? Ellin's hunger for learning was genuine, no doubt of it. But Garrick guessed that her desire to educate herself was largely motivated by a wish to please the earl's heir. Kerr, however, was eager to leave his island—always had been, according to Lavinia. A restless spirit, thought Garrick, recognizing a fellow rover.

"There's Lhondhoo," the young man said, "riding toward the mountain."

Garrick promptly abandoned his speculations about Kerr and Ellin when he saw the other person crossing the moors. Scrambling to his feet, he brushed the crumbs from his clothes. "Where's my coat?"

"I think you left it lying in the grass," Kerr replied.

"You don't mind my going?"

"*Immee royd*—away with you! I'll finish on my own."

The surefooted Fannag carried Lavinia up and down the fells and through rocky fords. Her mind travelled back to another day when she'd followed this same track before making her first trip to England. She remembered that the mountain before her had been cloaked in purple heather, and she'd been wearing her faded riding coat and rough woollen skirt.

Today all the surrounding hills were green, and the wildflowers bloomed profusely. She had a proper riding habit of fine burgundy cloth. But now, as then, marriage was very much on her mind. For if she didn't get a husband, and soon, she'd be adding to her father's distress—and his responsibilities.

"Lavinia—Lavinia, wait!"

She twisted in the saddle and saw Garrick vault over a stone wall and crash through thickets. What terrible event had sent him racing across the countryside? Kerr could have tumbled off the roof and broken his head—Kitty might be suffering a relapse.

She dismounted and rushed to meet him. "What's wrong?" she asked fearfully.

"My life is in danger," he panted. "You've got to save me. I'll make it worth your while, I swear. You'll have a share of my fortune, all the racehorses you want, my *palazzo* in Venice—"

"What *are* you talking about? If you're drunk again—"

"Not a bit." Gripping her hands, he said, "Remember what I said about playing piquet with Lord Everdon at Lady Buckinghamshire's, and my vow to give up cards? There's something I didn't tell you. I won a lot of money that night—twenty-six thousand pounds. Over thirty thousand in Manx currency."

"*Och*, Garrick."

His face fell. "You don't seem very pleased."

"Because you kept a secret. I hoped we were going to be honest with each other, always."

"Starting now," he pledged. "Lavinia, you *have* to marry me."

"Yes, I know. Three weeks for the banns," she said absently. "By then, everyone will know I'm—"

"Special license." He brandished a paper at her. "We don't have to wait—we can be wed today, if we want to. And I'm going to prove to you that I'm better than the jilt and rogue and gamester I was when we met."

With his wild eyes and unbound hair and laborer's garb, he seemed another being than the fashionable stranger who had accosted her in a London street—and kissed her. "You don't have to prove anything to me, Garrick."

"I may not be as rich as Newbold, but I can invest in your father's linen mill, and pay for Kerr's schooling and travel, and send Kitty to that spa. I want to help them. Before I came to this island of yours, I had no sense of belonging to a family. Joy and fulfillment always eluded me—until I met you.

Remember these?" He held out his hand and showed her the earrings he had given her at the Drover's Rest.

"Of course I do," she replied, wondering when he would give her a chance to tell her news.

"I've something else for you, *sposina mia*." The next item he took out of his pocket made her gasp— a long string of large diamonds.

"I'm a fortune hunter," she reminded him as he placed his glittering gift around her neck. "Everyone will say I married you because you've suddenly become so rich. Or because I'm—"

"The reason you're marrying me," he said intently, "is to preserve my life. Your father says that by Manx law, a dishonored maiden may punish her seducer with one of three instruments. A sword to cut off his head. A rope to hang him. Or a marriage ring. You hold my wretched, unworthy life in your hands, Lavinia. What is to be my fate?"

"The ring. And a hasty wedding." Blushing, she added, "I believe I might be carrying your child."

"*Dio*," he marvelled. "I'm going to be a father?"

"I'm not entirely sure, not yet."

His bright head bowed, and his fingers moved swiftly down the front of her burgundy jacket, unfastening the row of tiny, cloth-covered buttons. "Stop wriggling," he said.

"What are you doing?"

"Making the most of an opportunity," he answered, giving her a shamelessly wicked grin. "There is a way we can make your suspicion a reality."

Relief and love and happiness came spilling out in laughter. She let him lay her down upon the grass and the flowers, and silence her mirth with his eager, desperate kisses.

Epilogue

~~~∾⦿∾~~~

Suffolk, 1798

"**I** catched it!"

Lavinia smiled at her daugher, who was stalking tortoiseshell butterflies with a net.

Sir Bardolph Hyde, relying on his cane, crossed the lawn to investigate. "What d'you mean to do with it, Kat?"

"Give it to Jonafon. Birfday present." The child carried the prize to her brother, seated on a blanket at their mother's feet. "See the bufferfly."

"Butterfly," Lavinia corrected.

Her year-old son repeated, "Burfly."

"You'd better let it go, Kat. The wings are very delicate."

As the butterfly flitted across the sunny garden with the child in pursuit, the baronet said, "I'm glad I thought of that net. Her father used it when he was a lad."

"She's not used to his being away so long. She'll be most distressed if he doesn't return in time for Jonathon's party tomorrow."

372

"Garry shouldn't have gone to London." gentleman wagged his head.

"He felt he had to. He always regretted that hi. brother failed to support him when he was in trouble."

"I don't know what Edward was thinking. Absconding with a married woman, flaunting their liaison."

Lavinia was distracted by Fling, poking his black-maned head over the garden wall to nibble a tender vine. "Wicked animal! An opportunist—exactly like his master."

The baronet continued, "They would have done better to run away to Italy together. Like some people I could name."

Lavinia lowered her lashes, trying to look demure.

Garrick had carried her off to Venice as soon as they were wed. There Katherine had been born, and Jonathon conceived. After nearly two years of *la dolce vita*, they had judged it safe to return to England and now were comfortably settled at Monkwood Hall.

"I still say you should've gone to town with your husband. You can't keep away from London forever, m'dear."

"I'm trying."

"A carriage!" shrieked Kat. "Papa's come home!"

Lavinia rose in anticipation, and her hope gave way to joy when the traveller lowered the window glass and vigorously waved his hat.

"It *is* Papa!" Kat let her new toy fall to the ground and ran to meet him, nearly tripping over her long skirt and pinafore.

...th him," said Lavinia as she
...her arms. "He must have
...with him."

...ut of the vehicle and seized his
...r high. *"Katerina, cara mia!"*

...elight, placing her hot palms over
his cheeks. ...ched a bufferfly in a net."

"What's this all over your mouth, jam? *Molto
bene,* we've arrived in time for some tea and
scones."

"Where's Uncle Kerr?"

"In London still, chasing heiresses."

"Did you bring Jonafon a present for his birfday?"

"Most certainly, and so did this gentleman. My
lord, I am honored to present Miss Katherine Laura
Armitage. Kat, this is Lord Everdon."

"Efferdon," she repeated.

"Tell him what you want to be when you grow
up."

"A jockey. Just like Con."

Garrick set her down and took his son from Lavinia. "Here is Jonathon Hyde Armitage, who'll be
one year old on the morrow. And the beauteous
Lady Garrick Armitage."

"Welcome to Monkwood, my lord," said Lavinia.

The baron grasped her hand. "This reckless husband of yours said you wouldn't mind an unexpected guest. I wished to see for myself the miracle
that you've wrought. He stated, with impressive
conviction, that marriage has reformed him."

"He exaggerates," Lavinia replied. "His character
is unchanged."

Sir Bardolph shuffled over to greet the baron.

Soon they settled down on a garden bench, each dandling a child on his knees.

Meeting his wife's shining, silvery eyes, Garrick saw that Lavinia shared his elation. "Look at them. When I lured my father to Suffolk, I never imagined such a cosy scene as that." He slipped his arm around her slender waist and led her to a more secluded seat. "You might like to know that when Londoners refer to that 'shocking Armitage fellow,' they mean Edward. Mr. Fowler challenged him to a duel and he'll be charged as corespondent in the divorce."

Laying her head against Garrick's shoulder, Lavinia said, "We're fortunate that our happiness didn't come at so great a cost."

"Twenty-six thousand pounds is no small sum, *sposina mia*. Not to mention all those diamonds."

"You know perfectly well that you won me long before you had the money. Or that necklace."

His lips moved to her earlobe. "Wear it for me tonight," he whispered. "Only diamonds, and nothing else."

"You definitely have not changed," Lavinia said thankfully.

"And never will," he assured her, with a kiss.

Author's Note

As with all my books, my interests and obsessions and travel experiences found their way into *Kissing a Stranger*. I, like Garrick Armitage, adore Venice, and I share with Lavinia Cashin a strong connection to the Isle of Man, which I return to whenever I possibly can. Other settings in this book are places I have visited, either occasionally or often. Langtree is modeled on a specific Thameside mansion in Oxfordshire; Monkwood lies in an area of Suffolk where my own ancestors once lived.

While I do not in any way consider myself a gamester, I've experienced the thrill and the terror of testing my luck in gambling casinos—purely in the interest of research, of course! I've actually ridden to hounds, truly an exhilarating pastime. For many years I've studied and collected antique jewelry, and was always fascinated by the "lost" Marie Antoinette diamonds. What's more, I'm personally acquainted with Fling, as wonderful a horse in real life as he is in this novel!

I enjoy receiving and responding to mail from my

readers (legal-sized SASE appreciated) and can be contacted at P.O. Box 437, Epsom, New Hampshire 03234-0437. I also have an email address: *MargEvaPor@aol.com*. My website <*http://members.aol.com/MargEvaPor*> offers additional information about my novels and my interests, with book covers and photographs of favorite places, my dogs, and a special horse called Fling.

Hoping all your dreams come true,

Margaret Evans Porter

Dear Reader,

With a new year coming, don't miss a new year of exciting romances from Avon! We've got some of the writers you already know and love, along with some fresh voices you're sure to fall for.

A writer you know and love is January's Treasure author, Tanya Anne Crosby. *On Bended Knee*, Tanya Anne's latest, is an unforgettable love story of passion and promise, and she returns to the Scottish setting that her readers love so well. Don't miss this sinfully sensuous historical love story.

Rachel Gibson's first contemporary, *Simply Irresistible*, made readers sit up and take notice. Now, she returns with another witty and wonderful contemporary called *Truly Madly Yours*. When a young woman returns to her hometown of Truly, Idaho, she never dreams the handsome man she left behind would still be there...laying in wait for her!

If you're looking for a spectacular new writer, don't miss Gayle Callen, author of next month's *The Darkest Knight*. A young woman is on the run from a forced marriage, and is rescued by the one man she can never have in this sensuous, exciting medieval historical romance.

And with a title like *Once a Mistress* how can you resist buying the latest from Debra Mullins? A dark handsome rogue sweeps our heroine off her feet and rescues her from an evil abductor in this wonderfully swashbuckling romp.

Until next month, enjoy!

Lucia Macro

Lucia Macro
Senior Editor